Joanna Sims lives in [illegible] cory, and their three fabulous felines, Sebastian, Chester (aka Tubby) and Ranger. By day, Joanna works as a speech-language pathologist, and by night, she writes contemporary romance for Mills & Boon True Love. Joanna loves to hear from readers and invites you to stop by her website for a visit: www.joannasimsromance.com.

Sophie Pembroke has been reading and writing romance ever since she read her first Mills & Boon romance at university, so getting to write them for a living is a dream [illegible]ome true! Sophie lives in a little Hertfordshire market town [illegible]he UK, with her scientist husband and her incredibly [illegible]ginative six-year-old daughter. She writes stories about [illegible]nds, family and falling in love—usually while drinking [illegible]much tea and eating homemade cakes. She also keeps a [illegible] at www.sophiepembroke.com.

[illegible]**n Carlisle**'s love affair with books began when she made [illegible]rade in maths in the sixth grade. Not allowed to watch [illegible]il she brought the grade up, she filled her time with books [illegible]ame a voracious romance reader. She has 'keepers' on [illegible] to prove it. Because she loved the genre so much, she decided to try her hand at creating her own romantic worlds. She still loves a good happily-ever-after story.

When not writing, Susan doubles as a high school substitute teacher—she has been doing this for sixteen years. She lives in Georgia, with her husband of twenty-eight years, and has four grown children. She loves castles, travelling, cross-stitching, hats, James Bond and hearing from her readers.

Marriage On The Cards

JOANNA SIMS
SOPHIE PEMBROKE
SUSAN CARLISLE

MILLS & BOON

First Published in Great Britain 2018
by Mills & Boon, an imprint of HarperCollins*Publishers*
1 London Bridge Street, London, SE1 9GF

ISBN: 978-0-263-26714-3

05-0418

This book is produced from independently certified FSC™ paper to ensure responsible forest management.

For more information visit: www.harpercollins.co.uk/green

Printed and bound in Spain
by CPI, Barcelona

MARRY ME, MACKENZIE!

JOANNA SIMS

Dedicated to Aunt Gerri and Uncle Bill

You are loved more than words can say!

Chapter One

Mackenzie Brand parallel parked her 1960 Chevy sedan and shut off the engine. She leaned against the steering wheel and looked through the windshield at the swanky condos that lined Mission Beach, California. She checked the address that her cousin, Jordan, had given her and matched it with the address on the white, trilevel condo on the left. With a sigh, she unbuckled her seat belt and slipped the key out of the ignition.

"All right. Not exactly your crowd. But a job's a job and a favor's a favor." Mackenzie got out of her car, locked the door and dropped the keys into her Go Green recycling tote bag. She could hear a mixture of classic rock, loud talking and laughing as she walked quickly to the front door. It sounded like the Valentine's Day party that Jordan was throwing with her fiancé, Ian, was already in full swing.

Mackenzie rang the doorbell twice and then knocked on the door. While she waited, she stared down at her holey black Converse sneakers. They had passed shabby chic several months ago—definitely time to get a new pair. After a few minutes spent contemplating her pitiful tennis shoes, Mackenzie pressed the doorbell again. When no one opened the door, Mackenzie turned around to head to the beach side of the condo. She was about to step down the first step when she heard the door open.

"Hey!" Dylan Axel swung the front door open wide. "Where're you going?"

Dylan's voice, a voice Mackenzie hadn't heard in a very long time, reverberated up her spine like an old forgotten song. Mackenzie simultaneously twisted her torso toward Dylan while taking a surprised step back. Her eyes locked with his for a split second before she lost her balance and began to fall backward.

"Hey..." Dylan saw the pretty brunette at his door begin to fall. He sprang forward and grabbed one of her flailing arms. "Careful!"

Silent and wide-eyed, Mackenzie clutched the front of Dylan's shirt to steady herself. Dylan pulled her body toward his and for a second or two, she was acutely aware of everything about the man: the soapy scent of his skin, the strong, controlled grasp of his fingers on her arm, the dark chest hair visible just above the top button of his designer shirt.

"Are you okay?" Dylan asked. He didn't know who she was, but she smelled like a sugar cookie and had beautiful Elizabeth Taylor eyes.

If he hadn't caught her, she would have fallen for sure. Could have seriously injured herself. And Mackenzie's body knew it. Her heart was pounding in her chest, her skin felt prickly and hot, and her equilibrium was off-kilter. Mackenzie closed her eyes for a moment, took in a steadying breath, before she slowly released the death grip she had on his shirt.

"I'm fine," Mackenzie said stiffly. "Thank you."

"Are you sure?"

Mackenzie nodded. She forced herself to focus her eyes straight ahead on the single silver hair on Dylan's chest instead of looking up into his face.

"You can let go now." Mackenzie tugged her arm away from Dylan's hand.

Dylan immediately released her arm, hands up slightly as if he were being held up at gunpoint. "Sorry about that."

Mackenzie self-consciously tugged on the front of her oversize Nothin' But Cupcakes T-shirt. "No, *I'm* sorry."

Dylan smiled at her. "Let's just call it even, okay?"

That was classic Dylan; always trying to smooth things over with a smile. He wasn't as lanky as he had been in his early twenties. His body had filled out, but he was fit and had the lean body of an avid California surfer. And he still had that boyish, easygoing smile and all-American good looks. Even back in middle school, Dylan had been popular with absolutely everyone. Male or female, it didn't matter. He had always been effortlessly charming and approachable. Right then, on Dylan's porch, the last ten years melted away for Mackenzie, but she knew that he obviously hadn't recognized her.

Still smiling, Dylan stuck out his hand to her. "I'm Dylan. And you are?"

Instead of taking his offered hand or responding, Mackenzie stared at him mindlessly. It felt as if all of her blood had drained out of her head and rushed straight to her toes.

I'm not ready for this...

Dylan's smile faded slightly. He gave her a curious look and withdrew his hand. "You must be one of Jordan's friends. Why don't you come in so we can track 'er down."

Mackenzie was screaming in her mind, demanding that her stubborn legs take a step forward as she plastered a forced smile on her face.

"Thank you." She squeaked out the platitude as she skirted by Dylan and into the condo.

"Mackenzie!" Jordan wound her way through the crowd of people gathered in the living room and threw her arms around her cousin. "Thank *God* you could come! You're the *best*, do you know that?"

"Jordan!" Relieved, Mackenzie hugged her cousin. "Okay—first things first—I have to see this ring in person."

Jordan held out her hand and wiggled her finger so her large cushion-cut blue diamond engagement ring caught the light.

"Jordan, it's beautiful." Mackenzie held Jordan's left hand loosely while she admired the large blue diamond.

"I know, right? It's ridiculous." Jordan beamed. "It's way too extravagant. Ian really shouldn't have…but I'm glad he did."

"Dylan." Jordan draped her arm across Mackenzie's shoulders. "*This* is my *awesome* cousin, Mackenzie. She owns Nothin' But Cupcakes, home of the famous giant cupcakes. Look it up." To Mackenzie she said, "Thank you again for bringing us emergency cupcakes."

"Of course." Mackenzie kept her eyes trained on her cousin in order to avoid making eye contact with Dylan. For the first time in a long time, she wished she still had her thick tortoiseshell glasses to hide behind.

"Mackenzie—this's Dylan Axel… Dylan is the *Axel* in Sterling and Axel Photography. He's also a certified investment planner. He totally has the Midas touch with money, so if you ever need financial advice for your business, he's your man."

Mackenzie had to make a concerted effort to breathe normally and braced herself for Dylan to recognize her. But when she did finally shift her eyes to his, Dylan still didn't show even a *flicker* of recognition. He didn't seem to have the *first clue* that he was being introduced to a woman he had known in the *biblical* sense of the word. Instead, he looked between them with a slightly perplexed expression on his good-looking face. No doubt, he was wondering how she had managed to sneak into gorgeous Jordan's gene pool.

"Now I know your name." Dylan held out his hand to her once more. "Mackenzie."

The way Dylan lingered on her name sent her heart palpitating again. He was looking at her in the way a man looks at a woman he finds attractive. Dylan had never looked at her this way before. It was…*unsettling.* And yet, *validating.* It was undeniable proof that she had truly managed to eradicate the obese preteen with Coke-bottle glasses and tangled, mousy hair that she had once been.

Mackenzie forced herself to maintain the appearance of calm when she slipped her hand into his. She quickly shook his hand and then tucked her hand away in her pocket. Inside her pocket, where no one could see, Mackenzie balled up her fingers into a tight fist.

Oblivious to her cousin's discomfort, Jordan rested her arm across Mackenzie's shoulders. "Do you need help bringing in the cupcakes?"

Mackenzie nodded. "You wanted a ton. You got a ton."

Jordan walked with Mackenzie through the still-open front door. She tossed over her shoulder, "Give us a hand, Dylan, will you?"

"We can manage," Mackenzie protested immediately.

"I'm not about to let you ladies do all the heavy lifting by yourselves," Dylan said as he trailed behind them.

As they approached her car, Dylan whistled appreciatively. It was no surprise; men always commented on her car.

"The 1960 Chevrolet Biscayne Delivery Sedan painted with the original factory turquoise from back in the day. *Nice.*" Dylan ran his hand lovingly over the hood of her car. "She's yours?"

Mackenzie nodded quickly before she walked to the back of the delivery sedan; she unlocked, and then lifted up, the heavy back hatch of the vehicle.

"Who did this restoration?" Dylan asked as he leaned down and looked at the interior of the Chevy.

"A place up near Sacramento." Mackenzie wanted to be vague. Her brother, Jett, who had restored her Chevy at his hot-rod shop, had been friends with Dylan back in middle school. In fact, the last time Mackenzie had seen Dylan Axel was *at* Jett's wedding nearly eleven years ago.

"Well—they did an insane job. This car is *beautiful*. I'd really like to take a look under her hood."

"Hey!" Jordan poked her head around the back of the car. "Are you gonna help us out here, Axel, or what?"

"I'm helping." Dylan laughed as he strolled to the back of the vehicle. "But you can't blame a guy for looking, now, can you?"

"Here. Make yourself useful, will ya?" Jordan rolled her eyes at him as she handed him a large box of cupcakes. "And, no, I don't get the obsession with cars that went out of production *decades* ago. They don't make them anymore for a *reason*. Now, if you want to get excited about a motorcycle, I can totally relate to that!"

Dylan took the box from Jordan but smiled at Mackenzie. "Well—your cousin gets it, don't you?"

Mackenzie looked directly into Dylan's oh-so-familiar crystal-clear green eyes for a split second. "I get it."

"See!" Dylan smiled triumphantly at Jordan. "She gets it."

"Well—sure. Her dad and brother raised Mackenzie in a garage. Basically, she's been brainwashed. No offense, cuz."

"None taken." Mackenzie balanced the large cupcake box in the crook of her arm while she pulled down the heavy hatch door. Mackenzie gave the hatch door a bump with her hip to shut it completely.

"Okay," Mackenzie said, wanting to speed things along. "Let's get the troops out of the sun."

Dylan kept pace with her as they walked back to the condo. "I haven't heard someone say that since I was a kid."

"Really?" Mackenzie pretended to be fascinated with the neighbor's house. "I hear it all the time."

That was one of her father's favorite phrases; no doubt, Dylan had heard him use it a zillion times before he moved away from the neighborhood. Her father had restored vintage cars as a hobby in the garage behind her childhood home, and all of the neighborhood boys, including Dylan, had loved to hang out with him.

"This works." Jordan put her box down on the large marble slab island that separated the kitchen from the great room.

Mackenzie put her box down next to Jordan's and started to formulate an exit strategy. Dylan opened the top of his box and reached for a cupcake. Jordan slapped his hand playfully and put the box lid back down.

"Get your sticky paws off the cupcakes, mister! Ian isn't even here yet! I can't believe he's late for his own party."

"I'm still surprised he agreed to this at all," Dylan said. "You know Ian hates crowds."

"No. You're right. He does. But I'm determined to pull

that man out of his shell kicking and screaming if I have to." Jordan pulled her phone out of the back pocket of her dark-wash skinny jeans. To Mackenzie she said, "Give me a sec, okay? I want to see what's holding him up. The two of you haven't even met each other yet."

Jordan plugged one ear and held the phone to the other as she headed outside to call her fiancé. Even though there was a large group of people milling around in the great room, using it as a pass-through to the bathrooms or the deck outside, at the moment, Mackenzie and Dylan were the only two people in the kitchen. Dylan sent her a conspiratorial wink as he lifted the box top and snagged one of her giant cupcakes.

Dylan devoured the devil's food cupcake in three bites. "These are incredible. Did you make these?"

Mackenzie nodded. "There's another cupcake designer who works for me, but these are mine."

Dylan grabbed a second cupcake and sent Mackenzie a questioning look. "I can count on you not to tell Jordan, right?"

"She *is* my cousin," Mackenzie said as she scratched her arm under her long-sleeved shirt. Being around Dylan again was making her skin feel itchy and hot.

"Good call," Dylan said before he bit into the second cupcake. "You gotta pick family over some random guy you just met. I understand."

Before she could respond, a statuesque Cameron Diaz look-alike in a tiny bikini breezed into the kitchen like she owned it.

"Babe," Jenna said as she dropped a quick kiss on Dylan's cheek, "we're running out of ice out there *already*."

"Okay. I'll run down to the store and grab some more," Dylan said before he took another bite.

Jenna opened the refrigerator and pulled out a can of

diet cola. She popped the top, took a sip and put the can on the counter.

"Hi," she said to Mackenzie and then moved on.

Dylan gave his girlfriend a "look" and handed her a coaster to put under the can. Jenna rolled her eyes, but put the coaster beneath the can. Then she crossed her arms over her chest, her pretty face registering a combination of disbelief and disgust.

"Babe—*what* are you *eating*?" Jenna frowned at him.

"Cupcakes." Dylan took another bite of the giant cupcake and pushed a box toward his girlfriend. "Want one?"

"Are you *insane*?" Jenna asked, horrified. "Carbs, Dylan! I've got an audition tomorrow in LA—the last thing I want to be is all *puffy* and *bloated*. I don't know how you can put that poison into your body anyway."

"Happily." Dylan winked at Mackenzie.

"Whatever." Jenna walked to the door. She paused in the doorway and yelled, "Ice!"

"Got it." Dylan didn't look at Jenna as he wolfed down the final bite of the cupcake.

Instead of leaving to get ice, Dylan stayed with her in the kitchen. "So—did you grow up in Montana, too?"

Mackenzie looked up at Dylan—one part of her wanted to exit stage left without saying a word, but the other part wanted to rip off the Band-Aid and get the inevitable out of the way. It wasn't a matter of *if* she would confront Dylan about their past—it was a matter of *when*. She was impatient by nature, so perhaps, *when* she should bring up their past was *right now*.

Gripping the side of the kitchen counter to hold her body steady, Mackenzie asked quietly, "You don't recognize me, do you?"

Dylan's brow dropped and a question mark came into

his eyes. He stared at her face hard, and she could almost see the wheels in his brain turning, trying to place her.

"You're not going to believe this, you guys." Jordan threw her hands up into the air as she walked into the kitchen. "He's stuck at the studio—his editor needs him to do something for the new book. He won't be here for *at least* another hour." Jordan's shoulders sagged as she asked Mackenzie, "You can hang out that long, can't you? I've been so busy with my gallery show that I've hardly spent any time with you—"

"I really can't stay." Mackenzie shook her head. "I have to get back to the bakery."

"What a drag." Jordan sighed. "I know, I know...business first. Ian's *exactly* the same way."

"I'll text you," Mackenzie promised. "We'll figure out when we can sync our calendars."

"Okay. It's a plan," Jordan agreed as she hugged her cousin one last time. "Give Hope a kiss for me."

"I will." Mackenzie glanced nervously at Dylan, who hadn't stopped staring at her. Jordan's phone rang. She checked the number. "It's the caterer. Let me grab this first and then I'll walk you out."

"Don't worry about it." Dylan, still staring hard at Mackenzie's face, said to Jordan, "I'll walk her out."

"You're all right, Dylan—I don't care what they say about you." Jordan punched Dylan lightly on the arm, and then gave Mackenzie one last parting hug before she answered the call.

Mackenzie could feel Dylan's intent gaze on her as they walked the short distance to the front door. Dylan opened the door for her.

"You say we've met?" Dylan asked curiously after he shut the front door behind him.

Dylan studied the petite, curvy woman walking beside

him and he tried to figure out who she was before she had to tell him. He had had a lot of drunken hookups when he was in college and he hoped that she wasn't one of them.

It seemed to Mackenzie that her heart was pumping way too much blood, too quickly, through her veins. She was light-headed and for a split second, as she was coming down the front steps, it felt as if she might just pass out.

This is happening. After all these years. This is really happening.

"Yes. We've met," Mackenzie said as she walked quickly to her car, unlocked the door and then opened it so she would have something to lean on.

"You were good friends with my brother, Jett, back in middle school." Mackenzie gripped the frame of the open car door so hard that her fingers started to hurt.

"Jett…?" Dylan shook his head slightly as if he didn't connect with the name, but then recognition slowly started to dawn as a smile started to move across his face.

"Wait a minute!" Dylan exclaimed. "*Big Mac*? Is that you?"

Mackenzie blanched. No one had called her that horrible nickname since high school.

"I don't like to be called that," she said. When she was growing up, no one called her "Mackenzie." Jett and her friends always called her "Mac." Cruel kids at school had added the "Big" to it and the horrible nickname had followed her like a black cloud until she graduated from high school.

"Hey—I'm sorry. I didn't mean anything by it." He couldn't stop staring at her face. This was not the Mackenzie he remembered. The thick, old-lady glasses were gone, her hair was darker and longer, and she had slimmed down. She wasn't skinny; she was curvy, which was a pretty rare occurrence in California. The word *voluptuous* popped into his head to describe her now.

"Just don't call me that anymore, okay?"

"Yeah. Sure. Never again, I promise," Dylan promised, his eyes smiling at her. "Man. I can't believe it…Jett's little sister! You look great."

"Thanks," Mackenzie said.

"Man…" Dylan crossed his arms loosely in front of his body and shook his head. "How long has it been? Five, six years?"

"Ten," Mackenzie said too quickly and then added more nonchalantly, "Give or take."

"Ten years." Dylan nodded as he tried to remember the last time he had seen her. When it hit him, he snapped his fingers. "Jett's wedding, right? I can't believe I didn't recognize you right away—but, in my defense, Mackenzie, you've changed."

"Yeah, well…losing a hundred pounds will do that to a person," Mackenzie said. She was watching him closely; it still didn't seem to be registering with him that they had slept together after Jett's reception.

"A hundred pounds?" he repeated, surprised. "I don't remember you needing to lose that much."

"You'd be one of the few." Mackenzie heard that old defensiveness creep into her tone.

Several seconds of silence slipped by before Dylan asked, "So—how's Jett doing nowadays? Still married?"

"Uh-uh." Mackenzie shook her head. "The marriage didn't work out. But he's got custody of both kids, so that's the upside of that situation."

"Does he live around here, too?"

"No. He owns a hot-rod shop up in Paradise, California. He wanted to be closer to Dad and he thought a small town would be better for the girls."

"A hot-rod shop, huh? So wait a minute—did Jett do this restoration?" Dylan asked with a nod toward her car.

"Yep." Mackenzie nodded proudly. Her older brother had managed to build a lucrative career out of a passion he shared with their dad.

"Man—I'm telling you what, he did a *fantastic* job on this Chevy. I really respect that he kept it true to the original design. I've gotta tell you, this's pretty amazing timing running into you like this because I've been looking for someone to restore my Charger. I gotta get her out of storage and back out on the road."

"You should check out his website—High-Octane Hot Rods."

"High-Octane Hot Rods. I'll do that." Dylan hadn't stopped smiling at her since he'd realized she was Jett's little sister. "So, tell me about you, Mackenzie. Are you married? Got any kids?"

Instead of answering his question, Mackenzie slipped behind the wheel of the car. "Listen—I wish I could spend more time catching up, but I've really gotta go."

"No problem," Dylan said easily, his hands resting on the door frame so he could close the door for her. "We're bound to run into each other again."

Mackenzie sent him a fleeting smile while she cranked the engine and shifted into gear. Fate had unexpectedly forced her hand and now she was just going to have to figure out how to deal with it.

Chapter Two

Once out of Dylan's neighborhood, Mackenzie drove to the nearest public parking lot. She pulled into an empty space away from the other cars, fished her cell phone out of her pocket and dialed her best friend's number with shaky fingers.

"Rayna…?"

"Mackenzie? What's wrong? Why do you sound like that? Did something happen to Hope?"

"No." Mackenzie slouched against the door. "She's fine."

"Then what's wrong? You sound like something's wrong."

"I just ran into Dylan." There was a tremor in her voice.

"Dylan who?"

"What do you mean, Dylan *who*?" Mackenzie asked, irritated. "Dylan *Axel*."

"What?" Now she had Rayna's attention. "You're kidding!"

"No." Mackenzie rubbed her temple. She could feel a migraine coming on. "I'm *not* kidding."

"Where in the world did you run into him?"

"At his condo. In Mission Beach."

"He lives in Mission Beach?"

"Apparently so."

"What were you doing there?"

"Delivering cupcakes to Jordan's fiancé's birthday party," Mackenzie said as she tilted her head back and closed her eyes. "Dylan is *Ian's* best friend."

Rayna didn't respond immediately. After a few silent seconds, her friend said, "Oh. Wow. Are you okay?"

"I feel like I'm suffocating."

"Anxiety," Rayna surmised.

"Probably." Mackenzie put her free hand over her rapidly beating heart.

"Just close your eyes and take in long, deep breaths. You'll feel better in a minute."

"Okay..."

"Where are you now?"

"I'm parked. I didn't feel...stable enough to drive."

"That was smart," Rayna said. "Look—just take your time, pull yourself together and then come over. We'll figure this out. Hope's still at the barn?"

"Yeah. I pick her up at seven, after they bed down the horses."

"Charlie'll be home by the time you get here—we'll commiserate over pasta," Rayna said in her typical take-charge tone.

"Thank you." Comfort food with friends sounded like a great idea.

"And, Mackenzie?"

"Yeah?"

"It's going to be okay," Rayna said. "God is answering our prayers."

Rayna was one of the pastors for her nondenominational church of like-minded hippies and saw all life's events through the lens of a true believer.

"Hope's prayers," Mackenzie clarified. "Hope's prayers."

"Hope's prayers *are* our prayers. Aren't they?" Rayna countered gently. "Listen—I'll put on a pot of coffee and I'll see you when you get here. Be safe."

Mackenzie hung up the phone but didn't crank the engine immediately. Her mind was racing but her body was motionless. After ten minutes of taking long, deep breaths, Mackenzie finally felt calm enough to drive and set off for her friend's Balboa Park bungalow. Rayna was right. Her daughter's prayers *were* her prayers. She just hadn't been prepared for *this* prayer to be answered so quickly.

"Little one!" Molita Jean-Baptiste, the bakery manager, poked her head into the kitchen. "There's a young man out here who wants to talk to you."

"Okay," Mackenzie said as she slid a large pan of carrot-cake cupcakes into the oven. "I'll be right there."

Mackenzie closed the door of the industrial baking oven and then wiped her hands on a towel before she headed for the front of the bakery. She put a welcoming, professional smile on her face as she pushed the swinging doors apart and walked through. But her smile dropped for a split second when she saw Dylan standing next to one of the display counters.

"Hi," Dylan greeted her with his friendly, boyish smile. "Nice place."

"Thank you." Mackenzie glanced over at Molita who was restocking the cases and pretending to mind her own business. "Are you here to order cupcakes?"

"No." Dylan laughed. "I'm here to see you."

"Oh." Mackenzie frowned. "Okay."

For the last week, she had lost countless hours of sleep trying to figure out what to do about Dylan. And after so many sleepless nights, she *still* hadn't figured out how to blindside the man with a ten-year-old daughter.

"Would you like something to eat, young man?" Molita asked. Haitian-born and in her sixties now, Molita was as round as she was tall. Whether Molita was having a day of aches and pains or not, she always greeted the customers like family. She was the backbone of Nothin' But Cupcakes, and Mackenzie often joked that customers came to see Molita as much as they came for the cupcakes.

"No, thank you." Dylan put his hand on his flat stomach. "I'm trying to watch my girlish figure."

"Well..." Molita smiled warmly at Dylan. "You'll let me know if you change your mind. I just put on a fresh pot of coffee."

Dylan thanked Molita for the offer and then asked in a lowered voice, "Is there someplace we can talk?"

"Um...yeah. We can talk in my office, I suppose. But I only have a minute."

"This won't take too long," Dylan said.

"I'll be right back, Moll. I'm just going to step into my office for a minute or two."

"You know I'll call ya if I need'ja," Molita called out from behind the counter.

Dylan followed her to the office. She didn't typically take anyone to the office, and it struck her, when she opened the door, just how tiny and cluttered it really was.

"Sorry about the mess." Mackenzie shuffled some papers around in a halfhearted attempt to straighten up. "Believe it or not, I have a system in here..."

"I'm not worried about it." Dylan closed the door behind

him. If Jenna didn't use a coaster under a glass, it bugged him. But, for whatever reason, Mackenzie's untidy office didn't bother him so much.

Dylan squeezed himself into the small chair wedged in the corner on the other side of Mackenzie's desk.

"It smells really good in here." Dylan shifted uncomfortably, his knees pressed against the back of the desk.

Mackenzie hastily shoved some papers in a drawer. "Does it?"

"It does." Dylan looked around the office. "Now I know why you smell like a sugar cookie."

Surprised, Mackenzie slammed the drawer shut and stopped avoiding the inevitable eye contact with Dylan.

When Mackenzie looked at him with those unusual lavender-blue eyes, Dylan felt an unfamiliar tingling sensation in the pit of his stomach. There was something about Mackenzie's eyes that captivated him. He hadn't been able to get those eyes out of his head since the party.

"So..." Mackenzie said after an awkward lull. "What can I do for you, Dylan?"

Out of the corner of her eye, she could see the framed picture of her daughter, Hope, and resisted the urge to turn it away from Dylan.

"Actually..." Dylan tried to cross one leg over the other in the tight space and failed. "I wanted to do something for you."

Mackenzie pushed her long sleeves up to her elbows. "What's that?"

Dylan took the picture of Hope off the desk. "Cute kid. Yours?"

"Yes." Mackenzie's pulse jumped. "That's my daughter, Hope, at her fourth birthday party."

Mackenzie waited, anxiety twisting her gut, and wondered if Dylan would recognize his own flesh and blood in that picture. When he didn't, part of her was relieved and the other part was disappointed. Dylan put the picture back on the shelf without ever realizing that Hope was his. Mackenzie moved the frame to her side of the desk and turned it away from Dylan.

"Is Brand your married name? I remember you as Bronson." Dylan glanced down at the ring finger of her left hand.

"No." Mackenzie shook her head. "I decided to take my mom's maiden name when Hope was born. I wanted Hope to truly be her namesake."

Dylan's gaze was direct as he asked, "So, you're not married...?"

"No." Mackenzie wasn't subtle about looking up at the clock on the wall. As much as she knew that she needed to talk to Dylan about Hope, this wasn't the right time. They had three catering gigs set for the evening, and the afternoon lunch crowd would be lining up soon. She was already struggling to make payroll; she couldn't afford to lose one sale.

"Dylan...look, I don't mean to be rude..." Mackenzie started to say.

Dylan held up his hands and smiled sheepishly. "Okay... okay. I'll admit it. I'm stalling. It's just that, what I wanted to say to you seemed like a good idea this morning, but now..."

Mackenzie leaned forward on her arms and waited for Dylan to continue. Whatever it was that he wanted to say was making him turn red in the face and shift nervously in his chair. He had turned out to be a nice-looking man, with his dark brown hair and vivid green eyes. But Dylan wasn't classically handsome. He wasn't a pretty boy. Dylan's nose had been broken when they were kids and it hadn't healed back completely straight. There was a Y-shaped scar directly under his left eye from the time he'd caught a baseball with his face during a Little League game. These little imperfections didn't detract from his good looks for Mackenzie; they enhanced them.

"All right." Dylan rubbed the back of his neck. "I'm just going to say what I came here to say. I owe you an apology, Mackenzie."

Mackenzie's chair squeaked loudly when she sat back. "Why in the world would you need to apologize to *me*?"

"Because..." Dylan looked at her directly in the eyes. "I remember what happened between us the night of Jett's wedding."

Mackenzie ran her hand over her leg beneath the desk and gripped her knee hard with her fingers. "Oh."

"Obviously that wasn't the sort of thing that I wanted to bring up while we were standing on the street."

"No." Mackenzie shook her head first and then nodded in agreement. "I'm glad you didn't."

"But...I didn't want you to think that I had forgotten about...*after* the reception..."

"We both had a lot to drink that night..." Mackenzie said faintly.

"Yes—we did. But, I still think I owe you an apology..." Dylan leaned forward. "You were Jett's little sister, and no matter how much I had to drink that night, I shouldn't have...taken advantage of you."

"Taken *advantage* of me?" Mackenzie asked incredulously. "You didn't take advantage of me, Dylan. I knew exactly what I was doing."

"You had just broken up with your boyfriend..." Dylan said.

"And you had just broken off your engagement..." Mackenzie countered. "I think we both need to just give each other a break about that night, okay?"

Dylan took a deep breath in as he thought about her words. Then he said, his expression pensive, "I should've called you, Mackenzie. After that night, I should've called you."

"And said what?"

"I don't know..." Dylan shrugged his shoulders. "I could've checked on you, made sure you were okay." He looked down at his hands for a second before he looked back up at her. "I should've let you know that I'd gotten back with Christa. I look back and I think maybe I used to be kind of an insensitive jerk...I know I can't apologize to everyone, but at least I have a chance to apologize to you."

"Well..." Mackenzie crossed her arms in front of her body. "I appreciate the apology, Dylan. I do. But, I never thought that you'd *wronged* me in any way. And I don't ever remember you being a jerk, at least not to me. You were the only one of my brother's friends who never ignored me. You never treated me like the weird *fat* girl."

"I never saw you that way," Dylan said, surprised. "And it'd make me feel better if you'd accept my apology..."

"Then I accept." It felt as if she just might be laying the groundwork for him to accept *her* apology later. "Of course I accept."

"Good." Dylan smiled at her. "Thank you."

"You're welcome." Mackenzie stood up. "Listen—I'm sorry that it seems like I'm always cutting things short, but..."

"No. No. That's okay." Dylan's chair knocked into the wall when he stood up. "I'm holding you up from work. But before I take off, I really want to show you something outside. It'll only take a second, I promise. And, trust me. You're gonna want to see what I have to show you."

"Okay. But then I really need to get back to work. I have a ton of special orders to fill." Mackenzie walked through the door that Dylan held open for her. "And let me tell you, there's a seedy underbelly of sugar addicts in San Diego and they all start to line up for a lunchtime fix." Mackenzie stopped at the counter and checked on Molita. "Are you doing okay, Moll?"

"Don't you worry about me, now. I've got everything under control." Molita sprayed glass cleaner on the front of the display case. "You go handle your business."

"I'll be right back," Mackenzie said.

"I wanted to show you my baby." Dylan held open the bakery door for her. "My girlfriend doesn't understand old school, but I knew you'd appreciate her."

Mackenzie stepped onto the sidewalk, but halted in her tracks just outside the door. "Is that what I *think* it is?"

Dylan smiled triumphantly at her as he walked over to his car. "Didn't I tell you you'd want to see her?"

Mackenzie couldn't take her eyes off Dylan's rare, vintage car. This car could easily sell for one hundred and fifty *thousand* dollars. "You do know that this is the stuff of legends, right?"

"You know I do," Dylan said. "And *you* know exactly what you're looking at, don't you?"

"Of course I do. I took Old School 101 with Dad and Jett...which I aced, by the way," Mackenzie bragged as she walked over to his car. "This sweet girl is a 1963 split-back Chevy Corvette. Super rare because the split window went out of production in 1964."

"You got it." Dylan's smile broadened.

"Basically, the Holy Grail." Mackenzie ran her hand along the curved hood of the car.

"That's right." Dylan nodded his head, his arms crossed loosely in front of him. "See? I *knew* you'd be excited to see her."

"You have no idea." Mackenzie walked around to the

back of the car. "Dylan—this's all original. Jett would die to get his hands on this car. She's not for sale, is she?"

"Not a chance." Dylan shook his head as he walked up to stand beside her. "But I really want Jett to restore my Charger."

Mackenzie found herself smiling at Dylan. "That would mean a lot to Jett, Dylan. It really would."

"I was thinking about giving the Charger this same silver-flake paint job with flat black accents. What do you think?"

Mackenzie's phone rang. "Hold that thought."

"Sure." Dylan leaned casually against his car.

"Hi, Aggie." Mackenzie leaned her head down and plugged one ear. "Wait a minute—what happened?" Mackenzie's face turned pale. "Tell Hope I'm on my way."

"Everything okay?" Dylan asked.

"No." Mackenzie headed back to the bakery. "My daughter got hurt at the barn."

"I hope she's okay," Dylan called after her.

"Thanks." Mackenzie pulled the bakery door open. Inside the bakery now, she stopped and threw up her hands in the air. "Tamara has my car! Molly—did you drive today?"

"My granddaughter dropped me off." Molita put a cupcake in a box for a customer.

Mackenzie made a quick U-turn and pushed the bakery door back open. "Molly—I have to go get Hope. Hold down the fort, okay?"

"What happened?" Molly asked, concerned.

"She hit her head at the barn." Mackenzie pushed the door open. "I'll call you later with an update as soon as I have one!"

Dylan had his blinker on and he was about to ease out onto the street when he saw Mackenzie bolt out of the cupcake shop and run toward his car. He braked and rolled down the passenger window.

Mackenzie bent down so she could see Dylan. “Can you give me a ride? My car is out with the deliveries.”

Dylan reached over, unlocked the door and opened it for Mackenzie. “Hop in.”

The thirty-minute ride out to the barn was a quiet one. Mackenzie’s entire body was tense, her brow wrinkled with worry; seemingly lost in her own internal dialogue, she only spoke to give him directions. And he didn’t press her for conversation. He imagined that if he were in her shoes, he wouldn’t be in the mood for small talk, either.

“Turn left right here.” Mackenzie pointed to a dirt side road up ahead. “You’ll have to go slow in this car—with all the rain lately, there are potholes galore on the way to the barn. Not many Corvettes brave this road.”

“I can see why not.” Dylan slowed way down as he turned onto the muddy dirt road. He looked at the large sign at the entrance of the road.

“Pegasus Therapeutic Riding—is that where we’re heading?”

“Yes.” Mackenzie unbuckled her seat belt.

Dylan glanced over at Mackenzie. “What’s wrong with your daughter?”

“There’s *nothing* wrong with Hope. She’s perfect,” Mackenzie snapped. After a second, she added in a tempered tone, “Hope loves horses and she loves helping people. Volunteering here is what she wants to do with her free time.”

“She must take after you.” Dylan drove up onto the grassy berm in order to avoid a large pothole. “I remember you were always busy with a cause…collecting canned goods and clothing for the homeless, volunteering at the animal shelter…you were never satisfied with playing video games and hanging out at the beach like the rest of us…"

Mackenzie's shoulders stiffened. She had been picked on mercilessly when she was a kid about her causes. "There's nothing wrong with caring about your community."

Dylan jerked the wheel to the left to avoid another pothole. He glanced quickly at Mackenzie; her arms were crossed, her jaw was clenched. He'd managed to put her on the defensive in record time. Usually he was pretty good at navigating his way around women.

"I meant it as a compliment," Dylan clarified. "And Hope sounds like a really good kid."

"She is." Mackenzie stared straight ahead. "She's the best kind of kid."

"How old did you say she was?"

"I didn't say." Mackenzie spotted the weathered brown barn up ahead. "You can pull in right there between the van and the truck…"

As Dylan eased the car to a stop, Mackenzie already had her hand on the door handle. With her free hand, she touched his arm briefly. "Thank you, Dylan. You've managed to rescue me twice in one week."

"Do you want me to wait here for you?" Dylan shifted into park.

"No!" Mackenzie pushed the door open and climbed out of the low-slung car. "I mean…no. That's okay. You've already done enough."

Dylan leaned down so he could see her face. "Are you sure?"

"Yes. Really. We'll be fine." Mackenzie closed the car door and hoped that she had also closed the subject of Dylan sticking around. Now that she was at the barn, she couldn't imagine what she had been thinking. This was *not* the time or place for Dylan to meet his daughter. Something that life-altering took planning. And she didn't have a plan. Not for this.

Dylan shut off the engine, pulled the keys out of the ignition and jumped out of the car. He wanted to follow Mackenzie, but she was sending out some pretty obvious back-off signals.

"I could just hang right here…."

Mackenzie spun around and walked backward a couple of steps. "I'll catch a ride from someone here. Really. I'm sure you have a day."

Dylan stared after Mackenzie. It didn't seem right just to drop her off and then leave, no matter what she said. But, on the other hand, she hadn't exactly been diplomatic about telling him to shove off. Reluctantly, Dylan climbed back into his car and shut the door. He rolled down the window, slipped the key in the ignition and turned the engine over. Mackenzie had been right about one thing. He did have a day. And he needed to get back to it.

Chapter Three

Dylan shifted into Reverse, but he just couldn't bring himself to back out. Instead, he shifted back into Park, shut off the engine and got out of the car. Whether or not Mackenzie wanted him to make certain she was okay before he took off, it was something he felt he needed to do. Dylan set off toward the barn entrance; he carefully picked his way through long grass, weeds and sun-dried horse manure.

"You need some help?" Dylan was greeted by a young man in his early twenties leading a dark brown mare to one of the pastures. The young man appeared to have cerebral palsy and walked with a jerky, unsteady gate.

"I'm looking for Hope and her mom," Dylan said.

"They're in the office." The young man pointed behind him.

"Thanks," Dylan said just before he felt his left shoe sink into a fresh pile of manure. "Crap!"

"Yes, sir." The young man laughed as he turned the mare loose in the pasture. "That's exactly what it is."

Dylan shook his head as he tried to wipe the manure off his shoe in the grass. Today of all days he had to put on his Testoni lace-ups; he had spent some time this morning, polishing and buffing them to just the right amount of shine. Once he managed to semiclean his pricey leather shoes, he got himself back on track and found his way to the office. Dylan quietly stepped inside the disheveled hub of Pegasus. Dirt and hay were strewn across the floor and a large, rusty fan was kicking up more dust than circulating air. Mackenzie, a girl who must have been her daughter and a tall woman with cropped snow-white hair were gathered near a gray metal desk at the back of the rectangular office.

"Mom—I'm okay. When I bent down to grab a currycomb, I hit my head on the shelf. It's no big deal," Dylan heard Hope say.

Mackenzie brushed the girl's bangs out of the way to look at the bump on Hope's forehead. "Well—you've got a pretty good knot up there, kiddo."

"Here." The older woman held out a Ziploc baggy full of ice. "This'll hold her till you can get her checked out."

"But we still have more riders coming," Hope protested.

Mackenzie took the bag of ice. "Thanks, Aggie."

"They need my help, Mom! I'm *fine*. Really. I don't need to go to the doctor." Hope tried once again to reverse her fortune.

"Honey—I'm sorry." Mackenzie held her daughter's hand in hers. "We've gotta get this checked out. If the doctor gives you the green light, I promise, you'll be right back here tomorrow."

Hope sighed dramatically and pressed the ice to the lump on her forehead. "Fine."

Not wanting to interrupt the mother-daughter negotiation, Dylan hung back.

"Can I help you?" Aggie was suddenly in his face and confronting him like a protective mama bear with a cub.

Dylan slipped off his sunglasses and hooked them into the collar of his shirt. "I'm just checking on Mackenzie."

Mackenzie jerked her head around when she heard his voice. She swayed slightly and heard ringing in her ears as sheer panic sent her blood pressure soaring. "Dylan… why are you still here?"

"I'm just making sure you're okay before I leave." Dylan couldn't figure out why Mackenzie was freaked out about him looking out for her. Her overreaction struck him as odd.

Trapped, Mackenzie turned to face Dylan and blocked his view of Hope with her body. "That's my ride, Aggie."

"Oh!" Aggie wiped the sweat from the deep wrinkles etched into her brow. "If I'd known that, I would've made it a point to more cordial. I thought you might be one of them developers the Cook family's been sending around here lately…."

"Developers?" Mackenzie asked, temporarily distracted from her immediate problem.

Aggie waved her hand back and forth impatiently. "I don't want to borrow trouble talkin' about it right now.

"Agnes Abbot." Agnes stuck out her hand to Dylan. "You can call me Aggie or Mrs. Abbot—take your pick. But if you call me Agnes, don't expect an answer."

"Nice to meet you, Mrs. Abbot." Aggie's hand was damp and gritty. "Dylan Axel."

"And when I said that you could take your pick, I meant for you to pick Aggie."

"Aggie," Dylan repeated with a nod.

"Who's that, Mom?" Hope peeked around Mackenzie's body.

Realizing that there was no way out of this trap except forward, Mackenzie suddenly felt completely, abnormally, calm. This *was* going to happen. This meeting between father and daughter was unfolding organically, out of her control. Wasn't Rayna always preaching about life providing the right experiences at the right time? Maybe she was right. Perhaps she just needed to get out of life's way. So she did. She took a small step to the side and let Hope see her father for the first time.

"Hope—this is my friend Dylan." Her voice was surprisingly steady. "Dylan—I'd like you to meet my daughter, Hope."

Mackenzie zoomed in on Dylan's face first, and then Hope's, as they spoke to each other for the first time. If she had expected them to recognize each other instantly, like a made-for-TV movie, they didn't.

"Hi, Hope. How's your head?" Dylan had walked over to where Hope was sitting. For Mackenzie, it was so easy to see Dylan in Hope—the way she walked, the way she held her shoulders. Her smile.

"It doesn't even hurt," Hope explained to him.

Hope had Mackenzie's curly russet hair, cut into a bob just below her chin, as well as her mother's violet-blue eyes. But, that's where the resemblance ended. Her face was round instead of heart-shaped like her mother's; her skin was fairer and she had freckles on her arms and her face. The thought popped into his head that Hope must take strongly after her father's side of the family.

To Aggie, Hope said, "I think I should stay here. Don't you think I should stay?"

"No, ma'am." Aggie shook her head while she riffled around in one of the desk's drawers. "Your mom's got the right idea. They'll be just fine without us while we get you checked out."

"Nice try, kiddo." Mackenzie held out her hand to Hope. "You're going."

"Man..." Hope's mouth drooped in disappointment. But she put her hand into Mackenzie's hand and stood up slowly.

"Come on, kiddo...cheer up." Mackenzie wrapped her arm tightly around Hope's shoulders and kissed the top of her head. "We've been through worse, right?"

"Right." Hope gave her mom a halfhearted smile and returned the hug.

"Found one." Aggie pulled a pamphlet out of the pencil drawer and tromped over to Dylan in her knee-high rubber boots.

"Here." Aggie pressed the pamphlet into Dylan's hand, then she tapped on the front of it. "Here's the 411 on this place. We're always looking for volunteers. Do you have any horse experience?"

Dylan looked at the pamphlet. "Actually, I do."

"Perfect! We can always use another volunteer with some horse sense," Aggie said to him, hands resting on her squared hips. Then to Mackenzie, she said, "Well—let's get."

While Dylan skimmed the pamphlet quickly, it occurred to Mackenzie that she had just survived a moment that she had dreaded, and worried herself sick about, for years. Dylan and Hope had met and the world hadn't fallen off its axis. It gave her reason to believe that when the truth about their relationship came out, things would be okay for all of them.

Dylan folded the pamphlet and tucked it into his front pocket.

"Are you going to volunteer?" Hope asked him.

Mackenzie and Hope were standing directly in front of him now, arm in arm, the close bond between mother and daughter on display. It didn't surprise him that Mackenzie had turned out to be a dedicated and attentive mother. The way she had always taken care of every living thing around her when they were young, he didn't doubt it had been an easy transition into motherhood.

"I don't know." Dylan shifted his eyes between mother and daughter. "Maybe."

"You should." Hope tucked some of her hair behind her ear. "It's really fun."

From the doorway, Aggie rattled her keys. "We're burning daylight here! Let's go!"

"We're coming," Mackenzie said to Aggie, then to Dylan, "Thank you, Dylan. I'm sure you had a lot of things to do today. I hope this didn't put you behind schedule too much…"

"I was glad I could help." Dylan found himself intrigued, once again, by Mackenzie's unique lavender-blue eyes.

"Well…thank you again." Mackenzie sent him a brief smile. "Come on, kiddo. Aggie's already got the truck running."

"Nice to meet you, Hope," Dylan said.

"Bye." Hope lifted her hand up and gave a short wave.

Dylan waited for Mackenzie and Hope to turn and head toward the door. As Hope turned, something on the very top of her left ear caught his eye. Instead of following directly behind them, Dylan was too distracted to move. Dylan's eyes narrowed and latched on to Hope as he reached up to touch a similar small bump at the top of his own left ear.

"Are you coming, Dylan?" Mackenzie had paused in the doorway.

"What?" Dylan asked, distracted.

"Are you coming?" Mackenzie repeated.

Dylan swallowed hard several times. He couldn't seem to get his mouth to move, so he just nodded his response and forced himself to remain calm. Hands jammed into his front pockets, Dylan followed them out. He watched as Mackenzie and Hope piled into Aggie's blue long-bed dual-tire truck. Aggie backed out, Mackenzie waved goodbye and Dylan's jumbled thoughts managed to land on one very disturbing truth: the only other time he had ever seen a small bump like Hope's was when he was looking at himself in the mirror.

Instead of heading to the studio, which was his original plan, Dylan drove home on autopilot from the barn. His mind was churning like a hamster on a hamster wheel, just going around and around in the same circle. No matter how hard he tried, he couldn't remember if he'd used a condom when he'd slept with Mackenzie. He had always been religious about it, but he hadn't expected to sleep with anyone at the wedding. He had still been licking his wounds from his breakup with Christa, and ending up in Mackenzie's hotel room that night had been a completely unplanned event. And, unless Mackenzie was in the habit of carrying condoms, which seemed out of character, there was a real good chance they'd had unprotected sex that night. In that case, it was possible, *highly* possible that Mackenzie's daughter was his child.

Dylan pulled into the garage and parked next to his black Viper. He jumped out of his car and headed inside. He walked straight into the downstairs bathroom, flipped on the light and leaned in toward the mirror. He touched the tiny bump on his ear with his finger. He hadn't been imagining it—Hope's bump matched his. What were the odds that another man, the one who'd fathered Hope, would have the same genetic mark?

"I wouldn't bet on it," Dylan said as he left the bathroom. He went into the living room and pulled open the doors of the custom-built bookcases. He knelt down and started to search through the books on the bottom shelf. He found what he was looking for and pulled it off the shelf. His heart started to thud heavily in his chest as he sat down in his recliner and opened the old family photo album. On the way home, an odd thought had taken root in his mind. There was something so familiar about Hope and he couldn't get a particular family photo, one of his favorites, out of his mind.

Dylan flipped through the pages of the album until he found the photo he'd been looking for. He turned on the light beside the recliner and held the photo under the light.

"No..." Dylan leaned over and studied the photo of his mother and his aunt Gerri sitting together on the porch. His mom had to be around twelve and Aunt Gerri looked to be near eight or nine. Hope was the spitting image of Aunt Gerri. Yes, she had Mackenzie's coloring, but those features belonged to *his* family. That bump on Hope's ear came directly from *his* genes. He'd stake his life on it.

"No..." Dylan closed his eyes. A rush of heat crashed over his body, followed by a wave of nausea. He had a daughter. He was a father. Hope was *his* child.

What the hell is going on here?

"Babe!" Jenna came through the front door carrying an empty tote bag over her shoulder. "Where are you?"

"In the den." Dylan leaned forward and dropped his head down.

"There you are..." Jenna dropped her bag on the floor. She climbed into his lap and kissed him passionately on the mouth.

"I've missed you, babe." Jenna curled her long legs up; rested her head on his shoulder.

"I've missed you, too," Dylan said in a monotone.

"Whatcha lookin' at?" Jenna asked.

Dylan reached over with his free hand and shut the album. "I was just checking something out for Aunt Gerri."

"Be honest." Jenna unbuttoned the top button of his shirt. "Are you upset with me?"

"Why would I be upset with you?" Dylan felt suffocated and wished Jenna wasn't sitting on him, but he didn't have the heart to push her away.

"Because I'm going to be staying with Denise in LA… didn't you get my message?"

Dylan tried to focus on what Jenna was saying. "When are you leaving?"

"Tomorrow. Remember the audition I had this week? I got the pilot!" Jenna squealed loudly as she hugged him tightly. "Can you believe it?!"

"Congratulations, Jenna. I'm really happy for you."

"And not mad?"

"No." Dylan rubbed his hand over her arm. "Of course not."

"I mean—we can still probably see each other on weekends."

"Sure."

"And…" Jenna kissed the side of his neck. "I think the sex'll be even hotter when we *do* see each other, don't you think?"

Dylan tried to muster a smile in response, but he just wanted her to get off his lap.

"Do you want to go upstairs for a quickie before I grab my stuff?" Jenna slipped her hand into his shirt so she could run her hand over his bare chest. "I only have, like, an hour because I have to finish packing over at my place, but…we still have time. If you want…"

Dylan patted her leg. "Not now, Jenna. I'm…beat."

Jenna shrugged nonchalantly. "That's okay. But at least come up and keep me company while I pack."

Jenna uncurled herself from his lap, held out her hand and wiggled her fingers so he'd take her hand. Dylan followed Jenna up the stairs. He sat on the edge of the soaker tub while Jenna cleaned out the drawer he had cleared out for her. He listened while she chattered excitedly about her new job, but he couldn't focus on her words. His mind was fixated on one thing and one thing only: Hope. Usually he enjoyed hanging out with low-demand Jenna. But today she was grating on his nerves, and he had never been so happy to see her go. He had gone through the motions of carrying her bag out to her BMW and then kissing her as if he meant it before she drove away. There was an unspoken goodbye in that kiss; he had the feeling that it was only a matter of time before their relationship fizzled under the pressure of distance. They had both always known that neither one of them was playing a long game.

After seeing the last of her taillights, Dylan closed the front door and went outside on the balcony so he could look at the ocean waves. He needed to clear his head, figure out his next move. The best way he knew to clear his head was to get on his surfboard. The waves were small, but he didn't care. He just needed to blow off some steam and get his head screwed back on straight. After he spent several hours pounding the waves, Dylan jumped into the shower with clarity of mind—he knew exactly what he needed to do. He wasn't about to let this thing fester overnight. He was going to have to confront Mackenzie. He was going to ask her point-blank if Hope was his child. *Direct* was the only way he knew how to do business. Dylan dried off quickly, pulled on some casual clothes and then dialed a familiar number.

"Jordan. I'm glad I caught you." Dylan held a pen in his hand poised above a pad of paper. "Listen—I think I may have a job for your cousin Mackenzie. Can I grab her number from you real quick?"

Mackenzie put all of Hope's medicine bottles back in the cabinet. Even though Hope had fought it valiantly, getting injured at the barn, however minor, had worn her out. After she ate and took her medicine, Hope had gone to bed early.

"So tell me what happened," Rayna said over the phone. "They actually met today?"

Mackenzie pushed some recipe boxes out of the way and sat down on the love seat. "I needed a ride. He was there. It just happened."

"Well...you know I don't believe in coincidences..."

"I know..."

"So...what are you going to do?"

Mackenzie slumped down farther into the cushion and rubbed her eyes. "I'm going to get myself through this week, and then I'm going to call him. Ask to meet."

"I think you're doing the right thing. Do you know what you're going to say?"

"No. Not a clue." Mackenzie stared up at the ceiling. "I have a couple of days to think about it. What's the etiquette on something like this?"

"I don't know. We could look it up online."

Mackenzie kicked off her shoes and pulled off her socks. "I was joking, Ray."

"I know. But I bet there's a ton of stuff out there about how you tell your baby daddy that he *is* your baby daddy..."

Mackenzie curled into the fetal position on the love seat. "Ugh. I hate that term. *Baby daddy*."

"Sorry. But you know what I mean. You know someone had to write a 'how to' manual. There's probably a *DNA for Dummies* out there..."

Mackenzie's phone chirped in her ear, signaling call waiting. "Hold on, Ray. Someone's calling."

Mackenzie took the phone away from her ear and looked at the incoming call.

Dylan Axel was the name that flashed across the screen.

"Dylan's on the other line," Mackenzie told Ray.

"I'm hanging up," Rayna said quickly. "Call me back!"

Dylan couldn't sit still while he waited for Mackenzie to answer. He had been staring at Mackenzie's number for nearly an hour. Before he dialed her number, he began to question his own logic. Yet, after nearly an hour of careful consideration, his gut just wouldn't stop prodding him to place the call. If Hope *was* his daughter, then he had a right to know.

"Hello?" Mackenzie picked up the line.

"It's Dylan, Mackenzie." It was work to control his tone. "How's Hope?"

"She's worn out, but doing fine. The doctor cleared her to return to the barn tomorrow..."

"I'm glad to hear it." Dylan was pacing in a circular pattern.

After an uncomfortable silence, Mackenzie asked, "Um...did Jordan give you my private number?"

"Yes." Dylan needed to get to the point. "She did. Look—there's something that I need to ask you, Mackenzie."

There was a razor-sharp edge in Dylan's tone that brought her to the edge of the love seat.

"What's that?" Her attempt to sound casual failed.

"And I need you to give me an honest answer…"

Dylan stopped pacing, closed his eyes and tried to control his out-of-control heartbeat, as he posed his simple, straightforward question:

"Is Hope my child?"

Chapter Four

Mackenzie sat like a statue on the edge of the love seat, but bit her lip so hard that she could taste blood on her tongue. Once again, fate had snatched control away from her grasp. She had wanted to broach the subject with Dylan gently, calmly, at the right moment and in the right setting. This wasn't how she wanted it to go at all.

Dylan waited impatiently at the other end of the line. But he had heard Mackenzie suck in her breath when he asked the question, followed by silence. For him, he already had his answer. Hope was his daughter.

"Mackenzie." Dylan repeated the question, "Is Hope my child?"

Mackenzie stared in the direction of Hope's room, grateful that she had gone to bed early. "I..." She whispered into the phone, "I don't think that we should discuss this over the phone."

"You're probably right," Dylan agreed. "You pick the place and time and I'll be there."

"I can meet after work tomorrow." Mackenzie pushed herself to a stand. "But I don't know where we should meet."

"Let's meet at my place." Dylan's forehead was in his hand, his eyes squeezed tightly shut.

Mackenzie pressed her back against the wall and crossed one arm tightly over her midsection. "I'll get my friends to watch Hope. I can be at your place around six-fifteen, six-thirty."

"I'll see you then." Dylan opened his eyes. "Good night, Mackenzie."

"Good night." Mackenzie touched the end button and slowly slid down the wall until she was sitting on the floor. She wrapped her arms tightly around her legs and rested her forehead on her knees. From the moment she had held Hope in her arms at the hospital, she had *felt*, like a splinter under her skin, this day would eventually come. And now that it had, she felt undeniably shell-shocked and strangely…*relieved.*

But with the relief came another strain of uncertainty. She prayed for Hope's sake that Dylan wouldn't reject her. But what if Dylan decided that he wanted to play a larger role in Hope's life? She had raised Hope on her own for ten years. It had always been Mackenzie and Hope against the world. And she knew she was being selfish, but she *liked it* that way.

When Dylan ended the call, he started to straighten up the condo to keep his body busy and his mind occupied. He moved restlessly from room to room, cleaning surfaces and pounding pillows into submission. He wound up back in the kitchen and began to unload the dishwasher even though the housekeeper would be there in the morning. One by one, he put the glasses in the cabinet, setting them down hard and then shutting the cabinet doors a little bit more firmly than he normally would. Finished with the chore, Dylan tried to push the dishwasher drawer back in, but it caught.

"Dammit!" Dylan rattled it back into place and then with a hard shove, slammed it forward. He lifted up the dishwasher door and shut it, hard. Stony faced, he leaned back against the counter, arms crossed over his chest. Still frustrated and restless, Dylan headed down to the beach and once his feet hit the sand, he started to run. He was grateful for the cover of the night. He was grateful that there were only a few souls on the beach with him. He started to run faster, his feet pounding on the hard-packed sand. Pushing his body harder, pushing himself to go faster and farther than he had ever gone before. His lungs burned, but he didn't let up. His leg muscles burned, but he didn't let up. He didn't let up until his leg muscles gave way and he stumbled. His hands took the brunt of his body weight as he fell forward into the sand. Fighting to catch his breath, he sat back, and dropped his head down to his knees. He pressed his sandy fingers into his eyes and then pinched the side of his nose to stop tears from forming.

He'd never wanted to be a father and he'd worked damn hard to make sure it never happened. That he never had a slipup. He had been *vigilant* all of his sexual life to make sure that he never got anyone pregnant. Even if he had been dating someone for a while, even if he saw them take the pill every day, he *always* wore a condom. But the one time he didn't—the *one* time he *didn't*—he'd gotten caught. And now, he had to face the one fear he had never intended to face: Was being a bad father genetic?

"I'm here." Mackenzie pulled into a parking spot a couple of doors down from Dylan's condo. She was on speakerphone with Rayna and Charlie.

"Mackenzie—you've got this," Charlie said.

"And don't forget—" Rayna began.

"Rayna," Mackenzie interrupted her. "Please, please, *please* don't give me another spiritual affirmation. I just can't take it right now."

After a pause, Rayna said in her "let's meditate" voice, "I was just going to say—don't forget that we're always here for you, anytime, no matter what."

"Oh. Sorry. Thank you," Mackenzie said. "I'll be by to pick up Hope after I'm done."

Mackenzie hung up with her friends and then got out of the car. She stood by her car for several minutes, staring at Dylan's condo, before she forced herself to get the show on the road. Stalling wouldn't help. She needed to face this conversation with Dylan head-on and get it out of the way.

Mackenzie took a deep breath in and knocked on the door. This time, unlike the last time she stood in this spot, Dylan opened the door seconds after she knocked.

"Come on in." Dylan stepped back and opened the door wider.

Mackenzie walked, with crossed arms, through the door and into Dylan's world. She noticed, more so than she had the first time she was here, how neat and organized Dylan's home was. His home was sleek, expensive and masculine: the ultimate bachelor pad. It was a sharp contrast to her 1930s Spanish-style Balboa Park rental with an interior decor that was cobbled together with flea-market finds and garage-sale bargains. The lives they lived, the lives they had built for themselves, couldn't be more different.

"Can I get you something to drink?" Dylan stood several feet away from her, hands hidden in his front pockets. He looked different today. The boyish spark was gone from his eyes. The features of his face were hardened, his mouth unsmiling. Today, he seemed more like a man to her than he ever had before.

"No. Thank you." Mackenzie shook her head, wishing she were already on the back end of this conversation.

"Let's talk in the den." Dylan slipped his left hand out of his pocket and gestured for her to walk in front of him. "After you."

Mackenzie waited for Dylan to sit down before she said, "I'm not sure where to begin…"

"Why don't we start with an answer to my question." Dylan was determined not to let this conversation spiral out of control. He had always been known for his cool head and he wanted to keep it that way.

"I think you've already figured out the answer to your question, Dylan. But if you need to hear me say it, then I'll say it," Mackenzie said in a measured, even voice. "Hope is your daughter."

Instead of responding right away, Dylan stood up and walked over to the large window that overlooked the ocean. He stared out at the waves and rubbed his hand hard over his freshly shaven jawline. With a shake of his head, he turned his back to the window.

"I'm just trying to wrap my mind around this, Mackenzie. It's not every day that my friend's sister turns up with my kid."

"I understand." Mackenzie wished that she could stop the sick feeling of nerves brewing in her stomach.

"How long have you known that she's mine, Mackenzie?" Dylan asked pointedly. "Have you always known… or did you think that she was your ex-boyfriend's child?"

Mackenzie's stomach gurgled loudly. Embarrassed, she pressed her hands tightly into her belly. "I've always known."

"How?" Dylan asked quietly, his face pale. "How did you know?"

"You were the only one I'd slept with in months, Dylan. It couldn't've been anyone else *but* you."

Dylan leaned back against the window; he felt off balance. "That's not what I expected you to say."

"It's the truth...." Mackenzie said.

Dylan didn't respond; he didn't move. He didn't trust himself to speak, so he didn't.

"I have a question for you." Mackenzie turned her body toward him. "What made you think she was yours?"

"The bump...on her ear. It matches mine."

"Oh..." Mackenzie said faintly. Dylan had always worn his hair long when they were kids—she never noticed that birthmark before.

"And then there was this." Dylan retrieved the photo album, opened it and held it out for Mackenzie to take.

"Look familiar?" Dylan pointed to the picture of his aunt Gerri.

Mackenzie nodded, stared closely at the picture.

"Who needs a DNA test, right?" Dylan nodded toward the picture.

Mackenzie stared at the old black-and-white photograph. "This little girl...she's the spitting image of Hope." Mackenzie looked up. "Who is she?"

"That's my aunt Gerri when she was nine."

"I remember your aunt Gerri. We went to their horse farm a couple of times. She played the organ for us."

Dylan's jaw set. "Hope should be able to remember my aunt Gerri, too. Uncle Bill's the closest thing to a father I've ever had. He *deserved* the chance to know my daughter."

Dylan's well-crafted barb hit its intended mark. And it hurt. Because Mackenzie knew that he was right. Silently, she carefully closed the photo album and handed it back to Dylan.

Dylan put the photo album on the coffee table and sunk down on the couch a cushion away from Mackenzie. He leaned forward, rested his elbows on his legs and cradled his head in his hands.

"So…" Dylan said quietly. "We both know she's mine. The next question I'd like answered is…why did you know ten years ago and I'm only finding out *now*?"

Mackenzie leaned away from Dylan. "I found out I was pregnant really early on. I'm regular…like clockwork. So when I didn't get my period after the wedding…I knew."

"And you didn't think it was important to share this information with me, because…?"

"I was going to tell you. It never occurred to me *not* to tell you."

"But you didn't…" Dylan lifted his head, looked at her. "Why not?"

"Jett told me that you were back with Christa…"

"Jett knew?"

"No. Not back then. And not until long after the two of you had already lost touch."

Dylan nodded and Mackenzie continued her story.

"After I found out that your engagement was back on, I thought it was the best thing for both of us if I didn't tell you…"

"No." Dylan shook his head. "You should have told me. I had the *right* to know."

"You forget, Dylan. I knew how much you loved Christa. That's all you talked about the night Jett got married. And you and I both know what would've happened if she found out you'd gotten someone *pregnant* at the wedding! She would've broken off the engagement and you would have lost the love of your life because of me!

I couldn't see any *reason* to screw up your life, Dylan… not when *I* didn't even know if I wanted to keep the baby."

"I didn't *marry* Christa," Dylan challenged her. "But, you *did* keep the baby."

"Yes. I did. I thought about adoption. I thought about… abortion. In the end, I decided to keep her."

Dylan stabbed his leg with his finger. "That's a decision we should have made *together*."

"I admit that I may have called it wrong…"

"Called it wrong…?" he repeated incredulously.

"But I was young and I thought I was doing the right thing for all of us." Mackenzie touched her finger to her chest. "I got Hope and you got to marry the woman you loved."

"I didn't even know what love was back then…" Dylan shook his head. "At least now I know why you were so anxious to get rid of me at the barn the other day. You didn't want me to meet my own daughter."

"Not like that I didn't." Mackenzie set the record straight. "I didn't want that for Hope…and I didn't want that for you."

In a rough voice, Dylan asked, "Were you ever going to tell me, Mackenzie? Or were you just going to let me go the rest of my life not knowing?"

"No." Mackenzie clasped her hands together. "I was going to tell you. I had decided to start looking for you this year…"

Dylan's eyes were glassy with emotion. "You're telling me…that if we hadn't run into each other at Ian's party, you were going to track me down? Why? Why now?"

Mackenzie took a deep breath in and when she let it out, her shoulders sagged.

"It's what Hope wanted. When we were filling out her

Make-A-Wish application, she wrote—I wish I could meet my dad."

"Wait a minute..." What she had just said didn't sink into his head right away. "Make-A-Wish? Isn't that for sick kids?"

"Yes." Mackenzie waited for Dylan to ask the next logical question.

"Are you trying to tell me that Hope is sick?"

"Hope has been battling leukemia for the last two years." Mackenzie managed to say those words without tearing up.

As Dylan often did, he went silent. He stared at her for a long time with puzzled, narrowed eyes.

"Do you need a drink?" he finally asked. "I need a drink."

Dylan stood up suddenly and walked toward the kitchen. He stopped when he realized that she was still sitting on the couch. "Are you coming?"

Wordlessly, Mackenzie stood up on shaky legs and followed Dylan into the kitchen.

"Can I interest you in a cold malt beverage?" Dylan pulled a bottle of beer from the side door.

"Sure. Why not?"

"Why not, indeed," Dylan said cryptically as he popped the tops off the beers and handed her one. "We're both consenting adults here."

"Thank you," Mackenzie said. She brought the bottle up to her mouth but Dylan stopped her.

"What should we toast to?" He held out his bottle to her.

"Anything you'd like," Mackenzie said tiredly. She was exhausted. She was exhausted all the time, and had been for years. The stress of Hope's illness and the stress of trying to run a business had been catching up with her for a long time. And now she had a sinking feeling that dealing with Dylan was only going to add to her exhaustion.

Dylan tapped her bottle with his. “To Hope.”

“To Hope,” Mackenzie seconded.

“Could you go for some fresh air?” Dylan asked.

Mackenzie nodded and Dylan opened the French door leading out to the deck. “After you.”

Mackenzie stepped onto the large deck and was immediately drawn to the edge of the railing that overlooked the beach. She stared at the sun setting over the small, rolling waves and tried to relax her shoulders. Dylan, who used to be so simple to read, wasn’t so easy for her to read tonight. She had no idea what type of emotional shift she might encounter. Next to her, but not too close, Dylan rested his forearms on the railing, bottle loosely held in one hand.

“So…” Dylan said in a calm, almost contemplative tone. “Hope has cancer.”

“Yes…” Mackenzie nodded. “She has acute lymphoblastic leukemia. ALL. She was diagnosed when she was eight.”

“Leukemia. What is that? Blood cancer?”

Mackenzie nodded. “At first I just thought that she was pushing herself too hard between school and the barn. She was tired all the time, losing weight. She just wasn’t herself. When she started to complain about an ache in her bones and a sore throat…” Mackenzie lifted one shoulder. “I thought she was coming down with the flu. I mean… who would immediately jump to cancer?”

Dylan sat down in one of the chairs encircling a fire pit. Mackenzie joined him.

“I remember being really stressed out that day…the day we found out. I had to rearrange my entire morning so I could get Hope to the doctor. Traffic was ridiculous, I was on the phone with the bakery…on the phone with clients…I remember thinking that it was the worst possible time for Hope to be catching something on top of everything else." Mackenzie pushed strands of hair out of her face. "And all I could do was start adding things to do to my already gigantic to-do list—stop by the pharmacy, arrange for someone to stay with Hope…blah, blah, blah…"

Mackenzie stopped to take a swig from her beer. She shook her head as she swallowed the liquid down. "I had no idea how frivolous *everything* I'd just been obsessing over was about to become."

Dylan listened intently, while Mackenzie talked. "The doctor sent us to the hospital, tests were run and she was diagnosed that day. And just like that…literally in what seemed like the blink of an eye…our world imploded. No parent is ever prepared to hear the words *your child has cancer*." Mackenzie rubbed fresh tears out of her eyes. "But even more than that, I'll never forget the look on Hope's face when she asked me—'Did she just say that I have cancer?' I've never been that scared in my life. Hope was admitted to the hospital, and ever since then, our lives just became this never-ending revolving door of chemo and steroids and tests and checkups and hospital stays…"

When Mackenzie realized that she was the only one talking *and* that she had said much more than she had ever intended, she stopped herself from blurting out more by taking a swig of her now-tepid beer. She picked at the label on the bottle, wishing that Dylan would do something other than sit in his designer lounge chair and stare at her.

"I don't know why I just told you all of that," Mackenzie said to fill the silence.

At first, Dylan really didn't know what to say. He had been dragged from one emotional spectrum to the next in the span of an hour. At the beginning of their meeting, all he felt for Mackenzie was anger. But while Mackenzie was telling her story, and with the ocean wind blowing the wispy tendrils of her hair across her pretty face, she reminded him of the girl she had once been. The girl he remembered so vividly from his childhood—the chubby bookworm with thick glasses who used to read her books in the backseat of one of her father's vintage cars. All the boys in the neighborhood ignored Jett's sister, but he never did. Maybe it was because he liked how different she was than the rest of the girls. Or maybe it was because he had only seen her smile once after her mom died. He had never thought to analyze it. He had always just *liked* Mackenzie.

"Because we used to be friends," Dylan said.

"Were we?" Mackenzie asked.

"I always thought so." Dylan caught her gaze and held it. "And I tell you this, Mackenzie. If I had known that you were pregnant…if you had just trusted me enough to give me a chance, I never would've let you or Hope go through any of this stuff alone. I would have been there for you… both of you…every step of the way."

Chapter Five

It took Dylan a couple of weeks to make a decision about Hope. He had gone about his daily life trying to focus on business. He hadn't told anyone about Hope, not his girlfriend, his aunt or his best friend. He needed to get right with it in his own head before he could open up to other people. And after many distracted days and restless nights, he had an epiphany of sorts: Didn't he have a moral obligation to Hope? Yes, the idea of becoming an "instant parent" terrified him. But if he was brutally honest with himself, the idea of repeating his father's mistakes scared him even more. Once he came to a decision, he took the only next logical step: he called Mackenzie.

"Hello?" Mackenzie answered the phone.

"Hi, Mackenzie. It's Dylan. How are you?"

"I'm fine. Busy. But fine," Mackenzie said. "Hope's doing really well. Her recent blood tests came back clear. She's still in remission."

"That's good to hear."

When he didn't add anything more, Mackenzie asked, "How are you doing, Dylan?"

"I'm okay. Still sorting through this thing, I think." Dylan rested his forehead in his hand. "Look, Mackenzie, I've been thinking a lot about Hope…are you sure that getting to know me is what your daughter wants?"

Mackenzie hated that she hesitated before she said, "I'm sure."

"Then, let's set it up." Dylan stared out the window at the calm ocean in the distance. His tone was steady but his heart was pounding.

"Um…" Mackenzie rubbed her temples to prevent a migraine from flaring up. "I haven't told Hope that I found you yet. I was waiting to hear from you. I didn't want to get her excited and then…well, you know…"

"Understood." Dylan sounded as if he was arranging a business meeting rather than a meeting with his newly discovered daughter. It was his comfort zone and it helped him stay sane. "When can you get that done?"

"Not tonight," Mackenzie said distractedly. "She has chemo tomorrow and she'll be sick all weekend…but maybe next week sometime when she's feeling better…"

"That's fine." Dylan nodded his head. "Once that's done, give me a call and we'll figure out the next step. Does that work for you?"

"Yes," Mackenzie said after she cleared her throat. "I'll call you once I've spoken with my daughter."

After they ended the call, Mackenzie stared at the phone for several seconds.

"Well?" Rayna was staring at her like a cat gearing up to pounce on a catnip toy. "That had to be Dylan, right? What did he *say*?"

"He wants to meet Hope."

Rayna turned the burner on the stove down. “See? Look at that! Prayers in action! This is *great* news!”

“What’s great news?” Charlie walked through the front door wearing mint-green scrubs. She hung her keys on the hook just inside the door.

“Hi, honey.” Rayna smiled at her wife, Charlotte. “Dylan finally came to his senses and called. He’s agreed to meet Hope!”

Rayna was the yin to Charlotte’s yang. Rayna had shoulder-length wispy blond hair, pretty, Slavic features and alabaster skin. Charlotte, who preferred to be called Charlie, was an attractive mix of Irish and Mexican heritage with light brown eyes, golden-chestnut skin and thick black wavy hair worn loose and long. At first, Rayna and Charlie were just her landlords, but they had become family after Hope was diagnosed. Rayna and Charlie had been in the trenches with them right from the start—cooking meals, running errands and pulling all-nighters watching Hope while Mackenzie caught a few hours of sleep. And Rayna’s church had held fundraisers to help raise money to help pay for Hope’s burgeoning medical bills. It was hard to imagine how she would have gotten through the first year of Hope’s treatment without them.

“Huh…” Charlie kissed Rayna on the lips. “How come you’re happy and Mackenzie’s not?”

“You know Mackenzie resists change.” Ray held out a wooden spoon to Charlie. “Here. Taste this.”

Charlie tasted the sauce. “That’s really good.”

“I don’t think I *resist* change,” Mackenzie said.

A sleepy-eyed, rotund gray tabby cat named Max appeared. Charlie scooped him up, kissed him on the head. “I thought this was the call you’ve been waiting for all week…?”

“It’s not that I’m *not* glad that he called. I am. It’s just a lot to take in, that's all. It's always just been Hope and me." Mackenzie rested her chin on her hand. "I like how things are between us now..."

"Resistant to change," Rayna said in a singsong voice.

Charlie got some water and then joined Mackenzie at the kitchen table. "But maybe this will turn out to be a great thing. You yourself already said that he's a good guy. What could it hurt to have another person share the load? Between the bakery and managing Hope's leukemia treatments, let's face it...you've got your hands full."

At Mackenzie's feet, Max was preparing for a leap onto her lap. Mackenzie patted her legs for encouragement.

"Oh, my dear lord, what have you been feeding this cat, Ray?" Max landed on her leg with a grunt. "I thought he was on a diet."

Charlie sent Rayna an "I told you so" look. Rayna was immediately defensive. "He *is* on a diet! Don't listen to them, Max-a-million. You're just big boned!" Rayna pointed a spatula at her. "And don't change the subject. What's really scaring you?"

Rayna could read her like a book. "I don't know. I suppose I am, a little scared. I mean...what if...

"What if..." Mackenzie hadn't admitted this private thought aloud. "What if Dylan ends up wanting custody of Hope? What if Hope decides that she wants to live with him down the road?"

Charlie and Rayna both shook their heads in unison.

"Nope. Not gonna happen." Charlie twisted her thick wavy hair into a bun.

Rayna came to the table. "Not a chance."

"I feel stupid admitting that out loud..." Mackenzie scratched behind Max's chops.

"It's not stupid," Rayna said. "It's human."

"I suppose so..." Mackenzie helped Max to the floor

safely. "You know what, guys? If it's all the same to you, I think I'm just gonna skip dinner."

"Are you sure?" Rayna asked, disappointed. "I was going to try out a new recipe on you! And I have wine..."

"Yeah. I'm sure." She stood up, glad that she lived next door. "I just need some time to...decompress before Hope gets back from the movies."

"Bath salts, candles and a hot bath." Rayna hugged her tightly at the door. "Everything always looks better after a bath."

Dylan drove slowly up the winding, tree-lined private driveway that led to his aunt's farm. When he was growing up, and Uncle Bill was still alive, the farm had been bustling with activity. Now the place felt lifeless. The horses were gone, the stable hands and horse trainers were gone. The only thing left were empty pastures, empty stables and Aunt Gerri's sprawling two-story 1900s farmhouse with its wraparound porch and old tin roof. At one time, Forrest Hanoverians claimed over a hundred acres and were renowned for the quality of their Hanoverian breeding program. Over the years, Aunt Gerri had sold off much of the farm's land until only the central twenty acres of the farm remained.

Dylan parked his car in the circle driveway in front of the house. Aunt Gerri swung open the front door and waved at him.

"I was just getting ready to play the organ, when I saw you coming up the driveway!" Aunt Gerri called to him from the door. Just shy of her eighty-third birthday, Geraldine Forrest was a petite woman with intelligent bright blue eyes, a steel-trap memory and a kind-hearted disposition. Dylan always marveled at her energy; she kept herself busy going to garage sales, playing the organ at her church and socializing with her long list of friends.

"How are you, Aunt Gerri?" Dylan walked up the porch steps.

"Well…I'll tell you…I'm fit as a fiddle." Aunt Gerri held out her arms to him. "Oh! I'm so happy to see you!"

"I'm glad to see you, too, Aunt Gerri." Dylan hugged her and kissed her on the cheek.

"Okay…so let's go inside." Aunt Gerri turned to head back into the house. "You'll have to shut the door real hard—it's been sticking lately."

Dylan ran his hand up the edge of the door. "I'll fix it for you before I leave."

"Oh! Would you?" Aunt Gerri beamed. "That would be such a big help. I was finally going to break down and call someone about it tomorrow. You'll be saving me the trouble. Do you want coffee?"

"No, thanks. I'm good." Dylan stopped to straighten a picture of Uncle Bill hanging in the foyer. After his mom died, this became his permanent home. Uncle Bill and Aunt Gerri took him and raised him. This house, with its creaky wide-planked wooden floors and thick crown molding, was his home. It was the one place that never really changed. The one thing he could always count on, especially when something significant happened in his life.

"Let's go to the sitting room, then. I want to show you my brand-new organ." Aunt Gerri headed into the large room to the left of the foyer.

"It's a Lowrey Holiday Classic…" Aunt Gerri stood proudly by her organ. "I just traded my old one in. This is my seventh organ and this'll probably be the last one I buy…"

Dylan sat down in his grandmother's rocking chair. "It's nice. I like it."

"I'll be sure to play it for you before you go." Aunt Gerri settled herself in another rocking chair. "So..." Her sharp blue eyes were curious. "What's the news?"

"Can't I visit you without being accused of having an ulterior motive?"

"Oh, I think I know you pretty well," Aunt Gerri said. "There's gotta be something real important going on to bring you all the way out here on a business day."

"You've always had my number ever since I was a kid." Dylan fiddled with the loose rocking-chair arm before he looked back at his aunt. "And you're right. There is something I need to tell you."

"Well, go on and tell me what it is so we can talk it out."

"I found out a couple of weeks ago that I have...a daughter." Dylan watched his aunt's face to gauge her reaction. "Her name is Hope. She's ten."

"Did you just say you've got a daughter?" Aunt Gerri stopped rocking. "Who's the mother?"

For the next half hour, Dylan talked and his aunt listened. He told his aunt about the first time he'd ever seen Hope at the barn and he recounted his recent conversation with Mackenzie. Like a confession, he didn't leave anything out. Not even the fact that he hadn't been sober the night Hope had been conceived or the fact that he had never dated Mackenzie. And when he was done, he felt as if a weight had been lifted. Now that Aunt Gerri knew about Hope, it was real. No matter what happened, no matter how tough it got, there was no going back.

When he had said his piece, Aunt Gerri thought a bit before she spoke. She rocked back and forth, mulling things over.

"Now that I think about it, I remember Mackenzie. She was a heavyset girl, wasn't she? But she had beautiful blue eyes."

Dylan nodded. "She still does."

Violet eyes.

"She was such a sweet little girl," his aunt said. "But so serious."

"She still is."

"Well…what does she want from you, Dylan? What does she expect?"

"She wants me to spend time with Hope. That's all. She doesn't want money…"

"Not even for the medical bills? Good gracious, cancer treatment can't be cheap." Aunt Gerri had always held the purse strings for the farm.

"I know," Dylan responded to his aunt's skeptical expression. "I thought it was strange, too. But she was adamant about the money. More than that, she doesn't want me to be a parent to Hope, either."

Aunt Gerri frowned. "But is that what *you* want? You're the child's father."

"Honestly, Aunt Gerri? I have no idea what I want."

"Well…I suppose that's where you need to start then, don't you? If you don't know what you want, how in the world can you figure out what you're going to do?"

Hope had picked Pegasus as their first father-and-daughter day. It seemed like a better idea than a restaurant, and he wanted Hope to feel comfortable, so he had agreed. Now that he was here, he started to doubt the soundness of that decision. Perhaps they should have met in private, at his house, *before* they went public. Dylan parked his car next to Mackenzie's Chevy and shut off the engine. Instead of getting out, he stayed in the car. He'd never felt capable of having a panic attack until today. His heart was racing, his mouth was dry and beads of sweat were trickling down the side of his face. He was a mess. The thought of spending the day with Hope made him feel panicked. He had absolutely no idea what to say to a ten-year-old girl; ten-year-old girls hadn't exactly been his target demographic.

"Quit being a coward," Dylan said to himself. "And get out of the stupid car."

After convincing himself to leave the car, Dylan headed to the office. Lucky for him, Aggie was the only one there.

She greeted him with a broad smile and a loud, booming voice. "I heard you were comin' out to lend us a hand today!"

Aggie stomped over to him in her crusty, knee-high black rubber boots and pumped his hand a couple of times. "Come on over here and take a load off. I've got your papers all ready to be filled out. Nothing fancy—but the long and short of it is, you're agreein' that if one of our horses kicks you in the privates or eats your pinkie for a snack, you're on your own. We volunteer at our own risk around here…so if you can live with that, I'll be more than happy to put you to work."

"I can live with it." Dylan sat down at the cluttered picnic table in the middle of the room and resisted the urge to start straightening it up. Instead, he forced himself to focus on reviewing the papers.

"I'll make you a badge so you'll feel official. We don't have riders today—just barn work. But anyone who wants to ride after the chores are done can saddle up."

Aggie handed Dylan a badge and Dylan handed her the filled-out forms. Dylan stood up and Aggie looked down at his pristine boots.

"If you're gonna hang with us, you're gonna have'ta get you some good old-fashioned muckers. Those fancy boots aren't gonna survive a fresh steamin' pile of manure, I guarantee *that*." When Aggie laughed, one eye stayed open and the other one shut completely. "I'm done with ya, so head to the barn. There's always plenty to be done and not enough hands to do it."

Dylan walked out of the office, around the corner, and bumped right into Mackenzie.

Their bodies hit together so hard that Mackenzie had the breath temporarily knocked out of her.

Concerned, Dylan held on to her arms to steady her. "Are you okay?"

"I wasn't expecting anyone to come around that corner," Mackenzie said, slightly annoyed. "But I'm okay now. You can let go."

Dylan released her arms quickly, as if he was pulling his hands away from hot coals. "Sorry. I did it again."

Dylan stared hard at Mackenzie. Something had just happened between them. When their bodies came together, they were a perfect fit. She was curvy and voluptuous and petite; not what he would normally gravitate toward. But he liked the way her body had felt against his. He had enjoyed the feeling of having Mackenzie in his arms. She felt like…home.

Mackenzie tugged on the front of her oversize, long-sleeve T-shirt. "I'm glad you came."

"I said I would," Dylan said defensively.

"I know." Mackenzie had worry etched into her forehead. "I know you did…but I was…"

"Worried that I wouldn't show?"

"Yes…I'm sorry. But, yes. Hope could hardly sleep last night. She's so excited to meet you." Mackenzie was speaking in a low, private voice. "But I think she's more scared than anything."

"Scared? Why is she scared of me?"

"She's not scared *of you.* I think that she's scared that you won't like her." Mackenzie pushed some wayward strands of hair away from her face.

"Well, then, that makes two of us, because I've been really worried that she won't like me, too." Dylan looked down at his outfit. "I changed my clothes three times before I finally put this together."

Mackenzie's eyebrows rose. Dylan was wearing a pressed Ralph Lauren button-down dress shirt, new dark-wash jeans and his spotless boots.

"I did mention that you were going to be doing barn work…didn't I?" Mackenzie asked.

"You mentioned it. I just wanted to look nice for Hope." Dylan frowned down at his outfit. "I look ridiculous, don't I?"

"No. You don't look ridiculous, Dylan. You just look…kind of dressy for the barn. That's all," Mackenzie tried to reassure him. "But stop worrying. Trust me. Hope doesn't care what you're wearing. So…are you ready?"

"Nope." Dylan's stomach started to feel a little queasy.

"What happened to the fearless Dylan Axel I used to know?" Mackenzie tried to tease his nerves away.

"He was too young to know better."

"Come on, Dylan." Mackenzie offered him her hand. "The best way to get something done is to start…"

Dylan took her hand, soft and warm, and let her gently tug him in the right direction. Their hands naturally slipped apart as they walked side by side through the barn's dusty center aisle. As they walked along, Mackenzie greeted the ragtag bunch of secondhand horses and the handful of volunteers working that day. With thirty geriatric horses to care for, Dylan understood why Aggie was so eager to sign him up. Organizations that relied entirely on donations, grants and volunteers were in a constant state of borderline panic and flux. Pegasus was no different.

"This way." Mackenzie tucked her fingers into the front

pocket of her jeans. "Hope's out back washing feed buckets."

Dylan could hear the water running from the hose and he stopped walking. "Wait."

"What's wrong?"

Dylan backed up a step. "Maybe this isn't the best place for this to happen."

"Oh, no, no, no, no, *no.* You're not backing out." Mackenzie's demeanor changed. She walked over to him and grabbed his hand. "This is happening *right now.*"

Mackenzie pulled Dylan forward a couple of steps, into an open area with concrete slabs set up for washing the horses.

"Hey, kiddo!" Mackenzie slapped a bright smile on her face. "Look who I found..."

Under her breath, and only for Dylan's ears, Mackenzie said, "You're up."

Hope looked up from her task of washing out a large group of blue feed buckets. She looked at him directly and what he saw in her eyes was something he hadn't experienced with anyone other than his aunt Gerri: total acceptance. Hope's pretty face lit up with excitement as she smiled nervously at him. She dropped the hose and wiped her hands off on her jeans while she headed over to where they were standing. Hope wrapped her arm around her mom's waist for security. She looked up at Mackenzie, Mackenzie looked at Dylan, and Dylan looked at Hope.

"A*www*kward." Hope was the first to break the uncomfortable silence.

Dylan liked how Hope broke the ice. "You're right. It is."

Mackenzie ran her hand over the top of Hope's head. "Sometimes this one doesn't have a filter."

"That's okay." Dylan was immediately hooked by

Hope's shy, brief smile. "I have that same problem sometimes."

"Do you know who I am?" Hope asked him.

"Hope..." Mackenzie started to correct her.

"No. That's okay," Dylan said to Mackenzie before he looked down at Hope. "Yes. I do know who you are. You're my Hope."

Chapter Six

"Here..." Hope slipped a blue-and-yellow rubber-band bracelet off her wrist and handed it to him. "I made this for you."

"Hey...thanks." Dylan slipped it over his hand onto his wrist. He held it out for Hope to see. "Does it look good on me?"

Hope nodded. "It's a friendship bracelet."

It took the child of the group to ease the tension, but it took the mom in the group to get things moving along.

"Come on..." Mackenzie squeezed Hope's shoulder. "Let's get back to work. Aggie would have a fit if she saw us all standing around getting nothing done."

The three of them put their nervous energy into finishing Hope's chore together. And it turned out that having a common goal to accomplish eased the tension between them. Of course, it wasn't perfect and there were some odd lulls in conversation. And Dylan caught Hope in the act of studying him when she thought it was safe. Dylan understood her fascination, because he had to resist the urge to stare at his daughter. Mackenzie, on the other hand, made no bones about blatantly watching the two of them interact. But by the time all of the feed buckets were washed and drying in the sun, the tension between them had slowly given way to a more relaxed, fun vibe.

"What next?" Dylan unbuttoned his cuffs and rolled up his sleeves. His shirt was soaked, his boots were already caked with mud, and it made him feel less out of place than when he had arrived.

"Now we have to put all the feed buckets back into the stalls." Hope grabbed some buckets. "Carry as many as you can so we can get done quicker. Then, I get to ride Gypsy."

"Her favorite horse," Mackenzie explained.

Dylan grabbed as many buckets as his fingers could hold. "Lead the way, boss."

His words made Hope laugh, spontaneously and loudly. She smiled at him again, this time without the nervousness. Hope's smile, Dylan decided, was a million-dollar smile. It was addictive. He wanted to see it again and again.

"While you guys do this, I'm going to help Aggie in the office," Mackenzie said. She looked at Hope specifically. "Is that okay?"

When Hope gave a small nod to her mom, Dylan felt as if he had managed to accomplish something pretty major: Hope felt comfortable enough with him to spend time alone. One by one, Hope introduced Dylan formally to the horses and it was obvious that Hope had a special connection with each and every one of them. The horses, some of whom pinned their ears back and gnashed their teeth at him, all came to Hope for some love and attention. It made him feel proud that, at such a young age, she had a special way with these horses. They weren't pretty. They weren't young. But she loved them just the same. In that, she took directly after kindhearted Mackenzie.

"This is Cinnamon." Hope rubbed her hand lovingly over the mare's face. "She's a sweet girl. Aren't you, Cinnamon? When you work with her, make sure you only approach her from her left side, because she's missing her right eye. See?"

Dylan nodded. There was a deep indent where the mare's eye should have been.

"If you walk up to her on her right side, she might get spooked and accidentally knock you over. But she wouldn't mean to hurt you."

After putting the feed bucket in her stall, Hope kissed Cinnamon affectionately on the nose.

"I've saved the best for last," Hope said excitedly. "This...is *Gypsy*."

The word *Gypsy* was said with flair, as if Hope were introducing the most amazing horse in the history of the equine. Dylan read the large plaque on Gypsy's stall: Warning! This horse will bite! Dylan then took a step back from the gate. Hope wrapped her arms around the mare's neck and hugged.

"What's with the sign?" Dylan asked.

"Oh," Hope said nonchalantly. "She's just looking for food, is all. That's why Aggie won't let us carry treats in our pockets. And we can only give them treats in their buckets, never by hand.

"Isn't she great?" Hope rubbed the space between Gypsy's sad brown eyes.

Gypsy was a spindly-legged barrel-bellied mare with giant, fuzzy donkey ears, a dull brown coat and an unusually long, bony face. Even in the best of times, Dylan knew that Gypsy had *never* been a prize.

Wanting to be diplomatic on his first day hanging out

with his daughter, Dylan said the only *noncommittal* thing he could say, "If you like her then I like her."

"I knew you'd like her, too." Hope nodded happily.

In between stuffing envelopes for the upcoming fund-raiser, Mackenzie periodically checked on Hope and Dylan by poking her head around the corner. She didn't feel good about spying, but she *had to* check on Hope. And she was glad she did. If she hadn't spied on them, she would have missed a hallmark moment: the expression on her daughter's face when she introduced Dylan to Gypsy. Hope was beaming at him. She knew all of her daughter's many expressions by heart. That one? It was only reserved for those that Hope *really* liked. For Mackenzie, bearing witness to this moment confirmed for her that bringing Dylan into Hope's life was the right thing to do. It didn't nullify her fears for what a future with Dylan in it would mean for *her*, but for Hope? Her trepidation was erased just like words being wiped away on a whiteboard.

"Done!" Hope attached Gypsy's clean feed bucket to the hook in the stall and then exited the stall.

"Nice work." Dylan held up his hand.

Hope high-fived him. "Do you want to help me get Gypsy's tack?"

"Of course I do. I cleared my entire Sunday just for you."

"You did?"

Dylan nodded. He'd managed to win another smile from Hope. He was on a winning streak and felt like hugging her. But he didn't.

"That's cool," Hope said.

Hope grabbed the bridle, girth and saddle pad, while Dylan hoisted the heavy Western saddle onto his hip. With two of them working, they made quick work of grooming Gypsy before tacking her up. By the end of it, Dylan felt proud of the fact that he'd managed to get the job done without being on the losing end of Gypsy's teeth.

"You can ride, too, you know," his daughter said as she walked Gypsy down the breezeway.

"That's okay...I'd rather watch you," he said. He hadn't been on a horse since high school.

Mackenzie heard her daughter's voice in the breezeway and she met them at the barn entrance. There was a moment when she had a front-row seat to Hope and Dylan walking together, side by side, as if they had known each other all their lives. They had the same swing in their walk, these two. The same way of holding their shoulders, the same easygoing, couldn't-possibly-ignore-it kind of smile.

"Hey, Mom!" Hope greeted Mackenzie enthusiastically. "I was just telling Dylan all about the riding school I want to open up after college."

"I didn't even know they made ten-year-olds like this." Dylan smiled at them.

"Sometimes I don't believe that she's ten." Mackenzie handed Hope a bottle of water. "Hydration, sunscreen and helmet, please."

Mackenzie raised her eyebrows at Dylan over Hope's head. Dylan smiled at her and gave her the "okay" symbol.

"Sunscreen." Mackenzie exchanged the water bottle for the sunscreen bottle.

Hope put sunscreen on her arms and her face. She handed the sunscreen bottle back to Mackenzie along with Gypsy's reins.

"I'll be right back." Hope jogged over to the tack room to grab a helmet.

"How's it going?" Mackenzie asked quietly.

"Good," Dylan said. "Really good..."

"I was hoping that the two of you would...you know... figure each other out if I gave you some space."

"I think we did okay," Dylan said. "She's an incredible kid, Mackenzie. I mean…my God. So smart."

"Straight As," Mackenzie said with pride. "Even when she was at her worst with the chemo."

"I like her." Dylan's thoughts became words.

Mackenzie wasn't a crier. But when Dylan quietly said that he liked Hope, she felt like weeping with relief.

"Well…" Mackenzie turned her head away from him until she could put a halt to the waterworks. "I can tell that she's already crazy about you."

"Yeah? Do you think so?" Dylan was temporarily distracted by how the sunlight was reflecting on Mackenzie's face. It looked dewy and flushed and pretty. Her lips, lips that he'd never really noticed before, were naturally pink and plump. Kissable lips.

"I do." Mackenzie nodded. "I do."

Mackenzie liked how disheveled Dylan looked now. Gone was the catalog model posed in a barn. Part of his shirt was untucked, his jeans were dirty and the once-pristine boots were caked with mud and manure. He was sweaty and grimy and she liked him like that.

Irritated with her own musings about Dylan's masculine appeal, she decided to razz him the way she did when they were kids. "I bet your manicurist is going to have a heck of a time cleaning your nails."

Dylan checked his nails. "Yeah…you're probably right."

"I was just *kidding*! Don't tell me you really *do* have a manicurist, Dylan!"

"In my line of business, being well groomed is a matter of survival."

"Oh, dear Lord…" Mackenzie rolled her eyes. "I can't believe I've actually seen the day when Dylan Axel willingly submitted to a manicure. What happened to the guy who used to love to have grease up to his elbows?"

"Hey…there's nothing wrong with a guy taking care of himself. In fact…*ow*!" Dylan swung his head around quick. "She *bit* me!"

"What?"

Dylan glared at the mare accusingly. "You *bit* me!"

"Where'd she get you?" Mackenzie looked him over. "I don't see any teeth marks."

"That's because she didn't *bite* me on the arm." Dylan scowled at the mare. "Did you, you glue factory reject?"

Hope interrupted their conversation when she returned with a helmet. "What happened?"

"Nothing worth talking about. Here, kiddo." Mackenzie handed Hope the reins. "Why don't you get started and we'll be right behind you, okay."

"Okay. Come on, Gyps!" Hope led Gypsy to the riding arena.

When Hope was out of earshot, Mackenzie said, "She bit you on the butt, didn't she?"

"Let's put it this way…" Dylan said sourly. "It's going to be a long painful drive back to the city."

"Wait here." Mackenzie tried very hard to stifle her smile but failed. "I'll be right back"

Mackenzie returned with Aggie in tow.

"All right." Aggie held a first-aid kit in her hand. "Where'd she getcha? I swear that mare gets meaner every year…"

Mackenzie blurted out, "She bit him in the butt."

"Once a tattletale…" Dylan muttered.

"I'm not a bit surprised," Aggie said. "That's one of her favorite spots… She's gotten me on the fleshy part a couple of times. Do you want me to take a look? See if she broke the skin?"

"No, thank you!" Dylan stepped back.

"Oh, come on, Dylan…" Mackenzie teased him. "Don't be such a baby. Let Aggie take a look."

"Thank *you*," Dylan said to Aggie, then to Mackenzie, "But *no*."

"Suit yourself. But I suggest you grow eyeballs in the back of your head so you can see for yourself if she broke the skin." Aggie handed him the first-aid kit and headed back to the office. "And remember…you volunteered at your own risk."

"Which way to the bathroom?" Dylan asked Mackenzie.

"This way." Mackenzie smirked.

"I suppose you think this is funny…?"

"Not at all."

"Liar!" Dylan smiled at her. "What happened to the girl who used to have a little integrity, huh?"

"Here's the bathroom." Mackenzie pointed. "Light switch on the left."

Dylan went into the bathroom and examined his backside by turning his back to the mirror and straining his neck to look over his shoulder.

"Damn if she didn't break the skin." Dylan ripped open a packet containing an alcohol wipe. He dabbed the wound and then closed his eyes when the alcohol hit it. "And that smarts…"

"How's it going in there?" Mackenzie called through the door.

"She got me good." Dylan tossed the used wipe into the trash.

"Make sure you put some ointment on it and a Band-Aid."

"I'm not a contortionist, Mackenzie." Dylan pulled up his underwear carefully.

After a pause, Mackenzie asked, "Do you want me to do it?"

"It's fine."

"If you don't put something on it, won't it hurt worse when you drive home?"

"I'll manage." Dylan pulled up his jeans.

Mackenzie knocked on the door. "Why don't you let me help you?"

Not waiting for his response, Mackenzie turned the doorknob. "I'm coming in."

Dylan tried to lock the door but the lock failed.

"That lock's been broken for about a year now." Mackenzie leaned her hand against the doorjamb. "Will you stop pretending to be a prude and let me help you?"

"Really? You just open the door and waltz right in? What if I had been in the *middle* of something?"

"I could see your boots near the sink, okay? Now, quit whining and turn around."

"Mackenzie…" Dylan said. "The bite is on my *ass*."

"So? Do you think that I haven't seen your butt before? Give me a break! You and my brother and all of your stupid friends mooned everyone in the neighborhood! Remember?"

"Oh, yeah…I forgot about that."

"What did you idiots used to call yourselves again?"

"The Moonshine Gang."

"I'm sorry…" Mackenzie cupped her ear. "I didn't quite catch that?"

"The Moonshine Gang," Dylan said loudly.

"Thank you. I rest my case. Now, turn around, drop trou, then hand me the ointment. Please."

Grudgingly, Dylan turned around and dropped his jeans just enough to expose the wound.

"She got you, all right." Mackenzie squeezed some ointment onto the wound. "Hand me one of the big, square Band-Aids, will you?"

Mackenzie ripped open the package with her teeth.

"What's going on back there?" Dylan asked impatiently.

"I'm baking a cake...what do you think's going on?" Mackenzie pulled the Band-Aid out of the packet and tossed the empty wrapper into the trash.

"Voilà!" Mackenzie quickly applied the Band-Aid. "Done!"

Mackenzie left the bathroom while Dylan straightened his clothes.

"You're welcome," Mackenzie said when he joined her.

"*You* should be apologizing to *me* for barging into the bathroom like that," Dylan countered with feigned indignation.

"*You* should be apologizing for having a manicurist!" Mackenzie retorted.

Dylan stuck out his hand. "Call it even?"

"Fine. Even." Mackenzie shook Dylan's hand. "Come on...let's go watch Hope ride."

They walked out to the riding arena and both of them leaned up against the fence. Dylan watched Hope canter Gypsy. "She's got a great seat for riding."

"She definitely doesn't get that from me. I've always been a little afraid of horses."

"No. *That* she gets from me."

Mackenzie glanced at Dylan. They had known each other in another lifetime, when they were just kids. But there was something comfortable in their silences when it was just the two of them. That *something* was familiar, unrehearsed, effortless and impossible to fake. There was a shared history; they came from the same neighborhood. There was a common thread of values that transcended the years they had spent apart.

When Dylan spoke, it was in a lowered voice and for her ears only. "I know you told me that Hope has leukemia. But it doesn't seem possible. Just look at her. She's... perfect. She acts like a typical kid."

"She's been in remission for two years, so she's gained weight. And even though it's different and that bothers her, her hair finally grew back. But we aren't out of the woods yet. When she was diagnosed, she was put in the high-risk category, which means she has a greater risk of the cancer coming back."

"You know, when you told me about Hope, about her diagnosis, I've really tried to educate myself about her type of leukemia."

"ALL..."

"Right..." Dylan nodded. "But I still don't know what any of it means for Hope."

"What do you mean?"

Dylan turned his body toward her. "Is she going to be okay or not?"

Mackenzie looked at her daughter, so happy to be riding Gypsy again. "I don't know, Dylan. There's no guarantee. Her prognosis is good, but until we hit the three-year mark without a relapse, *I'm* not going to feel like we're out of the woods yet. She takes daily doses of medication, she goes in for regular testing and she still takes chemo. And let me tell you, when she does have chemo, she's not the same kid. She can't get out bed, she's sick to her stomach, I can hardly get her to eat." Mackenzie watched her daughter. "That's why she pushes herself so hard in between..."

"Because she knows what she's in for..."

"Exactly." Mackenzie smiled and waved at Hope, who cantered in a circle directly in front of them.

"She never mentioned it to me." Dylan rested his foot on the bottom of the fence. "I sort of thought she would."

"She doesn't like to talk about it much anymore, and I

try to respect that. All she wants is to be a normal kid. Who can blame her? No kid should have to go through this…"

Dylan wasn't certain what had changed inside him. But something had. A switch had been flipped, an indelible mark had been made, and there wasn't any going back. When he had awakened this morning, he hadn't been a father…and perhaps he really wasn't still. But he *wanted* to be. He saw it now just as plainly as if it had been written across the cloudless blue sky…he had a chance to do better for Hope. He had a choice…he could reject the legacy left to him by his biological father and embrace the lessons he had learned from Uncle Bill. And it took Hope, sweet, honest, tenderhearted Hope, to make him see the light. Hope slowed Gypsy to a jog and then an animated walk. Gypsy's neck was drenched with sweat, her mouth dripping foam from engaging with the bit.

Cheeks flushed red, eyes bright with joy, Hope patted Gypsy enthusiastically on the neck. "Good girl, Gypsy! I'm going to take her for a walk to cool her down before I rinse her off." Hope dropped her feet out of the stirrups and let them dangle loose.

"I'll grab the gate for you," Mackenzie said.

Hope guided Gypsy through the arena gate and headed to an open field; Mackenzie and Dylan walked slowly back toward the barn.

"Have you told Jordan yet that I'm Hope's father?" Dylan asked in a low, private voice.

"No." She had led her family to believe that her college boyfriend was Hope's father. Only her father and brother knew the truth. It was hard to come clean on a lie, especially one as big as this one.

"I haven't told Ian yet, either." Dylan slipped his sunglasses back on. "I'll call him and see if we can get together with them tonight. We may as well tell them together."

Chapter Seven

Mackenzie and Dylan took the elevator up to Ian Sterling's penthouse. Dylan, Mackenzie noted, was impeccably dressed in pressed khaki slacks, a custom-tailored navy blazer and spotless shoes that had to have cost more than one month's rent. She, on the other hand, still had on her baking clothes: an oversize Nothin' But Cupcakes polo, new black Converse and an old pair of baggy chinos that were permanently stained with food dye.

Mackenzie took a small step away from Dylan. Whenever she was near him, she felt like a dumpy bag lady. She caught her reflection in the highly polished brass elevator fittings. Had she been having an odd Alfalfa moment this whole entire time? She quickly tried to smooth the out-of-control curls.

Mackenzie glanced over at Dylan, who was standing stiffly next to her. He looked as nervous as she felt. "So… how's your backside?"

Her attempt to get him to loosen up a little worked. He cracked a smile. “Sore. Thank you for asking.”

“Well…you’re not the first victim.”

“And I won’t be the last…” The elevator came to a slow stop, the light dinged. “This is us.”

In front of the condo’s ornate door, Mackenzie started to feel queasy from nerves. Telling your family that you’ve been lying to them for ten years didn’t exactly seem like a fun time. When Dylan opened the unlocked door, she wished she were anyplace other than where she was.

“Anybody home?” Dylan announced their arrival.

“Dylan! Mackenzie!” Barefoot, dressed in faded low-slung boy jeans and a simple white tee, Jordan appeared at the top of the stairwell leading up to the main floor.

“Come on up! I apologize in advance for the renovation mess…”

At the top of the stairs, Jordan hugged Mackenzie first, and then Dylan.

“Jordan…this view…”

“I know, right? Crazy good. Once it’s remodeled, it’s going to be heaven on earth…”

“She’s taking advantage of the fact that I can’t see the invoices,” Jordan’s fiancé, Ian, commented as he walked into the room.

Mackenzie had seen pictures of Ian Sterling, world-renowned photographer and ex-model, but to see him in person was an entirely different experience. He was tall and built, high cheekbones, strong jawline. Sculpted lips. He was a perfect physical match for tall, athletic, naturally beautiful Jordan.

Jordan went immediately to Ian’s side and linked arms with him. “Knock that off, *GQ*… Mackenzie doesn’t know you’re kidding. I’m just warning you guys. He’s been cracking a lot of blind jokes lately…” Jordan confided to

Mackenzie as she nonchalantly guided Ian over to where Dylan and Mackenzie were standing.

"And Jordan is determined to suck all the fun out of this little adventure..." Ian said about his blindness.

Even though it was dusk, Ian wore dark sunglasses. Diagnosed with a rare form of macular degeneration called Stargardt disease, Ian was legally blind.

Jordan had a glow about her that Mackenzie envied. No man had ever made her all girlie and dewy and *flushed.*

Jordan introduced Mackenzie and Ian. They shook hands, and then Ian and Dylan gave each other a hug.

"Let's talk in the study...it's the only room Jordan hasn't torn apart..."

"Yet..." Jordan wrapped her arms around Ian's body and squeezed him tightly. "You know you love me."

Ian dropped a kiss on the top of Jordan's head. "Yes, I do..."

They all grabbed drinks and then headed to the study. There were two love seats on either side of the coffee table. Jordan curled up next to Ian on one love seat, which left the other one for Mackenzie and Dylan. Dylan waited for her to be seated before he joined her. No matter how she tried, she couldn't avoid touching Dylan's body. They were shoulder to shoulder and leg to leg on the tiny love seat.

"Okay..." Jordan got the conversation started. "I'm about to keel over with curiosity. What are the two of you doing here...*together*?"

Mackenzie and Dylan exchanged looks.

"Do you want to tell them?" Dylan asked her. "Or should I?"

"I'll do it. I'm the one who got us into this mess..."

"Well...I hardly think that's the case. It took both of us to—"

Exasperated, Jordan interrupted. "For the love of God

and all that is holy in the world…will you *please* tell us what's going on?"

Ian touched Jordan's leg to get her attention. "What?"

"Let them talk," Ian said gently.

Jordan frowned at Ian but gave Mackenzie and Dylan the floor.

"I have to set the record straight about something." Mackenzie wiped more sweat from her palms onto her pant legs. "Dylan is Hope's father."

Mackenzie's abrupt confession was followed by silence. Like a pretty kaleidoscope, Jordan's facial expression changed from confusion to shock to disbelief.

"I'm sorry…what did you just say?" Jordan leaned forward a bit.

"Hope is Dylan's child," Mackenzie repeated. It actually felt good to get this out in the open. She had never liked lying to her family. She had wanted to keep it from her father and Jett so they wouldn't tell Dylan, but the lie had metastasized to the rest of the family.

Jordan stared at the two of them, speechless in her contemplation, and Ian hadn't said a word. He was just listening, taking it all in.

"I'm Hope's father." That was the first time he had uttered those words aloud to anyone other than himself. "Hope is my daughter."

Jordan sat back. "Wait a minute…you mean…*Hope* Hope? As in, *your* daughter, Hope?"

Mackenzie nodded silently.

"But…I thought Hope's father was your boyfriend from college…the one with all the Star Wars toys…"

"Star Trek," Mackenzie corrected. "He was a Trekkie…"

Jordan rolled her eyes. "Whatever…same difference."

"Not to a Trekkie," Ian said. "They're completely different."

Jordan twisted around to look at Ian. "Really? Now you decide to chime in?"

"He's right," Dylan agreed. "Two completely different things."

"Can we get back to the important part of this conversation, please?" Jordan looked at everyone questioningly. "I mean…how do the two of you even *know* each other?"

The conversation that followed took longer than Mackenzie had originally anticipated. She was hoping for a more "drive-by" kind of deal that didn't require much emotional energy. That didn't happen. While Ian remained quiet for the entire conversation, he appeared to be listening intently to every word. Jordan, on the other hand, decided to earn her junior Perry Mason badge.

"Look…" Mackenzie finally said, exasperated. "I wasn't signing up for the Spanish Inquisition here, okay? I was young and I thought I was doing the right thing for all of us. Would I do it this way again?" Mackenzie caught Dylan's eye and held it. "No. I wouldn't." Mackenzie broke the gaze. To her cousin, she said, "But I can't go back. All I can do is say that I'm sorry for lying to you. I wasn't trying to hurt anyone. I was just trying to do the best I could for Hope. That's what I'm still trying to do…"

"Oh…hey…" Jordan crossed the short distance to Mackenzie's seat and wrapped her arms around her cousin's shoulders. "I didn't mean to upset you. I'm just surprised, that's all. I love you, Mackenzie. And I love Hope…no matter what. Okay?"

Jordan knelt down beside Mackenzie. "Hey…let me give you the five-cent tour of this place. I want to show you all the finishes I've picked…hand-scraped wide-plank hardwood…new custom cabinets throughout…"

"Hey—I *heard* that," Ian told his fiancée. "I still have excellent hearing."

Jordan laughed and returned to Ian's side. She leaned down, took his gorgeous face into her hands and kissed him on the lips. "I love you, my handsome man…"

"I love you more." Ian squeezed her hand, kissed it affectionately before letting it go.

Dylan watched Mackenzie and Jordan leave the room. He waited several seconds to make certain they were out of earshot before he said to Ian, "You haven't had much to say."

"Not much to say, I don't think." Ian pulled his wallet out of his pocket. He pulled a card out of the wallet, brought the card close to the side of his face so he could use his still-intact peripheral vision to read the name, then he held it out to Dylan. "Here. You might need this."

Ben Levine, Attorney-at-Law.

After looking at it, Dylan slipped the card into his wallet.

"You have a child." Ian twisted the cap off his bottle of water. "How do you feel about that?"

"Terrified." Dylan could be honest with Ian.

"You need to know your rights. We have the photography business to think of…we're launching the modeling agency in a couple of months…"

"I know. Mackenzie doesn't want child support, but…"

"People change their minds all the time. Call Ben."

"I will." Dylan nodded pensively. "You know…I spent the whole morning with her today. Hope. She's a great kid. Looks just like Aunt Gerri."

"Is that right?"

"Yeah…" Dylan smiled when an image of Hope's sweet, expectant face popped into his head. "Do you want to meet her?"

"Of course I do. She's your daughter." Ian finished off his water. "I'm not saying you shouldn't get involved...I'm just saying that you should cover your bases. That's all."

"Expect the best..." Dylan said.

Ian finished their motto. "But prepare for the worst."

After their visit with Jordan and Ian, Mackenzie and Dylan rode the elevator down to the ground floor together. Through the lobby of the building and out onto the city sidewalk, they paused for a moment just outside the front door. Noticing a large group of tourists heading their way, Dylan put his hand on the small of her back and guided her to the left. Then he put his body between hers and the group so she wouldn't get bumped.

Once the boisterous group passed them by, Mackenzie said, "You didn't have to leave when I did. You could have stayed."

Dylan had his hands in his front pockets, his blazer thrown over his arm. "It was time for me to head out, too. Did you walk here from the bakery?"

Mackenzie nodded.

"I'll walk you back," he said. Even though downtown San Diego was a pretty safe place, even at dusk, he didn't like the idea of her walking back to the bakery alone.

"It's not that far..." She looked over her shoulder toward the direction of her business.

But once she saw that Dylan was going to insist on seeing her safely back to Nothin' But Cupcakes, Mackenzie stopped protesting and started walking. At a crosswalk, waiting for the light to turn, she asked, "What does your girlfriend think of all this?"

The light turned and Dylan stepped into the crosswalk at her side. "Actually, Jenna and I had an amicable parting of the ways..."

"Not because of Hope?" She stepped up onto the curb.

"No. Not because of Hope." He reassured her. "She decided to finally make the move to LA, and I support her decision. It's what's best for her career. The breakup was inevitable."

"Well…I'm still sorry. She seemed really—" she searched her brain for a positive comment that she could say truthfully "—energetic."

Dylan shot her a quizzical look before he laughed. "Yes…you're right. She is very energetic."

They reached her storefront and Mackenzie pulled the keys out of her tote bag. "Well…this is me. Thanks for walking me back."

"Are you heading home or sticking around here?"

She slipped the key into the lock. "I have some work to do before I head home."

Mackenzie opened the door and walked quickly to the alarm keypad. She punched in the code and the beeping sound stopped. The only light in the front of the bakery was from the cases that had been emptied the night before by Molly.

"Thank you again for making sure I got here safely," she said to Dylan, who had followed her in and locked the door behind them. "But I'm sure you've got things to do. I'll be fine here by myself."

Sometimes she liked to come to the bakery after hours just to have some time alone—Ray and Charlie were always happy to watch Hope for her. She liked the bakery when it was quiet and dark the way it was now. She could be by herself with her thoughts while she baked. It was therapeutic, especially when she had something worrisome on her mind.

He knew she was politely trying to send him on his way, but he wasn't ready to leave just yet. He was enjoying her company. He felt relaxed around her; she made him laugh in a way that most women didn't.

"My schedule's pretty clear, actually. How about a quick tour?"

He heard her let out her breath and knew she was about to cave. "There's not much to see…and I really do have work that I've got to get done."

"I promise I'll stay out of your way…" He held up one hand as if he was taking an oath.

For the second time that night, Mackenzie gave in to Dylan's persistence. She was wasting time talking to him when she really needed to be working on the cupcakes. Molly had called to tell her that they were about to run out of one of their bestsellers, red velvet with cream cheese frosting. It was her mother's recipe, so she guarded it. She was the only one who made them; she needed to make several large batches and freeze some of them for later.

"I could help you," Dylan offered.

Mackenzie slipped into her white baking coat. "You can help me by sitting over there and not moving."

He smiled at her no-nonsense way of bossing him around her kitchen and obediently sat down on a stool out of the way. It was interesting to see Mackenzie in her element. Here, in the kitchen, she was absolutely sure of herself. She gathered the ingredients for the cupcakes first, and then measured each ingredient carefully before adding them, one by one, to an industrial mixer. While the batter mixed, she prepared the baking pans, deftly dropping specially designed Nothin' But Cupcakes cupcake cups into the pans. In the zone now, she didn't even seem to notice that he was sitting nearby.

Dylan had never really cared about watching someone cook before, but watching Mackenzie was different. He was fascinated by how easily she moved from one area of the kitchen to the next; it was like watching a well-choreographed dance.

"What kind of frosting are you going to make?" he asked.

Mackenzie glanced up at him, with a somewhat surprised expression in her pretty eyes. He had been so quiet, and she had been so focused, that she forgot for a moment that she wasn't alone.

"Cream cheese." She switched off the mixer and then set to the task of filling the cupcake pans.

Once the cupcakes were baking in the ovens, she made the frosting, which she could store in the refrigerator until morning. Now all she had to do was wait for the cupcakes to cook and cool. With a satisfied sigh, hands on hips, Mackenzie nodded to herself. Then she looked over at Dylan, who hadn't really bothered her at all.

"Do you like cream cheese frosting?"

Dylan had been leaning on one elbow. He sat upright. "Yes. I do."

Mackenzie took a large spoon out of a drawer, scooped up a large helping of freshly made frosting and handed it to him. Dylan ate all the frosting at one time; he closed his eyes happily and then licked the spoon before he handed it back to her.

"Good?" she asked, but she could tell by his smiling lips that he approved.

"Mackenzie…" he said seriously. "You are an artist."

His sincere praise for her baking made her entire body smile. When someone truly enjoyed her baking, it made the struggle to keep her business afloat worth it. Mackenzie felt herself relaxing with Dylan; after all, this wasn't the first time he had loitered in her kitchen. He was always hanging around with Jett when she had baked with her mother.

"Do you want to wait for the cupcakes to finish baking? I'll frost one just for you."

He looked more like the young boy she remembered when he asked, "Just one?"

The month after he first met his daughter sped by for Dylan. And even though he hadn't intended to become a regular fixture at Pegasus, that's exactly what had happened. It started out innocently. It was an opportunity for him to spend time with Hope on the weekends. Then something unexpected happened: the place got to him. The kids, the horses, the other volunteers…the parents… all of them had an impact. He discovered that he was surfing less and mucking out stalls more. He was handy with a hammer and Aggie had him on her radar. On the weekends, he traded his Testoni lace-ups for rubber muckers and his polo button-ups for Pegasus T-shirts. Instead of going out with his friends, he went to bed early on Friday night so he could be up early and fresh for the riders on Saturday morning.

And always, *always*, there was Hope. She was the main event. He found himself missing her during the week and regretting having to say goodbye on Sundays. He didn't mind the status quo for now, but this arrangement wouldn't work in the long term. He wanted to have a say in Hope's future; he wanted to be her *dad.*

"Hey…" Mackenzie appeared at the entrance of the feed room. As usual, she was dressed in oversize clothing, long sleeves, and her hair was haphazardly pulled up into a ponytail. Dylan wished she would fix herself up every once in a while.

"Hey…" Dylan pulled a bale of hay off the tall stack in the corner and dropped it on the ground.

"Where's Hope?"

Dylan used the bottom of his T-shirt to wipe the sweat that was dripping off his face, exposing his stomach. She was human. She looked. And her eyes latched on to the barely visible trail of hair leading from Dylan's belly button directly to his…

Dylan dropped his shirt; when she looked up at him, he was smiling at her. His expression told the story; he'd caught her red-handed.

"She's helping Aggie with Hank—he's got a pretty nasty gash on his fetlock and you know how he feels about anyone messing with his hooves." Dylan hoisted the bale of hay onto his shoulder. "Excuse me."

Mackenzie stepped to the side so Dylan could move through the door. She had watched Dylan closely over the past couple of weekends. She couldn't deny that he had a special way with all the kids, especially Hope. They all loved him. When they could, they trailed after him, and he was happy to let them. He had become the Pegasus Pied Piper. It was…endearing. And Aggie, who was pretty tough to impress, had come to rely on Dylan as part of her small circle of trusted volunteers.

"Do you feel like lending a hand?" Dylan cut the twine holding the bale of hay together.

"Sure."

Loaded down with armfuls of hay, Dylan tackled one side of the barn and Mackenzie tackled the other. When Mackenzie reached Hank's stall, she tossed the hay over the stall fence for the old gelding.

"Hey, Aggie. Time to wrap up, kiddo," Mackenzie said to Hope, who was watching Aggie treat Hank's wound. "You have school tomorrow."

"Okay, Mom…I'll be right there."

Mackenzie waited for Hope at the barn entrance and watched the sun set on the horizon. All day, every day, it seemed as if she was running around like a chicken with her head cut off—monitoring Hope's health, helping Hope with homework, working in the bakery, paying the bills, shopping for groceries, doing the laundry…one chore led into the next, one day bled into the other. She couldn't remember the last time she had actually allowed herself to just stop and enjoy a sunset.

"It's going to be a full moon." Dylan came up beside her.

Not wanting to expend her limited resource of energy on small talk, Mackenzie only nodded. She wanted to enjoy the view just a little bit longer before she had to rally the energy to cook dinner and do a load of laundry. She was having a perfectly lovely time until she felt something crawling on her neck. Startled, she slapped at the side of her neck and tried to spot the offending bug.

Dylan, looking sheepish, held a piece of hay in his fingertips. "You had a piece of hay stuck in your hair."

"Don't *do* that!" Mackenzie punched Dylan hard on the arm. "I thought it was a bug!"

Dylan rubbed his arm. "Man…you really know how to pack a punch…"

"Of course I do… You and Jett and the rest of your idiot friends thought it was hilarious to ambush me with dead bugs all the time! I *had* to learn how to defend myself."

"I never did that to you!"

"Yeah…you did."

"Well, I don't remember doing that, but if you said that I did, then I suppose I'm sorry."

"Your apology, however halfhearted, is accepted."

Dylan glanced over his shoulder; Aggie and Hope were coming out of Hank's stall and his window of opportunity was about to close.

"Mackenzie…" Dylan crossed his arms to give them

something to do. "I was wondering...do you want to come over for dinner Friday night?"

"Um...we can't. Hope's spending the weekend with one of her friends from Relay For Life. I don't normally let her spend an overnight, but this family knows the drill because their daughter has ALL as well, so..."

"I know. Hope told me. That's all she talked about today was her sleepover, which she *never* gets to do. What I meant was...do *you* want to come over Friday night for dinner...with me?"

Mackenzie lifted her brows questioningly. "Why?"

Dylan looked at her as if he couldn't quite figure her out. Perhaps he was used to automatic yeses to all his invitations.

"Because..." he said. "I think it'd be good for us to spend some time together. There are a lot of things we still need to figure out. Don't you agree?"

"I suppose." Up until now, she had been very good at dodging Dylan's attempts to sit down and discuss how they were going to move forward as coparents.

Dylan tucked his hands into his pockets and lifted his shoulders questioningly. "Oh, come on, Mackenzie... what's the worst that could happen? If nothing else, you'll get a free meal out of the deal. And, I really didn't want to brag..."

"Of course not..."

"But I *have* been told that I'm pretty amazing with my grill."

Chapter Eight

Mackenzie stood in front of her closet, staring at the sad collection of old clothing hanging askew on wire hangers. After several attempts at finding something even remotely fashionable to wear to Dylan's house for dinner, Mackenzie groaned dramatically and threw herself face down on her unmade bed. Dylan always looked so put together; she wanted at least to *try*, for her own sake, to look halfway decent for a change. But, in truth, she didn't really want to go at all. What she *really* wanted to do with her first kid-free weekend was to procure a bag of ranch-flavored Doritos and to watch the Food Network in bed. When her cell started to ring, she reached out with her hand and felt around on the nightstand for the phone. Not lifting her head up, she put the phone to her ear.

"Hello?"

"What are you doing?" It was Rayna calling.

"Slowly suffocating myself with my hypoallergenic pillow..."

"I take it the hunt for an outfit isn't going so well?"

Mackenzie rolled onto her back and wrapped herself in her comforter like a burrito. "I think I'm going to call him and tell him I'm too tired..."

"I'm coming over..."

"Is that gangsta rap?" Mackenzie took a time-out from her own crisis and tuned her ear to the loud music blasting through the phone.

"Yes. Charlie had a bad day at work. Max and I are coming over."

Moments later, Rayna and her rotund feline arrived in her bedroom. She peeled the comforter back and found Mackenzie inside. Max jumped up onto her bed with a grunt. He nudged her hand so she would pet him.

"Mackenzie...you can't back out. How long has it been since you've done anything remotely fun?"

Mackenzie tried to remember but couldn't.

"If you have to think about it for *that long*, then it's been *way too* long. And do you know what I think? I think that hidden beneath these rumpled, oversize clothes is a beautiful, curvy woman just dying to come out and play." Rayna tugged on Mackenzie's arm until she was upright. "Now... you go take a shower because you smell really sweaty. Max and I will try to find you something less...boxy to wear."

Needing to clean up anyway, Mackenzie took a quick shower and shrugged into her bathrobe. She wiped the moisture from the bathroom mirror and frowned at her own reflection. She looked tired. Dark circles, a little bit of stress acne on her chin.

Lovely.

When Mackenzie returned to her bedroom, her dirty

clothes had been collected and deposited in the hamper. And Max was happily lounging on her freshly made bed.

"What did you do in here?" Mackenzie asked.

"Oh…I just picked up a little so I could see what we're working with," Rayna said offhandedly. "You do know that *square* isn't a flattering shape for a woman's body, right?" Rayna had pulled several tops out of her closet. "Why are all your clothes two sizes too big?"

"I don't have time for shopping, Ray…you know what I *do* have time for?" She sounded defensive. "Payroll. And hospital visits. So, no offense, but having a fashion *moment* just isn't high up on my priority list."

"I know how busy you are." Rayna's hands stilled and she looked over her shoulder at Mackenzie. "But you're still buying clothes for your *old* body. And you may not believe me, but a good pair of jeans and a pretty blouse can change your whole outlook on life."

Mackenzie caught her reflection in the dresser mirror. Yes, she had lost a ton of weight. But when she looked in the mirror, all she saw was *fat*. And, with Hope's illness and always struggling to make ends meet, it was easier just to buy oversize, comfy clothes and avoid reflective surfaces. She couldn't remember the last time she had actually tried something on in a fitting room.

"Now, *this* is pretty!" Rayna spun around and held up a deep purple short-sleeved blouse that Hope had convinced her to buy. "What do you think? It still has the price tag on it."

Mackenzie shook her head. "No. I don't do short sleeves. My arms are too…" She wrinkled her nose distastefully. *"Jiggly."*

Disappointed, Rayna hung the blouse back in the closet. "You're your own worst enemy…you're hot and you don't even know it."

Mackenzie opened her dresser drawer and pulled out her favorite long-sleeved San Diego Padres shirt. "It's ridiculous that I've even been spending *one second* stressing about this...it's *Dylan*. Not a *date*. So I'm not gonna get all gussied up, when I *never* get all gussied up, and make Dylan feel all weirded out because *he* thinks that *I* think that this evening is something more than it is. Which it's not."

"It's a date." Rayna sat down on the bed next to Max. "Friday night. And he's cooking you dinner at his place? It's a date."

Refusing to indulge in Rayna's fantasy, Mackenzie stepped into the bathroom to slip into the Padres shirt and a pair of jeans. Mackenzie sighed. The jeans were tighter around the waist than they used to be. Why did it always have to be such a battle? If she didn't watch every bite, consider every carb or exercise several times a week, the scale would turn against her.

Whatever.

"Trust me, Ray...I'm not Dylan's type." Mackenzie grabbed her comb and began the chore of untangling her thick, wavy hair. "And he's not really mine."

"You actually have to *date* to have a type...and besides, you guys have a daughter...you must've been attracted to each other at some point. Right?"

"That was—" Mackenzie stopped combing her hair for a second to think. "I don't know what that was."

"A night of unforgettable passion?" Rayna raised her eyebrows suggestively several times.

Mackenzie scrunched up her face. "Uh-uh. Honestly... it was...really, really *awkward*."

"Oh..." Rayna wilted. "See...judging from pictures, I would've thought Dylan would be good in bed. For a man. He's got that sexy, squinty-eye thing going on."

"I don't know what you're talking about." Mackenzie had never noticed Dylan having a sexy, squinty anything. It was *Dylan*. Annoying, mooning, bug-throwing *Dylan*.

Rayna held up her pinkie and wiggled it. "Is he really… you know? Tiny?"

"What?" Mackenzie looked perplexed at Rayna's bouncing pinkie for a minute before she caught Rayna's meaning. "No…*no*. He's *fine* in that department. It's just that we had way too much to drink…"

"Which never works in a guy's favor…"

"And I didn't want him to touch me anywhere because I was *bulgy* all over…."

Rayna's brows lifted. "Now I'm actually kind of surprised the two of you managed to procreate."

"That's what I've been trying to tell you." Mackenzie twisted her hair up into a bun and secured it with a clip. "I can guarantee you that neither one of us wants a repeat of that night."

Deflated, Rayna said, "So…not a date."

"No. Definitely not a date."

Dylan met her at the door, stylish, freshly showered and shaved. Not a surprise; he even managed to make sweaty and dirty at the barn look good. What *was* a surprise was the table setting. Dylan had obviously put some thought into setting the table for two. There were two lit candles on the table that caught, and held, her attention.

"Now that you're here, I'm going to throw the salmon on the grill. You said you liked salmon, right?"

Mackenzie slipped her tote off her shoulder. "Yes…"

"Make yourself at home and I'll be right back. Unless you want to keep me company…?"

"No." Instead of putting the tote down, Mackenzie clutched it to her body. "I'll wait here."

I'm on a date.

Panic. Sheer unadulterated panic. Mackenzie quickly texted Ray: I'm on a DATE!

Ray shot a text back: Told U so! Yippee!

"Yippee? That's the sage advice I get?" Mackenzie turned the phone on Vibrate and tucked it into her pocket.

Now what?

Should she leave or should she stay...*that* was the ultimate question.

"All right..." Dylan reappeared and headed for the fridge. "I hope you like sweet red wine...?"

Mackenzie nodded. She was still trying to figure out how to back out of this situation gracefully. Could she fake a stomachache? Menstrual cramps? It's not that she didn't want to be on a date with *Dylan* per se...she didn't want to be on a date with *anyone*. Relationships took time and energy and she had very little of both of those resources to spare.

Dylan poured the wine, handed her a glass and then held his glass up for a toast. "To Hope's continued health..."

Mackenzie touched her glass to his. "To Hope's continued health..."

"And to new beginnings," Dylan added.

Mackenzie hesitated before she took a sip of the sweet wine. She put her glass down on the counter. Dylan quickly pulled out a coaster and put it under her glass.

"How's the wine?" Dylan asked.

"Good..." Mackenzie stared at the coaster for a moment. "Good. Um..."

"I'm glad that you showed, Mackenzie...I was actually pretty sure you were going to cancel on me..."

Mackenzie blurted out, "I almost did."

"See..." Dylan laughed. "That's one of the things I really like about you…you're honest. Why don't we go sit down, get comfortable."

"No," Mackenzie said tentatively, then more strongly, "No."

"That's okay. We don't have to sit. I read somewhere that standing is actually better than sitting. Better for the circulation, I think."

"I need to clear something up between us, I think…"

"What's that?"

"I mean…there's the table and the wine and the candles…it's Friday night." Mackenzie had one hand resting on her tote. "This feels kind of like a…date."

Dylan put his glass down slowly on a coaster. "That's because I thought it *was* a date."

"Oh…"

"But you didn't." Dylan stared at her for a moment before he blew out the candles.

Crap! She had hurt him. And now Mackenzie was at a rare loss for words as she watched the two twin ribbons of smoke rise from the extinguished candles.

"This is embarrassing." Dylan gulped down his wine and put his glass in the sink.

Both hands clutching the tote, Mackenzie said, "If I'd known that you thought this was a…date…I would never have said yes."

This wasn't the first time he'd embarrassed himself in front of a pretty woman he liked, but in this case, with Mackenzie, it stung just a little bit more than usual.

"I need to check on the salmon," Dylan said.

How she had managed to land on the defensive in this scenario, Mackenzie couldn't figure out…but on the defensive, she was. She followed Dylan to the outdoor kitchen. She sat down on the very edge of a built-in bench; Dylan pushed open the lid of the grill a bit harder than he normally would.

"The salmon looks good," Mackenzie said for lack of anything more helpful to say.

Dylan flipped the salmon steaks over, seasoned them and then shut the lid tightly. Mackenzie felt like a grade-A heel; all she wanted to do now was to smooth things over with Dylan and to get the heck out of Dodge.

"Why would you think this was a date, Dylan?" Guilty, Mackenzie switched from contrite to accusatory.

"Just forget it, Mackenzie." Dylan started to walk back to the house. But then he stopped. "No. You know what? *Don't* forget it. Why *wouldn't* you think this was a date?"

"Because...you're *that*..." Mackenzie waved her hand up and down. "And I'm *this*...I'm not your type."

Dylan sat down on a bench across from her. "How do you know what my type is, Mackenzie?"

"Christa? Jenna? Tall, blonde, skinny." Mackenzie held up three fingers. "And, me? Short, chubby, brunette. Not exactly rocket science."

"You forgot pretty..."

Mackenzie held up a fourth finger. "Pretty goes without saying."

"No," Dylan clarified. "I meant *you*. I think *you're* pretty. And funny and sweet and a really great mom to Hope."

Mackenzie crossed her legs and crossed her arms protectively in front of her body.

Dylan continued, "You know...Jenna and I both loved to surf. And I managed to sustain a relationship built on a mutual love for surfing for nearly a year. You and I have a child together..."

Now Dylan had her full attention.

"And I look at you and I look at Hope...and I think...

maybe I have a chance at what Uncle Bill and Aunt Gerri had together."

"You can't force a family." Mackenzie pulled her sleeves down over her hands and recrossed her arms.

"No, you can't. But you can try to build one." Dylan leaned forward, forearms resting on his thighs. "This doesn't have anything to do with *my* type, does it? That's just an excuse. This has to do with the fact that I'm not *your* type, right?"

"My friend Rayna says that you actually *have* to date to have a type…and I don't. Date, I mean."

"I know. Hope told me. Your friend set you up with a socialist three years ago?"

"He was a *social* worker. A very nice *social* worker. You and Hope certainly cover a lot of subjects, don't you?"

"She likes to talk to me. I like to listen. But let's not get off topic here. I like you, Mackenzie. I want to spend more time with you. And I get that I'm not the obvious choice for you because I don't have a five-page *community service* section on my résumé…but you've gotta admit, I'm a changed man."

Mackenzie thought about Dylan at Pegasus, mucking out stalls, caring for the elderly horses and bonding with the kids. Mackenzie thought of Dylan with Hope; how sweet and kind and patient he was with her. Hope loved him.

Mackenzie held up her pointer finger and her thumb an inch apart. "You've got about this much community service street cred."

The timer next to the grill buzzed. Dylan checked the fish and then pulled them off the grill.

"Come on! Just look at these bad boys." Dylan showed her the steaks. "I can't believe you're really going to let them go to waste."

Mackenzie tugged at the front of her jersey; he had gone to some trouble to make her a healthy meal. “I didn’t dress right…”

“Hey—” Dylan sensed that Mackenzie was caving “—if that’s the only thing holding you back from hanging out with me tonight, then I’ll change. And we can eat out here.”

The salmon and broccoli did smell really good. And she *was* really hungry.

“And let’s be honest.” Dylan’s dimples appeared. He was teasing her. “You think I’m sexy when I cook, right?”

“I’ll admit…that I *like* a man who can cook.”

“See there?” Dylan grinned at her triumphantly. “We can *build* on that!”

Good as his word, Dylan had changed into shorts and a short-sleeved polo, and they dined outside with the ocean as their view. Once Mackenzie stopped focusing on the “date” aspect of the evening and just focused on Dylan, she started to relax and have a good time. They laughed as much as they talked. And there was never a lull in the conversation. They reminisced about their childhood. They talked about Hope and her future aspirations. They talked baseball and surfing and cupcakes. Mackenzie couldn’t believe it, but she was sad when the clock on her phone flipped over to nine.

“It’s not too late…how about a short walk on the beach? Work off some of this dinner?” Dylan leaned against the island while Mackenzie loaded the last dish in the dishwasher.

“I wish I could…but I’ve got an early morning at the bakery.” Then she surprised herself by adding, “Can I take a rain check?”

From the look on his face, she had surprised Dylan, as well. “Sure.”

Mackenzie slipped her tote onto her shoulder and Dylan walked her to the door. They walked down to her car together; Mackenzie pulled her keys out and unlocked the car door. Not wanting to linger in that uncomfortable “end of the night, should I go for the kiss?” moment, Mackenzie wrapped her arms around Dylan’s waist, hugged him quickly and then stepped back.

“Thank you…I’m glad that I decided not to go home early…”

Dylan rocked back on his heels. “That’s very flattering, thank you.”

Mackenzie felt an internal cringe. “That didn’t come out right.”

“That’s okay, Mackenzie.” Dylan reached out and opened her car door. “I was just teasing you.”

Mackenzie climbed behind the wheel and Dylan closed the door firmly behind her. He tapped on the window so she would roll it down.

Hands resting on the door, Dylan asked, “How ’bout we fill that rain check tomorrow? Say, around seven? We can order in, watch a movie.”

“Okay.” Mackenzie nodded. She had just accepted a second date with Dylan without one millisecond of hesitation.

“Don’t back out,” Dylan said.

“I won’t…” Mackenzie cranked the engine. “Good night, Dylan.”

Dylan nodded his head goodbye as she rolled up the window, shifted into gear and pulled out slowly onto the darkened street. She felt odd driving away from his house—like something significant had just happened to her but she wasn’t exactly sure *what*. And, even the next day, as she moved through normal business at the bakery, she still wasn't quite sure what had happened the night before. Dylan hadn't made his thought process a secret: he wanted to see if there was a chance for the two of them, along with Hope, to become a family. That thought had never crossed her mind. But now…was Dylan onto something? *Could* they be a family? If it worked, wouldn't that be the best thing for Hope?

"You're okay to close up, Molly?" Mackenzie untied her apron and lifted it over her head.

"In my sleep, little one." Molly continued to wipe down one of the café tables near the front of the small bakery.

Mackenzie boxed up two of the best-looking giant cupcakes in the case, and gave Molly a kiss on the cheek before she headed out. It was rare that she left the bakery early on a Saturday night, but for once she didn't feel guilty. She felt *anticipation*. She had caught herself thinking about Dylan off and on all day. That just didn't *happen* to her. She had never had a really big crush or even fallen in love, not the way she had seen her friends do—the head-over-heels, can't-sleep, can't-eat, can't-talk-about-anything-else kind of love. In fact, she couldn't remember ever feeling *lust* for anyone before. She had felt a very strong affection for her college boyfriend, but her inability to commit to *Star Trek* had ultimately ended their three-year relationship.

When Hope was born, her entire focus, and all of her love, was aimed at her. She didn't care about dating or romance or marriage. She had Hope. That was enough. It wasn't until Hope was in elementary school that Mackenzie started to think that there might be something missing in her life: intimacy. Romance. *Sex*. But then Hope was diagnosed with ALL and thoughts of a relationship disappeared.

"Wear your hair down this time..." Rayna was on speakerphone.

"You're right. My hair does look good down."

"Are you going to wear the purple shirt?"

"Uh-uh...no. We're walking on the beach, Ray. I can just dress like me."

"Okay...but promise me you'll wear something smaller than extra-extra large! Give the poor man *something* to look at..."

"Bye, Ray!"

"Call me later!"

Unlike the night before, Mackenzie took a little extra time getting ready. She made sure that her long-sleeved V-neck shirt didn't have any stains and she rummaged through her drawers to find a newer pair of jeans. She tried on several pairs and finally selected the jeans that made her J.Lo booty look the best. She let her hair air-dry, leaving it thick and long and falling down her back. She had to admit, she did have beautiful hair. She dug through her messy bathroom drawer and fished out an old tube of mascara from the back. The mascara looked crusty and the brush brittle, so she gave up on that idea. But she did find a tube of lip gloss. Teeth thoroughly brushed for an extra couple of minutes, followed by a long gargle of mouthwash, Mackenzie applied lip gloss and headed out the door. This time when she left the house, there wasn't any confusion about the night. She knew that this was a *date*, and she couldn't wait to see what the night would bring.

Chapter Nine

She actually felt nervous at the thought of seeing Dylan. She had called Hope to say good-night and now she was standing outside his door, holding her cupcake offering. At some point, a flip had been switched and *just Dylan* had suddenly become *Dylan*. When Dylan opened the door, she thrust the box at him.

"Here."

Dylan pulled one long-stem lavender rose from behind his back and held it out for her. "For you."

Pleased and surprised by the romantic gesture, Mackenzie exchanged the cupcakes for the rose. She lifted the rose up to her nose and breathed in the strong, sweet scent.

"Thank you," she said with a small smile.

"You must've read my mind." Dylan stepped back so she could come inside. "I was craving your cupcakes today."

When they reached the kitchen, Dylan immediately opened the box and grabbed a cupcake.

"Are they both for me, or do I need to share?" Dylan removed the wrapper from the first cupcake and took a large bite.

"They're for you..."

"Hmm...always incredible." Dylan started in on the second cupcake. "I just realized, I've never even bothered to ask you how you got into the cupcake business in the first place."

Mackenzie crossed her arms protectively in front of her, those old, never-forgotten feelings of defensiveness shooting to the surface. "A lot of people ask me that. I always think that there's a built-in insult in there...like they're really asking why a woman with a weight problem would own a bakery..."

Dylan looked at her as if she had lost her mind. "But... that's not what *I* meant."

Ill at ease, Mackenzie tightened her arms around her body. "I'm sorry. Sometimes that old stuff creeps up out of nowhere and flies out of my mouth before I can stop it. Do you ever wish you had a rewind button on your mouth?"

"All the time." Dylan finished the cupcake and put the box in the recycling bin. "And can we just clarify something right now? I happen to think that you're a beautiful woman. Okay?"

"Okay." Mackenzie nodded.

"And I really like it when you wear your hair down like that."

"Thank you." Mackenzie uncrossed her arms. "Do you still want to hear about the bakery?"

"Of course."

"You remember that my mom and I used to bake cupcakes together before she died."

Dylan nodded as she continued, "I remember her always talking about opening up a cupcake shop, but she never got the chance to do it. When I got older, making cupcakes always made me feel happy, and for some odd reason, when I work with sugar and butter, I don't want to *eat* it." Mackenzie smiled a self-effacing smile. "So, when Dad saw me floundering after high school, he offered to send me to school to get my associate's in baking and pastry arts, which then led to a bachelor's degree in bakery and pastry arts management."

"And the bakery?"

"Dad's idea. He made the initial investment, but I'm not gonna sugarcoat it…no pun intended…it's been really tough being a single parent and running a business. After Hope's diagnosis…" Mackenzie paused before she confessed something to Dylan that only Ray knew. "I seriously considered closing. But I have employees to think about…"

"I think you're a really strong woman, Mackenzie. I know how hard it is to run a business."

Mackenzie pulled a small photo album out of her tote. "I brought something for you to look at."

"What's that?" Dylan took the album, flipped to the first page.

Once Dylan realized it was a photo album full of Hope pictures, he slid onto a stool to get more comfortable while he looked at it.

"Look how tiny she was!" Dylan stared at Hope's first baby picture. "'Hope Virginia Brand, 6 pounds 4 ounces, born 3:13 a.m., August 20.'"

"She was an early-morning baby."

"How come there aren't any pictures of you pregnant?"

"Are you kidding me? I would have killed someone if they tried to take my picture when I was pregnant! But, you know, Hope is the reason why I finally lost the weight…"

"How so?" Dylan flipped to the next page.

"After she was born, I knew that I had to get healthy. I

worked really hard to lose the baby weight and then I just kept on losing. The fact that I was doing it for both of us made it easier somehow."

"I would have liked to see you pregnant," Dylan said. "I wish I had been able to be there when Hope was born."

The photo album chronicled Hope's childhood. A childhood he had missed. The little girl in these pictures was lost to him, and a feeling of loss and sadness hit him out of the blue. Dylan used his thumb and forefinger to rub unexpected tears out of his eyes and then he pinched the bridge of his nose to stop more tears from forming.

Wide-eyed, temporarily struck dumb, Mackenzie hadn't expected this reaction from Dylan. When she had played the "photo album scene" over in her mind, she had imagined them laughing and smiling and talking about Hope. Instead, she saw grief. Not knowing what else she could do for him, Mackenzie wrapped her arms around Dylan's shoulders. She hugged him so tightly that the muscles in her arms started to shake. He sat, like a rock, still pinching the bridge of his nose. The sorrow that Dylan felt over having missed his daughter's life was palpable and profound. And, ultimately, she was the one to blame.

"I'm sorry," Mackenzie repeated over and over again. "I'm so sorry."

Dylan turned to her, reached for her and enveloped her in his arms. They clutched each other tightly, their arms entangled, their chests pressed together, their thighs touching. Without warning, Mackenzie's own guilt, her own sorrow and her own feelings of regret overwhelmed her.

"I'm so sorry..." Her tears were absorbed by the material of his shirt.

Dylan pulled back, caught her face between his hands and shook his head.

"Mackenzie..." Dylan wiped her fresh tears away with his thumbs, still holding her face in his hands. "It's okay."

Their eyes locked. And Mackenzie couldn't have looked away if she had the will to do it. Dylan's eyes were naked, raw, unshielded windows into his soul. She continued to stare into his eyes as he moved his thumb sensually over her lower lip. Then his mouth was on hers, without pretense, without warning. Dylan's kiss was soft, tentative, gentle, at first. Then demanding, possessive, sensual. He tasted like sugar; he slipped his tongue past her lips, pulled her body more tightly into his body. Her leg muscles turned to Jell-O; her breathing was quick and shallow. Dylan's arm cradled her back, his fingers fanned out between her shoulders. He kissed her again and again, going a little bit further, taking a little bit more. And then it happened to her. From somewhere deep inside her, untapped and neglected, Mackenzie felt *desire.* Like tiny electrical shock waves sent tingling and pulsing to the core of her body. Intuitively, Mackenzie pressed her groin into Dylan's... seeking...

The noise Dylan made in the back of his throat struck a primitive chord. And the feel of his arousal, rock hard, thick, searching...made her feel crazy inside. Out of control. She wanted to rip off her jeans, right there in the kitchen, and demand that Dylan use his body to put her out of this new, foreign, *torturous* misery. Mackenzie pushed back against his arm, pushed her hands against his chest. She had to put some distance between them before she let her body's driving needs overrun her reason.

Dylan's arms opened and they both took a step back. Chests rising and falling, desire still sparking in both of their eyes, they were silent. Stunned by what had just happened and uncertain of their next move. Mackenzie touched her fingers to her lips. She had never been kissed like that before; she thought those kind of kisses were for other women. Not her.

"I need to go to the bathroom," Mackenzie blurted out.

Dylan resisted the urge to adjust himself. "Down the hall—second door on the right."

Mackenzie headed to the downstairs bathroom and Dylan chose to head upstairs to the third-floor master bedroom. He took the stairs two at a time; he waited until he had reached his bedroom before he gave in to the need to make the necessary adjustments.

What the hell just happened?

Mackenzie had made him nuts: the sensual curves of her womanly body. The full breasts, the roundness of her hips. The way her hair smelled, the feel of her soft lips… the taste of her…it all drove him wild. And he'd wanted to take her right there on the kitchen floor; *would have* taken her, if she had only given him the green light. Dylan sat down on the edge of his bed; he needed some time to cool off before he went back downstairs. If he didn't, he wouldn't put it past himself to try to talk Mackenzie out of her pants and into his bed.

Mackenzie darted into the bathroom and locked the door.

What just happened?

She was shaking, not from being cold, not from fear… from *lust…desire…passion.* The most sensitive part of her body, between her thighs, was *throbbing*, for God's sake! She was…*embarrassed.* And hornier than she'd been since she was pregnant with Hope. She couldn't remember the last time she had wanted a man; she had mentally shut down her sexuality years ago. Eventually, her body had followed. But now? Now her body was turned back on with a vengeance. And she was hot for Dylan Axel. With few good options available to her, Mackenzie sat down on the edge of the tub until she could think of a better plan. What does one do in a situation such as this?

Run for your life?

"Mackenzie?"

Dylan's knock on the door startled her, made her jump. "Are you okay?"

"I'm fine!"

An unconvinced pause and then Dylan said, "Are you sure? You've been in there a long time…"

"I'll be out in a minute!"

Mackenzie splashed cool water on her face, glad now that she hadn't put on mascara. Yes, her eyes were watery, red and puffy…but at least she didn't look like a drowned raccoon.

She pointed at her own reflection. "You are *not* a coward. Just go out there and deal with this head-on!"

Determined to exit stage left as soon as possible, she open the door, marched back into the kitchen and prepared to deliver her excuse.

"I hope you like zinfandel…" Dylan had uncorked a bottle of wine.

"I do." That didn't sound like much of an excuse.

Dylan grabbed the bottle, two glasses and a blanket.

"Let's head down to the beach," he said.

Dylan seemed to know exactly what she needed, exactly how she needed it. And instead of making an excuse, as per the plan, she found herself following Dylan down to the beach. When they reached a good spot on the sand, he spread out the blanket. After they were settled, Dylan poured them both a glass of wine and they touched glasses.

"To first kisses." Dylan made the toast.

"First kisses?" Mackenzie didn't take a drink.

"Yeah…tonight was our first real kiss. I don't remember much from the wedding, but I *do* remember that you wouldn't let me kiss you."

"Oh…I'd forgotten about that." Not sure she wanted to repeat that toast, she took a sip of the wine instead. "Good wine."

Night had fallen and they practically had the beach to themselves. There was a party just kicking in to high gear several houses down, but none of the partygoers had wandered down to their small stretch of beach.

It took a second full glass of wine, but Mackenzie no longer felt the least bit awkward or embarrassed.

"Killer view, Dylan…"

"I like it…" Dylan nodded, his eyes focused straight ahead.

By the third glass, Mackenzie had kicked off her shoes, dug her toes in the sand, and she felt all swirly and dreamy like buttercream frosting atop a cupcake. By the fourth glass, Mackenzie was flat on her back, loose as a goose, admiring the stars.

"You're not going to be able to drive home now," Dylan noted.

"That's true," Mackenzie agreed nonchalantly.

Dylan finished his fourth glass of wine. They had finished the bottle. "And I'm not going to be able to *drive* you home."

"That's also true…"

"So…you'll have to spend the night."

Mackenzie giggled. "And here I thought I was too old for a sleepover."

Mackenzie was obviously three sheets to the wind and he was buzzed. It was time to get off the beach. Dylan helped Mackenzie stand up, helped her get steady on her feet and walked up the stairs behind her just in case she tipped backward. Back in the kitchen, Mackenzie folded her arms and laid her head down on the island.

"Come on..." Dylan said kindly. "I'll get you set up in the spare room."

Dylan made sure she had everything she needed for a comfortable night: new toothbrush, toothpaste, a comfortable bed...privacy. He even brought her the top of his pajamas to wear so she wouldn't have to sleep in her clothes. Languid and carefree from the wine, Mackenzie finished in the bathroom, tossed the decorative pillows onto the floor and rolled herself into bed. She sighed happily and snuggled into the downy pillows. Alone, in the dark, her mind drifted back to Dylan's kisses. Her body undoubtedly wanted more and more and more. But did she?

The next morning, she had the answer to that self-imposed question. Slightly hungover, and a little bit headachy, Mackenzie brushed her teeth and then, still in Dylan's pajama top, she left the guest bedroom. The house was quiet as she headed up to Dylan's third-floor master suite. Other than the unmade, empty bed, the room was spotless. The man really was a total neat freak. Her chronic messiness would drive him nuts! Mackenzie stood in the doorway for a moment, rethinking the soundness of her plan. Perhaps she should just turn around, sprint back to her room and catapult herself back into bed.

And she almost did, but then she heard a toilet flush and Dylan appeared, wearing the bottom half of the pajama set, stripped bare above the waist, hair mussed, scratching his chest hair. He didn't notice her as he walked sleepily back to his bed and flopped backward. Mackenzie, frozen to the spot, had been trying, since she had awakened, to formulate her best pitch line, and she had decided on, *Dylan—would you make love to me?*

"Dylan...?"

Surprised by her voice, Dylan bolted upright. "Geez… you scared the crap out of me, Mackenzie." Dylan collapsed back into his fortress of pillows.

"Sorry…"

"Don't worry about it…" Dylan yawned and stretched.

It took him a minute to focus his eyes and really get a look at Mackenzie. Standing shyly in his doorway, hands in the fig-leaf position, she was filling out his pajama top in a way that made his body stand at attention. He pushed himself into a sitting position and casually pulled the covers over the lower half of his body. He had to force himself not to stare at her legs; Mackenzie had really sexy, curvy legs.

"Are you hungry?" Dylan asked after he cleared his throat.

He needed to get her out of his bedroom. The last thing he wanted to do was go too far too fast and run her off the way he almost did last night.

"No." Mackenzie tugged on the bottom of the pajama top to cover more of her legs. "I mean…yes. I am. But no."

Dylan half smiled, half laughed at her odd response. "Say what?"

Mackenzie twisted her fingers together, losing faith in the sanity of her plan. She had been trying to keep things simple and uncomplicated with Dylan back in her life; what she was about to propose was a first-class ticket to *complicated.*

"Yes, I *am* hungry…but *no*, that's not the reason I'm here. In your bedroom…"

"I'm listening…" Dylan was intrigued…and hopeful. Perhaps Mackenzie didn't need to leave his bedroom after all.

"I was wondering…how you would feel about—" she

shifted weight from one leg to the other "—actually, what I'm trying to ask is…do you want to…make love to me?"

"Yes." Dylan took her up on her offer in record time.

"Yes?" Her voice had jumped an octave.

"Yes." He nodded. "I would…like to make love to you."

The man had said yes, which is what she wanted, right? But now she wished she could press Rewind and take back the offer. This couldn't be a good idea, could it? Sex complicated everything. And this situation was already complicated *enough*.

"Come join me…" Dylan peeled back the covers on the empty side of the bed.

Instead of taking the sane and safe option, she walked slowly toward him.

"You look really good in my pajamas…" It was a genius idea to lend her the top of his favorite pair.

Dylan found Mackenzie's nervous smile endearing. He had been used to women who were sexually confident, even aggressive at times. This was a nice change. When Mackenzie reached the side of the bed, she quickly slid beneath the covers and pulled them up to her chin. The tips of her fingers were white from gripping the covers so tightly.

"Did you know—" Dylan turned on his side, kept his hands to himself "—that most men are really nervous about sleeping with a woman for the first time?"

"Is that true or are you just making that up to make me feel better…?"

"I'm not making it up…it's true."

Mackenzie loosened her death grip on the covers. "Are you nervous now?"

"Yeah," Dylan admitted. "Sure I am…"

"Why?"

"Because…there's a lot pressure on a guy to perform, women just don't get it. We're always worried about are we big enough, are we hard enough, are we going to last? Not to mention the pressure of trying to give a woman *multiple* orgasms when it's hard enough just to figure out how to give her one. And trust me, all guys know that our performance, good or bad, is going to be discussed, and dissected, at length with their friends. I'm telling you…it's a lot of pressure to be on the guy end of things."

His attempt to make Mackenzie feel more comfortable with him must have worked, because she put her arms on top of the covers. They were still pinned tightly to her sides, completely blocking him from her body, but it *was* progress.

Dylan reached over, tucked her hair behind her ear and then lightly rested his hand on her arm. "We don't have to do this, Mackenzie. It's okay to change your mind."

"No!" Mackenzie protested. "I *want* to do it. I'm rusty, okay? And I would think," Mackenzie snapped, "that with all your vast experience, you'd know how to get the ball rolling. Aren't you the one with the bachelor pad and models-slash-actresses prancing about half-naked? I made the first move, why can't you make the—"

Dylan's kiss cut off the rest of her words. She liked the minty taste of his tongue; she liked the masculine smell of his skin—no cologne, just Dylan's natural scent. By the time Dylan ended the kiss, Mackenzie no longer felt like complaining. She wanted less talking and more kissing.

"Here…" Dylan tugged on the covers that were still pinned down with her arms. "Let me get closer to you."

Once he managed to coax the covers out of her control, Dylan pressed his body into hers. She continued to lay on her back, stiff and unmoving, when he wrapped his arm around her and draped his leg over her thigh. Dylan made a pleasurable noise as he nuzzled her neck.

"Aren't we supposed to do this *after*…?"

"Relax..." Dylan whispered near her ear.

Relax. Relax. Just relax!

"Open your eyes, Mackenzie..." Dylan was admiring her pretty face.

She opened her eyes; it was embarrassing. She only made love in the dark with her eyes closed. And now Dylan wanted them open?

"You have the most amazing eyes... Have I ever told you that before?"

She shook her head. She liked his eyes, too. In the soft morning light, they looked mossy green with flecks of gold around the irises.

He ran his fingers lightly over her lips. "Soft lips."

Those two simple words were followed by a kiss. Once he started kissing her again, he didn't stop. He seemed to enjoy the taste and the feel of her mouth. And she found herself responding to this gentle seduction. He wasn't in a hurry; he wasn't just going through the motions to get to the end zone as fast as he could. Dylan was making her feel special, beautiful...cherished. At first, she was a passive partner, timid and unsure. But his kisses started to change that and she began to touch his body—the hair on his chest, his biceps.

Dylan forced himself to go slow, take his time. Her touch was so tentative and she was so unsure of her own sexuality that it felt as if he was in bed with a virgin. Her body was so voluptuous, so soft, that all he wanted to do was to get rid of that stupid pajama top so he could feel her breasts. He wanted to hold them, massage them...kiss them. The scent of her hair and the feel of her silky skin were aphrodisiacs to him.

Dylan pressed his hard-on against her body, and that's when she felt it again: that throbbing, yearning sensation between her thighs. The next pleasurable sound she heard was her own. Dylan had slipped his hand into her panties and nudged his fingers between her thighs. When he felt how aroused she was, Dylan whispered into her ear.

"I want to be inside of you, Mackenzie." Dylan's voice had a husky, sexy quality now. "Do you want that, too?"

"Yes." Why was he talking so much? "Why are you *talking*?"

Chapter Ten

Dylan gently guided her onto her back. Her pretty lavender-blue eyes were filled with uncertainty and desire, lips parted, cheeks flushed pink, chest rising and falling quickly. She was…stunning. A goddess. And he couldn't wait to see all of her…to love *all* of her. He reached for the top button of her shirt. But Mackenzie stopped him.

"No. I want to leave it on…"

Dylan was disappointed but respected her wishes. A woman as sexy and beautiful as Mackenzie should be proud of her body, not hide it. He shifted his focus, peeled the covers back, exposing her simple white cotton briefs. He caught her eye as he traced the edge of the panties, starting at the inner part of her thigh up to the outer curve of her hip.

"But we will need to take these off…"

This time Mackenzie nodded. Not in a hurry, Dylan gradually inched the covers down, revealing her thighs, knees, and finally her tightly crossed ankles. Dylan noticed a small white scar on her upper thigh; he ran his finger across it.

"I remember when you got this. You cut your leg on a piece of glass in your father's garage."

Mackenzie nodded. Dylan leaned down, kissed the scar before he began to inch her panties down. He was so methodical and deliberate, dropping sensual kisses on her stomach, on the soft fleshy inner part of her thighs. He wasn't in a rush. She wanted to tell him to *hurry up*, but bit her lip instead.

"Mackenzie...you're stunning." Dylan knelt beside her, her underwear now on the floor.

He was the stunning one. Dylan's body was ripped and lean from pounding the waves. There wasn't an ounce of fat on the man; he was a thing of beauty. Dylan stood up, stripped off his underwear and reached for a condom. Mackenzie pulled the covers up over her body and watched, fascinated, as Dylan rolled the condom on. It was bizarre. Dylan had given her a child, but this was the first time she was seeing *all* of his body. The night they conceived Hope, she had insisted on a completely dark room.

Dylan joined her under the blanket and she was relieved that he got right down to business, covered her body with his. His weight felt good, pressing her down into the mattress. His hard shaft felt good, pressed into her belly. Dylan held her face in his hands, but she kept her eyes squeezed tightly shut.

"Mackenzie..." He said her name so sensually. "I wish you'd open your eyes."

Mackenzie opened her eyes. Why was he so patient when she felt as if she was suffering from a serious case of sexual frustration?

"I care about you, Mackenzie. I always have. And…I don't take what we're about to do lightly…"

Aching, throbbing, frustrated, Mackenzie sunk her fingernails into his shoulders. "Dylan! Stop *talking*!"

Dylan smiled down at her but followed orders. He kissed her and eased himself into her body, slow and controlled until he was fully inside of her. Their bodies completely connected now, Dylan didn't move. He dropped his head down, took a minute to compose himself. He didn't want to disappoint Mackenzie with a super-short performance. Mackenzie squirmed beneath him, begging him with her body to *move*.

"Mackenzie," Dylan whispered roughly. "You're driving me crazy…"

His fingers in her hair, his lips on her lips, Dylan began to move. But, slowly, as if he wanted to savor the moment, as if he didn't want this moment to end too soon. His long, deep strokes were exactly what her body had been craving. She lifted her hips to meet him halfway, to take more of him in.

"Wrap your legs around me." Dylan gently bit down on her earlobe.

She wrapped her legs around him, held on to his biceps. Dylan locked his arms to hold himself above her; he closed his eyes and let her watch him. They were starting to learn each other's bodies. Dylan was less cautious now, less gentle, and more demanding and intense. And she *liked* it. Dylan wrapped his arms tightly around her shoulders, curled himself around her, and drove his body into hers. And then he drove her right off the edge of reason and straight into the arms of ecstasy. All of the tension, all of the anticipation and frustration and *building* gave way to orgasmic ripples pinging pleasure signals all over her body. Her loud, vocal orgasm triggered Dylan's.

He thrust into her one last time, deep and hard, and then groaned loudly.

Dylan's breathing was heavy, his body felt heavy atop hers. He was still between her thighs, where she felt raw and wet. Dylan kissed her on the neck; he kissed her on the lips. He pulled the covers up over their still-connected bodies and held her tightly in his arms as if he sensed that she needed that reassuring pressure. She felt emotions, out of nowhere, surge through her. Dylan had just given her an amazing gift—her first *real* orgasm. After his breathing returned to normal, Dylan propped himself up on one arm so he could look at her.

"Are you okay?"

She nodded, still feeling a bit scandalized by her own behavior. She had never been so…*vocal*…in bed before. But she had to admit, that it had been…*liberating.*

"I should take care of this…" He reached down between them, secured the condom between his fingers, and then slowly pulled out of her.

Dylan returned to the bed quickly, propped himself up on the pillows and opened his arms for her.

"Come here. Let me hold you."

Mackenzie wanted to be close to him; she wanted to be in his arms after the lovemaking they had just shared. Dylan wrapped his arms around her, held her tight and sighed like a satisfied, contented man.

"This is a great way to wake up…" Dylan slid his fingers into her hair, a smile in his voice. "You're a wildcat…"

Mackenzie ran her fingers through his chest hair, smiled but kept quiet.

"I don't think anyone has surprised me the way you just did…" Dylan kissed the top of her head and rubbed her arm. "Hey…what are you doing today?"

"No plans, really. The bakery's closed on Sundays and I don't pick up Hope from her friend's house until four."

"And I already called Pegasus and told them that I wouldn't be there today, so my day is free. Why don't we spend the day together."

"What did you have in mind?"

"Breakfast, for starters."

"Agreed..."

"Then, surfing?"

"Negative."

Dylan laughed. "Okay...the hot tub, then."

"Uh-uh...I don't have a swimsuit."

"Skinny-dipping is encouraged."

"I never negotiate on an empty stomach. Let's eat first and then we'll talk."

Dylan was an organized, clean cook. She would drive him nuts; her bakery was spotless, but when she baked, she was a whirlwind—a *messy* whirlwind.

"You really do have a little OCD thing happening, don't you?" Mackenzie observed Dylan cleaning the counter throughout the cooking process.

"I guess. I just like things to be clean, organized. What's wrong with that?" Dylan twisted the rag dry and then dropped it over the faucet.

"We could never get married," Mackenzie said without thinking.

Really? You just brought up marriage?

"Oh, yeah?" Dylan flipped over the pancakes. "Why not?"

"Not that I was suggesting that *I* think that we *should* get married. It was just an observation..."

"You still haven't told me why not..."

"In the hypothetical?"

"If you'd like..." Dylan leaned back against the counter, crossed his arms in front of him.

"You are obviously a neat freak. And I am...*not* a neat freak."

"I know." Dylan smiled at her, set her heart fluttering. "I've seen your office, remember?"

"That's right." Mackenzie nodded. "So...you see my point?"

"No. I don't." Dylan put a stack of pancakes on a plate for her. "I have a maid. Problem solved."

Mackenzie could never imagine her life with a maid, which was yet another difference between them, but she decided to move on to a different subject. Dylan saturated her pancakes in butter and syrup, piled crispy bacon onto her plate and served her hot coffee. He ignored her calorie concerns, citing that everyone should allow themselves to have at least *one* cheat day a week and this was it. His logic, and the fact that he seemed to like a woman with a good appetite, encouraged her to devour the pancakes along with a second helping of bacon.

"I really don't normally eat like this," Mackenzie said, looking guiltily at her near-empty plate.

"Do you want more?" Dylan asked. "There're a couple of pieces of bacon left."

Mackenzie pushed her plate away from her and cringed. "Uh-uh...no. I've eaten too much already."

Dylan had managed to charm her into complacency and all she could think of now was how many calories she had just consumed.

"Hey..." Dylan leaned on his forearm and stared at her face. "Mackenzie...please stop beating yourself up about the food. Okay? Give yourself permission to have a little fun."

After they cleaned up after breakfast, Dylan convinced

her that the next logical step was to step down into his hot tub.

Mackenzie went to the guest room to change into a pair of Dylan's boxer briefs and a T-shirt. She called to check on Hope and then quickly sent Ray an I'm OK text message before she emerged from the room wearing Dylan's makeshift bathing suit.

"I look ridiculous," she complained to Dylan.

Dylan was in his surf trunks, bare to the waist, and barefoot. "Not to me you don't."

Dylan circled behind her and pulled the extra material of the T-shirt toward the back. "Here...let me tie a knot back here or the shirt will float up when you get in the water."

Now standing in front of her, he eyed her appreciatively. "There. Perfect."

Mackenzie looked down. Dylan's adjustment to the outfit pulled the front of the shirt tight over her breasts.

"Was that for my sake or yours?" she asked, half-teasing, half-serious.

"Both..." Dylan wasn't shy about admiring her with his eyes. "Definitely both."

She felt self-conscious walking out to Dylan's hot tub, but once she slipped into the hot, bubbling water, Mackenzie forgot all about her silly outfit. Dylan was right—this was bliss.

"Aaaaah." Mackenzie sank down farther into the water.

"Uh-huh...didn't I tell you?" Dylan slid in beside her.

"You did."

Beneath the water, Dylan reached for her hand. Pleased, she intertwined her fingers with his, dropped her head back, closed her eyes and let her mind go blissfully blank. Time moved but they didn't. Not for a while. Not until the sun, beating down on her scalp, finally became too hot to bear. Mackenzie sighed deeply, opened her eyes and moved to the middle of the hot tub. Dylan's interested eyes followed her every move. She leaned back and dipped her hair back into the water so she could cool off her scalp, and to slick her hair back. When she stood up and turned around, Dylan was smiling at her.

"What?" Mackenzie asked. "Why are you grinning at me like a Cheshire cat?"

Dylan's eyes drifted down to her breasts. "Can't I admire you?"

Mackenzie followed his gaze. The wet T-shirt had molded itself to her breasts, leaving nothing to the imagination. Mackenzie immediately sunk down in the water to her neck.

"No..." Dylan shook his head. "You've got to stop doing that."

Dylan was at her side, his arm around her waist; he kissed her as their bodies floated backward toward the side of the hot tub. Dylan lifted her into his arms, spun around and pulled her onto his lap. Then he kissed her again, his tongue taking possession of her mouth, his hand taking possession of her breast. He was already aroused; she could feel it against her thigh.

"When I take you back upstairs, Mackenzie..." Dylan whispered sensually into her ear. "I don't want there to be anything between us this time."

Mackenzie knew that Dylan was referring to the fact that she hadn't let him take off her top when they had made love. Her body wanted Dylan again, and so did she.

"Dylan..." Mackenzie moaned pleasurably into the sun-warmed skin on his neck. "Take me back upstairs..."

After they made love for a third time, Mackenzie took a shower, alone, in the guest bathroom. Dylan offered to share his shower with her, but for some reason, even after all of the lovemaking, a shower seemed somehow too...*intimate.* Mackenzie hurried through her shower, got dressed and made the bed. She tried to arrange the decorative pillows exactly as she had found them but finally gave up.

Dylan was lounging in the den, flipping through TV channels, waiting for her. "What would you like to do with your free afternoon?"

Mackenzie smiled a mischievous smile. "There is something that I'd really like to do."

"What's that?"

Mackenzie's smile widened. "Drive the Corvette."

She thought that Dylan was going to shut her down immediately. To guys like her brother, Jett, and Dylan, their cars were their babies. And they didn't let *anyone* get behind the wheel.

He shocked her when he said, "I'll let you drive her. We can take her down to Ocean Beach Pier. Have you been to the restaurant on that pier?"

Mackenzie shook her head no.

"Have you ever tried fish tacos?"

She wrinkled her nose distastefully. "No..."

"Then today is your lucky day, Mackenzie!"

They gathered their things and then Dylan handed her the keys to his pride and joy. She slid into the driver's seat and wrapped her hands around the steering wheel. As she backed out of the garage, she was half expecting him to have a change of heart and scream for her to stop. It didn't happen. They rolled down the windows, turned on the radio to a classic-rock station and headed to the pier. She wanted to open her up and really test the horsepower under the hood, but she didn't. The last thing she wanted to do was leave even so much as a scratch on a car this valuable. They parked and walked down to the beach. Dylan's phone had been ringing and beeping with texts and emails. He finally just shut his phone off and left it in the car. She didn't ask about who was trying to contact him, but she knew his recent history. He was a single, good-looking guy with deep pockets and a party pad. She didn't doubt his friends, both male and female, were missing one of their regular spots to party at the beach.

They walked side by side, but Mackenzie wasn't ready to hold hands in public. They never stopped talking, that's what she liked about hanging out with Dylan. She wouldn't have thought that they'd have much to say to each other, but they did. He made her laugh; he was silly and goofy and liked to joke around. He'd never really taken life too seriously when they were kids, and he still didn't. He still liked to have fun, and he wanted to take her along for that ride.

"Okay...be honest..." Dylan had just demolished five fish tacos. "You shouldn't have judged, right?"

The Ocean Pier Restaurant was built on the side of the pier. They were sitting at a small table with an incredible view, and Dylan insisted that she, at the very least, take a bite of their famous fish tacos.

Mackenzie chewed the small bite of fish taco thoughtfully.

"Well?" Dylan demanded impatiently. "Awesome, right?"

"It's...pretty good..." Mackenzie said, glad that she had refused the tacos and stuck with an egg-salad sandwich and water. She was still pretty full from breakfast and she couldn't just stop worrying about calories because he had encouraged her to do it. Calorie watching was her normal. Dylan, on the other hand, had been happy to tell her during the car ride that making love to her had left him famished.

"Pretty good?" Dylan acted as if she had just stabbed him in the heart. "You're killing me! These are *legendary.* Try another bite..."

"No!" She pressed her lips together and shook her head. "I wouldn't dream of taking even one more bite away from you..."

"Okay..." He was perfectly happy to polish off the rest by himself. "Are you sure?"

The taco had left a bad taste in her mouth that couldn't be washed away with water alone. She nodded yes while she dug through her tote to find her mints.

They finished their lunch, cleared their table and stepped out onto the pier. Dylan looked around. "Are you up for a walk?"

"Sure," she agreed. They had walked a little ways, when he gave her a curious look. "I thought you liked me."

"I do..."

"Then how come you're so far away?" He offered her his arm.

She took his arm and they strolled together along the pier. When the sun felt a little too strong on her face, the salty mist from the water crashing against the pier seemed to come just at the right time when her skin felt too hot. She couldn't remember the last time she had been to the pier. She had certainly never been here on a date. In this moment, she was content; happy to be walking beside Dylan.

At the end of the pier, Dylan asked, "Do you want to head back or sit down on one of these benches and people watch?"

"People watch, of course."

Like an old comfortable couple, they sat together on the bench. Dylan put his arm behind her shoulder; she leaned in just a little bit closer.

"Do you have the photo album with you? The one from last night?"

Mackenzie put her hand on her tote. "Right here."

"I'd like to finish looking at it."

"Are you sure?"

"I want to know more about our daughter."

Our daughter.

Dylan had never used that term before.

Dylan started at the beginning while Mackenzie told him the story behind each picture. Halfway through the album, they came to the pictures that chronicled Hope's cancer journey.

"Her face is so swollen in this picture. She doesn't even look like the same kid," Dylan said. Hope's face was puffy and round, her head completely bald, her eyebrows gone.

"Steroids," Mackenzie explained. "She could never seem to get enough food." Mackenzie pointed to the next picture. "This is when she first got her port put in for chemo. That was a…really bad day."

Dylan flipped through the rest of the photographs and then went back to the first picture—the one taken the day Hope was born.

"You know that I love her now, Mackenzie."

Mackenzie nodded. She did know.

"And, I'm…really worried about her. What if she relapses?"

Mackenzie didn't like to think about that. She put the album in the tote. "Then we fight it. That's all we can do."

They stayed at the pier for another hour; before they headed back to the car, Dylan insisted that he take her to his favorite ice-cream shop, which was famous for its waffle ice-cream sandwich. After the ice cream, Dylan drove them back to his place. Climbing out of the low-slung Corvette, Mackenzie couldn't remember having a better time with a man.

"Do you want to come in for a while? Or do you have to go?"

"I have to go. I pick Hope up at four. School tomorrow."

On the way back to the car, Dylan made her promise to return the favor and let him drive her vintage Chevy the next time they saw each other.

"I had a really good time with you, Mackenzie. And I know this is going to sound kind of strange, because we have Hope, so I *will* be seeing you again…but I want to see you again."

Dylan was leaning against her driver's door. For the whole entire day, right up until this moment, Mackenzie had felt really good about her decision to deepen the connection with Dylan. But now that she was getting ready to return to reality, her life…doubt was starting to creep in fast and loud.

"Why do I get the feeling something just went wrong here?" Dylan asked suspiciously. Mackenzie's body language, the expression on her face, had changed. Her eyes, which had been open and willing, were guarded.

"There's nothing wrong, Dylan," she lied. "It's just time for me to get back to real life."

He hadn't believed the lie. "I think we should make a date right now. How about if the three of us drive out to Aunt Gerri's house next Sunday? She's been asking for both of you."

"Um…let me check my calendar, okay? And I'll get back to you."

"Now, see…I feel like I need to get a commitment out of you…pin you down." Dylan frowned. "It seems like you're already having second thoughts about this weekend. I can feel you backing away from me…"

Mackenzie took a small step back. "I don't think I'm backing away from you…"

"Actually, you just literally *did* back away from me."

Dylan reached out, slipped his fingers through her hair to the nape of her neck and brought her lips to his. He kissed her until he felt her take a step back toward him. And he didn't *stop* kissing her, until she melted into his arms.

"So..." His lips were still so very close to hers. "Do we have a date?"

"You don't play fair, do you?"

"Not when it comes to you." Dylan kissed her again. "Do we have a date?"

"Yes, Dylan." He was a very persuasive kisser. "We have a date."

Chapter Eleven

"What do you think?" Mackenzie stood in the doorway of her room feeling *naked* in the short-sleeved purple blouse. It was Sunday, and they were scheduled to meet up with Dylan in an hour so they could all go out to his aunt's farm together. She wanted to look presentable, and even though she had been having misgivings about her weekend with Dylan, she wanted to look nice for him, too.

"I picked that out." Hope was a stylish kid. She loved jewelry and accessories; she cut pictures out of fashion magazines and couldn't wait to wear makeup. "You look pretty, Mom."

Mackenzie checked her reflection in the mirror again, tugged on the front of the blouse. It was strange seeing so much of her arms, and they still looked too *round* for her liking, but lately she'd started to think that she needed to force herself out of her baggy-fashion box. There was no doubt in her mind that Dylan's regular compliments had boosted her body image. She still had work to do, but at least she was able to finally cut the tags off this blouse and put it on her body. Mackenzie pointed to her reflection in the mirror.

"You look good," she said, then shut off the bathroom light and headed to the kitchen. She took a quick sip of her strong black coffee before preparing Hope's morning medicine.

"Did you make your bed?" Mackenzie called out to Hope.

She knew that she was never going to be a complete neat freak like Dylan, but she was starting to think that a little more organization wouldn't hurt. In fact, she was very proud of the fact that all their dinner dishes had made it directly into the dishwasher without their typical pit stop to the sink.

"Yeah." Hope showed up looking cute as a bug in a sparkly butterfly T-shirt, cuffed jeans and lavender tennis shoes. "But why'd I have'ta start doing *that* now?"

Mackenzie held out the pills for Hope. "It wouldn't hurt us to be a little neater around here...I made mine, too."

Hope made a face at the pills.

"I know, kiddo. But you gotta take them. Down the hatch."

Mackenzie handed Hope a glass of grape juice, watched her take her pills. When she was done, Mackenzie rinsed out the glass and put it in the dishwasher.

"You feeling okay today?"

"Uh-huh..." Hope nodded.

Mackenzie and Hope loaded into her Chevy and headed toward the bakery. She had agreed to meet Dylan there and she didn't want to be late. During the short trip from their house to the bakery, Mackenzie couldn't seem to get comfortable. She fiddled with the radio, the AC, her seat belt, the neckline of her blouse. She was fidgety and uncomfortable. Anxious. This would be the first time Dylan and she would be seeing each other after their weekend alone. He'd called, but she had made excuses: she was tired, she was working…bad reception, low battery. She just didn't know what to say to him, so it was just easier to say nothing at all. The farther away she got from the weekend, the more she beat herself up for jumping into bed with him. Yes, her body had been deprived in that area for years, but her brain knew better.

And, as often happened with spur-of-the-moment libido-driven decisions, by Monday night, Mackenzie was marinating in full-blown regret. It had been a *terrible* idea to sleep with Dylan. Their focus, their only focus, should have been on Hope—not on each other. She needed to tell Dylan how she felt when they were face-to-face and, hopefully, the two of them could agree to refocus their attention on Hope. If the right moment materialized today, she knew that she needed to have a talk with Dylan.

Dylan arrived at the parking lot behind the bakery ahead of schedule. He was usually early. While he was waiting for Mackenzie and Hope, he decided to try his attorney's private number. He was surprised when Ben actually answered.

"Hey, Ben! I was planning on leaving you a message."

"Do you want me to hang up?" Ben asked.

"No." Dylan laughed. "This is better."

"What can I do for you, Dylan?"

"I had a chance to look over the papers you emailed. Everything looks good, exactly as we discussed."

"That's what I like to hear. Just send a signed copy to the office and we'll have them in the mail to the mother this week."

"Actually…that's what I was calling you about. I'd like to hold off on sending the papers. Just for a little bit."

"May I ask why?"

"I'm hoping that we can work some of this stuff out on our own. So far, things have been pretty cordial between us. But if Mackenzie gets these papers now, I think she'll go ballistic and turn this into World War Three."

"I see. Well, ultimately, it's your decision." Ben paused for a moment of thought. "Why don't we do this…send over a signed copy and we'll hang on to the papers until you're ready to pull the trigger. How does that sound?"

Dylan saw Mackenzie's Chevy pulling into the parking lot and wanted to get off the phone quickly. "That sounds like a plan, Ben. Thanks for picking up on a weekend."

"Billable hours, my friend," Ben said jokingly. "Billable hours."

Hope hugged him hello and Mackenzie greeted him by handing him the keys to her Chevy. He didn't have a car with a backseat, so Mackenzie volunteered her car. And since he had let her drive his Corvette, it was his turn to drive her Chevy. The vintage Chevy had a bench seat in front big enough to fit all three of them. He was behind the wheel, Mackenzie was in the seat by the passenger door and Hope was seated between them. Dylan had the distinct feeling that Mackenzie was glad to put some distance between them in the car, especially since she had been giving him the cold shoulder all week. He'd thought they'd had a great weekend together. *She* came to *his* room. Not the other way around. But he'd blown off enough women when he was in his twenties to know when it was happening to him. He just didn't understand *why*. Luckily, they had Hope to fill in the large gaps in conversation between them.

"See this fence right here, Hope? All of this land belongs to my aunt." Dylan slowed down so Hope could see the farm.

Hope leaned forward, her eyes large. "Whoa…I wish she had horses still!"

Dylan made the turn onto the main driveway. He braked and stared at the For Sale sign posted at the entrance.

"I didn't know the farm was for sale," Mackenzie said.

"Neither did I." Dylan's forehead wrinkled pensively before he slowly let off the brake and headed toward the farmhouse.

Mackenzie saw the empty pastures and the weathered farmhouse in the distance and felt the memories stir inside of her. She had been Hope's age the last time she had seen this farm. Her mother had died the year before; Dylan had just lost his mother. Dylan's birthday party that year, the first without his mother, was one of those memories that had always stuck out in her mind when she thought of her childhood. Aunt Gerri and Uncle Bill had gone out of their way to make sure Dylan had the best birthday that he could possibly have. There was cake and presents and horseback rides and games. She remembered having a really good time; she remembered that Dylan's aunt had let her help in the kitchen. She also remembered that Dylan's smile, the entire day, had always been forced. The smile had never reached his eyes.

Dylan honked the horn and then shut off the engine. A few minutes later, Aunt Gerri swung open the door and came out onto the porch.

"There she is," Dylan said proudly.

Aunt Gerri waved both hands in the air, her bright blue eyes shining with a welcoming smile on her round face.

"Oh, my goodness! Let me look at you!" His aunt held

out her arms to Hope. "You're just the prettiest little girl I've seen in my whole entire life."

Unlike when Hope had met him, she didn't hesitate to hug his aunt straight away.

"And Mackenzie! I'm so glad to see you again."

Even though he wanted immediately to start questioning his aunt about the For Sale sign, he forced himself to wait. Aunt Gerri was brimming with things to say while she gave Mackenzie and Hope the tour of the place. Dylan followed behind them, biding his time until he could ask her about the sign.

"Here's a picture of Bill and me at our fiftieth wedding anniversary." Aunt Gerri stopped in front of a large portrait hanging in the formal living room. "It wasn't too long after this picture was taken that we found out he was sick."

They finished the tour in the front room. The last time he was in this room, he had told his aunt about Hope. Now Hope was here, admiring his aunt's year-round Christmas tree. He waited while his aunt showed Hope and Mackenzie her favorite ornaments. While he waited, he straightened the stacks of sheet music on top of the organ. And, then he got tired of waiting.

"Aunt Gerri…?"

"Hmm?" His aunt was showing Hope her favorite Olive Oyl ornament.

"There's a For Sale sign at the gate. When did you decide to sell?"

His aunt hung Olive Oyl back in her place. "Oh, a couple of weeks ago, I suppose."

Dylan breathed in deeply and then sighed. He'd been feeling anxious ever since he'd seen the sign. His aunt had always owned this farm, for as long as he could remember. It was a touchstone for him. It had always been there if he needed it.

"I didn't even know you were thinking about it…"

Aunt Gerri gestured for Hope and Mackenzie to have a seat. To Dylan she said, "Why do you look so surprised, Dylan? You had to know this would happen eventually."

"I don't know…" Dylan sat down in his grandmother's rocking chair. "I suppose I didn't think it would ever happen. Not really. I thought Sarah or Mary would want the property…"

"No," Gerri said of her daughters. "They both have big-time careers back East. They've never wanted the responsibility of the farm. None of you did…" His aunt smiled a wistful smile. "It's just time, I suppose. It's been time, really. Once Bill was gone, the place was never the same. And I want to be closer to town so I can see my friends. I want to be closer to my church. And I try to think about what Bill would want me to do. You know, your uncle was a black-and-white person, not an in-between person. I don't think he'd like to see what we worked so hard to build together shrink bit by bit until there's nothing left but this house. Better to let it go now. And you've got to remember, Dylan, this land is my retirement."

Sometimes the truth did hurt, Dylan thought. To his aunt, he said, "I'm just sad to see it go."

"I know you are, hon. You never were one for change. But unless you're in the market for a farm, it's got to be sold."

"You should buy it, Dylan!" Hope exclaimed, her face very hopeful. Dylan could see the dreams of horses dancing in her blue-violet eyes.

Dylan shook his head with a laugh. "Sorry, Hope. That's not gonna happen."

Hope jumped up from her seat, brimming with enthusiasm. She talked with her hands and her mouth. "But we could fix up the barn and rent out the stalls. We could give riding lessons out here and clinics and I could have my own horse…"

"I knew that was coming," Mackenzie interjected.

"And when I become a hippo-therapist, I could have my business here!"

"Now what do you want to be when you grow up? A hippa-what?" Dylan knew his aunt and she was getting a kick out of Hope's heartfelt plea.

That question was all the encouragement Hope needed. She sat down in the rocking chair next to Aunt Gerri's and told her all about her future plans. Mackenzie and Dylan's eyes caught occasionally while Hope and his aunt engrossed themselves in a conversation built for two. It reminded Dylan of a Norman Rockwell picture, the two of them together, sitting in rocking chairs in a well-lived-in farmhouse. His aunt had two daughters, both professionals, both living in big cities; his cousins had favored Uncle Bill. But his Hope? She favored his aunt to a T. And, right from the word *go*, they had hit it off, just as one would expect two peas in a pod to do.

"Well…you've definitely got your dad's imagination, that's for sure," Aunt Gerri said. Aunt Gerri didn't notice it, but there was a moment of discomfort between the three of them. No one had called him Hope's dad yet. "Do you remember, Dylan? You tried to convince Bill to turn one of the pastures into a skateboard park. He tried and tried, bless his heart," she said to Mackenzie and Hope. "I remember Bill coming to bed one night so impressed by Dylan. He said that he actually came up with a plan to charge kids so the skateboard park would pay for itself."

"I'd forgotten about that…" Dylan said.

"How about a tour of the farm, Hope?" Aunt Gerri asked. Dylan had a feeling she was just looking for an excuse to get the old golf cart out of storage.

Hope was more than willing to take a tour with his aunt. Aunt Gerri grabbed her keys and they all headed outside. Mackenzie watched Hope load into his aunt's golf cart, while Dylan sat down on the front-porch swing.

"If I know my aunt, they're going to be gone for a while. Come over here and keep me company."

Mackenzie waited until the golf cart disappeared from view before she took him up on his offer. She had wanted to catch Dylan alone, have a chance to set things straight between them. But now that she *did* have him alone, she wasn't exactly sure what she wanted to say to him.

"I'm actually glad that we have a chance to talk to each other without an audience."

Mackenzie nodded, tugged on the short sleeves of her blouse.

"I like that color on you, Mackenzie." Dylan complimented her blouse. "It matches your eyes."

Mackenzie didn't look at Dylan when she said thank-you.

"I wanted to tell you when I first saw you, but I was afraid that you'd be upset with me for complimenting you in front of Hope..."

When Mackenzie didn't say anything, Dylan continued, "And I guess I'm kind of confused here, Mackenzie. I thought we had a good time together last weekend. I know *I* did. I had a better time just hanging out with you than I've had with anyone else in a really long time."

Mackenzie examined her hands instead of returning his gaze. "I had a really good time, too, Dylan."

"Then what's wrong? You haven't been returning my phone calls. When I can get you on the phone, you're always rushing me off. Do you regret what happened between us? Is that it? Do you wish that we hadn't—" Dylan lowered his voice even though there wasn't a soul in sight "—made love?"

Mackenzie glanced at him. "I've been beating myself up about that all week…"

"Well…" Dylan gave a small shake of his head, looked off into the distance. "I'm really sorry you feel that way."

"This isn't about you, Dylan. It's not even about me. It's about Hope. Don't you think I've been lonely? Don't you think I'd like to have someone in my life? I would. But I can't even think about that now. All my energy has to be focused on getting Hope permanently well and keeping my business open. That's it." Mackenzie shook her head. "What happened between us last weekend…I take full responsibility for how far things went."

"Jesus…don't confess to me like you committed a crime! I don't regret what happened between us, either. I actually have some pretty strong feelings for you, Mackenzie."

And he did. Right there, on his aunt's porch, swinging on the porch swing with Mackenzie felt right. She was that missing piece of the puzzle, the one that completed the picture of his life. And from her demeanor…from her body language…it wasn't hard to read that his feelings weren't exactly returned.

"You don't have to say that," she said in a small, tense voice.

"Why shouldn't I say it, Mackenzie? It's the truth. And, from where I sit, we've got nothing standing in our way. You're single. I'm single. We already have a child together. Give me one good reason why we shouldn't *try* to be a family."

Mackenzie didn't feel as if she had one good reason. She felt as if she had a hundred good reasons. But at the core of all her reasons was Hope. What would it do to Hope if they tried to be a family and failed? She was closer to Hope than she had ever been to any human being in her life. And she knew, without a doubt, that Hope couldn't handle that kind of disappointment. Not right now.

Mackenzie stood up and moved to the railing. Putting some distance between them seemed like a good idea.

"If you don't have feelings for me, Mackenzie…that's one thing. But if you're just shutting me down because you're afraid…"

"*Of course* I'm afraid," Mackenzie snapped at him. "It's taken me a long time to get traction after Hope was diagnosed, okay? But I still feel like I've built a matchstick house…like the slightest move could make the whole thing burst into flames. I'm always dreading the next test results, always dreading the next medical bill…"

"But I told you that I want to help you with that," Dylan said.

The comment about the medical bills had just slipped out. Dylan had offered since the beginning to pay child support. He'd offered to help her with medical expenses. But she had always refused. For her, taking money from Dylan was like opening up yet another can of worms. There were a lot of legal strings that could come with that money…visitation, joint custody…and she just couldn't bring herself to wade into those waters just yet. The minute they sat down to establish paternity and child support, Dylan would have rights and she couldn't guarantee what he would do with them. She would have to consult him about educational and medical decisions. She had always prided herself on being able to care for Hope on her own. She had always prided herself on being a strong, successful single parent. The fact that change was already fraying the edges of her life only made her want to cling to how things "were" even more.

"I know you did," Mackenzie said more calmly. "And maybe that's what will happen…eventually. But for now, why can't we just take everything one day at a time?"

"I don't have any problem with taking things slow. But you've gotta be straight with me, Mackenzie. Is the only thing you think about what happened between us last weekend is that it was a mistake?"

Mackenzie rejoined Dylan on the swing.

"No. That's not what I think. What I think is that I have a responsibility as Hope's mom to think before I move. I owe that to her. And last weekend I lost sight of that."

She didn't want to hurt Dylan. She didn't. In her heart, she knew that she had never felt for another man what she had been feeling for Dylan this last week apart. And it scared her. She hadn't allowed herself to become vulnerable to someone in a long time and she wasn't so sure she had it in her to do it now.

"I want to be in a relationship, Dylan," Mackenzie confessed. "Not just for me. But for Hope. When she was younger, it didn't matter as much…now that she's old enough to have friends with two parents, she knows what she's missing…and I think…she wants a family. I wasn't able to admit it to myself for a long time because I wanted to be enough. I didn't want to think that I had made a mistake for all of us all those years ago. But I think…I know… that's why she wanted to find you in the first place."

"I want to try for that, too…"

"But what if we can't make it work between us? What would that do to Hope?"

"What if we *can* make it work?" Dylan answered her question with a question.

"If you're not closing the door on us…"

"I'm not." Mackenzie put her hand on his.

"Then we'll take it real slow... You're both worth the wait."

When Mackenzie saw Aunt Gerri's golf cart in the distance, she pulled her hand back from his.

"I think that if we always put Hope's best interests first, everything else will fall into place..." Mackenzie stood up and waved to Hope. She didn't look at him when she asked, "So, we have a deal?"

"Yes." Dylan stood up and stood next to her. He was close, but not *too* close. "We have a deal."

Chapter Twelve

Mackenzie came home late Wednesday night feeling worn-out and tired from the day. Her main goal was to spend some time with Hope, make sure the little girl was caught up on her homework and then go to bed.

"Hey, Mackenzie." Charlie was sitting on her love seat. The TV was on, but the sound was on Mute.

"Hey..." Mackenzie pulled her key out of the door and closed it behind her. She dropped her bag on the floor next to the door and slumped into a chair.

"You look tired."

Mackenzie dropped her head into her hand. "I am... We've had a ton of responses from the ad we ran in the trade magazine. A lot of special orders. This entire week is going to be crazy and Hope has chemo this Friday—" Mackenzie sighed "—so this weekend is going to be tough." Mackenzie looked toward Hope's bedroom. "Is she still working on her homework?"

"No," Charlie said quietly, shaking her head. "She went to bed early."

Mackenzie pushed herself up, looked at her watch. Hope usually fought going to sleep. She always wanted to stay up later than her official bedtime. "Is she sick?"

"She said that she was really tired and wanted to go to bed." Charlie stood up. "I've got an early morning tomorrow, Mackenzie, so I'm going to head home, okay?"

Mackenzie stood up, her mind on her daughter. She hugged Charlie. "Thanks for watching her."

"You know I love to hang with Hope." Charlie opened the door. Offhandedly, she said, "Oh…I put your mail on the kitchen counter."

Mackenzie locked and dead-bolted the door behind Charlie, grabbed the mail off the counter and went to check on Hope. Lately she had been getting a sickening feeling in her gut. Hope just hadn't been herself for a couple of days. Mackenzie sat down on the side of Hope's bed, ran her hand gently over Hope's head. She felt her forehead with her wrist. It was cool. Hope cracked open her eyes.

"Hi, Mom," she said groggily.

"Hi, kiddo. Are you feeling okay?"

Hope reached out for her mom's hand. "I'm tired."

"Are you having any other symptoms? Are you achy? Do you have a sore throat?"

Hope shook her head, pressed her face into the pillow. "Not really. Just tired."

Concerned, Mackenzie gently rubbed her daughter's back. "I think we should take you to the doctor tomorrow…"

Hope's eyes opened, she turned slightly. "No…" she begged. "Mom…we're going to finish making our birdhouses tomorrow in art class and then we get to hang them up around school! I'm already going to the doctor on *Friday*!"

Mackenzie stared down into her daughter's pleading eyes; it broke her heart that Hope had already missed out on so much after she was first diagnosed. So, against her better judgment, she agreed to let Hope go to school and wait until Friday to see the doctor as planned.

Mackenzie kissed her daughter on the forehead, stood up. "Okay, kiddo. Get some rest. If anything changes, you come get me, okay? I'll see you in the morning."

Mackenzie paused in the doorway for a second or two, watching her daughter drift back to sleep, before she quietly closed the door. Hope's blood would be tested on Friday. Maybe this was nothing to worry about, but she had learned from terrible experience not to minimize symptoms anymore.

She kicked off her shoes and flopped backward onto her pillows. She rested the pile of mail on her stomach, wanting to delay contact, for just a little while longer, with the stack of envelopes that had to be at least fifty percent medical bills. With a long, tired sigh, Mackenzie sat up and started to sift slowly through the mail. The second envelope had bright red paper showing through the cellophane. She ripped open the envelope, looked at the dollar amount and then started a separate "delinquent" medical bill pile. One by one, she separated the mail. As the medical bill pile grew in size, so did her anxiety. It was a daily ritual, with only a brief respite on Sundays. The mail, with its constant stream of bad news, now regularly triggered the feeling that she was slowly being buried alive in quicksand.

Mackenzie was glad to reach the last envelope in the pile; there wasn't any angry red paper glaring at her from behind the cellophane. But once she looked closer at the return address, her psyche shifted.

"Levine, Ernest and Seeger, PA"

She ripped the thick envelope open and pulled out the papers within. She didn't have to read the papers to surmise who had sent them. The only person in her life with a reason to retain an attorney was Dylan. And during their lengthy, private, *supposedly* open and *honest* conversation on Sunday, Dylan had failed to mention that his *attorney* would be contacting her.

Mackenzie began to read quickly through the lengthy documents. With each new written "demand" set forth by Dylan and his attorney, her shaky fingers tightened on the pages, crumpling the edges of the crisp linen paper.

She sat on the edge of the bed, stunned and still. Her brain was on fire: *Why* hadn't she seen this freight train coming?

Mackenzie slammed the papers down on her bed and picked up her phone. She scrolled through her recent-call list and stared hard at Dylan's name. She was tempted to call him right now; verbally blast him *right now.* But she didn't. She closed her eyes and tried to calm her body down: her brain, her heartbeat, her blood pressure. They were all out of control. As much as she wanted to confront Dylan about these papers, she didn't want to give him the advantage by being the out-of-control emotional one on the phone.

Instead of calling Dylan, Mackenzie got herself ready for bed. She doubted that she was going to get much sleep, but she knew she had to try. *This week* was not the week to be ragged from sleep deprivation. Now more than ever, she needed to be on her A game. Once she was in bed, and the lights were off, her mind wouldn't stop racing with thoughts. But there was one thought that ate at her the most: *How am I ever going to afford a lawyer?*

* * *

Mackenzie did her best to get through her day. She had gotten Hope to school, and she had gotten to the bakery early so she could start tackling the special orders that were starting to pile up. It was the first time she had ever wished to be *less* busy at the bakery. She had dozed off a couple of times, but when her eyes popped wide-open at 3:00 a.m., that was it for sleep. For the next two hours, she had stared into the darkness, frustrated and growing increasingly angry as time crept along. And now, thanks to Dylan, her eyes were burning and puffy from lack of sleep and her head was pounding.

"This is the last of them." Mackenzie boxed up the specialty cupcakes she had just frosted. She tiredly stacked the box with the rest of the special orders to be picked up by customers, and then took off her apron.

"Do you mind closing up for me today, Molly?" Mackenzie asked her manager.

"I don't mind a bit, little one. I've got nothin' but dirty laundry and drama waiting for me at home. I come to work to get away from it." Molly belly laughed. "Go home and get some rest. You're working yourself too hard."

Sitting in her car, Mackenzie truly wished she could take that advice. But she couldn't. She had ignored her phone all day in order to get through the special orders. Now she needed to deal with Dylan. He had called and she hadn't trusted herself to answer when she still had orders to fill. When she listened to his message, she was puzzled by the fact that he hadn't mentioned the letter from his attorney. He wanted to know if she was attending the emergency meeting at Pegasus.

"*What* emergency meeting?" she asked herself aloud.

Instead of dialing Dylan's number first, Mackenzie called Aggie.

"Aggie, it's Mackenzie… What's this I hear about an emergency meeting?"

"The owners've sold the property right out from underneath us. Our lease runs out in a month, we've gotten a notice to vacate and we've got no place to go. And even if we *did* have a place to go, we don't have enough money to get there. The grants've dried up, the donations've dried up… I was countin' on our annual fundraiser to pull us through another six months. Now that's off. We're in real trouble here…"

Rayna and Charlie had already agreed to watch Hope after school so she could get caught up at work and deal with Dylan. From Dylan's message, she knew that he intended to attend the meeting at Pegasus. She hadn't planned to confront him in a public venue, but at this point she didn't care. She would see what she could do to help Aggie and then she would find a way to handle her business *discreetly* with Dylan.

By the time she arrived at Pegasus, a record number of volunteers had crammed themselves into the narrow, dusty office. Everyone was tightly packed in the hot space, and the air was already muggy and stale. The volunteers wore worried tense faces as they wiped sweat from their brows and the back of their necks.

Mackenzie wound her way through the crowd to get closer to where Aggie was stationed. At the front of the pack now, Mackenzie spotted Dylan standing to Aggie's right. He was still dressed in business attire, complete with tie, slacks, cuff links and polished wing tips. She didn't imagine it. She knew she didn't imagine it. His eyes had lit up when he saw her and he had smiled at her in greeting. It amazed her how *cavalier* he could be about turning his attorney loose on her.

Jerk!

After the initial eye contact, Mackenzie refused to look at him. She kept her eyes aimed directly on Aggie, and did her best to focus on the crisis at hand. She would get to Dylan soon enough.

For a moment, Dylan was distracted by the daggers in Mackenzie's eyes that seemed to be aimed directly at him. And he was really certain that he hadn't done anything wrong. Maybe she was having a rotten day. Maybe she was understandably concerned about the fate of Pegasus. But she had looked at him as if he was enemy number one and now she was refusing to make eye contact with him at all.

What the heck did I do?

"The bottom line here is that we've got to relocate the horses and we've got a month to do it. We're gonna have to call all our riders and cancel this month's sessions so we can give this situation our total attention. I hate to do it, but it's got to be done. I need volunteers to start shaking some of our donors' trees to see if anything'll fall out. And I need everyone to start looking for a place where we can stable thirty horses." Aggie's sharp voice ricocheted in the small space. Her face was beet red, her deep-set eyes blazing mad. "If we can't get this done…if we can't find a place for all of 'em, we're not gonna have any choice but to split 'em up. And that'll be the end of Pegasus until we can regroup. That's what we're lookin' at. That's how serious this is."

Murmurs of concern and distress rippled through the group, while Aggie took a moment to collect her emotions. Dylan was standing close enough to her to see that her eyes, for a split second, had teared up.

"So…I appreciate all of you comin' out here today on short notice. All I can say now is let's get to work and make this happen."

Aggie abruptly ended the meeting and went through

the side door that led to the barn. Dylan went directly to Mackenzie's side; he waited patiently for her to finish talking to one of the other volunteers.

"I don't want Hope to know about this." Mackenzie was firm when she said this. "She's got enough to deal with right now."

"That's fine." Dylan took a step closer to her so a volunteer could walk behind him. "Hey…are you mad at me for some reason?"

Mackenzie shook her head in disgust. "You're joking, right?"

Surprised and confused, Dylan glanced around at the crowd and decided that they needed to go somewhere with fewer ears listening.

"Let's go outside," Dylan leaned down and said closer to her ear.

Mackenzie acknowledged everyone she passed, hugging some, commiserating with others, until she found her way out of the humid office and into fresher early-evening air. Dylan was on her heels, keeping pace with her as she made her way back to her car. She unlocked the doors.

"Get in." All of the anger and hurt she had been suppressing during the day was rushing to the surface, making it difficult for her to maintain a civil tone.

Dylan closed the door behind him; he had no idea what had set Mackenzie off like this. He hadn't done anything wrong!

"This week just keeps on getting better and better," Mackenzie muttered. She dug through her bag and pulled out an envelope. She thrust it toward him. "I got your little list of demands, Dylan. You want regular, *scheduled* visitation? You want to legally mandate that you're the only man Hope can call Dad? Are you *insane*? I'm not going to *force* my daughter to call you *Dad* if she doesn't want to do it!"

Astonished and confused, Dylan took the envelope. He pulled out the papers and studied them.

"These weren't supposed to be sent to you yet," he said.

"*Yet*? Why would you send them to me *ever*?" Mackenzie snapped at him. "What made you go behind my back and get an attorney? I've *never* put any pressure on you, I've *never* made any demands! All I asked was that you spend time with her. Get to know her. *Love* her…"

"I do love her." Dylan tucked the papers back into the envelope. "And I'm sorry that you got these papers. It was a mistake and I'll handle it. But the fact is, Mackenzie, you're the one holding all the cards. I wanted to know my rights, so I went to a lawyer. You had to at least suspect that I would…"

"Did you—" Mackenzie stopped talking for a minute to smile and wave at the volunteers walking past the car "—hire this attorney before or after we slept together?"

There was a long pause, a guilty pause, before Dylan admitted, "Before."

"That's just great, Dylan." Mackenzie pulled the envelope out of his hand and stuffed it in her tote. "That's just *great*." Mackenzie leaned back, gripped the steering wheel with her hands. She refused to look at him. "The worst part is that I had actually started to allow myself to care about you. I'd actually let myself start to think that maybe we could give Hope what she's been missing for a long time…a mom *and* a dad."

"We still can…"

Mackenzie bit her lip hard to stop tears from forming. She refused to cry in front of him over this.

"You *slept* with me knowing that you were going to serve me with papers! Why would I ever trust you again after you did a snake-in-the-grass thing like that?"

"You came to my room, Mackenzie. Not the other way around."

"You didn't have to say *yes.*"

"I wanted to say yes! You're a beautiful woman. You asked me to make love to you and I *did.* And I don't regret it!"

"I'm sure you don't…"

Dylan looked up at the roof of the car, shook his head and then said, "I'm sorry you got the papers. I am. But I'm *not* going to apologize for going to an attorney so I know my rights. I've tried to talk to you about this before and you've always shut me down. You shut me down all the time, Mackenzie. You know you do."

In response, Mackenzie grabbed her keys off the console and stuck them into the ignition.

"Just forget it, Dylan. We're not going to solve anything tonight. I have a ton to do to get the bakery ready for the weekend, Hope has chemo on Friday, Pegasus is falling apart, and now, thanks to you, I have to figure out how in the world I'm going to get the money for a lawyer. Can this week *get* any better?"

"You don't have to get a lawyer…"

"Oh yes, I do." Mackenzie cranked the engine. "Please get out of my car."

Dylan stood in the empty spot where her Chevy had been parked and watched Mackenzie's taillights disappear around the corner. He'd never in his life seen Mackenzie lose her temper like that. She was understandably furious and he knew he'd screwed up big-time with her. And so, apparently, did everyone else.

"What the hell did you do to Mackenzie?" This was Ian's greeting when he picked up the phone.

"I took your advice and went to see Ben."

Dylan could hear Jordan commenting loudly in the

background. "I didn't tell you to serve her with papers. And now Jordan's walking around all pissed off at me..."

"Mackenzie called Jordan...?"

"Of course she did. And Jordan knows Levine is one of my friends."

"Sorry, man..."

"Don't apologize. Fix it. I don't like it when Jordan's pissed off at me. And now she's determined for us to pay Mackenzie's legal fees."

"Oh...crap..."

"My sentiments exactly. I'm telling you, I do *not* want to be caught up in the middle of this. I love you, you're my best friend, but you need to straighten this crap out right now."

"She wasn't supposed to get the papers, okay? Ben told his paralegal not to file them and she made a mistake and mailed them instead."

"I hope he fired her," Ian snapped.

"What does it matter? The papers were sent. The damage is already done." Dylan rubbed his forehead. "Look... tell Jordan that I'll fix it, okay? But in the meantime, I need a favor..."

There was a long pause and in the background he could still hear Jordan blowing her top. "Can you *hear* what's going on behind me?"

"I hear it..."

"And you're still asking me for a favor?"

"Yes...I know my timing sucks...but, yeah."

Two days after Mackenzie had received the papers, she was still refusing to take his calls. He had intended to give her a couple more days to cool off. But he wasn't going to wait indefinitely. He knew Hope was scheduled to have chemo and he didn't want to be shut out of these critical moments in his daughter's life anymore. And even though he realized that Mackenzie had good reason to be mad at him, he had actually started to think that maybe he had a good reason to be upset with *her.* He wanted to be there for Hope in all the ways that mattered. But as far as the world was concerned, he wasn't her father and he didn't have any rights where she was concerned. That was Mackenzie's doing and he was justified in wanting it to be *un*-done. He had actually worked himself up pretty good, so he sounded less than conciliatory when Mackenzie surprised him with a phone call. If she wanted to start round number two, he was willing.

"Dylan?" There was a distinct waver in her voice. Mackenzie didn't sound mad. She sounded upset, as if she was fighting to hold herself together.

Dylan was on his way to meet Ian at their CPA's office to discuss the tax implications of expanding their business. His fingers flexed on the steering wheel hard when he heard the raw emotion in Mackenzie's voice. She wasn't calling to pick a fight.

"Hold on a minute, Mackenzie. I'm driving. Let me pull over so we can talk."

Dylan pulled into a parking lot, turned off the engine.

"What's wrong?" he asked.

"Hope was admitted into the hospital. She…relapsed." Mackenzie's voice cracked. "She's scheduled to have a lumbar puncture today…she wants to see you, Dylan. Will you come?"

"I'm on my way."

Dylan turned around and headed toward the hospital. He called Ian on the way and canceled their meeting. Never in his life had he felt the way he was feeling now. He had loved people before. He had loved friends, family…women.

Mackenzie. But what he felt for Hope…that was an entirely new type of love.

Dylan worked to look calm on the outside. He wanted to be an anchor for Hope. But on the inside he was panicked. Dylan had been walking quickly right up until he reached the wing that housed Hope's room. He slowed down, even stopped a couple of times, trying to collect himself before he went into her room.

Pull yourself together, man.

But it was a hard thing to do. He was scared out of his gourd, and completely out of his league. The antiseptic smell of the hospital made him feel sick to his stomach. The beeping of the blood pressure machines, the buzzing at the nurses' stations, the coldness of the hallways, all unearthed memories that he had tried to keep buried. His mom had died in a place like this. Would his daughter die in a place like this, too?

"Look who's here, Hope." Mackenzie's face was drawn and tight. Her eyes were bloodshot from stress and worry.

Hope looked so small, so fragile, in that hospital bed. She was hooked up to IVs and monitors. Dark circles ringed her dull eyes. Her sweet round face was pale; her freckles contrasted with the sallow coloring of her face. This was not the same girl he'd seen less than a week ago.

"Hey, Hope," Dylan said from the doorway.

Mackenzie pointed to the wall next to the door. "There's hand sanitizer right there."

Dylan sanitized his hands before he pulled a chair up to the side of Hope's bed.

"Are you going to go see Gypsy tomorrow?" Hope's lips were dry, her voice weaker than usual.

"Of course…" Dylan smiled at her. "Of course I am."

"Will you give her a carrot for me? I don't want her to think that I forgot about her."

Dylan swallowed hard several times, pushing his emotions down with each swallow. "I'll get some carrots on the way home tonight."

"But don't give them to her by hand. Put them in her bucket."

Dylan nodded, reached for her hand and squeezed it reassuringly. Hope looked at him in the eyes, and then her face crumpled. Tears streamed down his daughter's face, her eyes shut tightly. Paralyzed, Dylan didn't know what to do.

"I'm going to miss the field trip." Hope hid her face in the thin white hospital blanket that covered her bed. "And I'm going to lose all my hair again."

Hope collapsed into Mackenzie's arms. Above Hope's head, Dylan's and Mackenzie's eyes met. And a silent agreement passed between them. A truce. Their disagreement washed away by Hope's tears. They had to be on the same team. They both had to be on Hope's team.

Chapter Thirteen

Watching Mackenzie help get Hope ready for the spinal tap gave him a new perspective on the mother of his child. There was a moment when Mackenzie was able to rise above her emotions to help the medical team like a pro. She was calm, collected, a steady hand for their daughter. He was impressed…from a distance. In business meetings, he was usually the guy at the head of the table. The guy with all the answers. But here? He was useless. And it didn't feel good.

Hope was given medication to help her relax. The medication would help her stay motionless during the procedure but would also allow her rest afterward. Mackenzie helped the nurse gently guide Hope onto her side and curled her into the fetal position. Hope wasn't crying anymore; in fact, once the procedure began, she didn't move and she didn't make a sound. Mackenzie ran her hand soothingly over the top of Hope's head. Hope's bare skin was exposed for the nurse to sterilize the area and apply anesthetic cream to her lower spine.

"You're a champ, Hope. Just hang in there and we'll be done before you know it," the doctor said as she prepared to puncture Hope's skin with the long needle.

Dylan caught Mackenzie's eye right before he ducked out of the room. He'd chickened out; he couldn't handle it. He hadn't been prepared, mentally, for this part of Hope's life. Yes, he knew she had been diagnosed with leukemia. Yes, he knew that she had to take daily medicine and weekly medicine, that she had a permanent port just below her collarbone for chemotherapy and blood tests. But knowing about something and *seeing* something were two different things. He had never seen her port before today. And no one in his life had ever needed a spinal tap before.

Thankfully, the entire procedure, from start to finish, took less than forty-five minutes, but to Dylan, it seemed as if he had exiled himself to the hallway for a much longer time. He heard the doctor tell Mackenzie that they should have the results back from the lab in a few hours and then doctor and nurse walked hurriedly out of the room, one right after the other, and on to their next patient. Dylan poked his head into the room; Mackenzie was tucking the blanket tightly around Hope's body. Hope had her eyes closed when her mother kissed her on the forehead. Mackenzie turned off the light to Hope's room, left the door cracked open and joined him in the hall.

"Sorry…I couldn't watch…" Dylan hoped that she didn't think less of him because he had left the room.

"I know…it's hard. I never get used to it."

"It didn't seem that way to me. I didn't even see you flinch."

"Oh, well…I've learned how to fake stability." Mackenzie smiled weakly. “But don’t be fooled. My legs shake every time.”

“Every time? Has she had a lot of these?” Dylan asked, surprised.

Mackenzie nodded. “That’s how they check to make sure that the cells haven’t spread to the spinal fluid. All we can do now is pray that they haven’t.”

They fell silent, two pensive figures motionless in the midst of the bustling backdrop of the hospital. It wasn’t fair, to be standing here with Mackenzie. Hope should be in school and looking forward to riding Gypsy. She shouldn’t be in a hospital bed, preparing for an intense round of treatment.

“Have you eaten?” It was the only thing he could think to ask at the moment.

“Uh-uh. No. I haven’t had a chance. But I don’t want to leave in case Hope needs me.”

“I’ll stay with her. You’ve got to eat.”

“Are you sure?”

“I want to help you.” Dylan wasn’t used to feeling as if he didn’t have something important to contribute to a situation.

A break would be nice actually. She had skipped breakfast and her stomach was so empty that it hurt. And there were phone calls that still needed to be made. Hope could be in the hospital for a while so this was her new temporary home. Arrangements had to be made. She’d have to contact the school, maybe bring in extra help at the bakery so they didn’t fall behind. There was so much to do.

Mackenzie quickly grabbed her phone and wallet out of her tote. “Just make sure that she stays on her back, okay? I won’t be long.”

“Mackenzie…” Dylan saying her name made her stop.

She turned, took a step toward him, and he took a step toward her.

"I wanted to say…" He started to apologize, but the expression on her face stopped him.

"Can we just…not…right now?" Mackenzie asked him. She was exhausted, and stressed, and even though she was hiding it well, he knew that she was terrified that the cancer had come back. If she wanted to table the apology, he would table the apology. No questions asked.

"Sure…" Dylan had to put his hands in his pockets to stop himself from reaching out to her. She looked as if she desperately needed a hug; he wanted to comfort her. Was she receptive to that kind of support from him? He doubted it.

"Take your time." Dylan watched her walk down the hall. Mackenzie turned her head to look back at him, saw him standing there and smiled fleetingly before she disappeared around the corner.

Dylan closed the door behind him to keep the bright hallway light from flooding into the room. Sitting next to her bed, he marveled at the fact that anyone managed to rest in a place that made so much noise. Doctors being paged, nurses checking on patients, carts rolling loudly by. And if the noise didn't disturb you, the regular "vital signs" visits would. That's what eventually awakened his daughter. After a chubby nurse's assistant with a Minnie Mouse voice took Hope's vital signs, she looked up at him groggily, her eyes barely open.

"Where's Mom?" she asked. Her voice was weak, her lips very dry.

Dylan poured her a glass of water from the pitcher, took the straw out of the wrapper and dropped it into the disposable cup.

"She went to go get something to eat. She'll be back

soon. Here…" Dylan held the straw up to Hope's lips. Hope took a couple of small sips and then turned her head away to signal that she'd had enough.

Dylan put the cup down on the rolling table and sat down in the chair. Hope's eyes were closed again; he thought, for a moment, that she had drifted back to sleep. He reached through the metal bed rails so he could slip his palm under hers. Hope squeezed his fingers.

"Dad?" Hope's voice was so quiet and raspy that Dylan wasn't sure he'd heard her right. Had she just called him Dad for the first time?

"Dad?" Hope said again, this time more loudly…more distinctly.

"I'm right here, Hope…" Dylan couldn't have predicted what hearing that one word would make him feel. He knew he was Hope's father, but this was the first time that he truly felt like her dad.

"I'm cold."

Finally, something he *could* fix. Dylan flagged down a passing nurse and requested extra blankets. Dylan hovered by the door until the heated blankets arrived. Dylan quickly covered her with the blankets. He tucked the edges tightly around Hope the way he had seen Mackenzie do for her.

"Better?" he asked.

Hope nodded her response, never opening her eyes.

A few minutes later, Mackenzie came through the door.

"Everything okay?" she whispered from Hope's bedside.

Dylan gave one quiet nod. He almost told her about what had just happened. He almost did. But then he thought better of it. Mackenzie might not be so excited about the news and she had enough on her plate right now to deal with.

Dylan stood up so Mackenzie could take the most comfortable chair closest to the bed. He checked his watch. They still had another couple of hours before they would hear the results of the lumbar puncture. He picked up the chair by the door, moved it closer to the bed, sat down and started to scroll through his emails on his phone. Now he knew to bring his computer. In between reading and answering email, Dylan would look up from the task and watch his daughter sleep. Before today, he'd never tucked her into bed. Before today, she had always called him Dylan.

Dad, Dylan thought in amazement. *I'm Dad.*

Two weeks into Hope's hospital stay, Dylan started to feel like a seasoned hospital patron. He knew where he could find good hot coffee at just about any hour of the day or night. He knew when to eat at the cafeteria and when to avoid it like the plague. He knew the nurses, and custodians, and volunteers by name. And, unfortunately, he now knew more about steroids, and chemotherapy, and flushing ports than he had ever *wanted* to know. It was gut-wrenching to watch when Hope was at her worst. And, because of the relapse, the treatment protocol was much more aggressive. But the leukemia cells hadn't reached the spinal cord and that gave them reason to believe that a second remission could be on the horizon.

"I thought I'd find you out here." Mackenzie was wise to his best hiding spots. Sometimes he just needed to get away. Sometimes he just needed to *escape* the reality of the hospital.

Dylan scooted over so she could join him on the wrought-iron bench. This small, secluded courtyard was his favorite of his hiding spots. He'd eaten a lot of bag lunches under the shade of this old blue oak tree.

Mackenzie's hair was pulled back in a loose ponytail

and she was wearing the same Padres jersey she had worn the night they had kissed for the first time. There were so many times over these last weeks that Dylan craved Mackenzie. He wanted that physical connection with her. He wanted to love her and *be* loved by her, particularly during some of the worst moments with Hope. But she always kept him just an arm's length away. Close, but not *too* close.

Dylan reached inside his computer bag and pulled out a stack of her medical bills. He had come to her a week ago and insisted that she let him help her with the expenses. In the end, she couldn't argue with his logic. The stress of unpaid medical bills hanging over her head and ruining her credit was only funneling her vital energy away from Hope.

"These are paid."

Mackenzie stared at the large stack of envelopes on the bench between them. These envelopes had dogged her for years. They had robbed her of sleep; they had caused her so much stress and worry. And then, just like that…with no real fanfare, they were gone.

"Thank you…" Mackenzie reached for them. "Thank you."

"Thank you for letting me help." Dylan closed the lid of his laptop. "Is she still working with the tutor?"

She nodded yes. Hope was an overachieving kind of student, which she came by honestly from her mom. Other than her hair falling out again, the two things that really upset Hope about the relapse were missing school and missing out on Pegasus.

"Any updates from Aggie?" Mackenzie hated that she couldn't be more involved with solving Pegasus's crisis. As long as Hope was in the hospital, everything had to be put on hold. Even Pegasus.

"I think we've nailed down a viable option."

"Are you serious?"

When Dylan confirmed what he had just said, Mackenzie closed her eyes, her face tilted upward for a moment.

"Oh, thank goodness…" Now she could break *good* news to Hope instead of heartbreaking news.

"Where in the world did Aggie find a place that could take that many horses on short notice?"

When Dylan wasn't with Hope, he spent his wait time at the hospital trying to run down leads to place the horses. But what they really needed was more time, more money and a miracle.

"We're moving them out to Aunt Gerri's," Dylan said.

Mackenzie stared at him, shocked into silence. After a second or two, she asked, "Aunt Gerri is donating the farm to *Pegasus*?"

Dylan shook his head. "No. I would never ask her to do that. That's her retirement."

Dylan answered the question in Mackenzie's eyes.

"We're going to buy it from her."

"Pegasus is going to buy your aunt's farm? How? That land has to be worth…*millions*."

"It is…"

"They can't afford that! I've seen Aggie struggle to buy enough hay some months…."

Dylan rubbed the stubble on his chin and face. The stress in Mackenzie's voice matched the stress that he had been feeling for weeks. He had no real idea how to make the farm work in the long term for Pegasus; all he had was a short-term plan. He was the numbers guy and the numbers just didn't work. Not yet.

"My aunt's agreed to let us lease the land for now." Getting his kindhearted aunt to agree to lend a hand had been the easy part. It was the logistics of the move that were the problem. Yes, they had plenty of volunteers willing to help and they had enough trailers lined up to accommodate the horses. But the farm hadn't housed horses for years. The infrastructure had deteriorated, the two standing barns needed to be cleaned out and cleaned up. The fences needed to be mended so they could use the pastures. And all of that took money. They'd already raised a decent chunk of change, but they needed more to buy the land. Lots of it.

"And..." Dylan continued. "We've already raised right around two hundred thousand dollars, so we've got some capital to work with..."

"Wait a minute...did you just say...two hundred *thousand*?" When Dylan confirmed the number, Mackenzie said, "You did this..."

It was a statement, not a question.

Dylan stood up and held out his hand to her. "I really need something to drink. Walk with me?"

She put her hand into his but her eyes never left his face. This man had grown; he had matured. In just a short few months, he had begun to care more about the condition of the world around him. And he had been a tireless support these last weeks at the hospital. Everyone had noticed it: Rayna, Charlie...Jordan.

"How did you pull this off, Dylan?" Dry, brittle leaves crunched beneath their feet as they walked slowly across the courtyard.

"Trust me...I couldn't do that on my own. I'm just good at turning money into more money, not fundraising. Some of the money came from our regular donors, Ian's been contacting some of our previous clients looking for sponsors, and I think your cousin, Josephine, is it? Her boyfriend's parents have some pretty deep pockets..."

Mackenzie walked through the door Dylan held open for her. "How much did you donate?"

Dylan followed her through the door. "I donated some."

"How much?"

"Some..."

Mackenzie stopped walking. "Dylan...how much of that two hundred thousand came from you?"

Dylan sighed, stopped walking and made a small U-turn so he could stand directly in front of her.

"How much?" Her eyebrows lifted with the question.

Dylan glanced around before he said, "A hundred..."

"Dollars?"

"No..." Dylan lowered his voice. "Thousand..."

Mackenzie was dumbstruck. She studied Dylan's tired eyes and then it clicked in her brain.

"You sold your Corvette..." She said that and Dylan stopped meeting her gaze. "Oh, Dylan...you didn't..."

Dylan turned his head away from her. "Don't make a big deal out of it, Mackenzie."

"Don't make a big *deal* out of it? That car meant *everything* to you."

"No. It didn't." Dylan's eyes were back on her. "Hope means everything to me. Okay? *You* mean everything to me."

Mackenzie swallowed hard several times to keep her emotions in check. She refused to let herself cry in the middle of the hospital lobby. But she wanted to cry. Eyes watery with emotion, Mackenzie asked Dylan, "Can I hug you?"

The pain in his eyes when she asked that question made her feel like a genuine jerk. She knew that Dylan had wanted to be consoled by her for weeks. She knew it. And yet, she hadn't done the one thing for this man that he needed from her. It was such a simple thing and she had denied him.

Dylan didn't nod, he didn't say yes; he opened his arms to her instead. She was the one to close the distance between them. He had already taken nine figurative steps toward her over the past few months, and it was her turn finally to take that one *literal* step toward him. They embraced, right there in the middle of the busy hospital lobby. Dylan held on to her so tightly. And she held on to him. When they were face-to-face, body to body, arms intertwined, Mackenzie could feel that they were a perfect fit. A perfect match. Hugging Dylan…being hugged by Dylan… was the most comfortable, reassuring experience she could remember having. Everything but Dylan, and the feel of his body, faded far into the background.

"Thank you…" Mackenzie rested her head on his shoulder.

Dylan's arms tightened around her, she felt him kiss the top of her head. "I've missed you."

Mackenzie leaned back a bit so she could put her hand on Dylan's face. "You're such a good man, Dylan Axel."

Dylan reached up and captured her hand, pressed his lips to her palm and then held her hand next to his heart. "I've always wanted you to think so. Even when we were kids."

"I do think so…what you've done for Hope…what you've done for me." Even though she had called a truce with him that first day in the hospital, this was the moment when she was truly able to release her resentment over the attorney's letter.

Dylan took a chance. The way she was looking at him, he wanted to believe that there was an invitation in her eyes. He kissed her. Gently, sweetly, tenderly.

"People are staring…" Mackenzie said when the kiss ended.

Dylan glanced around for a second then grabbed her hand. Instead of heading toward the cafeteria, Dylan started walking back toward the courtyard. He led her through the door, across the courtyard and behind the large blue oak tree. Hidden behind the thick trunk of the tree, Dylan pulled Mackenzie back into his arms and kissed her. The first kiss had been a question. The second kiss was a lover's demand. He leaned back against the tree and brought her with him. He deepened the kiss, teasing her tongue with his.

Ultimately, it was Dylan who ended the kisses. He held her by the shoulders, pinning her with narrowed, intense eyes. "I have to stop."

Mackenzie agreed. They needed to stop. If only it hadn't felt so good. If only she didn't want to kiss him again… right now.

"You've never let me apologize for not telling you that I had gone to an attorney. I've tried…more than once."

"I know…" He had tried, but just as he had said to her during their disagreement at Pegasus, she always changed the subject.

"Do you forgive me, Mackenzie? Can we move on now?"

"I forgive you," she said, and meant it.

Mackenzie's phone chimed; she checked it.

"Hope's done with tutoring," she said. "I need to get back to her. Can we…talk more later?"

Dylan nodded his agreement.

"Are you coming?" Mackenzie paused when he didn't follow her.

"In a minute…" Dylan glanced down toward the bulge near his zipper.

She wasn't really a blusher, but she did then. "Oh…do you want me to wait, too?"

"No. You go ahead. I'll catch up in a minute." While he was waiting, he realized how much his reality had shifted since Mackenzie and Hope. A couple of months ago, he was a successful business owner with a lot of time for parties, surfing and hot blondes. Now? He hadn't thrown a party since Ian's birthday, he had become a philanthropist, a curvy brunette had replaced the blonde and the Corvette was gone.

But that was all superficial stuff and now he knew it. The biggest change was the change that had happened in his heart. He discovered that he liked having a daughter. He liked being a dad and he was pretty good at it so far. In fact, he had started to think that he'd like to have more children. This time he'd be there from conception to birth and beyond. And he wanted to have those children with Mackenzie. She was the one for him. He loved her and when the moment was right, he was going to propose marriage. She might not know it yet, but Dylan was determined to marry Mackenzie.

Chapter Fourteen

One week at the hospital could feel like a month. Dylan had passed exhaustion a while ago and was now operating in a zone teetering somewhere between comatose and hysteria. He had taken to sleeping on his favorite courtyard bench and didn't even care anymore that he must look like a homeless person sleeping off a bender. Mackenzie rarely left the hospital, and when she did leave, it was to get something done for the bakery or go to Hope's school for a meeting. She hadn't had a real break, or real sleep, in weeks. And they were both starting to fray around the edges. The littlest thing would make them snap at each other, and there was a bite in their tone that was a symptom of their extreme fatigue and chronic worry. Mackenzie had let Rayna or Charlie stay with Hope during the day, but she had refused to leave Hope overnight. Mackenzie needed to get some actual sleep in an actual bed, and he was going to force the issue today.

"Uh...*wow*! You look like total crap!" Jordan met up with him at the hospital entrance, carrying her motorcycle helmet under her arm.

He could tell by the look on her fact that Jordan was shocked by his appearance. He couldn't really blame her; he was usually the stylish guy in the group. Even on casual days, Dylan wore slacks, button-down shirts, his customary Rolex watch and expensive shoes. Today, he was in a T-shirt, jeans and sneakers. His hair was shaggy, as if he'd missed his bimonthly appointment with the barber, and she had never seen him with a five-o'clock shadow before.

"Thanks for coming." Dylan hugged Jordan, glad to see her.

"Of course. What else?" Jordan asked. "Is Mackenzie really going to let me take a shift? I've been offering for weeks."

Dylan opened the door for her. "I'm not going to give her a choice. If I have to, I'll throw her over my shoulder and carry her out of here."

"Well, all right, caveman." Jordan laughed at the thought. "That'll go over well. If I were you, when you put her down, run like hell. Mackenzie may be little, but she packs a punch."

"Trust me—" Dylan pushed the button for the elevator "—I know."

Just outside Hope's room, Dylan slipped on a paper hospital mask. "Wait here for a minute, okay?"

Jordan waited for Dylan while he went into the room. The room was dimly lit because Hope was resting. Mackenzie was doing her best to sleep curled up in the chair. He had tried to sleep in that chair himself, so he knew how uncomfortable it was. He knelt down beside Mackenzie and rested his hand on her thigh.

"Mackenzie..." he whispered.

"Hmm?" Mackenzie cracked her eyes open.

"Come outside with me for a minute..."

"Why?"

"Just come outside with me..."

Mackenzie pushed herself upright slowly, yawned behind her mask and rubbed her eyes. Finally, she stood up, stretched her arms above her head and followed him quietly out of the room.

Mackenzie slipped off her mask. "Jordan!"

The cousins hugged each other in greeting.

"I wish you'd let me know you were coming. Hope's asleep. She's going to be really upset that she missed you."

"She's not gonna miss me," Jordan said. "I'm spending the night."

Mackenzie looked between Dylan and her cousin. "You are?"

"You need to sleep in your own bed, Mackenzie. You haven't slept in weeks." Dylan put his hand on her shoulder.

"No..." Mackenzie shook her head. To Jordan she said, "Thank you, but no."

Jordan was a good match for Mackenzie. They didn't resemble each other, but they were cut from the same tough cloth. Jordan had a really good chance of winning this round.

"You're welcome, and *yes*. You're going home. I'm staying here," Jordan said in a no-nonsense tone. "Hope's my family. You're my family. I get to help."

Mackenzie wasn't a shrinking violet, but she was a *weary* violet. "All right."

Dylan was surprised at how quickly Mackenzie gave in to her cousin, but he wasn't about to wait around to let her change her mind. He hustled her back into the room to grab her tote and kiss a still-sleeping Hope goodbye. He handed Jordan a mask.

"You have to wear this all the time. No fruit, no flowers. I'm going to drive Mackenzie home. Call *me*, not her, if you need something."

"No...she needs to call me..." Mackenzie disagreed. Over her shoulder, she said to Jordan, "You need to call me."

"*Go*...both of you." Jordan had her mask on. "I've got this."

Jordan watched her cousin and Dylan walk away together. Mackenzie had her arm linked with his and Dylan had the look of a man in love. Dylan and Mackenzie? On paper, they seemed like a really odd match, but, when Jordan saw them together, they just *fit*. Sometimes opposites really did attract.

Dylan drove Mackenzie home in his car, leaving her car parked at the hospital. She twisted to the side in the bucket seat, facing him, and closed her eyes. He typed her address into the GPS. He knew that she lived near Balboa Park, but he'd never been to her house.

Mackenzie wasn't asleep on the way home; she was just too tired to keep her eyes open. She was so exhausted that she felt sick with it. When Jordan showed up, she knew that Dylan had arranged it and that he was right. It was time for her to get some rest. If she got sick, then she wouldn't even be able to go into Hope's room, much less stay with her overnight.

Mackenzie heard the robotic voice of the GPS say the name of her street. She sat up, yawned loudly and then pointed to her small Spanish-style bungalow.

"That's me right there on the left."

Dylan pulled up in front of her house and parked. He

walked quickly to her side of the car, opened the door and held out his hand to her.

"Nice place." Dylan walked beside her up to the front door.

"Thank you. Hope and I love it here." Mackenzie turned off the alarm remotely and then slipped the key into the door. "Do you want to come in?"

"Sure..." He had been hoping for an invitation but wasn't so sure he'd get one.

Mackenzie walked in first, and then stepped to the side so he could come in. "You may as well see what you're getting yourself into..."

The way Mackenzie had described her penchant for messiness, he had been worried about what he may find behind the door. He was relieved to find that the quaint, shabby-chic bungalow was a little cluttered—a little disorganized. But it was clean. He could work with that.

Mackenzie dropped her tote and keys on the kitchen counter. "I have to sit down for a minute."

Dylan looked at her small curio cabinet tucked in the corner. "What's this?"

"I collect hearts," Mackenzie said with a yawn. "My mom had a heart collection and I just kept it going. Do you want to sit down?"

She put all the recipe boxes off the love seat onto the floor so Dylan would have a spot to sit. He joined her on the love seat; they sat shoulder to shoulder, thigh to thigh in the quiet living room.

Mackenzie sighed. "This is what I'm going to do... I'm going to take a really hot shower and then get into bed."

"Sounds like a plan," Dylan agreed.

Mackenzie turned her head toward him. "You can either go home, or you can join me. It's up to you."

Her words were blunt, to the point and completely unexpected. But his decision was an easy one to make.

"I want to stay with you…"

Mackenzie stood under the steaming hot water for a long time, letting the heat beat down on her aching neck and back. Sleeping in a chair had taken its toll on her body. After the shower, she got Dylan a fresh towel and one of Hope's unopened One Direction toothbrushes from under the sink. Dylan showered, brushed his teeth and shaved his face with a razor Mackenzie had told him was dull from her shaving her legs. He didn't put his clothes back on; instead, he just wrapped the towel around his waist. It wasn't like Mackenzie hadn't seen the goods before.

He carried his clothes down the hall and found Mackenzie already in bed. "Can I throw these into the washing machine?"

Mackenzie had been dozing off. She nodded sleepily. "Behind the sliding doors right behind you. Detergent's on the shelf."

Dylan threw his socks, underwear and T-shirt in the washing machine. He had noticed that Mackenzie had left one side of her small bed open for him, and he was looking forward to occupying it. He'd been thinking about getting Mackenzie back into his arms for the longest time. And tonight…*finally*…was the night. Dylan dropped his towel by the side of the bed; if Mackenzie minded that he was getting into her bed in the buff, she didn't say. She watched him, eyes half-mast, while he got into her bed. He was the first man she'd ever had in this bed, and she was glad that she had invited him to stay.

"Do you want me to hold you?" Dylan asked.

Mackenzie turned over and scooted back into his awaiting arms. Dylan wrapped his arm around her body, buried his face in her sweet-smelling neck and closed his eyes.

It didn't take but a minute for his body to start getting worked up over having her in his arms. She was warm and soft and sexy, and even as tired as he was, his body still wanted to make love. Knowing how sleep deprived Mackenzie was, Dylan moved his hips back slightly away from Mackenzie's body. She needed sleep, and as much as he wanted to love her right now, he needed to let her rest.

"Good night," she murmured.

When she snuggled even more deeply into his arms, Dylan closed his eyes and sighed contentedly. Relaxed and at home lying next to her, Dylan fell asleep with the certain knowledge that wherever Mackenzie was, that's where he belonged. They slept for hours. It had been dusk when they arrived home, but it was late in the night when Mackenzie awakened. She heard Dylan snoring beside her in the narrow bed, and she could see in the faintly lit room that he had pushed all the covers over onto her side. Not wanting to wake him, Mackenzie carefully peeled the covers back and tried to get off the end of the bed without wiggling the mattress too much.

"Where're you going?" Dylan asked in the dark.

"Bathroom..." Mackenzie whispered.

She slipped into the bathroom, peed, rinsed out her mouth and then opened the door. The light to the bathroom was still on, so Mackenzie got a full-frontal view of a naked Dylan scratching his chest hair just outside the bathroom door. Dylan had been asleep, but the lower half of his body was wide awake.

"I'll meet you back there..." Dylan let out a long yawn before he changed places with her.

Mackenzie hid a smile as she hurried back to bed. She checked her phone. Jordan had sent her a text saying that Hope was doing well. It was 3:00 a.m., which meant she still had some more sleeping to do.

Dylan took care of business in the bathroom, dropped his clothes in the dryer and then came back to bed. He immediately pulled Mackenzie back into his arms. But this time, instead of letting her go back to sleep, he started to drop small butterfly kisses along the back of her neck.

"Mackenzie..." Dylan breathed in her scent.

"Hmm?"

"Do you know that I love you?"

Her eyes had been closed, but she opened them. She turned her head toward the sound of his voice. "No..."

His lips were next to her ear, the feel of his breath sending wonderful chills down her back. Mackenzie shifted her body so she was facing him in the dark.

"Do you know that I'm in love with you?" he asked.

"No." Mackenzie didn't flinch when Dylan's hand slipped under her T-shirt. He slid his hand behind her back and pulled her closer to him.

Dylan found her lips in the dark. Kissed her, long and slow.

"I do love you..." Dylan touched her face, his fingertips tracing the outline of the lips he had just kissed.

"Do you love me, Mackenzie?"

She gently bit the tip of his finger. Her body was already responding to his kisses, to the feel of his lean, muscular body next to hers.

"Yes..." she admitted to him, and to herself.

Over the past several weeks, her feelings had grown for Dylan. They had deepened. When she looked at him, her heart felt full. When he was gone, she missed him. Lately, she had caught herself waiting for his phone calls and texts, and staring at the hospital doorway, awaiting his return. The love that she now knew she felt for Dylan was different than the love she had for Hope, but it was just as strong. She was in love, for the very first time in her life.

"Thank God," he said before he kissed her again. He gathered her into his arms, holding her so tightly as he deepened the kiss.

Without words spoken between them, Dylan stripped off her shirt and panties. His mouth was on one breast, his hand massaging the other. He sucked on her nipple, drawing it into his mouth, teasing it with his tongue, until she couldn't stay quiet. She pressed his head tighter to her breast and moaned softly. She slipped her hand down between their bodies and wrapped her fingers around his long, hard shaft. He groaned and she smiled a lover's smile. Mackenzie pushed on his shoulder so he would lie down on his back.

"What are you doing?" he asked in the dark.

Intent on her mission, she ignored him. He would know her intentions soon enough. His shaft was thick and silky and warm; it felt so good in her hand. The head of his shaft was large, and tasted salty when she drew it into her mouth.

Dylan's next groan was even louder. His fingers were in her hair, his leg muscles tensed in anticipation; Mackenzie was emboldened. Right then and there, he was at her mercy, she was totally in control, while she loved him with her mouth.

"Mackenzie...I don't want you to stop..." Dylan's voice was strained. "But you've got to stop."

Dylan pulled her up on top of him, kissed her and then pushed her onto her back. He was down between her thighs before she could stop him. She hadn't let him do that when they had made love before; this part of lovemaking always embarrassed her. She could give, but it was harder for her to receive.

But the minute she felt his hot mouth on her flesh, she couldn't remember why she'd ever said no to him before. Dylan slid his hands beneath her hips, lifted her body up and loved her with his tongue until she was squirming and aching and crying out for him to put her out of her misery.

Like a stalking tiger, Dylan moved up her body until they were chest to chest. His shaft was pressed into her stomach; she needed it to be pressed inside of her.

"Where are your condoms?" Dylan's teeth grazed her shoulder.

"I don't have any..."

The moment she said those words, it occurred to her that he was asking because *he* didn't have a condom. Dylan's body became very still on top of her.

"You don't have one?" he asked, frustrated.

Mackenzie shook her head. "No."

Dylan dropped his head into her neck, tempted just to lift his hips and slide himself into her tight, wet, warm body, damn the consequences. After a moment of silent debating, Dylan rolled off her body and sat up on the edge of the bed. He hadn't had sex for a month and he'd been too stressed out to worry about masturbating. But now? His body *knew* it had been deprived and it wanted relief ASAP. He was so hard it felt as if the skin was going to split wide open. And even the thought of risking getting Mackenzie pregnant didn't soften it one bit. In fact, the thought of impregnating her again actually turned him on even more.

Cold without his body on top of her, Mackenzie pulled the blankets up over her body. She wanted to scream. Her body was so sexually charged that all she could think about was getting Dylan inside of her. She curled her legs up and tried to stop focusing on the throbbing he had started between her legs. Head in her pillow, she closed her eyes. She opened them when she felt Dylan lift the blanket.

He was on top of her again and he was still aroused;

the head of his shaft was poised just outside the opening of her body. He took her face between his hands.

"Mackenzie?"

A small stream of moonlight had wound its way through the window slats; she could see the strong planes of his face. More important, she could make out his eyes.

"Yes, Dylan?"

"I want you to be my wife. I want to have more children with you."

Mackenzie swallowed hard before she spoke. "Are you asking me to marry you?"

"Yes, I am." He hadn't expected to propose to her tonight. But the moment felt right. "Marry me, Mackenzie."

"Okay…" she said simply.

Dylan reached between their bodies and guided himself in. He slowly, carefully, slid deeper and deeper until he was as deep inside of her as he could be. He waited for her to protest, to be the voice of reason when they both knew the risk. But she didn't. He pulled back, teasing her with sensual, controlled strokes. Her frustrated sounds signaled that she wanted more from him. She wanted more passion, more intensity, more, more, more… So he stopped worrying and gave himself permission just to experience Mackenzie. He deliberately and methodically loved her longer, and with more passion, than he had ever loved anyone before. When he loved her slowly, she demanded that he go faster. When he gave her one orgasm, she pleaded for another. But it was her unbridled, uncensored cry at the peak of her second orgasm that destroyed his carefully manufactured control.

"I'm going to come…do you want me to pull out?" Dylan gritted the words out.

Mackenzie locked her legs around him and kept him right where he was. That simple gesture drove him crazy;

he braced himself above her, arms locked, head thrown back as he exploded inside of her.

Dylan didn't move; he dropped his head down and caught his breath. Then he lowered himself down on top of her.

"Holy Toledo, woman..." Dylan laughed into her neck.

Mackenzie hugged him and laughed, too. She felt satisfied and *sexy.* She didn't even bother to cover her body when Dylan rolled to the side. They both lay on their backs, holding hands, savoring the aftermath of their lovemaking. Each time with Dylan was just a little bit better than the last. She was more comfortable with her own body. She was more comfortable with him. He thought she was beautiful, and she'd only seen him date really gorgeous women. It had helped her to start owning the idea that she was an attractive, curvy woman.

"Do you think that I got you pregnant?" Dylan's question interrupted her own internal dialogue.

Her hand moved down to her abdomen. The timing in her cycle could be right. "I don't know. Maybe."

"And if I did?"

The thought of carrying Dylan's child filled her with an immediate rush of joy. She *wanted* to be pregnant with his child again.

"Then Hope won't be an only child anymore."

He squeezed her fingers. "Will you be happy?"

"Yes..." she reassured him. "I've always wanted another child."

Dylan lifted her hand and kissed it.

"What about you?" she asked. "Will you be happy?"

He propped himself up on his side, put his hand on top of hers. Now they both had their hands on her abdomen.

"I hope I did get you pregnant."

His words were the exact reassurance she needed. She

was the mother of Dylan's child, and now she was going to be his wife. That hadn't always been her dream, but it was now. Still tired from weeks at the hospital, they pulled the covers over their bodies and knew that they should try to get some rest. For now, they had had a temporary reprieve from the harsh reality of hospital life. Dylan held on to her tightly; the warmth of his hairy chest felt so good against her back. He brushed her hair back off her shoulder, tightened his arm around her and let his head sink down into the pillow. He was a father and soon he would be a husband. And, maybe, just maybe, their lovemaking had created a new life tonight. If they hadn't succeeded this time, Dylan was hopeful that Mackenzie would agree to keep on trying until they *did.*

Chapter Fifteen

Dylan's days of wearing expensive clothes and nice shoes were temporarily on hold. Until Pegasus was moved to the farm, he was relegated to jeans, T-shirts, work boots and a baseball cap. His partner, Ian, was taking charge of the business expansion while he split his time between the hospital and the farm. The new owners of the land Pegasus was currently occupying, investors with a plan to develop, had given them a two-week extension to vacate. It didn't seem like much, but it was actually a donation of sorts. As far as the investors were concerned, every day they delayed their project cost them money. The extra two weeks helped, but there was still a long list of things that needed to be done at the farm in order to keep the horses comfortable. As far as getting Pegasus operational again for riders, that was an entirely different problem for a different day.

He had found his uncle's old tool belt in the shed, and

wearing it made him feel like maybe Bill was watching, guiding him with his steady hand. He was actually surprised at how quickly he had fallen back into life at the farm. He'd even crashed a couple of times in his old room instead of driving back to his place.

"The delivery guy just called!" Doug Silvernail shouted to him from the far end of the barn. "You want them to stack the lumber out front?"

Doug was a contractor at his aunt's church who had donated his time to Pegasus.

"That works, Doug. Thanks!" Dylan shouted back. He pulled off his ball cap, wiped the sweat off his brow and then put the hat back on. He stuffed the sweaty rag back into his pocket and got back to the business of fixing the broken hinge on the stall door. When his phone rang again, which it had been doing nonstop all morning, Dylan cursed under his breath and pulled the phone out of his front pocket.

It was Mackenzie this time. He picked up the call immediately.

"Hey, sweetheart…" He smiled. Talking to Mackenzie was always the best part of his day. Because of his work on behalf of Pegasus, they hadn't been able to spend much time together, but they were in constant contact by phone.

"Dylan…?" The sound of her voice was different. She sounded emotional, and elated. "We just got the test results back…"

Dylan rested his hand on the stall door so all his attention could hone in on Mackenzie's next words.

"She's in remission!"

Relieved, Dylan squeezed his eyes closed for a moment and then looked heavenward. "Oh, thank God!"

He straightened back up, looked upward in gratitude

before he shouted out to the people scattered around the barn. "Hope's in remission! Hope's in remission!"

The people in the barn erupted in cheers. He needed to tell Aunt Gerri right away. On his way out of the barn, some of the volunteers slapped him on the back, shook his hand…it was a day they had all been praying for.

"When can she come home?" Dylan stepped out from the shade of the barn into the bright, hot California sun.

"Tomorrow…" Mackenzie was understandably emotional. He wished he were there to hug her. He wished he could hug both of his girls. "Here…Hope wants to talk to her dad."

Dylan stopped in his tracks. Mackenzie had never called him that before, and she had said it so casually, as if it was no big deal. Hope only called him Dad when Mackenzie wasn't around, so he'd thought that Mackenzie didn't know about it yet. Dylan knew that the subject would have to be broached at some point, but the right moment hadn't presented itself. And, for him, it wasn't urgent. He was going to marry Mackenzie and he was Hope's natural father. That's what mattered. The rest of the stuff would work out eventually.

While he was celebrating with Hope on the phone, Dylan continued on his way to the house. He found his aunt in the kitchen, surrounded by ingredients and pots and pans.

"Hold on, Hope…Aunt Gerri wants to talk to you…"

Dylan held the phone out to his aunt. "She's in remission."

Aunt Gerri's face lit up and she tossed up her hands in the air in excitement.

Dylan sat down at the kitchen counter while his aunt chattered excitedly with his daughter. The two of them seemed never to run out of things to say.

"Well, I'm just as happy as I can be, honey…I can't wait to see you. I love you, too," his aunt said before she hung up the phone.

She came around to Dylan's side of the counter and hugged him. "I can't wait until church Wednesday night. The whole congregation's been praying for her!"

His aunt had been in rare form ever since the revolving door of volunteers had started to come to the farm. Her solitary life had vanished and she was thriving. She was energetic and talkative and her kitchen was always open for business. Dylan covered the expense of feeding the volunteer crew, and Gerri was happy to have a reason to cook every day. She fed them and then she played the organ for them. She had been intending to move to town so she could be around people, but for now, the people had come to her.

"Okay…you go do what you know how to do so I can keep doin' what I know how to do. I'll ring the bell when lunch is ready." Gerri had reinstated the practice of ringing the dinner bell Uncle Bill had installed at the back kitchen door.

Dylan opened the back door, but he paused. "Aunt Gerri…?"

"Yes, honey?" Gerri was back to peeling potatoes.

"I'd like to marry Mackenzie here, on the farm. If she likes the idea, would you be okay with it?"

"Well, of course it's okay…this is your home."

It had been a nearly impossible task, but they had managed to pull it off. The two standing barns on the property had been brought back to life. They weren't pretty or perfect, but they were functional for the horses and that's all that mattered at the moment. Uncle Bill had an office space in the main barn, so that's where Aggie would store all of her Pegasus papers, forms and files. The fence around one of the larger pastures had been repaired; some of the horses couldn't be out together; they'd have to rotate the horses until the other fences were fixed. There were still some plumbing issues at both barns, so it was portable restrooms for now. If Dylan thought about all the things left to do, it would drive him nuts. Instead, he tried to concentrate on all the things they had already accomplished.

Even now, riding in the passenger seat of Aggie's truck as she turned up the driveway to the farm, it was still hard for him to believe that this long-anticipated day had finally arrived. He could see Mackenzie and Hope sitting on the porch swing waiting for the horses to arrive at their new home. His aunt appeared from inside the house as the large caravan of trucks, horse trailers, cars filled with volunteers and several rented moving trucks.

"My Bill would be so proud of this day…" Aunt Gerri beamed at Mackenzie and Hope.

Mackenzie put her arm around Gerri's shoulder, and they stood arm and arm, watching the procession head up the winding driveway.

Hope, whose hair had already started to fall out at the hospital, was wearing a bright purple bandanna on her head. Her eyebrows and eyelashes were gone. And she was still pale, thinner than before and still weak from the chemo. There were dark rings around her eyes that made them appear to be sunken into her puffy face. But some of the light, the fire, had returned to her wide lavender-blue eyes.

"I don't see Gypsy. Do you see Gypsy?" Hope leaned over the porch railing. Gypsy was all Hope could talk about for weeks. Mackenzie had taken Hope to the feed store so she could buy a large tub of special treats for all the horses.

"She's in one of those trailers, kiddo… They wouldn't

leave her behind..." Mackenzie saw Dylan through the windshield of Aggie's truck and, as was usual nowadays, her pulse quickened. She was simply head over heels crazy for that man. She could finally relate to the lyrics of sappy love songs and the tortured words of poems. She just *loved* him. He was her special somebody.

Dylan hopped out of the truck. He lifted up his arms with a tired, happy smile. "We did it. We're here!"

Aggie was already barking orders, directing traffic and setting the second phase of the move into motion. She had already moved some of her items into the office and she had spent quite a bit of time on the farm, getting familiar with their new digs.

"What can we do to help?" Aunt Gerri's bright blue eyes were dancing with excitement. Dylan turned to look at the cars, and trucks, and trailers and people. The farm was *alive* again.

"Just sit back and watch the show..." Dylan kissed his aunt on the cheek. To Hope, he asked, "Ready to see Gypsy?"

Hope nodded and slipped her hand into his hand.

Mackenzie and Dylan caught each other's eyes and held. "I'm going to help Gerri with the food. I'm sure everyone's going to be starved..."

With one last smile, a loving smile meant just for Mackenzie, Dylan took his daughter to the last trailer in the line. Hope was like the rock star of the day; this was the first time many people from Pegasus had had an opportunity to see her since she'd been in the hospital. But, because Hope was fresh off chemotherapy, and her immune system was still weak, all the people who wanted to greet her and hug her had to keep their distance. Hope's recovery was still too fragile for her to be exposed to viruses right now. It was already a risk to have her around this many people, but neither Mackenzie nor he had the heart to tell her that she couldn't be a part of this day.

Hope ran up to the last trailer when she spotted Gypsy. She stood on tiptoe so she could touch the white star on the mare's forehead.

"Hi, there, Gyps…you've got a new home now. A better home, with really big pastures and lots of grass and your very own stall…"

Hope looked at him. "She looks okay, doesn't she?"

"Yeah…I think she looks great."

"Hey! Axel!" Wearing faded jeans, motorcycle boots, a plain white V-neck T-shirt and a black paisley bandanna on her head, Jordan appeared from behind one of the moving trucks.

"Jordan…I didn't know you were going to make it today," Dylan said.

"Are you kidding me? Do you think I'd miss a chance to hang with my favorite second cousin?" Jordan reached out, gave Hope's hand a quick squeeze before she moved back a couple of steps to keep a safe distance.

Hope smiled up at Jordan. "I like your bandanna."

"I like yours." Jordan returned the compliment and then looked around. "Man…this is quite a posse you've assembled."

"I know…I still can't believe it," he agreed. "Mackenzie's in the house with my aunt if you want to say hi."

"Yeah…let me do that before you put me to work." Jordan blew Hope a kiss before she headed toward the house.

Jordan followed the sound of voices and the smell of good food cooking back to the kitchen. Mackenzie and Gerri were laughing and talking when she showed up. Mackenzie greeted her with a warm hug and then she introduced her to Dylan's aunt.

"Did Ian come, too?"

Jordan propped her hip against the counter, crossed her arms casually in front of her. "No. He hates crowds."

"That's too bad." Mackenzie frowned.

"Ian has always been a bit of an introvert," Gerri said. "He actually got a little worse when all the girls started to chase him senior year…"

"Hey…that's right!" Jordan exclaimed. "You know Ian!"

"Like he was another one of my own…" Gerri nodded. "He didn't really start to come out of his shell until he went to college. Modeling helped. But, now, with his eyes, I'm afraid he's slipping back into his old ways…"

Jordan leaned down, elbow on the counter, chin propped up by her hand. "I'm actually thinking about getting him a service dog. He'd die before he used a cane…"

"A service dog's a good idea. Get him a man's dog, like a black Lab. That would suit him." Gerri slid a pan of cookies into the oven.

"I'm gonna do it." Jordan nodded. Then she changed the subject. "So…I hear you're *engaged* now?"

Lately, Mackenzie had been blushing. And, now she was at it again. Mackenzie smiled shyly. "Dylan asked me to marry him."

"My nephew knows a good thing when he sees it…" Gerri smiled warmly at Mackenzie.

"I'm really happy for you… He's a really great guy." Jordan straightened upright. "Is Hope over the moon?"

"Totally over the moon…" Mackenzie put a bowl in the sink and ran water into it. "We already got our marriage license."

Jordan's jaw dropped. "Uh…*wow*! Where's the fire?"

"Dylan doesn't want to wait," she said. "And I guess I don't want to wait either. Dylan wants to get married here, in front of the old oak tree behind the house."

"Well, more power to you. I'd love to do a quickie wedding, but Mom is pulling out all the stops back home. Luckily, all I have to do is sit back, let her do her thing and approve the stuff she emails me."

"Aunt Barb knows how to throw a party..."

"She does...but honestly, Ian'd love to just elope, but he promised me we'd get married in Montana and I'm gonna hold him to it..." Jordan popped a chocolate chip into her mouth. "You've got to let me and Jo take you shopping for a dress. Jo dies for that kind of stuff. She's still trying to manifest a proposal out of *Brice*. Yuck." Jordan shuddered. "You *are* going to invite the Brand clan to this shindig, right? If you don't, trust me, you'll be able to hear Mom's hissy fit all the way from Montana!"

After the horses were all settled, the feed was in the new feed room and the tack was put away in the new tack room, his aunt's house filled up with hungry folks who had been working all day. One of the front rooms was set up with long tables for an all-you-can-eat buffet. Some of the food was brought in, but most of the food was home-cooked by Gerri. With their paper plates and plastic cups in tow, it was standing room only in Gerri's organ room. For this special occasion, and particularly for Hope, Gerri turned on the Christmas-tree lights.

"I haven't seen her this happy in years," Dylan whispered to Mackenzie. Mackenzie was perched on the arm of a chair and he was standing next to her. Hope had taken the seat of honor next to his aunt on the organ bench.

"Now..." Aunt Gerri said to her audience while she looked through a songbook. "I like to start off playing 'Do Re Mi' to limber up my fingers. I usually play it two times 'cause it has all the notes in the scale, plus you've got sharps and flats and it's a gay little tune so it puts me in a real good cheerful mood." Hope looked happy; she had even agreed to wear the white, protective mask that she hated just so she wouldn't miss out on the fun.

"And—" Aunt Gerri smiled at Hope "—once I'm all warmed up, I'll play 'Count Your Blessings' just for you!"

"Come outside with me for a minute." Dylan reached for her hand.

Mackenzie linked her fingers with his as he led her to the kitchen and through the back door. They walked down the back steps, across the yard, to the beautiful three-hundred-year-old oak tree that was growing behind Gerri's house. Under the tree, Dylan kissed her, slow and sweet.

"I love it here." Mackenzie was wrapped up securely in Dylan's arms, his chin resting lightly on the top of her head.

"Me, too…"

"I can't wait to marry you under this tree…." She rested her head on his shoulder, listened to his strong, steady heartbeat.

"Have I told you lately how much I love you?"

Mackenzie smiled. "Yes. You have. And I love you."

Dylan loosened his arms, took a small step back. Mackenzie looked so pretty in this soft, golden early-evening light.

"There's something I need to do…" Dylan knelt down at her feet, took her hand in his hand.

"What are you doing?" Mackenzie laughed nervously. "You already *asked* me to marry you!"

"You deserve a better proposal than that, Mackenzie." Dylan stared up into her eyes. "You're so beautiful to me, do you know that? I look at you and you take my breath away. I can't remember what my life was like before I met you…before I met Hope…and I don't want to remember, because none of that stuff matters anymore. You're everything to me, Mackenzie. Will you marry me?"

Dylan pulled a ring out of his front pocket and poised it at the tip of her ring finger.

"You know I will..." There was an emotional catch in Mackenzie's words.

Dylan slipped the heart-shaped diamond engagement ring onto her finger.

"It's a heart, Dylan!" Mackenzie admired the ring. "I collect hearts!"

"I remember." Dylan had her in his arms once again. He kissed her and she kissed him. They embraced in the spot where they would one day say their vows. They embraced in the soft dusky light with the sound of nickering horses drifting up from the barns. It was a perfect, stolen moment between two people who had fallen in love.

Night had fallen on the farm and there were only a few vehicles parked in the grassy area next to his aunt's house. The food had been packed up, the dishes cleaned, the tables broken down to be put back in storage and the trash had been removed. His aunt was taking requests on the organ for some of the folks who were too tired to get up and drive home. Dylan was sandwiched between Mackenzie and Hope on the porch swing. Hope was tuckered out from her day; she was leaning against him, eyes closed as they gently swung back and forth on the swing.

"I want to shave my head." Hope spoke after a long stretch of silence.

"What?" Mackenzie leaned forward to look at her daughter. "Why?"

"Because it's falling out anyway..." Hope said. "And, I'm tired of it falling in my food when I'm trying to eat."

"Are you sure?" Mackenzie asked.

Hope nodded. "Yeah...it's time."

Dylan hugged his daughter closer. "I feel like shaving my head, too. You can shave mine at the same time."

Hope perked up. "*Really*? I can?"

"No..." Mackenzie objected.

"Sure...why not?" Dylan ran his hand over his hair. "I need a haircut. That way we can both grow our hair out for the wedding."

Hope had been spending time with Dylan at his beach house. She loved the beach and she loved spending time with him. This switch was hard on Ray and Charlie because they were used to watching Hope, but their lives were changing. In fact—Mackenzie hadn't really discussed it with Ray yet—Dylan wanted them to live in his house after the wedding. She loved Balboa Park and didn't want to leave, but Hope was so happy at the beach. It was hard for her to say no.

"Where is everyone?" Mackenzie took the key out of the door. "Hello?"

She dropped her tote on the kitchen counter. There were two dirty plates on the island, not in the sink. There was a glass on the counter without a coaster. Mackenzie put the dishes and glass in the sink.

"Hello?" She checked in the den next. Maybe Dylan and Hope had gone down to the beach. But when she checked the French doors leading out to the deck, they were still locked. When she didn't find them on the lower floor, she headed up the stairs.

"Dylan! Hope!"

"We're up here!" Dylan shouted from his bathroom on the third floor.

Mackenzie heard her daughter laughing loudly. The higher she climbed, the louder a suspicious buzzing sound became.

"What are the two of you doing in here?" Mackenzie stood in the doorway, horrified.

Dylan was sitting cross-legged on the floor; Hope had a large electric clipper in her hand. Dylan's button-down shirt, his pants and his fancy marble floor were covered with his hair. Hope had used the clippers to buzz a thick, crooked line from his forehead to the back of his neck.

"I'm the barber and this is my client," Hope explained.

"Have you looked at yourself in the mirror?" Mackenzie asked him.

"I'm waiting to be surprised." Dylan winked at her.

"I have no doubt it will be a surprise," she said.

Dylan was blissfully unaware of how horrible his usually perfect hair looked. "Come join us… We've missed you."

"I've missed you…" Mackenzie leaned back against the doorjamb. "You do realize that you've come over to the dark side, right? Do you know how long it's going to take to get all of those little hairs up off the floor?"

"That's why he has a maid," Hope told her as if she said the word *maid* every day and twice on Sundays.

Mackenzie took a step inside the bathroom, arms crossed over her chest. She frowned severely at her fiancé and Hope. "Um…that would be a *no.* Dylan, we're not going to teach her that. When the two of you are done, the two of you are going to clean this up."

"Okay, Mom…"

"Okay, sweetheart…"

Hope proudly buzzed off the right side of Dylan's hair. Mackenzie covered her eyes. "I can't watch this."

Mackenzie left them to their little shaving party, grabbed a glass of wine and went out onto the deck. Her mind drifted back to their first date. She hadn't even considered Dylan date material at that point and now she was engaged to the man. Life had a way of surprising you all the time.

“It feels really cold up there now.” Dylan walked out onto the deck, rubbing his shorn hair. “What do you think? Do you still want to marry me?”

Mackenzie stood up and then reached up so she could rub her hand across his shaved head. “It’s like peach fuzz now…”

“Peach fuzz? And here I was thinking that I looked like a tough guy.”

Mackenzie shook her head and smiled. She hugged him. The fact that he had let Hope shave his head to make their daughter feel more comfortable about shaving her own head touched her. She liked him better with his hair, but she loved him more with his head shaved.

Hope came out on the deck and the three of them went down to the beach for a walk. Mackenzie knew full well that neither of them had bothered to clean up the hair in the bathroom, but she didn’t say so. The truth was, she didn’t want to miss a moment with them tonight. They could always clean tomorrow.

Chapter Sixteen

Several months had passed since the Pegasus gang had moved to Aunt Gerri's farm. Hope was still in remission and her hair had grown back enough to be styled into a cute pixie cut like her cousin Jordan's. Mackenzie was busier than ever between the bakery and the wedding plans. Dylan was an involved groom, which made the planning more fun than a chore. The invitations had been sent and many of her Montana relatives had RSVP'd. Her dad and Jett were coming down from Paradise with her nieces. Hope, Jordan, Josephine, Rayna and Charlie had helped her pick out a beautiful lace fit-and-flare wedding dress with a sweetheart neckline, capped sleeves and crystal embellishments. She had worried that she wouldn't be able to find a gown that would work with her curves, but she had. This dress gave her a perfect hour-glass figure while smoothing out the bulges and bumps. In all of the weeks leading up to the wedding, Mackenzie had been stressed out about the details, but she was never nervous about marrying Dylan. And now that the big day had actually arrived, she was excited to see her family and for Dylan to see her in her dress, but she still wasn't nervous.

The two of them had spent the night at Aunt Gerri's house, while Hope stayed with Rayna and Charlie. Dylan, having an old-fashioned moment, insisted that they sleep in separate rooms so he wouldn't see her before the ceremony. The morning of the wedding, Mackenzie awakened missing him. They had agreed not to move in together until after the wedding, and with their work and Hope, it wasn't always easy to find time to be alone. Mackenzie slipped on her bathrobe and tiptoed down the hallway to Dylan's room. She quietly opened the door and sneaked in. Dylan, as usual, was on top of the sheets, flat on his back. He was bare-chested but had worn pajama bottoms to bed. He was snoring lightly; she wanted her visit to be a surprise and now it would be.

Smiling at her own stealth, Mackenzie sneaked over to the bed.

"Dylan..." she whispered.

Dylan grumbled, stretched and rolled over onto his side. She poked his shoulder.

"Dylan..." This time a little bit more loudly.

Caught off guard and groggy, Dylan opened his eyes. When he realized she was standing by the bed, he smiled at her.

"Hey, baby..." he said sleepily. "What're you doing?"

"Happy wedding day..." She smiled at him.

Dylan yawned loudly while he roughed up his short hair, grown back now from his buzz cut, trying to wake up. He rubbed the sleep out of his eyes, and when the fog started to lift, he realized that this was the morning of the day he was going to marry Mackenzie.

“Hey…” Dylan propped himself up on his elbow. “What are you doing in my room? It’s bad luck for me to see you.”

Mackenzie shook her head. “No…it’s bad luck for you to see me in my wedding dress before the ceremony. I’m not *in* my wedding dress…”

There was a saucy glint in her eyes as she slowly untied the belt on her robe. She opened the robe and let it fall to the floor. The robe was the only thing she had put on to come to Dylan’s room. And now she was standing before him, completely naked.

Dylan’s eyes drank her in. She was such a sexy, beautiful woman. He loved her curvaceous Marilyn Monroe figure: the large natural breasts, the small waist, the flare of her voluptuous hips. He loved her inside and out and he wanted her all the time.

“How do you feel about your luck now?” she asked him seductively.

Dylan didn’t hide the fact that he was admiring every inch of her naked body. “I think I’m the luckiest man alive.”

Mackenzie laughed softly; he held out his hand to her. Her hand in his, and still standing, Dylan leaned over and pressed a kiss on her rounded belly.

“Your body’s changing already.” He rested his free hand on her stomach, over their growing child.

She smiled, nodded and placed her hand over his. “A little. We won’t be able to keep the secret much longer.”

“We’ll tell everyone after the honeymoon.” He swung his legs over the side of the bed, pulled her between his thighs and hugged her close.

His head nestled between her breasts and Mackenzie kissed the top of his head lovingly. They had discovered that she was pregnant soon after Hope was released from the hospital. Once she was past the first trimester, she would feel safe to share the news. But, for now, it was a sweet, private secret that she could share with her husband-to-be.

"How are you feeling?" Dylan knew that Mackenzie had started to have minor bouts with morning sickness.

"I feel great today." She pulled back a little. "I'm marrying you."

His hands began to explore her back, her hips, and the moment took a turn to the sensual. Dylan's mouth was on her breast, sending wonderful tingling to the most sensitive part of her body. She tilted her head back, raked her fingers through his hair and savored his attention unabashedly. This was her man, and there was everything right about their lovemaking.

"Do you want to go for a ride?" Dylan asked her suggestively.

Mackenzie laughed as she always did at his not-so-subtle sexual innuendos. She stripped off his underwear, knelt between his thighs and took him into her mouth. Dylan closed his eyes; he braced himself back on his arms and groaned, long and low. Dylan reached for her, hunger in his eyes.

"Come here…" Dylan lay on his back with a smile; hands behind his head and shaft hard and erect and ready for her pleasure.

Without any pretense, Mackenzie sunk down and took him as deep within her body as she could.

"Oh…" The inside of her body was tight, and wet, and so incredibly warm.

And, then she began to move. Dylan watched her ride him; she was a thing of beauty. Her head was tilted back, her lips parted as she moaned with pleasure. Her breasts, so round and full, with pink nipples moved sensually as she rotated her hips. He could feel her hair, long and loose, brushing his thighs. Dylan felt her start to tense, and he knew instinctively that she was starting to peak. He grabbed onto her hips, thrusting inside her faster and harder.

Mackenzie collapsed forward and tried to stifle the sound of her orgasm in his neck. Her orgasm triggered his and they held on to each other tightly as the waves of ecstasy crashed over their bodies. Dylan rolled her over onto her back and smiled down at her.

"God, I love you…"

She reached up to touch his face. "I love you, too, Dylan. More than I can say."

She had laid in his arms until she heard cars, *plural*, heading up the driveway. She had peeked out the blinds to discover a caravan of cars heading their way. It looked like the Montana Brands had arrived, along with the makeup artist, and *she* was still naked, post coitus, in her fiancé's bed! She quickly put her robe back on, and after a lengthy goodbye kiss, she sneaked back to her own bedroom.

"Hey, Mackenzie!" Jordan banged on her door. "We're here. Open up!"

Mackenzie had taken a shower to rinse off the evidence of their lovemaking and now she was back in her robe. She opened the door and Jordan reached out, grabbed her wrist and dragged her down the stairs.

"Come *on*!" Jordan wouldn't let go of her hand. "Dylan's aunt wants us to use the sitting room downstairs to get ready. We can close it off completely and that way the groom can't sneak a peek before you say *I do*!"

Laughing now, Mackenzie was whisked into the sitting room and the doors were closed behind her. Thanks to Ian's connections, a celebrity hairstylist and makeup artist would be on the scene later to do her hair. Her cousin

Josephine Brand was unzipping the garment bag holding her violet bridesmaid dress. Stylish, classic Josephine had helped her with every detail of the wedding, from dresses to tent rentals and everything in between.

Josephine stopped what she was doing and ran over to give her a hug. "Mackenzie! Have you seen the ceremony setup? It's gorgeous!"

Josephine was Jordan's twin, but when they stood side by side, it wasn't easy to know that. Jordan wore her hair short and switched colors every other month, while Josephine wore her hair long and wavy and naturally golden-brown.

Now that her relatives had arrived, the quiet of the farmhouse was shattered. In the hallway, Mackenzie could hear Aunt Gerri greeting her family in from Montana. She heard footsteps coming down the creaky wooden stairs, and then heard Dylan introducing himself to her family. The front door opened and the male voices disappeared. With flare, Barbara Brand slid the doors open wide and joined them in the sitting room.

"Oh, Mackenzie!" Her aunt Barb's arms were extended toward her for a hug. "I'm so happy that we're here to see you get married!"

She had always had a special connection with Jordan and Josephine's mom. Aunt Barb never forgot her on special holidays, sending her special little gifts. Many of the hearts in her heart collection had been sent to her by Aunt Barb.

Mackenzie hugged her aunt so tightly. She was the closest thing to a mom she had today, and she was so happy that they had made the trip all the way from their ranch in Montana to attend.

Barbara, very chic and trim, her platinum hair slicked back into her trademark chignon, smiled lovingly at her niece. She pulled a small box out of her Hermès bag. "Your uncle and I want you to have this… Your grandmother wore this on her wedding day…"

Mackenzie opened the aged, blue velvet box. Inside was a perfect string of antique pearls. She had seen these very pearls in a picture of her grandmother on her wedding day.

"Oh, Aunt Barb…they're beautiful. Thank you."

Her aunt helped her put on the pearls. "You're beautiful. They suit you."

Her cousins gathered around to admire the necklace, complimenting her and assuring her that it was going to go beautifully with her gown. Aunt Gerri came in with a plate of food, and then they started to prepare her for the wedding in earnest. She watched from her chair as trucks pulled up with chairs, tables and food. Her makeup was professionally applied; her hair was swept up away from her face with long, loose curls down her back. Dylan was going to love her hair this way.

She had never been fussed over so much before, but it wasn't half-bad. It was actually kind of fun and the end result would make Dylan a very happy man. Rayna, who was going to perform the ceremony, arrived with Charlie and Hope. Hope bounced into the room excitedly and hugged her mom right away.

"Look what Dad gave me!" Hope held out her hand and showed Mackenzie a ring with a small heart-shaped amethyst in the center.

"It's beautiful, just like you…" Mackenzie hugged her daughter hard. "Jordan's going to help you get ready, okay?"

There was so much commotion in the room, especially after Rayna and Charlie arrived, that no one noticed that she hadn't touched her champagne. They laughed and they talked and they reminisced and they all got gussied up in their beautiful dresses. Hope's flower-girl dress was lace with a satin sash and lavender flower embellishments; she was beaming because she was allowed to have a hint of makeup applied. When they were all dressed, Josephine, Jordan and Charlie looked gorgeous in tea-length lavender chiffon dresses, strapless with sweetheart necklines. The women in her life gathered around her and helped her put on her wedding dress.

She worried that her tiny baby bump would make the dress too tight around the waist, but it was a perfect fit.

"Oh, my goodness, you're so special..." Aunt Gerri admired her. "You're the best thing that happened to Dylan, Mackenzie, and I love you. I hope the two of you will have fifty years together like Bill and I did..."

The ceremony was set to start in less than thirty minutes. Mackenzie was filled with nervous excitement and she couldn't wait to see Dylan. She stood in front of the full-length mirror that had been brought especially for her, and she couldn't believe that the attractive woman in the reflection was actually *her*. Her dress, her hair, her makeup...the pearl necklace...made such a pretty picture. She was a bride. She was Dylan's bride.

Barbara slid open the pocket doors leading out to the foyer. Hank Brand, her uncle and her mother's older brother, was talking with Aunt Gerri in the foyer.

Uncle Hank was lanky and tall; he had thick silver hair and deep-set blue eyes. He owned and operated Bent Tree Cattle Ranch in Montana and had done for as long as she could remember. He was wearing a navy blue suit, and his cowboy hat was in his hand, cowboy boots on his feet.

"You look just like Hope did when you were her age..." Hank studied her face seriously. He was a hard man, a tough man, but there was always a kindness beneath his weathered exterior. Hank had been very close with her mother, and she could tell that it still stung, all these years later, that his baby sister had died.

As the time for the ceremony to start approached, and the majority of the guests had arrived and been seated by the old oak tree, Mackenzie went back into the drawing room so Dylan wouldn't see her before the ceremony. Alone in the room, Mackenzie put her hand on her stomach and closed her eyes. She needed to harness her roiling emotions; she could feel tears of joy and anticipation and relief gathering behind her eyes.

"You are not going to ruin your makeup!" Mackenzie whispered to herself sternly.

The door to the sitting room slid open and her father poked his head in. "I've been playing heck to find you! This place is like a maze."

"Dad!" Relieved to see him, Mackenzie threw herself into her father's big, burly arms. "Oh, my goodness! You *shaved*?"

Jim Bronson was a hefty, barrel-chested man who had worn a thick unruly beard since he had retired from the auto industry. She hadn't seen the lower half of her father's face for over a decade.

Jim smiled self-consciously as he touched his fleshy, freshly shaven face. "I have more chins now than I'd like to know about, but I wanted to look nice for your pictures."

"Thank you, Dad..."

"Now, I know I'm a handsome devil like this..." Jim said with a spark of humor in his deeply set brown eyes. "But don't go getting all attached. I start growing my beard back tonight."

Mackenzie laughed; she touched a couple of nicks on his chin. The lower half of his face was whiter than the part of his face that had always been exposed to the sunlight. "That's okay…I don't think you're all that good at shaving."

Jim captured her hand, kissed it, then stepped back and twirled her under his arm just the way he had when she was a little girl.

"You look like your mom on our wedding day." Jim's expression was more serious now, his eyes watery. Mackenzie hadn't seen her father this close to tears since her mother's funeral.

Mackenzie hugged her father again, careful not to get makeup on his white tuxedo shirt. Jim accepted the hug and then, as he always did, changed the mood from serious to joking. He stepped back and twisted from side to side.

"I'm hurt that you didn't even bother to mention my getup." Jim raised his arms to show off his black tuxedo. "Do you think it's easy to find a monkey suit in extra-big and not-so-tall?"

The door slid open and Josephine poked her head into the room. "Dylan's about to take his place and then you'll come out."

Jim looked down at his daughter proudly. He offered his arm to her and asked, "Ready?"

Mackenzie accepted her father's arm. "Absolutely."

Dylan looked out of his boyhood bedroom window at all the people taking their seats. He would be a married man soon, and he'd been looking forward to this day for months.

"Can you believe I'm taking the plunge before you?" Dylan asked Ian, his best friend and best man.

Ian was sitting in a chair next to the bed. "I didn't see this one coming…"

Dylan smiled. "Do you have the rings?"

"Right here in my pocket."

Mackenzie had wanted a small intimate ceremony and

she had wanted simple, classic gold bands. He would have preferred rings that were a little more ornate, but in the end, he just wanted her to be happy.

Dylan saw Rayna take her position beneath the oak tree, and heard his aunt start to play the organ. As they had rehearsed, that was his signal to come down for the ceremony.

"They're ready for us..."

"Showtime..." Dylan stood up, shrugged on his jacket and headed down the stairs.

Once outside, Dylan walked down the aisle and took his position next to Rayna, who smiled warmly at him. He was glad that he had Ian to stand with him. Most of the guests were Mackenzie's family from Montana. He, on the other hand, didn't have much family. He had half brothers and half sisters from his father's side that he'd never met. All he really had was Aunt Gerri and Ian. But, after today, he had a whole new family; and most important, he would have Mackenzie and Hope. The organ had been moved outside for the ceremony, and when his aunt began to play the classic wedding march, he knew his moment to finally marry Mackenzie had arrived. A hush fell over the guests, and Dylan actually felt his knees buckle.

First, he saw his beautiful Hope walking down the aisle toward him throwing petals. Over the last months, she had bounced back from her bout in the hospital. Her pixie-cut hairstyle fit her round, freckled face perfectly. And she looked so pretty in her lace dress and lavender sash. Down the aisle came Charlie, the matron of honor, and then Jordan and her twin sister, Josephine. And then finally, finally, he saw Mackenzie and her dad poised to come down the aisle toward him. He was awestruck by the beauty of his bride. He always thought she was pretty, but today, in that dress, she was an angel in white lace. The crystals on her veil sparkled in the late-morning sunlight as she walked slowly toward him carrying a bouquet of purple orchids. Through the delicate fabric of the veil, Dylan met her eyes. And, for a split second, they were the only two people in the world.

"Who gives this woman to this man?"

"I do," Jim Bronson bellowed. Mackenzie pressed her lips together for a moment so she wouldn't laugh out loud at the sound her father's booming voice disrupting the otherwise serene, tranquil setting.

Jim lifted the veil off his daughter's face and kissed her lightly on the cheek. To Dylan he said roughly, "Take good care of her."

"I will, sir. I love her." Dylan shook her father's hand and then reached out for hers.

"You are beautiful…" Dylan said to his bride.

Mackenzie's eyes were full of love for him. "I love you…"

Beneath that sprawling oak tree, and before a small group of their close family and friends, Dylan and Mackenzie exchanged their vows. The ceremony was simple and quiet and traditional, as were their vows to each other.

Rayna performed her duties admirably, but there were a couple of moments when she needed to calm her own emotions; she was so happy that her dear friend had finally met her match. Mackenzie handed her bouquet to Hope, and Ian handed the rings to Dylan. With their wedding bands securely in place, hands clasped together, Rayna said the words they had been waiting to hear.

"By the power vested in me, I now pronounce you man and wife. Dylan, you may kiss your beautiful bride…"

They leaned in to each other.

"I told them no lipstick so you can kiss me for real," his wife whispered to him.

And he did kiss her for real. He took her in his arms and kissed her on the lips, and then he hugged her so tightly that he let her know that he never wanted to let her go.

"Ladies and gentlemen, Dylan and Mackenzie Axel!"

Mackenzie took Hope's hand and the three of them walked up the aisle, as a family, while the crowd cheered for them. It had been a perfect ceremony, on a perfect California day, and Mackenzie believed to her core that this was the start of a long and successful marriage. They held the reception in a large tent beside the house. There was dancing and eating and drinking and pictures being taken. Mackenzie couldn't remember a day when she had laughed so much.

"Are you having a good time?" Dylan had just danced with Hope and now he was back in her arms.

"This is the best day of my life..." She laughed as he dipped her over his arm.

"It's almost time for us to leave for the honeymoon, you know..."

"I know." Mackenzie frowned at him playfully. "Why won't you tell me where we're going?"

"It's a surprise." Dylan twirled her around to make her laugh again. "But I'll give you a hint...it's warm, it's an island and we are taking the private company jet."

"Sounds like heaven..." Mackenzie said. "But anywhere is heaven when I'm with you."

Finally, Dylan had to pull her away from her friends and family. They did have a flight to catch. Mackenzie was having such a blast that she hated to leave, but she knew it was time. Her last duty as the bride was to throw the bouquet. All of the single women bunched together and Mackenzie counted, "one, two, three..." and tossed the bouquet over her shoulder.

Without trying very hard to catch it, the bouquet landed in Josephine's hands. Surprised, she looked over at her longtime boyfriend, Brice, whose expression didn't change when he saw her catch the bouquet.

"Josephine...you're next!" Mackenzie said.

"We'll see..." Josephine lifted the flowers up for Brice to see before she brought them to her nose to catch the sweet scent of the purple orchids.

After Josephine caught the bouquet, Mackenzie and Dylan hugged and kissed Hope goodbye with a promise to bring her something back from their honeymoon. They climbed into the backseat of Ian's chauffeured Bentley, rolled down the window and waved to their friends and family who had gathered in the driveway. Aunt Gerri came up to the car and kissed both of them.

"I love you both..." Her eyes were damp with unshed tears.

"Thank you, Aunt Gerri...for today...for everything," Dylan said.

To Dylan she said, "Bill always kissed me good-night and told me that he loved me. You do that for Mackenzie and you'll have fifty years like we did."

Gerri had the last word before the window was rolled up and the car drove away. Mackenzie waved through the tinted back window of the car until the house was out of sight. Dylan draped his arm around her shoulders and pulled her into his body.

"Are you happy?" he asked her.

"So happy..." She leaned her head back on his shoulder.

She was Dylan's wife now; he was her husband. They had a daughter and another child on the way. Mackenzie turned in his arms so she could kiss her husband. Dylan kissed her sweetly, gently, his hand on her face.

"Have I told you lately that I love you?" His eyes locked with hers.

"Yes…" she said. "But tell me again."

* * * * *

A PROPOSAL WORTH MILLIONS

SOPHIE PEMBROKE

For Pete and Kate,
for a truly wonderful, memorable holiday.

CHAPTER ONE

SADIE SULLIVAN BLINKED into the sunshine and waved goodbye to the rental car pulling away from the Azure Hotel. If she squinted, she could just make out Finn's tiny face pressed up against the rear window, and his little hand waving back. Her father, in the driver's seat, was obviously concentrating on the road, but Sadie spotted the glint of her mother's ash-blonde hair beside Finn, and knew she'd be holding him in place, making sure his seat belt was secure.

He was in good hands. She had to remember that. Even if her heart ached at the thought of being separated from her little boy.

The car turned the last corner at the end of the drive and disappeared out of sight, behind the row of juniper trees, onto the road that led up the coast then back inland towards the main roads and Izmir airport. Sadie sucked in a deep breath and wiped the back of her hand across her eyes, quickly, in case anyone was watching. The last thing she needed right now was talk about the boss breaking down in tears. Professionalism, that was the key.

'It's one week, Sullivan,' she muttered to herself. 'Get over yourself. In seven days you'll be in England with him, getting ready to bring him back. Enjoy the peace until then.'

Except next time it might be for longer. A whole term, even. And what if he didn't want to come home to her in the holidays? No, she wasn't thinking about that. Whatever her father said about British schools, about having family around, Finn's place was with her. The local schools were great, and Finn's Turkish was really coming along. He'd be fine.

She swallowed, and stepped back into the coolness of the Azure lobby. Even in late September Kuşadasi still enjoyed the warmth of the Turkish climate. In a few weeks, she knew, the locals would start pulling on sweaters and mumbling about the chill in the air—while she, and the few remaining tourists in town at the end of the season, would still be down at the beach, enjoying the sun.

This time next year Finn would have started school. The only question left to answer definitively was, where?

'Did Finn and your parents leave for the airport okay?' Esma asked, looking up from the reception desk, her long red nails still resting on her keyboard.

Sadie nodded, not trusting herself to speak just yet.

'He's so excited about having a holiday with his grandparents,' Sadie's second in command carried on, regardless. 'And the timing is just perfect, too.'

Sadie kept nodding. Then she blinked. 'It is?'

Esma tilted her head to study her, and Sadie tried to pull herself into her best boss posture and expression. She had the suit, the hair, the make-up—all the things she usually hid behind when she didn't quite know what to do. That armour had got her through her husband's death, through taking on his ridiculously ambitious business project that she didn't have the first clue about. Why on earth would it fail her now, at the prospect of a mere week without her son?

It obviously worked, because Esma shrugged and pushed the work diary across the reception desk towards her.

'I just meant with that potential investor arriving this week. Without Finn to worry about, you will have more time to spend winning him over, yes?'

'Yes, of course,' Sadie responded automatically, her eyes fixed on the red letters spelling 'Investor Visit' written across the next five days. How could she have forgotten?

Her priority for the week. The only thing she had time to worry about, at all, was this investor and all his lovely money.

She hadn't wanted to resort to outside help, but things were getting beyond desperate, even if only she and Neal knew the true extent of the Azure's problems. When their hunt for local investors had failed, Neal had suggested seeking investment from abroad—with similar results. But he'd had a last-chance possibility at the ready when she'd asked where on earth they went next. A business acquaintance, he'd said, who had interests in the hotel industry, and might just be interested enough to send an employee over to check out the Azure.

Sadie had been doubtful, but she was also running out of options. She trusted Neal—he was more than her accountant, he had been one of her late husband Adem's best friends. And she had no doubt that Neal would have asked his acquaintance to go easy on her. Everyone always did.

She's a widow. They always shook their head sadly as they said the word 'widow'. *Lost her husband in a car crash, tragically young.*

These days, that was often the only thing people knew about her at all. Well, that and the fact that she was saddled with a white elephant of a hotel renovation that might never be finished at the rate things were going.

Sadie was almost sure there used to be more to know about her once.

Behind the reception desk Esma's eyes were wide and worried, so Sadie reinforced her 'in control of everything' smile. She had to shake off the negativity. She loved the Azure, just like Adem had, and just like Finn did. It was her home, and she would make it a success—one way or another.

She'd made promises. Commitments. And she had every intention of fulfilling them.

She just might have to accept a little help along the way.

'Did Neal call with the name of the guy the company is sending over yet?' Sadie asked. 'And we have a car collecting him from the airport, correct?'

'Yes, at four o'clock,' Esma confirmed. 'I sent Alim.'

'Good.' Alim was reliable, and his English was great—far better than her Turkish, even after four years of living in the country and working hard to learn. Finn was a much quicker study than her, it turned out.

And just like that, she'd forgotten all her business worries again and was back to fretting about her son. Part of being a mother, she supposed.

She checked her watch. It was already gone five.

'Has Alim texted to say they're on their way?' Sadie asked.

'Almost an hour ago. They should be here any moment.' Esma bit her lip. 'It will all be fine, Sadie,' she added after a moment. But it sounded more like a question than reassurance.

Sadie smiled broadly. 'Of course it will! I'm certain of it,' she lied. Then something occurred to her. Esma had only answered half her question. 'And the name?' she pressed. 'Neal gave it to you, yes?' How embarrassing would it be to greet this guy with no idea what to call him?

Behind the desk, Esma squirmed, shuffling an irrelevant stack of papers between her hands, her gaze fixed firmly on her nails. Something heavy settled in Sadie's stomach at the sight. Something heavier even than her guilt about Finn being away all week. Something more like the magnitude of the fears and nightmares that kept her awake at night, wondering how on earth she would achieve everything she'd promised her husband and son.

'Esma? What's his name?'

Her face pale, Esma finally looked up to meet Sadie's gaze. 'Neal said it might be better if you…' She trailed off.

'If I what?' Sadie asked. 'Didn't know the name of the person who might hold the future of this place in his hands? Why on earth would he—? Unless…'

Behind her, she heard the swoosh of the automatic doors and the clunk of a heavy suitcase on the marble floors. Her heart beat in double time, and that heavy feeling spread up through her chest, constricting her breathing and threatening her poor, laboured heart.

Sadie turned, and suddenly it was thirteen years ago. She could almost sense Adem beside her—younger, more nervous, but alive—hopping from foot to foot as he introduced his new girlfriend to his two best friends. Neal Stephens and Dylan Jacobs.

Except Adem was dead, Neal was in England—where she couldn't yell at him yet—and only Dylan stood in the lobby of her hotel. Dylan, who was supposed to be thousands of miles away in Australia, where he belonged. Instead, he was at the Azure, as self-assured and cocky as ever. And every inch as handsome.

No wonder Neal hadn't told her. She'd have been on

the first flight out with Finn, and he knew it. He might not know everything, but Neal had to at least have noticed that she'd made a concerted effort *not* to see Dylan since the funeral.

But now she couldn't run. She had commitments to keep—and she needed Dylan Jacobs of all people to help her do that.

Sadie plastered on a smile, stepped forward, and held out a hand that only shook a bit.

'Dylan! How wonderful to see you again,' she said, and prayed it didn't sound like the lie it was.

Dylan's chest tightened automatically at the sight of her. An hour's drive from the airport and hours on the plane before that, and he still wasn't ready. In fact, as he stepped forward to take Sadie's hand he realised he might never be ready. Not for this.

Five minutes ago he'd been moments away from calling the whole visit off. Sitting in the car, as they'd come up the long, winding hotel driveway, he'd almost told the driver to turn around and take him back to the airport. That the whole trip was a mistake.

But Dylan Jacobs never shied away from an opportunity. And, besides, it was Sadie. So instead he'd checked his phone again—emails first, then messages, then voicemails then other alerts—his habitual order. Anything to distract him from thinking about Sadie.

He hadn't seen her in two years. Two long years since the funeral. Hadn't even heard a peep from her—let alone a response to his card, telling her to call, if she ever needed anything.

And now, apparently, she needed everything and she was calling in that promise.

He just wished she'd done it in person, instead of via

Neal. Wished he could have spoken to her, heard her voice, sensed her mood.

Wished he had a better idea what he was walking into here.

She's coping, Neal had said. *Better than a lot of people would. But...she lost Adem, Dyl. Of course she's not the same. And she needs you. The Azure is all she has left of her husband, and you can help her save it.*

So in a rapid flurry of emails Dylan had been booked on the next plane into Izmir and now there he was. At Adem's dream hotel. With Adem's dream woman.

Glancing at the sign above the hotel doors, Dylan had winced at the name. The Azure. Why did it have to be that name? There were a hundred perfectly decent generic hotel names on offer. Why on earth had Adem picked that one?

A half-forgotten memory had flashed through his brain. Adem's excited phone call, telling him all about his next big project, how he and Sadie were moving to Turkey to save some ramshackle old hotel that had once belonged to his Turkish mother's grandfather or something. What he remembered most was the sharp sting that had hit his chest at the name—and the utter irrationality of it.

It's just a name. It doesn't mean anything, he'd reminded himself.

But symbolism was a bitch, and to Dylan the Azure would always mean loss. The loss of his father, his freedom, so many years ago. Loss of hope. Lost chances and opportunities.

Except maybe, just maybe, this time it could be different. So much had changed... And this was a different hotel, thousands of miles and more than two decades away from the Azure where the man who had raised him had walked out on his entire family and never looked back.

This was Sadie's hotel now.

He'd never told Adem the whole story of his father, and had certainly never mentioned the name of the hotel. If he had, his friend would probably have changed it, just to make Dylan feel more comfortable. That was the sort of man Adem had been, the good, caring, thoughtful sort.

The sort of man who had deserved the love of a woman like Sadie.

Unbidden, images of the last time he'd seen her had filled Dylan's vision. Dressed all in black, instead of the bright colours she'd always loved, standing beside that coffin in a cold, rainy, English graveyard. She'd been gripping her tiny son's hand, he remembered, and he'd known instinctively that if she'd had her way Finn wouldn't have been there, wouldn't have had to witness any of it. He'd wondered who had insisted he take part, and how lost Sadie must have been to let them win.

Lost. That was the right word for it. She'd looked small and tired and sad...but most of all she'd looked lost. As if without Adem she'd had no compass any more, no path.

It had broken Dylan's heart to see her that way. But standing outside her hotel...he had just wondered who she would be now.

And then it was time to find out.

Heart racing, he climbed the steps to the hotel entrance and let the automatic doors sweep back to allow him in. He squinted in the relative cool darkness of the lobby, compared to the bright sunlight outside. But when his vision cleared the first thing he saw was Sadie—standing at the reception desk, her back turned to him so he couldn't make out her face. But there was never any doubt in his mind that it was her, despite the plain grey suit and shorter hair.

So many memories were buttoned up in that suit—of the friend he'd lost and the woman he'd never even had a chance with—that his chest tightened just at the sight of her.

He braced himself as she turned, but it wasn't enough. Nowhere near enough to prepare him for the shock and horror that flashed across her familiar face, before she threw up a pleasant, smiling mask to cover it.

She didn't know I was coming. Oh, he was going to *kill* Neal. Painfully, and probably slowly.

Reflex carried him through the moment, the old defences leaping back into place as she smiled and held out her hand. Her hand. Like they really were new business acquaintances, instead of old friends.

'Dylan! How wonderful to see you again,' she said, still smiling through the obvious lie. And Dylan wished that, for once, he'd ignored the opportunity and headed back to the airport like his gut had told him to.

But it was too late now.

Ignoring the sting of her lie, Dylan took her cool fingers between his own, tugging her closer until he could wrap his other arm around her slim waist, his fingers sliding up from hers to circle her wrist and keep her close. Just the touch of her sent his senses into overdrive, and he swallowed hard before speaking.

'It's so good to see you, Sadie.' And that, at least, was the truth. Dylan could feel his world move back into balance at the sight of her and the feel of her in his arms… well, it just told him what he'd known for years. That the feelings for his best friend's girl he'd tried so hard to bury had never been hidden all that deep at all.

He really was going to kill Neal for this.

Sadie pulled back, still smiling, apparently unaware of how his world had just shifted alignment again, the same way it had thirteen years ago when Adem had said, 'Dyl, this is Sadie. She's…special,' and Sadie's cheeks had turned pink as she'd smiled.

A real smile, that had been. Not at all like the one she gave him now.

'Let's get you checked in,' Sadie said, and Dylan nodded.

Even though he knew the most sensible thing to do would be to run, as far and as fast as he could, away from the Azure Hotel.

Maybe his dad had had the right idea after all.

Sadie's hands shook as she climbed the stairs to her tiny office—the one that used to be Adem's—and reached for the door handle. Instinctively, she checked back over her shoulder to make sure Dylan hadn't followed her. But, no, the stairs were clear and she was alone at last, and able to process what had already been a difficult day.

Hopefully by now Dylan would be happily ensconced in the best suite the Azure had to offer—which was probably still nowhere near the standard he was used to. He hadn't let her escape without making her promise to meet him for dinner, though. Of course, she'd said yes—she was hardly in a position to say no, now, was she? She just hoped he had no idea how much she'd wanted to.

Stepping into her office, she slumped into her desk chair and reached for the phone, her fingers still trembling. Dialling the familiar number, she let it ring, waiting for Neal to pick up. He'd be there, she was sure, waiting by the phone. After all, he had to know she'd be calling.

'I'm sorry,' Neal said, the moment he answered.

'So you bloody well should be. What were you thinking? Why didn't you tell me? Never mind, I think I know.' Which didn't make her any happier about the subterfuge. Not one bit.

'You'd have said no,' Neal explained anyway. 'But, Sadie, he really wants to help. And you need him.'

'I *don't* need a pity save.' Sadie could feel the heat of her anger rising again and let it come. Neal deserved it. 'I'm not some bank that's too big to fail. I don't need Dylan Jacobs to sweep in and—'

'Yes,' Neal said, calm but firm. 'You do. And you know it.'

Yes, she did. But she wished that wasn't true.

'Why did it have to be him, though?' she whined.

'Who else do we know with millions of pounds, a tendency to jump at random opportunities and a soft spot for your family?' Neal teased lightly.

'True.' Didn't mean she had to like it, though. Although Neal was right about the jumping-at-opportunities thing. Dylan was the ultimate opportunist and once he'd jumped it was never long before he was ready to move on to the next big thing. This wasn't a long-term project for him, Sadie realised. This was Dylan swooping in just long enough to give her a hand, then he'd be moving on. She needed to remember that.

'Is this really a problem?' Neal asked. 'I mean, I knew your pride would be a bit bent out of shape, but you told me you wanted to save the Azure, come hell or high water.'

She had said that. 'Which is this, exactly?'

There was a pause on the other end of the line, and Sadie began to regret the joke. The last thing she needed on top of Dylan Jacobs in her hotel was Neal showing up to find out what was going on.

'Why does he bother you so much?' He sounded honestly curious, like he was trying to riddle out the mystery of Sadie and Dylan. The same way Neal always approached everything—like a puzzle to be solved. It was one of the things Sadie liked most about him. He'd taken the problem of her failing hotel and had started looking for answers, rather than pointing out things she'd done wrong. 'It can't be that he reminds you of Adem too much or you'd have kicked me to the kerb after the funeral, too. So what is it?'

Sadie sighed. There was just no way to explain this that Neal would ever understand. His riddle would have to go unsolved. 'I don't know. We just...we never really managed to see eye to eye. On anything.'

Except for that one night, when they'd seen each other far too clearly. When she'd finally realised the threat that Dylan Jacobs had posed to her carefully ordered and settled life.

The threat of possibility.

'He's a good man,' Neal told her. 'He really does want to help.'

'I know.' That was the worst part. Dylan wasn't here to cause trouble, or make her life difficult, or unhappy. She knew him well enough to be sure of that. He was there to help, probably out of some misguided sense of obligation to a man who was already two years dead, and the friendship they'd shared. She could respect that. 'And I need him. I should have called him myself.' She thought of the sympathy card sitting with a few others in a drawer in her bedroom. The one with a single lily on the front and stark, slashing black handwriting inside.

I'm so sorry, Sadie. Whatever you need, call me.
Any time.
D x.

She hadn't, obviously.

'So we're okay?' Neal asked.

'Yeah, Neal. We're fine.' It was only her own sanity she was worried about. 'I'll call you later in the week, let you know how things go.'

'Okay.' Neal still sounded uncertain, but he hung up anyway when she said goodbye.

Sadie leant back in her chair, tipping her head to stare at the ceiling. All she needed to do was find a way to work with Dylan until he moved on to the next big thing—and from past experience that wouldn't take long. Jobs, businesses, women—none of them had ever outlasted his short boredom threshold. Why would the Azure be any different? The only thing Sadie had ever known to be constant in Dylan's life was his friendship with Adem and Neal. That was all this was about—a feeling of obligation to his friend, and the wife and child he'd left behind. She didn't need him, she needed his money and his business.

A niggle of guilt wriggled in her middle at the realisation that she was basically using her husband's best friend for his money, milking his own sense of loss at Adem's death. But if it was the only way to save the Azure…

She'd convince him that the Azure was worth saving, and he'd stump up the money out of obligation.

Then they could both move on.

CHAPTER TWO

DYLAN WAITED A while before calling Neal to yell at him. After all, he figured he owed Sadie a fair crack at their mutual friend first.

In the meantime, the wait gave him the opportunity to settle into his suite, his frequent flyer business traveller mind assessing the space the way he always did in a new hotel room. Bed: king-size—always a good start. The linens were crisp and white, and part of his weary brain and body wanted to curl up in them right away and sleep until dinner. But he was there to do a job, and that job required him to be awake, so he pushed on.

The room itself was a good size, but Dylan figured this was probably the biggest the hotel had, so he'd have to explore some of the smaller, ordinary rooms before making a judgement on room size. Wandering through to the bathroom, he clocked fluffy towels, good tiling and lighting, and a shower he very much looked forward to trying out later. If that shower head was as effective as it looked, and the water pressure as good as Dylan hoped, his aching muscles would appreciate the pummelling before bed.

Back in the main room, Dylan ran his fingers across the small table and chairs by the window in the bedroom then strolled into the lounge area through the open arch of a doorway. Again, the size was good, the sofas looked comfy enough, and the coffee table was stacked with magazines and brochures detailing things to do in the area. He flicked through them quickly before deciding the mini-bar and desk were far more interesting.

Crouching down, he yanked open the fridge door and nodded his approval. A decently stocked mini-bar—even if he never used it—was a must in Dylan's book. Then he dropped into the swivel chair by the desk, tugged his phone from his pocket and checked for the complementary WiFi the girl at the desk had assured him was part of his room package. To his amazement, it worked first time and with minimal fuss over the password.

He smiled to himself. He shouldn't be so surprised. After all, this was Adem's place, for all that Sadie was running it now. And Adem had always been vocal about the individual's right to easy-access WiFi at all times and in all places. Something else he and Dylan had always agreed on.

Twirling around in his chair, Dylan split his attention between checking his mail again and surveying the room as a whole—and spotted something he hadn't noticed before. Getting to his feet, he crossed the room, pulled aside the curtains and stepped out onto the suite's small balcony.

Now this was worth travelling all those miles for. Breathing in deeply, Dylan savoured the warm sun on his face and forearms, and stared out. He could see now why Adem had been so evangelical about the place, right from the start, quite apart from his family connection to the hotel.

The view was magnificent. Down below, the Aegean Sea lapped against the rocks, bright and blue and entrancing, sending up puffs of white spray with every wave. Above the rocks, scrubby bushes and juniper trees twisted up towards the clear azure sky, all the way up the peak where the hotel sat. Overhead, a bird called out as it passed, and Dylan thought for the first time all year, since he spent the holidays with his sister and her family, that he might actually be able to just switch off and enjoy the moment.

Except he still had to deal with Sadie—and find out how bad things at the Azure really were for Neal to have sent him here when she so obviously didn't want his help.

Eventually, he figured enough time had passed that even Sadie would have finished yelling at the hapless accountant and, leaving the sunny warmth of the balcony behind him, Dylan headed back inside to sit at the desk and call Neal.

After just a couple of rings Neal answered the phone with a sigh.

'You can't possibly be surprised by this call,' Dylan pointed out.

'I know, I know.' Neal sounded stressed, in a way Dylan wasn't used to hearing from his old friend. That alone put his nerves on high alert. 'Trust me, I've already heard it all from her.'

Her. Sadie. The memory of her expression, the shock and horror that had flashed across her face at the first sight of him, rankled all over again.

'I bet you have,' Dylan said. 'So? Is she going to kick me out on my ear or let me help?' It wasn't what he'd expected to ask—he'd expected there to be a lot more yelling first, apart from anything else. But now he had Neal on the phone it seemed like the only thing that really mattered.

'She'll let you help.'

'Because she's desperate.'

'Pretty much.'

'Great.' Dylan put as much sarcasm as he could muster into the word. 'I just love being a last resort.'

Neal let out another, world-weary sigh. 'You know Sadie, Dyl. She's proud. And she thinks it's her responsibility to fulfil Adem's dreams all on her own.'

'She let *you* help.' Which, Dylan had to admit, still irked him a bit.

'Yeah, but I'm less smug than you.'

Smug? 'I'm not—'

'Yes. Yes, you are. And you need not to be this week, okay?' Neal wasn't joking any more, Dylan could tell. And that worried him more than anything else that had happened that day.

But, to be honest, being too smug and alienating Sadie wasn't really what Dylan was concerned about. He was far more worried about being obvious than smug. Worried that Sadie still thought she knew more about his feelings than she could reasonably expect to after so many years—and might refuse to let him help because of it.

'Things are that bad here?' he asked.

Neal huffed impatiently, a far more familiar sound than his concern. 'Didn't you read the info I sent over?'

'Of course I did.' Well, he'd scanned through it on the plane, which was practically the same thing. It wasn't that Dylan wasn't interested in the stats for the Azure Hotel, it was just that he had a lot of other projects on his plate, plus new opportunities coming in. Besides… he hadn't really been able to imagine any of it until he was actually here.

'She needs more than your money, Dyl. She needs your business brain.'

And, okay, yes, it was bad timing, but it wasn't really

his fault that his brain's automatic response to a comment like that was a feeling of smug pride, right? 'Doesn't everyone?'

'Okay, that? That's exactly what I don't want you to do this week.'

The puff of pride disintegrated as fast as it had appeared. 'Fine. So I'm here in a business advisor capacity only?'

'No, she needs your money, too,' Neal said. 'She's insanely committed to Adem's dream of making the Azure a successful hotel. Doesn't matter that he's not there to see it—she's going to make it happen anyway.'

Only Sadie. Other people walked out on commitments every day—families, marriages, financial and business obligations—and never looked back. Only Sadie would remain committed to a dead man's schemes. And only because she had loved Adem so much.

Dylan sighed. 'That's not going to be easy.' He knew that much from the information Neal had sent him—and the fact Sadie had agreed to let him help at all. If she'd thought she could do it herself, she would have. Sadie was nothing if not bloody-minded and determined.

'Probably not,' Neal allowed. 'But it might save Adem's dream. And Sadie.'

And so, of course, he would do it, without question. He just hoped no one ever pressed him to say exactly which of those motivations was strongest for him.

'I'm having dinner with her tonight.' He tugged a sheet of writing paper branded with the Azure logo closer to him and grabbed a pen. 'Where do I start?'

'She needs this to be business,' Neal said. 'Not a pity save, even if that's what it is.'

It was more than that, Dylan knew. This wasn't just pity. He couldn't bear to see Sadie struggling, so he'd do whatever it took to save her. He suspected that Neal knew that too.

'So how do I convince her it's not?'

'By letting her pitch the Azure and Kuşadasi to you as a real investment opportunity. As something you'd want to put money into even if she wasn't involved. Let her present her proposal for the place, then decide if you will invest.'

Suddenly, a plan began to form, right at the back of Dylan's brain, where he always got his most inspired ideas.

'I can do that,' he said, and smiled.

Standing in front of her wardrobe, Sadie shifted her weight from one foot to the other, squinted, then sighed and gave up. Nothing she could do right now changed the clothes hanging there for her to choose from. If Neal had told her Dylan was coming, she'd have had time to go shopping. Not that she would have done. The last thing she wanted to do was give Dylan Jacobs the impression that his presence was new-clothes-worthy.

Either way, her options now were limited.

She flicked through the hangers again, dismissing each outfit in turn. Black suit? Too conservative for dinner with someone who was, business opportunities aside, an old friend. Navy shift dress? Might have worked, if it didn't have hummus smeared down the front of it, courtesy of Finn. She tossed it in the laundry hamper. Grey shift dress? She supposed it could work. The neckline was demure, the fit okay… It was just boring and made her look even greyer than she felt.

Hadn't she once had more interesting clothes? The sort with colour and pop and stuff? She was sure that once upon a time she'd dressed to fit her happy and in-love mood. Maybe that was the problem. When Adem had died he'd taken all her colour and brightness with him—and it even showed in her wardrobe.

Trapping her lower lip between her teeth, Sadie reached right to the back of the closet and felt slippery satin slide through her fingers as she tugged one more dress to the front. *The* dress. The bright red, sexy dress her sister had talked her into buying on their last shopping trip to London before she and Adem had left for Turkey. She'd never yet found the courage to wear it, for all of Rachel's suggestions that it would be the perfect dress to wear if she wanted to convince Adem they should give Finn a little brother or sister.

She let it fall from her grasp. Definitely *not* the right dress for tonight.

Instead, she pulled out her standard black function dress—the one she'd worn for every single event since she'd arrived in Kuşadasi, and the dress she'd known she'd end up wearing all along, if she was honest with herself. It was well cut, didn't reveal too much, looked more dressy than a work dress, but still had the aura of business about it.

Sadie sank to sit on her bed, her hands clutching at the fabric of the dress. Business. She had to focus on that. This was her last and only chance—she couldn't afford to think of Dylan as Adem's twenty-two-year-old university buddy, or the best man who'd brought Adem home from his stag night with an almighty hangover, a blow-up sheep and no recollection of where they'd spent the last two days. Dylan wasn't that person any more.

She swallowed, blinking away sudden tears of guilt and loss at the memory of her husband. Because that was the problem. She wasn't thinking of *that* Dylan at all. Instead, she couldn't help remembering another one, sitting up too late in a bar after someone else's wedding, talking too much and too deeply.

Despite herself, she couldn't help remembering the man who had once asked her if she'd ever imagined what might have happened if he'd met her first, instead of Adem.

Rushing to her feet, too fast, Sadie shook off the memory with the resulting light-headedness. She loved her husband—now, then and always. And she planned to preserve his memory for their son by saving the hotel. Business, that's all any of it was for her now. And she was sure that was all it was for Dylan too.

She knew business now, and she needed to show Dylan that—needed him to see that she wasn't the same girl she had been then either. She'd grown up, learned and changed. She could save the Azure all by herself—she just needed his money.

Nodding to herself, Sadie pulled on her black dress and added her work jacket and heels. A business-casual compromise, she decided. It was perfect.

Heading down to the bar, Sadie was pleased to realise she'd beaten Dylan there, despite her clothing dilemma delay. After a moment's thought she ordered them both a glass of a local white wine—showcasing the specialties of the region had to be a good way to convince Dylan that Kuşadasi was worth his time and interest. Following her theme, she also asked the bartender to check in with the chef on the menu. He returned in short order, carrying both wine and a daily menu. Sadie scanned it quickly and told him to instruct the chef to serve them both the best local food on offer, once they made it through to the restaurant.

She settled back onto her bar stool and took a sip of her wine, feeling in control for the first time that day. Dylan may have caught her off balance when he'd arrived, but it took more than that to rattle Sadie Sullivan. She had everything in hand now—and it was the upper one.

Then he appeared in the doorway, looking far too good in his navy suit and open-collared shirt, and she struggled to swallow her wine without spluttering. Dylan, Sadie was sure, hadn't bothered agonising over what to wear at all. He'd just thrown on what he liked and looked… *perfect* in it.

It was strange; she didn't remember him being quite so attractive. Oh, he'd always been good looking, but it had been in a single-guy-about-town, flirt-with-the-girls-and-take-them-home way. Whereas Adem had always been more steady, less striking—but so gorgeous when he'd smiled at her. It had felt like he'd saved all his best looks just for her, and she'd loved that.

But now Dylan looked more grown up, more reliable, like he'd grown into his looks and out of his bad habits. Sadie shook her head lightly—it was an illusion. She knew from Neal's more recent stories that Dylan was just as much of a playboy as ever.

'You look beautiful.' Reaching her stool, Dylan bent to kiss her cheek, and Sadie ignored the thrill it sent down her spine.

'And you're just as much of a flirt as ever,' she chastised him, earning the reward of a positively rakish grin that made it hard not to laugh. 'Have a seat,' she said, waving at the stool next to her. 'Drink wine.'

He did as he was told for once, fishing his smartphone from his pocket and placing it on the bar before he reached for his glass.

'This is good,' Dylan said, after the first mouthful. 'Local?'

She nodded. 'Everything you're going to taste tonight is from the area. Just another host of reasons why you want to be investing in Kuşadasi and the Azure.'

'Down to business so soon?' His smile was a little lop-sided this time, like he knew something she didn't, but since he was already swiping a finger across his phone screen to check his emails Sadie didn't think he should complain about talking business in a bar.

'Isn't that what you're here for?' Best to be blunt, she decided. History aside, this was a business dinner—for both of them.

'Of course.' Dylan leant against the wooden back of the bar stool, his arms folded behind his head. 'Go on, then. I'm ready to be convinced.'

'About the food?' Sadie asked, suddenly thrown off balance. Surely he didn't expect her to convince him to invest a ridiculous amount of money based purely on one sip of wine and the promise of dinner?

'About this hotel. You're right, this is a business trip. As much as I'd personally be happy to hand over whatever money you need, I have shareholders and board members who might not be so keen. So I need you to convince me that the Azure is a sound investment before I can agree to come on board.' His tone was perfectly matter-of-fact, even as he admitted he'd give her a pity save if he could. A very small part of Sadie wished it was that easy.

But no. This was exactly what she'd wanted—no pity save, no charity for the poor widow. Business.

She just hadn't expected him to agree so fast—or for it to be a requirement for him too.

But she could do this. She could show him. She had a

plan—Adem's plan for the Azure—and she intended to follow it to the letter. All she needed to do was convince Dylan it was a good plan.

'Right, then,' she said, briskly. 'Where do you want to start?'

CHAPTER THREE

THE MOMENT THEY were settled at their table—obviously the best seat in the house—Sadie launched into what had to be a rehearsed sales pitch. Dylan tried to pay attention as she listed the details of room numbers and styles, amenities and so on, but in truth very little of it went in. He couldn't keep his eyes off her—and apparently he'd lost the ability to stare and listen at the same time.

Sadie was beautiful as ever, he'd known that since he arrived at the Azure. Before, even. Sadie was Sadie, and her beauty was an intrinsic part of her—and had very little to do with what she actually looked like at all. But now, soaking her in over the candlelit table, he had a chance to catalogue the changes. She was more fragile now, he decided, more closed off. Somehow more off limits than she'd ever been, even after she'd married Adem. Now she was The Widow, and he couldn't seem to help but let those two words—and the tragedy they encompassed—define her in his mind.

Her spark seemed dimmed, and it hurt him to see it. Maybe this week could be useful in more than one way. He'd help her with her hotel, of course. But how could he not try to bring that spark back too? To make sure she was really okay here, alone with a crumbling hotel, a small boy and her memories.

Just as a friend. Obviously. Because there was no way she'd let him close enough for anything else now, if she never had before. Besides, given the position she was in, he wouldn't risk it. Not if it would just make things worse for her. All he had to offer was the money she needed and business support maybe. Then he would be on his way. He wasn't Adem and he never had been.

Dylan knew himself too well—at least as well as Neal, Adem and Sadie always had. He was too like his father to ever settle to one life, one set of possibilities—not when the next big thing could be just past the horizon. So this was temporary, and that was fine with him.

It just meant he only had one week to find the promise in the Azure Hotel and come up with a plan to make it good. He needed to get started on that, pronto. *Priorities, Dylan.*

Their starters arrived without him ever seeing a menu, but as he examined the seafood platter he decided he didn't mind at all. If all else failed, at least he could honestly say the food and drink at the Azure were good. It was a start.

'Did Adem make you memorise all that?' he asked, as Sadie reached the end of her spiel and reached for a calamari ring.

'No,' she said. 'Well, just some of it.'

'But it's all his plan, right?' He'd known Adem since they'd been eighteen. He'd recognised his friend's touch before Sadie had reached the second bullet point.

'How can you possibly…? We worked on it together. Of course.'

'Of course. But this was his dream.' He followed her lead with the calamari, hoping it tasted as good as it looked. One piece of rubbery calamari could ruin a whole meal. But, no, it had the perfect mixture of crunch in the batter and melting seafood. He reached for another.

'His heritage.' She shrugged, her shoulders slim and delicate now she'd taken her jacket off, and more tanned than he remembered. 'He wanted a future here for our family.'

Family. *Stop thinking about her shoulders, Jacobs, and focus on what really matters to her.* 'Where *is* Finn, anyway?'

A shadow crossed her face, and he almost regretted asking. 'He's staying with my parents for the week. I'm flying over to England to collect him after you leave.'

'Because I was going to be here?' That stung. He may not have seen much of the boy since he'd been born, but that didn't make him any less of an honorary uncle.

Sadie gave him a look—the sort she used to give him in the pub when they'd been twenty-two and he'd been acting like an idiot. 'To be honest, I didn't know *you* were the one coming, which I think you must have guessed. Besides, that wasn't it. He's due to start school next year, and my parents wanted to spend some time with him outside the holidays before then.'

There was something else, hiding behind the lightness of her tone, but he couldn't put his finger on it, and it was still too early to press too hard for information—frustrating as that was. He had to have patience. Eventually she'd open up to him again.

A waiter cleared their starter platters, even as another brought their main course—some sort of delicious, spicy, lamb stew thing that Dylan vowed to find out the name of before he left. But right then he had bigger priorities than his stomach.

'Okay, so, I've heard all the grand plans,' he said between mouthfuls. 'How far have you actually got with them?'

Sadie put down her fork and ticked the items off on her fingers as she spoke. 'The lobby, restaurant and bar are finished, as you've seen. So is the spa. Of the bedrooms, the top floor with the penthouse suite—your suite—and the other family suites is done, and the first floor of luxury doubles.'

'So that leaves you, what?' He tried to recall the floor numbers from the lift. 'Another four floors to go? Plus any other reception and function rooms?'

She nodded. 'We had a timescale planned but…'

'The money ran out.' Not a surprise. He'd seen it often enough, even in projects less plagued by tragedy and uncertainty.

'Yes. So we opened anyway, to try and get enough funds to keep going. But at least one of the floors is uninhabitable as it stands, so occupancy is never very high.'

'What about the outside space?' That had to be a selling point in a climate like this.

'The outside pool needs retiling and the path down to the beach needs some work. Fortunately the inside pool is attached to the spa, so got done in the first wave, before…' She trailed off, and he knew exactly what she wasn't saying. Some days, he thought that if he didn't say it, it might not be true, too.

'There's a lot left to do,' he finished for her, cutting short the moment.

'That's why we need your money.'

His fork hit china and he looked down to see he'd eaten the whole bowl without tasting anything beyond that first delicious mouthful. What a waste. He put his cutlery down. 'Dinner would be worth investing in alone. That was truly delicious.'

She blushed, just a little. 'I'm glad you enjoyed it. Somehow I suspect one meal isn't quite enough to win over your shareholders, though.'

'Maybe not. Okay, listen. I'm going to tell you a bit about my company, and you can decide if you want us involved. If you do…then we can discuss what else I need to see and do, what questions I need answered, before I can take a proposal to the board.' She'd been straight with him, as far as he could tell. Time for him to do the same.

'Okay.' Eyes wide, her nerves were back, he realised, pleased to still be able to read her so well.

'My company isn't generally interested in long-term investment. Mostly what we do is take on a failing business, tear it down or build it up until it's successful, then sell it on.'

'In that case, I'd think the Azure would be perfect. We have "failing business" written all over us.' She reached for her wine—a local red, he assumed—and took a gulp.

'The key is, the business has to have the *potential* to be a huge success,' he clarified. 'In the right hands.'

'Yours, you mean.' She sounded more sceptical than Dylan felt was truly necessary.

'Or whoever we put in charge. In this case…we'd need to be sure that you could turn this place around on your own, with just money and guidance from us.' Make it clear upfront that he wouldn't be staying around—not that he imagined she wanted him to.

'I see.' This time her tone gave nothing away at all, and he found himself talking just to fill the silence that followed.

'Unless, of course, you're in favour of taking a bulldozer to the place, putting someone else in charge of the rebuild and taking a back seat until the money starts rolling in?' He knew she wouldn't say yes, but part of him couldn't help but hope she would. It would be the easy way out—but since when had Sadie ever taken that?

She shook her head. 'Sorry. This is personal for me. I made a commitment to make this hotel a success. For Adem.'

'I guessed you'd say that. Don't suppose you'd consider changing the name either?'

'No,' she said, giving him a curious look. 'Why? What's wrong with the name it has?'

'No reason.' She stared and waited. He sighed. He should have known that wasn't a good enough answer for her. 'I had a bad experience at an Azure Hotel once.'

Her wide grin made the admission worthwhile. 'Let me guess. Some woman's poor husband showed up at the wrong moment?'

Of course that's what she would think. And, really, who could blame her? 'You know me.' But not all his secrets—which was probably for the best. For both of them.

'Okay, so if we're not going to knock this place down, what do I need to show you to convince you we're worth your time, money and effort?'

Honestly, he could probably make the decision based purely on the numbers. But that would have him flying back to Sydney tomorrow, instead of spending time with Sadie. He had to give her a real chance to convince him.

'Here's my proposal. I want a proper tour of the hotel. Then I need to see the local area—get a feel for the economy and tourist potential. Numbers are all well and good, but you need to visit a place to get a real feeling for it.' All true, up to a point. 'Then we'll sit down together and see if I can help you save this place.'

She nodded. 'Okay. Do you want me to set you up with the local tour company we use?'

Where would be the fun in that? 'No. I think this will

work much better if you show me yourself.' Not to mention give him a clearer idea of how Sadie was really coping after her husband's death. Multitasking was the key to any successful business, after all.

Sadie nodded her agreement, and Dylan sat back to anticipate dessert, hoping his smile wasn't too smug. Everything was going to plan.

After a restless night, full of dreams that were half memory, half fantasy, Sadie met Dylan in the lobby the next morning, dressed in her best black suit and determined to impress with her business skills. His proposal had been more than fair. Neal must have told him what dire straits they were in at the Azure, but still Dylan had agreed to spend time on the ground, studying and evaluating everything himself, before he made his decision.

Sadie suspected that had more to do with friendship than good business sense. Still, he'd made it very clear over dinner what he needed from her—professionalism—and she intended to give it to him in spades.

Except Dylan, when he arrived, was dressed in light trousers and a pale blue shirt with the sleeves rolled up, sunglasses tucked in his pocket, making her feel instantly overdressed—even though *she* was the one who was appropriately attired. *How does he* always *manage that?*

'Right, let's get going,' he said, as he approached. 'Lots to see today!'

'Before we start our tour,' she said, stalling him, 'I realised there was something I forgot to show you yesterday, and I'd hate you to miss it.'

Striding across the lobby, she led him to the windows at the far side of the elevators. Dylan wasn't the sort to stop and sniff the roses, unless someone reminded him to, and she couldn't have him missing the most magnificent thing about the Azure, just because he forgot to look.

'Oh, really? What's that?' Dylan asked, following, his eyes on the screen of his smartphone.

'Our view.' Sadie stared out across the bright blue waters, the sea almost the same colour as the sky, white foam echoing the wispy clouds overhead. They were high enough to see for miles, out along the coast and out to sea. Her heart tightened the way it always did when she looked out over the water and coast beyond the Azure. Whatever had happened here, she was lucky to have had the chance to live in such a beautiful country. She had to remember that.

'There's a path from the back door that leads straight down to the beach,' she murmured, but Dylan's eyes remained fixed on the view, just as she'd known they would.

It was this view that Adem had used to convince her, back when buying a crumbling hotel had just been a pipe dream.

Look at it, he'd said. *Who wouldn't want to be here?*

And in that moment she hadn't been able to imagine anywhere she'd rather be than in the Azure Hotel, making Adem's dreams a reality.

Dylan looked similarly entranced, his phone forgotten in his hand. Sadie allowed herself a small smile. Perhaps this would be easier than she'd thought.

'Of course, the view would still be there, even if you knocked this old place down and rebuilt it,' he said, turning his back on the view, but his tone told her he was joking. Mostly. 'You could put in a whole glass wall in the lobby, and rooms with a sea view could have folding glass doors and balconies. Really make the most of the asset—and change the name while you're at it…'

Sadie rolled her eyes. Some woman—or her husband—had really done a number on him in an Azure Hotel, hadn't she? Funny that Adem or Neal had never told her that story, when they'd shared so many others.

Was that why he couldn't see it? The romance of this place? This old building was more than just its stones and its view. It was the heart of the place.

'Time for the rest of our tour, then. But I want you to remember—this is all business.' Sure, he'd said it himself the night before, but it couldn't hurt to hammer the point home. 'I want you to treat me and the Azure like you would any other business proposition. We're here to impress you, our client. So, what do you want to see first?'

'I'm the client, huh? My wish is your command. Sounds good.' Giving her a lopsided smile, Dylan stared around him, obviously thinking. 'Let's start with the bedrooms.'

'The suites? Or the luxury doubles?' Which would be best? He'd already seen the best suite in the place—he was staying in it. So maybe the doubles…

'The uninhabitable ones,' Dylan said, cutting short any hopes of impressing him that morning. Sadie silently cursed her loose tongue over dinner. It had to be the fault of the wine.

'Right this way,' she said, her smile fading the moment she turned away to press the 'Call Lift' button.

The bedrooms were worse than she remembered. A lot worse.

'Lot of work needed here,' Dylan said, winning the prize for understatement of the year. Sadie sighed as she took in the broken tiles, missing bed, ripped wallpaper and strange black marks on the carpetless floor.

'Yes,' she agreed. 'And a lot of money to do it.' If there were anything guaranteed to send Dylan running…and she'd brought him straight there. Why had she even given him the choice?

But Dylan just shrugged and smiled. 'But I've seen worse. Okay. Now let's see the ones you've done up.'

Sadie wanted to ask what sort of hotels he'd been staying in, to have seen worse, but instead she decided to grab the life belt with both hands and swim for the shore. 'Luxury doubles coming up,' she said, with a smile that made her face ache.

At least she knew they had carpets.

By the time they were done viewing the hotel, Sadie was exhausted from excessive smiling and from scraping around in her brain for the answers to Dylan's incredibly detailed questions. At least she could never complain that he wasn't taking this business proposal seriously. For all his tourist clothes, he'd been professional to the hilt, asking questions she'd never even imagined she'd need to know the answers to.

Back in the lobby, she looked over her scribbled list of things to look up for him. It was up to two pages already, and he'd only been there less than a day.

'I'd better get back to the office and type up my notes from this morning,' she said. 'I should have answers for you by this evening…'

'Oh, I'm not done with my tour yet, Mrs Sullivan.' He flashed a smile. 'I want to see the town next.' He looked her up and down, and Sadie resisted the urge to hide behind her clipboard. 'Why don't you go and get changed into something more suitable for sightseeing?'

Something more suitable… What had happened to this being all business? What was he imagining—a Hawaiian shirt and a bumbag? But she had said he was in charge, so she bit her tongue. Hard. 'Give me ten minutes.'

He nodded, but since he was already frowning at the screen of his phone she wasn't sure he noticed her leave.

As she dashed up to her room she ran through the morning again in her head. Dylan had seemed somewhat underwhelmed by the hotel as a whole, with far more questions than praise, but Kuşadasi was bound to impress. The local economy and the blossoming tourist trade was what made the Azure a safe bet. She just had to make sure he saw that.

Dylan was so like Adem, in so many ways, she thought as she slipped into a light sundress. Adem had always worked on gut instinct, trusting his feelings to lead him to the right decisions. And instinct mattered to Dylan too—so that was what she needed to win over.

Hadn't he made it clear his business specialised in short-term, in-and-out projects? All she needed to do was hold his attention long enough to get him to invest. Then the Azure would take off, she'd be able to pay him back or buy him out in no time, and it would be back to just her and Finn again.

Grabbing her sunglasses and bag, Sadie took a deep breath and headed down to wow Dylan Jacobs. Whether he liked it or not.

CHAPTER FOUR

IT ALMOST FELT like a date, Dylan thought as they sped down the Turkish roads towards the town centre. The Azure Hotel wasn't quite close enough to walk in—another point against it—but with Sadie sitting beside him in a pale cotton sundress, her dark hair loose to her shoulders, he found it hard to be objective.

Because this—being alone with her, exploring a new place, relaxing in her company—was everything he'd dreamed about once, in the secret places of his mind he'd never fully admit to. Back in the days when he'd let himself think about a world without his best friend, or one where he'd met Sadie first.

He hadn't let the fantasies into his mind often—he'd learned early in life there was no point wishing the world to be any different than it was unless you were willing to do something to change it. And he hadn't been willing, not in the slightest. If even imagining it had felt like betrayal, the idea of acting on those fantasies had been beyond contemplation.

Adem had been the right guy for Sadie—he'd always known that. Known he couldn't offer her half as much, so he'd never considered trying—not that he'd have risked or betrayed his friendships that way anyway. A woman like Sadie needed love, commitment—she deserved forever. And he didn't have that in him.

But now, with Sadie in the driver's seat, sunglasses on and legs bare under that sundress, he could feel those imagined possibilities rising again. And just for a moment he let himself believe that she wanted him here—for more than just his money.

A light turned red and they pulled to a stop, the jerk breaking the moment, and reality sank back in. If this were a date he'd planned, he'd know where he was going. Sadie would be smiling at him, not looking tense and nervous and sad. The familiar guilt wouldn't be sitting in his chest—smaller than when Adem had been alive, sure, but still ever present.

Plus he'd probably be driving.

The lights changed again, and Sadie manoeuvred expertly past waiting cars and swung into a suddenly vacant parking spot by the marina that Dylan hadn't even noticed. He had plenty of experience driving abroad himself, but for once he was glad to be driven. It was nice to see Sadie so in control in this place.

'Come and look at the ocean,' she said, sliding out of her seat and into the sunshine. 'It'll give you a feel for the place.'

They stood by the railings together, staring out at the Aegean, and Dylan felt a comfortable warmth settle into his bones—one he wasn't sure was entirely due to the sunshine. He was enjoying Sadie's company just a little too much. He'd always found her presence relaxing, to a point, but before he'd never allowed himself to indulge in that feeling too much. Here and now, though, it felt all too natural.

He shut his eyes against the sparkle of the sun on the

water. Business. That was what he was here for, and that was what he needed to concentrate on. He couldn't afford to forget himself here—he needed to keep on top of his other projects while he was away, as well as work on the Azure proposal with Sadie. Already that morning he'd had enough emails from his assistant back in Sydney to remind him that things never worked quite as smoothly when he was away. He had to stay on top of everything.

Eyes open again, he shut his mind to the view and the warmth of the sun, and turned his attention instead to the practical aspects of the place. A marina, filled with top-end private yachts—and further up, cruise ships. Suddenly he understood exactly why Sadie had parked where she had.

'So, this is your subtle way of telling me that Kuşadasi is a popular cruise-ship destination?' he said, turning his back on the marina to lean against the railing and study her instead.

She gave him a perfectly innocent smile. 'Pure coincidence, I assure you. But as it happens, yes, it is! Tourism is the heart blood of this place. The ships stop here regularly, filled with people ready to explore the town—and spend their money on souvenirs.'

Which all sounded good until you studied the logic behind it. 'But how many of them make it up the hill to the Azure?'

'That's not the point.'

'Of course it is. If the bulk of the tourists visiting this place are only here for the day, what do they need with a hotel?' She winced at his words, but recovered quickly. He had to admire her tenacity, even if her argument was weak.

'The cruise ships are only a small part of the tourist industry here—and, actually, they're the gateway to a whole new market. Some of the people who visit for a day might never have even considered Turkey as a holiday destination before—but after a few hours here they may well decide to come back for a longer stay. Or to tell their friends that it was a great place to visit. Or even look into buying holiday apartments or hotel time shares here.'

A slim possibility. People who liked cruises—like his mother and her third husband—tended to take more cruises, in Dylan's experience. But who knew? Maybe she was right. He'd need more figures before he could make a value judgement.

'Okay, then,' Dylan said, pushing away from the railings. 'So what is it about this town that will make them come back?'

'The history,' Sadie replied promptly. 'The shopping. The atmosphere. The food. The views. Everything.'

'So show me everything.'

'That could take a while.'

Dylan shrugged. 'We've got all day. So, what's next?'

Sadie looked around her then nodded to herself. 'Let's take a walk.'

That date-like feeling returned as they walked along the seafront towards a small island, linked to the mainland by a walkway. Dylan resisted the urge to take her arm or hold her hand, but the fact it even needed to be resisted unsettled him. Not just because this was *Sadie* but because he'd never really thought of himself as a hand-holding-in-the-sunshine kind of guy. He tended to work better after dark.

Sadie turned and led him along the walkway leading out into the sea towards the island, and Dylan distracted himself by reading the signs of fishing tours on offer and checking out the tourist trap stalls set up along the way, selling bracelets and temporary tattoos.

'What is this place?' he asked, nodding to the island up ahead. Covered with trees, it appeared to have a fortified wall running around it and plenty of people wandering the path along the edge of the island.

'Pigeon Island,' Sadie replied promptly. 'You see over there, above the trees? That's the fortress of Kuşadasi—built in the thirteenth century. It was there to protect the Ottoman Empire from pirates—including Barbarossa himself.'

'I didn't realise I was here for a history lesson, as well as a tourism one.'

'There's a lot of history here,' Sadie pointed out. 'And a lot of tourism to be had from history. Wait until you see the *caravanserai*.'

'I look forward to it.' History wasn't really his thing, but Sadie seemed so excited about taking him there he was hardly going to mention it. Maybe it would be more interesting than he thought, looking back instead of forward for once.

'There's a seafood restaurant and café and stuff inside,' Sadie said, as they reached the path around the island, 'although I thought we'd head back into town for lunch. But I wanted you to see this first.'

She stopped, staring back the way they had come, and Dylan found himself copying her. He had to admit, Kuşadasi from this angle was quite a sight, with its busy harbour and seafront. He could see what Adem had loved about the place.

'Does Turkey feel like home now?' he asked, watching Sadie as she soaked up the view.

She turned to him, surprised eyebrows raised. 'I suppose. I mean, we've been here for a few years now. We're pretty settled. I can get by with the language—although Finn's better at it than me.'

'That's not the same as home.' At least, from what little Dylan knew about it.

'Well, no. But, then, I never really expected that *anywhere* would be home again after Adem.'

One quiet admission, and the whole mood changed. He was wrong, Dylan realised, and had been all along. This was nothing like a date at all.

He looked away, down at the water, and tried to imagine what kept her there in Kuşadasi. It couldn't just be history and sheer stubbornness, could it? Especially given how strange and lonely it must be for her there every day in Adem's place, without him beside her.

She shook off the mood, her hair swinging from side to side as she did so, and smiled up at him. 'What about you? Where's home for you these days? Neal says you're operating mostly out of Sydney?' Changing the subject. Smart woman.

'Mostly, yeah. My mum left Britain and moved back home to Australia when she remarried again, and my sister is out there too now, so it makes sense.' And this time, finally, he had faith that they might both stay there now they'd each found some happiness in their lives. He felt lighter, just knowing they were settled.

'Do you see them often?' Sadie asked.

Dylan shrugged. 'It's a big country. We catch up now and then.'

'Between business trips.' Was that accusation in her tone? Because he wasn't going to feel bad for running a successful business, even if it meant always being ready to jump at a new opportunity and run with it—often in the opposite direction from his family.

'Pretty much. Between the office in Sydney and the one in London, I probably spend more time in the air than in my apartments in either city.'

He'd meant it as a joke, but even as the words came out he realised he'd never thought of it like that before. All those years trying to get his family settled, and he'd never stopped to notice that he didn't have the same grounding at all. He'd just assumed his business—solid, profitable and reliable—was enough to give that security. But in truth he was no more settled than Sadie was, in this country she'd never chosen for herself.

Maybe they were both drifting.

'We're both very lucky to live in such beautiful places, though,' Sadie said.

He tried to return her smile. 'Yes, I suppose we are. So, why don't you show me some more of the beauty of this place?'

'Okay.' She stepped away, back towards the promenade to the mainland. 'Let's go and take in the town.'

Home.

Sadie considered Dylan's question again as she led him into the town of Kuşadasi proper. She took him by the longer back route to give him a true feel for the place. In comfortable silence they walked through narrow cobbled streets filled with shops. Half their wares were hung outside—brightly coloured belly-dancing costumes and leather slippers butting up against shops selling highly patterned rugs, or with rails of scarves and baskets of soaps on tables in the street. The smell of cooking meat and other dishes filled the air as the local restaurants prepared for lunch, the scent familiar and warming to Sadie.

As they walked she could see Dylan taking everything in—reaching out to run his fingers over the walls, his eyes darting from one shop display to the next. Had she been so fascinated when she'd first visited? It seemed so long ago she could barely remember.

Would this place ever truly be home? Could it? Or would it always just be the place where she'd lost the love of her life?

When she thought of home she thought of her family—and so, by default, of the pretty English village where she'd grown up, just outside Oxford. She remembered playing in the woods with her sister Rachel, or taking walks on the weekend with their parents and stopping for lunch in a country pub. And she thought of later meeting Adem and his friends in Oxford, when she'd travelled in every day for her first proper job after training in a small, independent spa and beauty salon there. She thought of the first flat she and Adem had rented together in London, after they'd been married.

She didn't think of the Azure. Not because she didn't love it but because it seemed so alien to all those other things. Like a permanent working holiday.

She loved Turkey, Kuşadasi, the Azure. And maybe Dylan was right in an odd, roundabout way. If she wanted to stay there, she needed to find a way to make it feel like home.

They emerged from a side passage out onto the bigger main street, with larger stores and the occasional street vendor stall. Here, after the charm of the old town streets, Kuşadasi looked more modern, ready to compete in the world tourist market. It was important to show Dylan that they had both here.

Suddenly, Dylan stopped walking. 'Hang on a minute.' Turning, he walked back a few paces to a stall they'd just passed. Curious, Sadie followed—not close enough to hear his conversation with the stallholder but near enough to see what had caught his attention.

She rolled her eyes. A sign advertising 'Genuine Fake Watches'. Of course. In some ways Dylan really was just like Adem—they had the same absurd sense of humour and the same reluctance to let a joke lie untold.

Still, she smiled to see that Dylan wasn't pointing out the error to the stallholder, and instead seemed to be striking up a friendly conversation with him as he took a photo on his phone and examined the watches. Another way he was like her husband, she supposed—that same easy nature that made him friends everywhere he went. She'd never had that, really, and couldn't help but envy it.

'Enjoying yourself?' she asked, as he returned.

Dylan grinned. 'Immensely. What's next?'

She'd planned to take him to the *caravanserai*—she just knew his magpie mind would love all the tiny shops and stalls there, too, and it was a huge tourist attraction with plenty of history. But it was getting late and her stomach rumbled, nudging her towards the perfect way to remember why she was so lucky to live in Kuşadasi—her favourite restaurant.

'I think lunch,' she said, watching as Dylan slipped his own no doubt authentic and ridiculously expensive watch into his pocket and replaced it with the genuine fake he had just bought.

'Fantastic. I can show off my new toy.' He shook his wrist and, despite herself, Sadie laughed, feeling perfectly at home for the first time in years.

From the way Sadie was greeted at the door of the restaurant with a hug from an enthusiastic waitress, Dylan assumed she was something of a regular. Despite the queue of people ahead of them, they were led directly to a table right in the centre of the glass-roofed portion of the restaurant, with vines growing overhead to dull the power of the sun as it shone down.

He couldn't catch the entire conversation between

Sadie and the waitress, but he did notice it was conducted half in English, half in Turkish, with the waitress particularly shifting from one to the other with no sense of hesitation at all.

'Adem's second cousin,' Sadie explained. 'Or third. I forget. Most of the Turkish side of his family moved over to England at the same time his mum did, as a child, but one cousin or uncle stayed behind.' She handed him a menu. 'So, what do you fancy?'

'I get to order for myself today, then?' he teased, and she flashed him a smile, looking more comfortable than she had since they'd left the Azure that morning.

'I think I can trust you not to choose the burger and chips. But if you're fishing for a recommendation...'

'No, no. I think I can manage to choose my own food, thanks.'

She shrugged. 'Sorry. I think it's the mother thing. Finn always wants to debate all the options on the children's menu before he makes his choice.'

The mother thing. It still felt weird, identifying Sadie as a mother. Maybe because he'd spent far more time with her before Finn's birth than since. Just another reminder that she was a different woman now from the one he'd fallen so hard for in Oxford all those years before.

'So, what do you fancy?' she asked, folding her own menu and putting it to one side. Dylan got the feeling she had it memorised.

'The sea bass, I think.' He put his own menu down and within seconds their waitress was back to take their orders.

'Can I have the chicken salad today, please?' Sadie asked, smiling up at her friend. 'With extra flatbread on the side.'

'Of course. And for you, sir?'

As he looked up Dylan spotted the specials board behind the waitress. 'Actually, I think I'll have the lamb *kofta* off the specials, please.'

Sadie frowned at him as the waitress disappeared with their menus. 'I thought you wanted sea bass?'

He shrugged. 'Something better came along.'

She didn't look convinced, but rather than press the point she pulled a notepad from her bag and opened it to a clean page. Apparently they were back to business.

'So, while we have a quiet moment—what do you think so far?'

'Of Kuşadasi? It's charming,' he said.

'Not just the town.' Frustration creased a small line between Sadie's eyebrows. Despite himself, Dylan found it unbearably cute. 'Of everything. The tourist potential here, my plans for the hotel…the whole lot. Consider it a mid-visit review.'

'I've only been here less than a day,' Dylan pointed out.

'Really? It seems longer.' She flashed him a smile to show it was a joke, but Dylan suspected she meant it. After all, he was feeling it too—that feeling that he'd been there forever. That they'd never been apart in the first place.

A very dangerous feeling, that. Maybe Sadie was right. It was time to focus on business again.

Leaning back in his chair, he considered how to put his comments in a way that she might actually listen to rather than get annoyed by.

'Your plans…they're the same ones Adem mapped out when you moved here, right? And that was, what? Three years ago?'

She nodded. 'About that, yes. And, yes, they're his plans. He put a lot of time, energy and research into developing them. I was lucky. When he… When it all fell to me, I already had a blueprint to follow right there. I don't know if I'd have managed otherwise.'

'I think you would have done.' In fact, he rather thought she might have to. 'The thing is…are you sure that sticking to Adem's plans is the wisest idea?'

Her shoulders stiffened, and Dylan muffled a sigh. He should have known there wasn't a way to broach this subject without causing offence.

'You knew Adem as well as I did, almost anyway,' she said. 'Do you really think he wouldn't have triple-checked those plans before putting them into action?'

'Not at all.' In fact, he was pretty sure that Adem would have taken outside counsel, considered all the possibilities, and covered every single base before he'd committed to the Azure at all. Despite his enthusiastic nature and tendency to jump at opportunities, Adem had always been thorough. 'But what I mean is, the best plans need to be flexible. Adem knew that. Things change in business all the time—and quickly. Three years is a long time. The world economy, the tourist trade, even this place, aren't the same as they were then. That's why you need to review plans regularly and adjust course where necessary.'

'I thought you were here to provide investment, not business advice.' Her words came out stiffer than her frame.

Time to put his cards on the table. 'Sadie, I'm here to provide whatever it is you need—to survive here, to save your hotel, or just to be happy. But you have to trust me in order to get it.'

CHAPTER FIVE

TRUST HIM. WHAT A strange concept.

In the years since Adem had died Sadie had grown very good at relying on and trusting nobody but herself. After all, who else could she trust to care as much about Finn and the future of the Azure? Neal had helped, of course, but he'd always deferred to Adem's plan.

She should have known it wouldn't be as simple with Dylan.

Their food arrived and she picked at her salad and flatbread, loving the crunch against the soft gooeyness of the freshly baked bread. Eventually, though, she had to admit that she couldn't hide her silence behind food forever—and Dylan was clearly waiting for her to talk first. Either that or whatever information kept flashing up on his phone really was more interesting than lunch with her.

Actually, that was probably it. Still, she had to try and keep his attention.

With a sigh, she put the piece of bread she'd just torn down on her side plate.

'Look, I know what you mean—about the market changing, and all that.' Dylan looked up as she started to speak. She'd caught him just as he forked another mouthful of lamb between his lips, so at least she knew he wouldn't interrupt her for a moment or two. 'But sometimes you have to stick with a plan for a while to see its full potential. You have to give it time to work.'

There was silence again for a moment while Dylan chewed. Then he said, 'What if you don't have that kind of time?'

And wasn't that the nightmare scenario that kept her awake at night? But it was also why he was supposed to be here—to buy her the time she needed to make things work. He just had to give her that chance.

'You know, just because you're always chasing after the next big thing, that doesn't mean it's always the right thing to do.' Frustration leaked out in her tone. 'Jumping at every new trend or idea would just make us look unsteady and inconsistent. Some people like someone who can see things through—like Adem would have done with this plan. He'd have given it a chance to succeed, I know he would.'

Dylan winced at her words and Sadie realised that her comments could possibly be construed as more of a personal attack than a professional one. But it was too late to take them back now.

'Okay, I admit Adem was always better at committing than I was,' Dylan said. 'To a plan, or anything else for that matter. But he always knew when changes needed to be made, too. That's what made him such a good businessman.'

The most frustrating part was that he was probably right. In this one area Dylan had known Adem better than she could have—they'd worked together straight out of university, until Dylan had left to start his own business abroad, and Adem, newly married and planning a family, had declined to join him after a long talk with her. But until then they'd been the company's dream team, working completely in sync. Dylan was the one person in the world who truly knew what Adem would have done in her situation, and that irritated her.

'So what? You're going to give me a list of changes for the Azure and just enough pocket money to do them, then disappear for six months and let me get on with it?' she asked. 'But what happens next? I bet I can guess. You come back and move the goalposts again—because the market's changed or whatever—and give me a whole new list of changes.' She shook her head. She wouldn't do it. 'I can't work that way, Dylan. I can't *live* that way either. It's not fair to ask me to.'

'I never would,' Dylan shot back. His fork lay forgotten on his plate now, and the intensity in his gaze as he leant across the table was almost intimidating. 'That's not what I'm saying at all. All I mean is…let's go through Adem's plans together, see what needs tweaking or updating. I'm not throwing the baby out with the bathwater here, Sadie. I'm certain that Adem's plans are solid—or were three years ago. But just because you've made one plan doesn't mean you can't adapt or improve it when a better idea comes along.'

'Like switching from sea bass to lamb.' He made it all sound so simple and sensible.

Dylan smiled, relief spreading out across his face. 'Something like that.'

'Okay. I'll think about it.' And that was all the commitment she planned to make to this man.

'That's all I ask.'

They finished eating in silence. Sadie settled up the bill and they were back out on the street before Dylan asked where they were going next.

'The *caravanserai*,' Sadie said, with a faint smile.

'Another tourist site with a lot of history. I think you'll like this one.'

'I'm sure I will.'

The *caravanserai*, a fortified marketplace dating back to the seventeenth century, loomed up above them, its crenellations making it look more like a castle than a shopping centre.

'So, what is this place?' Dylan asked, squinting up at the tall walls.

'These days, part marketplace, part hotel and entertainment venue.' Sadie strolled through the marble arch, the splash of the fountains and the greenery surrounding the inner courtyard helping her relax, just like they always did. 'But back in the day it was a protected place for merchants and such passing through the town—they could be sure they and their merchandise would be safe behind these walls.'

'So I can see.' Dylan placed a hand against the stone wall. 'Solid.'

'Come on. Come and look at some local wares.'

There were fewer goods on offer now that the *caravanserai* was mainly a hotel, but Sadie suspected Dylan would enjoy what there was. She gave him a quick tour of the ground floor, slipping through stone archways into shady stores hung with rugs and other fabrics. Once she was sure he had his bearings, she left him examining some beautifully painted bowls and pottery and escaped back out to the courtyard and the refreshing sound of the falling water from the white fountain in the centre.

She needed a moment to think, a moment alone, without Dylan's presence scrambling her senses. She wasn't sure if it was because she associated him so closely with Adem, or because it felt at once so strange and yet so natural to have him there in Turkey with her, but either way it confused her. She couldn't think straight when he was smiling at her, talking apparent sense that only her personal knowledge of his history and her gut instinct could counter.

She settled down to sit on the edge of the fountain, letting the coolness of the marble sooth her palms, and circled her neck a few times to try and relieve the tension that had spread there over lunch.

Of course, it was possible she'd only grown so defensive with him because he'd been criticising Adem's plan—because it had felt like betraying the man himself, even if she knew intellectually Adem would never have seen it that way. But Adem's plan was the only thing she had left to tell her what her husband would have wanted for her, for their son, and for their dream hotel.

In the absence of anything else she'd clung to it like a life raft. Except it hadn't worked—and she had to face the fact that, whatever Dylan said, that failure was more on her than the plan. She had no doubt that if Adem had been there, with all his charm and enthusiasm, he'd have made it work—and they'd never have been in the position of having to beg Dylan Jacobs for help at all.

If they needed a new plan, then she needed help. She hadn't trained for this, hadn't ever planned to take it on. She could run her spa business with military precision and a profit every quarter—she knew what it needed and what worked. But a whole hotel? She was lost. And she was going to have to confess that to Dylan—not a conversation she relished.

But if she couldn't trust herself to come up with a plan to save the Azure, could she really trust Dylan? Wasn't he just another short-term sticking plaster? Oh, he meant well, she was sure enough of that. But he didn't see things through. Everyone knew that. Why would the Azure be any different for him?

Suddenly, a shadow appeared on the stone floor in front of her—dark and lengthening in the afternoon sun. Sadie looked up to see Dylan standing over her, a contrite expression on his face and a paper-wrapped parcel in his hands.

'For you,' he said, handing her the package.

'Why?' she asked, unwrapping the paper. 'I mean, thank you. But you shouldn't have.' The wrapping fell aside to reveal a beautiful silk scarf—one from the rack she'd shown him inside, but not one she'd ever have looked at for herself. Not because she didn't love it, or because it wouldn't suit her. The bright, vibrant colours were exactly the sort that her sister Rachel was always telling her she should wear, but she rarely did these days.

It was too bright, too bold for her. But, holding it, she wished more than anything she still had the guts to wear it.

'It's just a token,' Dylan said. 'An apology, I guess.'

Sadie shook her head, wrapping the scarf back up loosely in its paper. 'You don't have to apologise to me.'

'I feel like I do. I didn't mean to offend you, at lunch I mean.' He sighed and sat down beside her at the fountain. In an instant all the cool serenity Sadie usually found there vanished. 'You know I'd never badmouth Adem—you do know that, right? I know it's not the same as for you but…you know what he meant to me too.'

'I do.' Guilt trickled down inside her chest. Dylan and Adem had been best friends before she'd even met them. Miles might have separated them, but she knew Adem had stayed in close contact with both Neal and Dylan until the day he'd died. She didn't hold the monopoly on grief over his death.

'I'm not just doing this for him, though—helping you, I mean.' Dylan twisted to look her straight in the eye, and Sadie found it strangely difficult to look away. What was it about this man that was so captivating, so compelling? 'But you have to know I wouldn't give up on this—not on something that was so important to my best friend.'

'I know that,' Sadie said, but she knew it lacked the conviction of her previous agreement.

Yes, Dylan would want to do this for Adem. But she also knew that all he could really offer was a short-term solution at best. The money would keep them afloat, give them another chance, and his thoughts on the plans for the future of the hotel would be invaluable, she was sure. But it was going to take more than that to save the Azure. She needed to find a way to do that herself, once Dylan's money had been spent and the man himself had moved on. She couldn't rely on him to be there for anything more than cash and brief excitement at the start of a new project.

With a sigh Dylan reached across and took the scarf from her lap, unwrapping the paper again. Then, gently, he placed it around her throat, knotting it loosely at the front. The soft silk felt luxurious against her skin, and she couldn't help but smile at the bright pop of colours around her neck. Then she raised her chin, and her gaze crashed into his, heating her cheeks until she was sure she was bright pink. His fingers straightened the fabric of the scarf, brushing against her throat, and her skin tingled under his touch.

How long had it been since she'd felt a tingle like that? She could say exactly, to the day.

Not since her husband had died.

Sadie swallowed, hard, and shuffled back along her stone seat.

'I know I'm not Adem,' Dylan said, his voice softer now. 'And you know me, I don't do long term or commitment, not in my personal life. But if I say I'll take on a work project, I see it through to the end, whatever happens. You can trust me on that.'

Sadie nodded, knowing it was true as far as it went. But it wasn't the whole truth. 'Which is why you only ever take on short-term projects,' she pointed out, as gently as she could.

'Yeah. I suppose it is.' Dylan looked down at his hands, and a coolness spread across Sadie again now he wasn't staring at her.

He looked so forlorn that Sadie felt obliged to try and build him up again. After all, he *was* doing his best, and that had to be worth something. Besides, she needed him.

'Okay,' she said, 'we're in this together, then—if you can convince your stakeholders to invest.'

He glanced up again, a faint smile on his lips. 'I'll be as persuasive as I can with whatever proposal we come up with. So what's next?'

'I don't know about you, but I need some coffee.' She got to her feet, smoothing down the skirt of her sundress and adjusting the scarf. The bright colours looked just right against the pale dress somehow. 'Proper Turkish coffee.' She offered him a hand to pull him up.

'Sounds like just the tonic,' he replied, his fingers closing around hers.

Sadie hoped so. With the strange way she was feeling today she needed some sort of medicine. Or a slap upside the head.

Sadie chose a small coffee shop overlooking the marina. Dylan sat back and let her order while he took in the view. Still, the aroma of thick, burnt coffee beans took him back through the years—to epic coffee-fests with Adem and Neal at university, when they'd drink buckets of the stuff to get through revision or a particularly tough assignment. Or later, lounging around in Sadie and Adem's first flat in London, when they had all just been starting out—and burning the candle at both ends working full time and studying for MBAs or accountancy qualifications at night. They'd passed whole weekends just drinking coffee until it had been time to switch to beer.

'So,' Sadie said, as the waiter disappeared to fetch their coffee, 'you think I need to change direction with my plans.'

Yeah, he should have known that conversation wasn't over. The scarf apology seemed to have worked in the short term, but it didn't really change anything. Her plans were still stuck in the past.

'I think you need to consider new opportunities as they present themselves.' That sounded better, right? 'Adem always knew how to keep an eye out for a new opportunity—and when to jump at it.'

She pulled a face, her mouth twisting up into a grimace that would have been ugly on anyone else. Apparently his new approach didn't sound all that much better after all. 'I suppose you taught him that.'

Dylan frowned. What, exactly, was that supposed to mean? Stupid to pretend he didn't know. And she was right—she'd seen him jump at the chance of new work, new women, new places, new everything too often not to be. Dylan Jacobs didn't stick at anything—except success. And even then he'd found a way to make it fit his own natural tendencies towards the short term.

His sister Cassie always claimed he was just making sure to run first—before he could be left or hurt. Dylan had never had the heart to tell her that he was more afraid of hurting than *being* hurt. He might be his father's son in many ways, but he had a better handle on his own failings. If he couldn't give forever—and he couldn't—it was better never to promise more than just for now.

It had worked so far, anyway.

Sadie was still waiting for an answer. 'Maybe. We both learnt a lot from working together.'

No response. The waiter returned, carrying two tiny cups of thick, black sludge and little sugar pellets to sweeten it. Dylan busied himself stirring some into his coffee while he tried to figure out what he'd said now.

And then, when it became clear he wasn't going to work it out alone, he asked, 'Okay, what did I say this time?'

Sadie looked up from twirling her spoon anti-clockwise in her coffee and shook her head. 'Nothing. Really.' She faked a smile—and Dylan had seen enough of her real ones to be sure this one was fake. 'But we're letting our history colour our business discussions again, don't you think?'

Were they? Not really, Dylan decided. Which meant that whatever discussion she was having with herself in her head probably was. God, he really wished he knew what she was thinking.

'That's kind of inevitable, don't you think?' he asked. 'We've known each other a long time, after all.'

'I've barely seen you in the last five years,' Sadie pointed out.

'Which only makes it worse. We've got a lot of catching up to do.' Instinctively, he reached out to place his hand on hers, where it rested beside her coffee cup. 'And, Sadie, just because we haven't seen each other, that doesn't mean we're not still friends. That we're not still connected.'

She had to feel it too, that connection, tying them together through the years, however far he strayed. Surely she did, otherwise, he was all on his own out on this limb. He might not be able to stay, but it felt like he'd never truly left her either.

Sadie pulled her hand away, and Dylan's heart sank an inch or two.

'What would you like to do for dinner tonight?' she asked, not looking at him. 'I could book a table for you somewhere in town, if you'd like.'

For you. Not us. Yeah, that wasn't going to work for him.

Clearly the history thing was still bothering her. But as much as she wanted this to be all business, the truth was he wouldn't be there at all if it wasn't for their past. So maybe they needed to address that history head-on so they could move forward. On to a new business relationship, even if that was all it could ever be. At least he'd be able to help her.

He just had to find a way to get her to open up and talk to him about those five years he'd missed. And maybe, just maybe, what had happened before then.

Unfortunately, Dylan only knew one way to get those kinds of results. It worked with most of his clients' stumbling blocks—and it had always, always worked with Adem. Like the night he'd shown up pale and troubled, ring box in hand, trying to pluck up the courage to propose to Sadie, even though they had been far too young. Dylan had applied his usual technique, talked it out, and convinced Adem to do it—ignoring any cracking of his own heart as he'd done so.

The method was foolproof. It had precedent. No reason at all to think it wouldn't work with Sadie, too.

He needed to get her drunk.

Dylan drained his coffee, trying not to wince at the still-bitter taste. 'Town sounds good. But don't bother booking anywhere. I think tonight you need to show me the Kuşadasi nightlife.'

CHAPTER SIX

THE SAME WARDROBE, the same clothes—still nothing to wear. Sadie sighed and dropped to sit on her bed and study the contents of her closet from afar. What was she supposed to wear for a night out on the town anyway? She wasn't sure she'd ever had one in Kuşadasi—since they'd arrived she and Adem had always been too busy with the hotel. Tonight would be the blind leading the blind.

Except, of course, Dylan was probably the expert at wild nights out in towns and cities across the globe. If she was lucky, maybe she could wait until he inevitably started chatting up some blonde at the bar then slip away home without him even noticing. That would be good. Sort of.

But even that incredibly depressing plan still required her to get dressed.

Eventually she settled on her smartest pair of jeans, a black top that had enough drape at the front to look vaguely dressy, and a pair of heels. She'd just have to rely on the make-up and jewellery she'd picked out to do the rest.

Sadie checked her watch—she still had half an hour before she needed to meet Dylan. The calculation of the time difference between Turkey and England was so automatic these days it was barely seconds before she'd fired up the laptop ready to Skype Finn, glad to see that her parents' computer was already online.

Finn knew the sound of the Skype call well enough that Sadie wasn't surprised when the video picture resolved to show his cheeky face already there, ready to chat. His cheeks were red and his hair a little sweaty around the hairline, as if he'd been doing a lot of racing around. From the shouts and laughs in the background Sadie guessed that his cousins were visiting, too. Good. He had little enough interaction with other children in Turkey; she'd hate to think of him getting lonely over in England, too.

'Hi, Mum!' Finn waved excitedly across the internet. 'Wow! You look really pretty tonight.'

Guilt poured over her in a rush, threatening to wash away her carefully applied eyeliner and lipstick. 'Thanks, little man,' she said, the words coming out weak. She shouldn't be dressing up for Dylan, shouldn't let her son see her looking pretty for another man, even if he was only a friend. She should be with Finn, sorting their future.

That's what I'm doing, part of her brain argued back. She needed Dylan to save the Azure.

When had it all grown so complicated?

'Are you having fun with Grandma and Granddad?' she asked. 'What are you up to?'

'Lots. CJ and Phoebe are here with Auntie Rachel. We've been playing in the garden, and next we're going to build the biggest Lego fort in the world ever!' Finn's eyes brightened with excitement, and Sadie felt a wave of love rush over her, the way she always did when she saw him happy. Whatever else seemed crazy in her life at the moment, Finn at least was as wonderful, perfect and precious as always.

'Sounds fun.' She was just about to ask him something else when the sound of two high-pitched voices yelling Finn's name cut her off.

'Sorry, Mum. Gotta go. CJ needs me for the fort. Otherwise Phoebe will make it a pink princess castle again.' Finn's words came out in a rush as he moved further away from the screen. 'Bye, Mum!'

'Love you,' Sadie called after him, but all she could see was the back of his head, disappearing through the door to the other room. Well. Who was she to try and compete with a Lego fort, anyway?

Before she could end the call her sister Rachel appeared on the screen, settling into the chair Finn had just vacated. 'Sorry. They're just having so much fun together. It's lovely.'

'That's okay,' Sadie said with a smile. 'I'm just glad he's not missing me.'

'Liar.' Rachel grinned back. 'At least part of you wishes he was pining away without you. Go on, admit it.'

'Maybe a very small part.'

Rachel nodded. 'You wouldn't be human otherwise.' She squinted at the screen, and Sadie tried not to duck away under her sister's scrutiny. 'He's right, though. You *do* look pretty. What's going on there worth dolling up for?'

She groaned inwardly. She should have called *before* she'd got ready. She couldn't lie to Rachel—she'd tried often enough over the years, but her sister always saw through it. But how to tell the truth?

'I've got a potential investor visiting,' she said in the end. 'He wants to see the Kuşadasi nightlife. Does this look okay for bar-hopping? It's been so long I can't remember.'

'Stand up and give me a twirl,' Rachel instructed, and

Sadie did as she was told. 'It's perfect. So…this potential investor. Is he cute?'

Sadie sat back down with a bump. Cute wasn't exactly the word she'd use to describe Dylan. Heartstoppingly gorgeous but totally untouchable? Closer to the mark. Still, she wasn't saying that to Rachel.

'I suppose so,' she said, as neutrally as she could.

'And is there…dare I risk to hope it? Is there fizz?'

Fizz. The word they'd used as teenagers to describe that intangible connection, that feeling that you just had to touch that other person, be close to them, feel their smile on your face or you'd just bubble over and explode. Did Dylan have fizz? Silly question. He'd always had fizz. That was the problem. And when he'd placed that scarf around her neck and his fingers had brushed her skin…

'There *is* fizz!' Rachel announced gleefully. 'Don't try and deny it. I can tell these things. Psychic sister skills.'

Sadie shook her head. 'It doesn't matter if there is or isn't fizz. The investor…it's Dylan. You remember Adem's best man? He's just here because he wants to help out with the Azure, but he needs to convince his stakeholders we're a good investment so I'm trying to give him enough plus points to present a great proposal to them.'

'Dylan? Of course I remember Dylan. If I hadn't been already married at your wedding…'

'Then you could have lined up behind the other bridesmaids for a shot at him.'

'He was more than cute, Sadie,' Rachel pointed out. As if she hadn't noticed.

'He's an old friend.'

'So? There's fizz.'

'He's *Adem's* old friend,' Sadie stressed, hoping her

sister would just figure it out without her having to spell it out.

'Which means Adem trusted this guy,' Rachel countered. 'Which means you can too.'

'With my hotel, maybe. Not with any fizz.' Even if she *was* ready to throw herself back into romance with a one-night stand or something, Dylan Jacobs would not be a good choice. And if she was even *thinking* about anything longer term, he'd be the worst choice in the world. He'd said it himself, he didn't do commitment. And she couldn't be in the market for anything less. She had her son to think of.

But Rachel clearly didn't get that. 'Why not?'

'Rachel…'

Her sister sighed, the sound huffing across the computer speakers. 'It's been two years, Sadie. Adem wouldn't want you sitting out there all alone, you know that. He'd understand.'

'Maybe,' Sadie allowed. Her husband had been loving, generous and wonderful. He probably would want her to be happy again with someone else. On the other hand… 'But I'm sure he wouldn't want me with Dylan Jacobs either.' He'd want her settled and stable—not things on offer from Dylan, even if he was interested.

'Why on earth not?'

'He's not that sort of guy, Rach. Besides…' She trailed off, not wanting to put the thought into words.

'Now we're getting to it. Tell me.'

Sadie took a deep breath, and confessed. 'If I admit to feeling…fizz with Dylan now, isn't that the same as admitting I felt it when Adem was alive, too?'

'Oh, Sadie.' Sympathy oozed out of Rachel's words and expression. 'Fizz, attraction…it's just that. We all feel it from time to time, with all sorts of people. It's what we do with it that counts. Sometimes we ignore it, and sometimes we act on it and see what happens next.' She paused. 'You didn't, right? Act on it with Dylan, I mean, before?'

'No!' An easy truth. But it didn't stop the niggling guilt reminding her that she'd thought about it.

'Then don't beat yourself up about it. Go out with the guy tonight. Relax. Enjoy a little fizz…'

Sadie groaned. 'I'm going to pretend you're talking about prosecco.'

'Ha! Whatever helps you loosen up a bit.'

'I'd better go.' Sadie checked her watch to be sure. 'Tell Finn I love him. And that I'll call tomorrow.'

'Will do,' Rachel said with a nod. 'Now, go and have fun.'

With a weak smile Sadie clicked the 'end call' button. A whole evening watching Dylan flirt with barmaids and blondes. She had a feeling that fun was the last thing she should expect tonight to be. Maybe more some sort of weird torture technique devised purely to drive her insane.

'And yet I'm going anyway,' she murmured to herself as she gathered up her light jacket and handbag. 'The things I do for this hotel…'

Tipping his chair back against the wall behind him, Dylan watched Sadie's slim form as she made her way across the bar from the bathrooms, wondering if she'd notice he'd replenished their drinks in her absence. Operation Drunk Conversation was now officially two drinks in, and he still felt a little uneasy about it. Apparently Bar Street was the place to go and get drunk in Kuşadasi, although with its range of Irish and British bars, as well as some Turkish ones, Dylan wasn't sure this was necessarily the local colour he'd be trying to sell to the stakeholders. On the other hand, it clearly brought in plenty of tourists—and money. It almost reminded him of their student days.

She looked younger in jeans and heels, he decided. Almost like she had back in London as a twenty-something. She'd filled out a little since then, he supposed, but only in the best ways. Her slender curves enticed him as she swerved through the crowds to reach him. His head filled with music, the way it had the first time he'd ever met her—the Beatles' 'Sexy Sadie' playing on a loop through his mind.

'You're still alone. I'm amazed.' Sadie slipped into her seat and took a sip of her wine without commenting on the level in the glass.

'Why amazed?'

'Well, five minutes always used to be more than enough time for you to find a girl to flirt with when we used to go out.' There was no bitterness or censure in her voice, more amusement, but Dylan felt the words like paper cuts all the same. Probably because they were true.

'Times have changed.'

'Not that much,' Sadie said. 'Neal keeps me updated on your exploits, you know.'

He bit back a curse. But, on the other hand, she'd given him the in he'd been waiting for—the first reference to the good old days. 'I was just thinking how much younger you look in jeans, actually. Like you used to, back in London. I half expected Adem to appear and put his arm around you.'

Sadie's smile turned a little sad. 'Would that he could.'

'Yeah. It must be hard, being here without him. The memories, I mean.'

'We never came here, actually,' Sadie said, looking

around her curiously at the crowded bar. 'But you meant Turkey itself. The Azure.'

'I did, yeah,' Dylan agreed. Dare he push it yet? Just a little? 'No one would have blamed you for selling up and leaving, you know.' He needed to understand why she hadn't. What made her commitment to this place so strong? What was it about Sadie that made her so able to commit and stick? And what was missing in him?

'It wouldn't make any difference where we were anyway,' Sadie said, which didn't answer the question he hadn't asked, but Dylan supposed he couldn't really blame her for that. 'I see Adem every day when I look at Finn—and, to be honest, I love that reminder.'

Of course she did. He'd never seen any couple as in love as Adem and Sadie. He didn't really need her to answer—he knew. The Azure was her way of holding onto the love of her life. Just because he'd never felt like that about someone didn't mean he couldn't see it in others.

'I'm glad you have that.' The truth, even if it carried a little pain with it. 'I'm sorry. I should have visited more. Spent more time with Finn.'

'Yes, you should,' she said, mock-sternly. 'Why didn't you?'

Did she really not know why? After that night at Kim and Logan's wedding he'd been sure his motives for staying away had been more than clear—and that she'd be grateful he had. Unless she didn't remember? She *had* been pretty drunk. So had he, of course, or it never, ever would have happened in the first place.

Misgivings began to creep up on him when he thought again about his plan. The two of them, drunk alone together, hadn't ended well in the past. But he didn't know another way to get her to loosen up around him.

'Work, mostly,' he lied, realising she was still waiting

for an answer. 'But I'm ready to fix that now.' He raised his glass. 'To absent friends.'

'Absent friends,' Sadie echoed. Lifting her own glass, she drank deeply, unconsciously giving him exactly what he wanted. It was too late for misgivings now anyway. It was time to put the plan into action.

'Hey, do you remember the time Neal got locked out of that hotel wearing nothing but a corset and stockings?'

Sadie burst into laughter, putting her glass down too hard on the table so wine sloshed over the edge. 'Of course I do—it was my corset! What I don't remember is how he persuaded me to lend it to him.'

'You've always been a soft touch for Neal,' Dylan said. 'Besides, he had a very good story. I should know, I made it up.'

She slapped his arm. 'You deviant. Tell me the whole story, then—the truth this time.'

It was going to work, Dylan could tell. By morning they'd have exorcised all their ghosts and memories and be able to move on. To be the friends and business partners Sadie needed them to be.

And nothing more.

He took a glug of his beer and started the story.

'Well, there was this girl, see…'

Several bars later Sadie could feel the alcohol starting to get to her—in that pleasant, slightly buzzy way that meant it was time to stop before another drink seemed like a really good idea. Otherwise tomorrow would be no fun at all. *Now* she remembered why she didn't do this any more.

'I need to call it a night.' She pushed her still half-full glass across the table away from her.

'Not a bad idea.' Dylan drained the last of his pint. 'You always were the sensible one.'

'Somebody had to be.'

She gave him a friendly grin and he returned it, his smile all at once totally familiar and yet somehow new. It made that buzzy feeling in her limbs turn a little more liquid, like honey.

They'd talked all evening, almost without pause. She'd worried, when he'd suggested this night out, that it would be awkward, the conversation stilted. But instead they'd fallen into old patterns, chatting about the past in the way only friends who'd done their most significant growing up together could. The conversation had covered everything from the day they'd met until the last time they had all been together before Adem had died.

Everything except one night—the night of Kim and Logan's wedding.

Did he even remember? And, if so, how much? Curiosity was burning inside her with the need to know. Had *she* remembered wrong? It had been so long ago she was starting to doubt her own memories. They'd both been pretty drunk that night…

But she wasn't drunk tonight. Just tipsy enough to be a little daring.

'What's the plan for tomorrow?' Dylan asked, getting to his feet and grabbing his jacket. 'I've got a business call first thing, then I'm all yours for the day.'

Tomorrow. Had she even made a plan for tomorrow? 'I thought maybe the beach?'

'Lying prone in the sun sounds like the perfect way to deal with my inevitable hangover.' He groaned as they headed for the door. 'I am officially too old for this.'

Sadie smiled. 'I never thought I'd hear you admit to that.'

'We all have to grow up some time,' Dylan said with a shrug, and somehow it felt like he was saying far more than just the words.

Outside, the autumn evening air had turned a little chilly, and Sadie shivered as they walked along the sea-front, looking out for an empty cab.

'Cold?' Dylan asked. Then, without waiting for an answer, he slung an arm around her shoulder for warmth. A friendly gesture, Sadie knew. That was all it was—and nothing he and Neal hadn't done often enough in the past. But suddenly, here and now, as the fabric of his jacket brushed her bare neck she felt it. Fizz. Undeniable, impossible to ignore, fizz.

It was no good; she needed to know. And she was just drunk enough to ask.

'I've never asked you. Do you remember Kim and Logan's wedding?'

Dylan squinted out towards the ocean. 'That was the one up in Scotland, right? Where we all stayed in that weird hotel down the road and kept the bar open all night.'

'And Adem and Neal got into a drinking competition and passed out on the sofas in the next room.'

'I remember,' Dylan said, and even the words sounded loaded. 'You and Adem had been together, what? About a year?"

'Something like that. Do you remember what you asked me that night?'

He was standing so close, his arm around her shoulders, that she could feel his muscles stiffen. Oh, yeah, he remembered. 'Do you? We never… You never mentioned it again, so I always figured you must have forgotten. We weren't exactly sober that night.'

She'd gone too far to back out now. 'You asked me if

I'd ever wondered what might have happened if I'd met you first instead of Adem.'

'Yeah.' He let out a long breath. 'You said you hadn't.'

'And I truly hadn't, until that moment.'

The words hung there between them, the implication both clear and terrifying. They'd stopped walking without Sadie even realising, and suddenly a taxi pulled up beside them, the driver rolling down the window to ask where they wanted to go.

'The Azure, please,' Sadie said, shuffling along the back seat to let Dylan in beside her.

They rode in silence for a long moment before Dylan asked, 'And after?'

'After?' She knew what he was asking, but she needed a moment before she answered.

'After that moment. Did you…?'

She looked away. 'I wondered.'

'Huh.' Dylan slumped back against the car seat, as if all the tension had flowed out of his body with her words. Then he shook his head, laughing a little—Sadie got the impression it was at himself, rather than her. 'And then, of course, I tried to kiss you like a total idiot and—'

'Wait. What? I don't remember that bit.' And surely, surely that was the part she *would* remember, however much she'd had to drink.

'Don't you?' Dylan smiled, the expression shaded in the darkness of the cab. 'It was after we'd lugged Adem and Neal up to our rooms. You gave me a hug goodnight and…' He shrugged, trailing off. 'You pushed me away, of course.'

'I can't believe I don't remember that.'

'I'm glad you didn't,' Dylan said. 'Not my finest hour. I felt absolutely awful the next day—and was very glad one of us had been sober enough to be sensible.'

Sadie turned away, searching her memory for the lost moment and coming up blank. How different might their world have been if she'd remembered the next day? If she'd confessed to Adem? A thousand different paths spiralled from that moment, all but one untaken. And she wouldn't want to change it, she realised, not really. She wouldn't give up the years she'd had with Adem, or having Finn, for anything in the world. Things had worked out exactly as they were supposed to.

But that didn't stop her imagining what it might have felt like. And, God, did that bring a bucketload of guilt with it, right there.

Before she'd had time to work her way through half her emotions, they were back at the Azure. She paid up in a daze and walked inside, heading for the lift with Dylan beside her.

'You okay?' he asked, as the doors opened.

She nodded, and stepped inside, pressing the button for her floor on autopilot. 'Fine. So, tomorrow. Meet you in the lobby at ten?'

'Perfect.' He leant across her to press the penthouse button as they started to move. 'Sadie—'

'Don't worry about it,' she said, too fast. 'It's all in the past now.'

The lift dinged as it reached her floor, and she stepped towards the doors before they were even open.

Suddenly there was a hand at her waist, spinning her round, and Dylan was closer than she'd imagined, so close she could feel the heat of him.

'I might be about to be an idiot again,' he said.

Sadie swallowed, her mouth too dry. God, she wanted it. Wanted to feel his lips on hers, to see what she'd missed all those years ago. But the guilt that filled her had sobered her up and was already moving her feet backwards as the lift doors opened.

'Goodnight, Dylan.' She pulled away, stepping out, watching the frustration and fear crossing his face as the doors closed behind him and the lift whisked him away.

CHAPTER SEVEN

DYLAN WOKE UP the next morning to the sound of his phone alarm buzzing, far too early, and his head throbbing in time with the beeps. As if he needed the physical reminder of last night's exploits to give him a bad feeling about the day ahead.

He fumbled for the phone and switched off the alarm, his poor, tired brain trying to catch up with the day. He had a conference call. He had to deal with Sadie. He really needed a shower.

Deciding that the last might help with the previous two items, he hauled himself out of bed and into the bathroom, thoughts flying at him as fast as the water from the wonderfully powerful showerhead.

If he was feeling bad this morning, chances were that Sadie was feeling worse. And not just physically. He knew her tendency to beat herself up about things that weren't her fault, or weren't even all that wrong in the first place, and he had a feeling this morning would be a doozy.

Still, as bad as he felt for making her life more difficult than it already was—or at least more morally and emotionally complicated—he couldn't help but smile, remembering that for the first time since he'd met her he knew he wasn't in this alone. Not completely.

Switching off the water, he dried, dressed and managed to make it through the conference call—hopefully without any obvious signs of his hangover or his preoccupation. As he hung up, scribbling a last few notes to himself for later, he checked the clock. Still twenty minutes before he was due to meet Sadie. Should he work, nap or…?

He picked up his phone and hit the familiar key combination to call Neal. Yeah, it was early in Britain, but Neal had always been an early bird anyway. Except after nights out with him and Adem.

'How's it going?' Neal asked, in lieu of an actual greeting. 'You signed over your life savings to her yet?'

If he thought that would work… 'Nah. I got her drunk and told her the whole story about you and her corset instead.'

'Cheers. I'll look forward to that coming up next time we have a business meeting,' Neal said. 'But, seriously, how is she?'

'Probably hungover but otherwise fine.' He hoped.

Neal sighed. 'What did you do?'

'Nothing.' Much.

She'd try and pull back now, he could feel it. Try and put that distance they'd crossed last night back between them. Unless he could convince her not to.

'Although…' Dylan said, and Neal groaned.

'Here we go. Tell me.'

'I might have questioned Adem's plan for the Azure a bit. It needs updating.'

'So what? You're going to stay in Turkey and develop a better one?' Neal sounded sceptical.

'I'm going to work with her to develop one before I leave,' Dylan corrected him. She didn't have time to pull back. He only had a few more days to help her; they had to keep working. She'd see that, right?

Maybe the best thing was for them both to pretend that last night had never happened, just like last time. At least, once the headache faded.

'Are you, now?' Dylan didn't like the sudden raised interest level in Neal's voice.

'I am. What about it?'

'Just sounds like more involvement than you'd planned on,' Neal said. 'A lot more.'

Since Dylan's original plan had been get in, get out, send Sadie cash afterwards and never have to think about the Azure again, Neal had a point. He hadn't wanted to torment himself more than necessary by staying in her presence when she was more available than ever but still every bit as untouchable.

But all that had changed with two words. *I wondered.*

'She needs more help than I expected,' Dylan said, hoping his friend would accept the excuse.

'She needs every bit of help she can get,' Neal agreed with a sigh. 'I'm glad you're there.'

'So am I.'

Yes, he was still leaving in three days. And, yes, he knew he'd never be Adem, never be the love of Sadie's life. He wasn't imagining some perfect golden future for them together or anything.

But just knowing that she'd thought about it—about them—too? Well, that gave him hope.

And sometimes that was all a guy needed to get through the day.

The first thing Sadie registered when she woke up was her dry mouth. Next came the crushing weight of what felt like a boulder on her chest.

Last night had been everything she'd planned to avoid. How was she supposed to go back to All-Business Sadie after admitting that she'd imagined them together? And for the last twelve years…

After learning he'd tried to kiss her, too.

After almost letting him kiss her last night.

She pulled the pillow over her head and hoped it muffled her agonised groan.

And now she had to spend a whole day on the beach with him. In swimwear.

It all just went to prove that there really *was* a special hell for women who ogled their husband's best friend.

Escaping from her pillowy cage, she took deep breaths and tried to let the morning air soothe her—and her hangover. She needed to be calm and reasonable about this. As she had been about everything else she'd dealt with since Adem had died. She—and the Azure—needed Dylan. They needed his money, his investment and, much as she hated to admit it, his business brain, too. So she needed to find a way to make this right.

And, hopefully, considerably less awkward.

As she kicked off the covers and contemplated, Rachel's words from the night before floated back through her distracted brain. In some ways her sister had been right—as usual. Adem wouldn't want her to be alone or lonely. Which wasn't to say he'd want her to be rushing into the arms of another man either, but Sadie knew he wouldn't expect her to be alone forever.

She had, though. For the last two years the very idea of being with someone else had felt completely alien, the sort of thing that could only happen to other people. Adem had been the love of her life. Where was there to go from there really?

But last night, for the first time, the idea of moving on had seemed like a possibility. The thought of kissing another man had, for once, not filled her with revulsion or even confusion.

She'd wanted to kiss Dylan. And that was absolutely terrifying.

Because even if she was ready to *maybe* think about *possibly* moving on and *perhaps* just *thinking* about dating again, Dylan Jacobs was not the man to move on with.

If she had been after a fling or a one-night stand, something to get her back in the dating game, then maybe. But she wasn't a one-night stand sort of girl, never had been. And now…she had responsibilities. Commitments that had to come before a little personal pleasure.

She had Finn.

She wouldn't be another notch on Dylan's bedpost—and with a guy like Dylan she knew that was all she could ever be.

No, last night had taught her something far more important than the fact he'd tried to kiss her once. It had taught her that they still had history, and friendship, even with Adem gone. Sadie wanted Dylan to stay part of her life—and part of Finn's. She wanted her son to learn about his father from the people who had loved him most—and that had to include Dylan.

Another reason, if she'd needed one, why she couldn't risk anything more with him. She knew him, too well perhaps. One night in his bed and he'd hit the road, not coming back until he was good and certain that she wasn't getting any ideas about things between them going anywhere.

Better to keep things simple. Maybe they couldn't be just business—but they could definitely be just friends.

Now she just needed a way to get that across to Dylan.

Lying back against her cool sheets with the covers off,

she let the breeze from the open window caress her skin as she considered her options. This wasn't a conversation she wanted to have with him while she was wearing a bikini. She needed to stall a little before they got to the beach. Then he could sunbathe, nap, explore, ignore her the rest of the day, whatever he wanted. As long as he understood how things were going to be.

Sadie smiled to herself as the perfect solution presented itself. And it might just solve both of their hangovers, too.

It was hard to tell what Sadie was thinking or feeling when Dylan met her in the lobby. Her eyes were hidden behind oversized dark glasses, her hair pulled back from her face, and she wore a light skirt and tee shirt. From the large straw bag she carried, with towels peeking out the top and a bottle of suntan lotion in the front pocket, he assumed they were still on for the beach. Beyond that, he had no idea how the day might play out—and she didn't seem inclined to tell him.

'Ready to go?' she asked, the moment he approached. When he nodded, she spun on her heel and headed out, slipping behind the wheel of her car and waiting for him to join her.

They drove in silence for about ten minutes, while Dylan thought up a dozen conversation starters in his head. But every time he turned to use one of them Sadie's cool indifference to his presence stopped him.

He had to let her go first.

The first rumblings of doubt started in his mind when Sadie pulled in at a tumbledown farmhouse on the side of the road. There was no sign of anyone else around, but she jumped out of the car all the same and waited for him to follow.

A terrace sat outside the house itself, covered with vines and greenery, right next to the road. Sadie climbed the rickety wooden steps up to it and, after a moment, Dylan did the same.

'Um, did we add something to today's itinerary?' he asked, as they stood alone on the terrace.

'Trust me,' Sadie replied. 'We need this.'

What he really needed was a few more hours of sleep and some mega-painkillers, but she'd asked for his trust, so he'd give it to her.

After a moment the door to the farmhouse opened and a man walked out, smiling widely at Sadie, hands open in welcome. Sadie grinned back, and the two of them spoke in Turkish for a moment or two. Dylan didn't even try to guess what they were saying.

The man motioned to a nearby table, bare wood with benches to match, right at the edge of the terrace with a great view of the passing cars and the dusty fields beyond. But Sadie sat without question, so Dylan did the same.

'So this is…?' he asked.

Before Sadie could answer, a woman in an apron appeared, her dark hair coiled at the back of her head, and placed a strange metal pot, two glass teacups and a basket of bread on the table.

'Breakfast,' Sadie answered, reaching for the bread. 'Told you we needed it.'

Dylan started to relax. Maybe the woman had a point after all. He hadn't managed to make it down to the restaurant that morning, and his stomach definitely needed food.

The dishes kept coming, carried out by the man and the woman while Sadie explained about Turkish tea and waited for it to brew before pouring it. Dylan salivated at the sight of sweet, thick honey for the bread, bowls of olives, scrambled eggs with chorizo, chunks of salty feta cheese and a huge fruit platter. It might not be the full English he'd usually rely on to finish off a hangover, but Dylan had a feeling it would be more than up to the task.

They ate mostly in silence, Dylan savouring every mouthful of the delicious and obviously freshly cooked food. And as they ate, Dylan's hangover wasn't the only thing that started to recede. Somehow, without talking about it or even acknowledging it was there, the tension that had been pulled tight between them since they'd met in the lobby that morning started to loosen, just enough for him to relax.

The powers of good food truly were transformative.

As Sadie mopped up the last of the chorizo and eggs with the end of the bread, Dylan poured out the final dregs of the tea, knowing that things were about to change.

It was time for The Talk.

God, he hated The Talk.

Steeling himself, he waited for her to begin.

'Okay. So, I thought we needed that before we could deal with…' Sadie trailed off.

'Last night,' Dylan finished for her. No point beating around the bush now. 'Good call.'

Sadie picked up her paper napkin and began twisting it between her fingers. 'Here's the thing. I figure you wanted to go out last night to remind me that we're not just business. We have history.'

'I guess, a bit. Perhaps.' It hadn't been much of a plan, but it still discomfited Dylan a bit to have it seen through so easily.

'And you're right,' Sadie went on, apparently unconcerned by his manipulations. 'I get it. We're friends—and I don't want to lose that.'

'I'm glad to hear it.' Ah, so this was the way it was. She was actually giving him the old 'I don't want to ruin our friendship with sex' talk. He'd never been on this side of it before.

It kind of sucked.

But her friendship mattered to him—no, just having her in his life mattered to him. Any way that worked for her. So he'd go along with it, despite the stinging pain that had taken up residence in his chest. Because what else did he have to offer her, really?

'I want you to be part of Finn's life.' She leant across the table, shifting plates and bowls out of her way. Dylan rescued the remains of the honey, which were perilously close to her elbow. 'I want him to know about his dad from the people who really knew and loved him—and that includes you.'

She sounded so earnest, so determined that he couldn't even find it in himself to be mad or frustrated. Because, of course, it was all about Adem in the end. He should never have imagined that it could be otherwise.

'But as for the rest of it,' Sadie said, sitting back again, the distance between them yawning open, 'there's no point dwelling on the past. Right?'

'I've always tried not to,' he said mildly. Tried not to think about how different his life might have been if his father hadn't walked out and left them, if he hadn't spent his youth protecting his mother and sister, taking care of them, finding the money for the household bills each week. How different *he* might be. Life was what it was—no point pretending otherwise.

Except, of course, that was exactly what he was doing every time he thought about Sadie and imagined what could have been, maybe. What they could have had if he'd been the one she'd run into with a full cup of coffee one rainy Oxford day instead of Adem.

Stupid, really. It wouldn't have made any difference. They'd have flirted perhaps. Maybe even dated for a bit. But if she thought he wasn't the settling-down sort now, it was nothing compared to how he'd been at twenty-one. He'd have sabotaged things within a month—and Sadie would probably have cried on Adem's shoulder, and they'd have fallen in love anyway.

Just the way it was supposed to be.

'I'm ready to face the future now, I think.' Bravery shone out of Sadie's face, and Dylan tried to shake away his melancholy thoughts and listen. 'I'm really ready to build a new future out here for me and my son—not just keep living Adem's dream and his plan.'

Did she really think that counted as moving on? She'd still be here, in the place Adem had chosen for them. She might think this was a big step forward, but to Dylan it still looked like clinging to the past.

The past was all well and good, but living there wasn't going to help Sadie find her spark again. For that, she needed to move on to her own dreams. And he was there to help her do that.

'So, what does that mean?' he asked.

'It means I'm ready to listen to your plans, instead of insisting on following Adem's,' Sadie said. 'You tell me what we need to do at the Azure, and we'll do it. Whatever it takes to save this place for Finn.'

For Finn. That was why she thought she was doing this. Interesting.

'Great.' It wasn't moving on, not really. But it might be the best he got from her, and at least it gave him a way to help her. It could be worse. 'Then let's get to the beach.'

'The beach?' Her nose crinkled up adorably, and Dylan looked away to stop himself staring at it.

'I always do my best brainstorming when I'm relaxing,' he said, faking a smile.

CHAPTER EIGHT

LADIES' BEACH WAS comfortingly familiar to Sadie. As they walked from the car down onto the soft sand she took deep breaths and let the salt air fill her lungs, while the sound of gulls and families playing in the sand and surf echoed in her ears. But even as she let the comfort of the seaside wash over her, the feeling that something was missing ached in her middle.

She missed Finn. He loved the beach so much—especially this one. They could play for hours, searching for shells to decorate sandcastles or jumping over the waves as they lapped against the shore. When they'd first moved here they'd spent almost every weekend at the beach the whole summer.

'It's a nice beach,' Dylan commented, his trainers dangling from his fingers as he walked barefoot beside her.

'Nice?' Sadie said disbelievingly. She took another look around her at the perfect yellow sand and bright blue water. 'It's perfect.'

Dylan chuckled. 'Okay, yeah. It's pretty gorgeous. I can see why this, at least, is a big draw for the tourists. Finn must love it here.'

'He does.' The heavy weight of a pebble of guilt joined the ache in her middle. When was the last time she'd brought Finn down to the beach? Things had just been so busy… 'We haven't made it down here together for a while, though.'

She flinched with surprise as Dylan's hand came up to rest against the small of her back, rubbing comfort through her tee shirt and steering her around a hole some enterprising young child had clearly spent some hours digging. She needed to pay more attention to where she was going. But Dylan's hand stayed at her back and the warmth of it, so much more heated than the bright sun overhead, was too much of a distraction in itself.

Friends, she reminded herself. That was what they'd agreed. And beyond one drunken attempt at a kiss she had no evidence at all he wanted anything more. A hand on the back was not seduction—however much it felt like it right now.

'When we get the Azure back on track, you'll be able to hire more help,' Dylan said, apparently oblivious to the effect his touch was having on her. 'Give you more time with Finn.'

'That would be perfect.' Finn deserved so much more than an overworked, stressed mother. She needed to be both parents to him now, and that meant being there all the time. A reduced workload would definitely help with that.

She just hoped it wouldn't be too reduced. After all, what else was she going to do once Finn was in bed or at school? And once Dylan was gone. All the times when she was alone again. She would need something to distract her then, and work was perfect.

Sadie almost laughed at herself. From one extreme to another—it seemed she'd always find something to worry about. They had to actually save the Azure first anyway, and that by no means felt like a sure thing.

Everything was so much harder without Adem there

to help—even if it was just someone else to help build sandcastles or explore seaweed clumps.

Suddenly Dylan stopped walking, right in the middle of an open patch of sand unmarred by castles or holes and a decent distance from any of the other beachgoers.

'This looks like the perfect spot,' he said, dropping his bag and towel to the sand.

'To brainstorm?' Sadie asked, one eyebrow raised.

He flashed her a smile. 'To sleep off the remains of my hangover.'

'I suppose that *is* the first step to saving my hotel,' Sadie said, only half sarcastically. After all, it was going to take Dylan on top form to help the Azure.

'Definitely.'

Without warning, he reached for the hem of his tee shirt and pulled it over his head, revealing more muscles and hair than she'd expected—and definitely more skin than she felt comfortable with as a friend. Sadie's mouth dried up and she swallowed painfully as she tried not to stare. God, but the man was gorgeous. She'd known that, of course, objectively. But she'd never spent much time with such upfront and undeniable proof, certainly not in the last decade.

Dylan had always been good looking, but now he'd grown into his looks completely. He wasn't a play*boy* any more, Sadie decided. He was all man.

She needed to get out of there. 'I'm going to go and swim.'

'Okay.' Dylan looked up from laying out his towel and grabbed for her wrist before she could turn away. His proximity and the feel of his skin on hers sent every sense she had into overdrive. How did anyone ever manage to be just friends with someone who looked like Dylan Jacobs? She needed some sort of handbook.

'Sadie,' he said, staring down into her eyes, his gaze so compelling she couldn't even think of looking away. 'I will find a way to save the Azure. You know that, right?'

Sadie swallowed again, her throat dry and raspy. 'I believe you.'

His mouth twisted up into a half-smile. 'Millions wouldn't, right?'

'This is business,' Sadie said with a shrug. Something she would do well to remember. 'And you know business. If anyone can save the Azure, it's you.'

'Only for you,' he murmured.

It was too much. 'Right. Swimming.' Sadie pulled her hand away from his and tugged down her skirt and pulled off her tee shirt, leaving her in just her sensible purple tankini. Then, with what she hoped was a friendly smile, she headed straight for the water.

She couldn't afford to be swayed by fizz, or touch, or the way he looked at her. Dylan looked at every woman he met that way, she was sure. He was a walking chemistry experiment for the female half of the human race. She couldn't read any more into that.

Money and business advice was all he had to offer her, and only for the short term. Once he got bored he'd be on the move again. She really needed to remember that.

Settling onto his towel, Dylan propped himself up on one elbow in the sand and watched Sadie's tankini-clad form sashaying towards the sea. He doubted she knew she was doing it, but her hips swayed as she walked all the same, her feet sinking into the sand. All those slender curves she kept so well hidden under dark suits and shapeless jackets were on display now and, friends or not, he wasn't going to miss a minute of watching them.

Friends. She'd sounded so certain over breakfast that friendship was all she wanted from him. After the night before, and her escape from the lift, he'd almost believed her. Until he'd touched her wrist on the beach and watched the colour flood her cheeks as their skin had met. Until he'd watched her watching him and known that whatever she thought she wanted, her body had other ideas.

Bad ideas, admittedly. She was a single mother with more responsibilities than money and a rigid sense of commitment that was in complete opposition to his own. But she wanted him. Maybe even half as much as he had always wanted her.

He couldn't give her what he knew she needed—what she'd always wanted since they'd met. Sadie was the kind of woman you settled down for, that you built a life with. Another reason why Adem had been perfect for her. Despite his own fears and apprehensions, he'd put aside every reason not to and jumped at the chance to have Sadie with him for life.

Even if that had turned out to be far shorter than any of them had imagined.

No, Dylan wasn't the man to replace Adem in her life, if anyone even could. He couldn't commit to forever, and he knew that Sadie deserved nothing less. And even if he wanted to try…what would it do to her, not to mention Finn, when he failed? It wasn't worth the risk.

But he could offer her something else. After all the sorrow and stress in her life over the last couple of years, he could see shoots of new growth in her—the first hints of spring ready to return to Sadie's world. She was ready to get out there again, to blossom into a new life.

He could be a friend and business partner in that new life. But right now, in this brief time of transition, maybe he could be something more. Something temporary. A first step, perhaps. Something that would waken that new Sadie completely.

It might be the worst idea he'd ever had—and if he told Neal what he had planned he had no doubt his old friend would be on the first plane out there to stop him. But it had been over a decade now—thirteen years of watching her, wanting her and wondering about her. Who could really blame him for wanting to taste that forbidden fruit, just once, now he knew how much she wanted it too?

Just one night. How bad a sin would that be, really? As long as he was honest and upfront with her, and they both knew what they were getting out of it. They were adults now. If Sadie knew exactly what he was offering, she could make her own decision.

It just might take a while for her to talk herself into it, knowing Sadie.

He watched her lean legs disappearing into the water and shifted to keep a better eye on her as she dived under the waves. She looked so at home out there, like a sea nymph returning to her natural environment after being cooped up on land for too long. She looked free in a way she hadn't since he'd arrived in Turkey.

Dylan wanted to make her look that way on land. Preferably in a bed.

Eventually, Sadie emerged again from the waves, slicking her dark hair back from her face with her hands. With water droplets shining off her skin in the sun, she began walking back towards him, and Dylan found himself putting a lot of effort into keeping his body calm and relaxed in the face of such a sight. God, she was beautiful.

The sound of his ringing phone was an almost welcome distraction. Fumbling in the pocket of his rucksack, he pulled it out and answered, only half listening to what his assistant had to say as Sadie arrived, rolled her eyes at him, and began towelling off with a spare towel.

By the time he ended the call Dylan wasn't entirely sure what he'd agreed to, but he trusted his assistant to email him all the pertinent details. He'd deal with them later, when there were fewer distractions around.

'Honestly. Who brings work to the beach?' Wrapping a flimsy scarf thing around her waist, Sadie dropped to sit on the towel beside him.

'You brought me,' Dylan pointed out. 'This week, that's practically the same thing.'

Sadie laughed, high and bright, a sound he'd almost thought lost. She was so much more relaxed out here; he could tell it from the lines of her shoulders, the absence of the crease between her eyebrows that he'd thought was permanent. This was the Sadie he remembered.

'Seriously, though,' she said, 'what's so important that it can't wait a few hours? Why not just let it ring—or, better yet, turn it off?'

Dylan shrugged—and realised she was watching his shoulders rise and fall. Interesting. 'Guess I don't want to risk missing an opportunity. I've missed too many in my life already.'

He'd been talking about the years spent taking responsibility for his family, saying no to chances and opportunities because they'd needed him. But as the words hung in the air between them he realised she thought he meant something else entirely. And maybe, he admitted to himself, maybe he did. *Did you ever wonder what might have happened if you'd met me first, instead of Adem?*

I wondered.

Sadie looked down at her hands, damp hair hanging forward across her cheek. 'I'm not the same girl you asked that question all those years ago,' she said, her voice soft.

'You think I don't know that?' he asked. 'Look at me, Sadie.' She did as he asked, and Dylan took a long moment just absorbing everything she was now. Slowly, obviously, he looked over every inch of her, from her hair—shorter now than when they'd met by a good foot—down over her body, past every added curve or line, every soft patch and every muscle, all the way to her feet.

Did she really not know? Not realise how much she'd grown up since then—and how every year had only made her a better person? Who would want the twenty-year-old Sadie compared to the one who sat before him now?

'You are so much more now than you were then,' he murmured, knowing she'd hear him anyway. 'You're stronger, more beautiful, more alive…more than I ever dreamt any woman could be.'

Sadie stared down at him, captivated by his gaze as confusion, guilt and hope fought for space in her head. Did he really think that?

Yes. The answer came fast and true as she looked into his eyes. This wasn't Dylan making a move, the way he did with all those other women. This wasn't a seduction attempt. It was him stating a fact—something that was true and obvious to him, even if she found it hard to believe.

The knowledge that he believed it warmed her damp skin far more than the sun overhead. And his gaze on her body…well, that felt even hotter.

She broke, forcing her gaze away from his, and reached for a dry towel to lay out on the sand. Whatever this was between them, she wasn't ready to deal with it just yet. She needed time to process his words—to examine them, pick them apart and find some sense in them, somewhere. And that was all but impossible when he was lying there next to her in nothing but a pair of swim shorts.

'You should go for a swim,' she said, not looking at him. 'The water's glorious.'

'You looked very happy, splashing about out there.' He didn't make any move towards the water, though.

'I love it,' Sadie admitted. A truth for a truth perhaps. 'The sea always makes me feel…free somehow.' Like all her promises and commitments, all her obligations and the weight of her worries might just float away on the tide.

'I can see the appeal.' With a groan, Dylan hauled himself to his feet, brushing off the stray grains of sand that clung to his legs. 'Okay. I'll go for a swim.' He flashed her a smile. 'Just for you.'

'Great. Enjoy.' Sadie sat down on her fresh towel with a bump, staring after him as he walked towards the water's edge, the sun turning his skin golden across his broad back and trim waist.

She needed to think, she reminded herself, not ogle. With an act of willpower much harder than it should have been, she lay down and closed her eyes. There was no way she could think sensibly about that strange moment with Dylan while she could still see him. His very presence was distracting.

Unfortunately, she'd failed to account for her late night and exercise in her plan. The next thing she knew, cool droplets of water were dripping onto her and a sun-warm towel was being laid across her body. Her eyes flew open to find out why.

'Sorry.' Dylan tossed his head back, sending more

water droplets flying. 'But it's pretty warm out here. I was afraid you'd burn.'

Personally, Sadie thought his presence might be more of a threat of that than the sun, but she wasn't telling him that.

'Thanks.' She sat up. 'Good swim? How long was I asleep?'

Dylan shrugged, fished in his bag for his phone and checked the time. 'Half an hour or so, I guess? It's nearly two.'

'Wow. We missed lunch. Are you hungry?' It wasn't like they hadn't had a substantial breakfast to keep them going, but all of a sudden her stomach was grumbling.

'You know, amazingly, I am.'

'Come on, then. There's a great seafood place just off the beach. And it's in the shade.'

Together, they packed up their small camp. Sadie pulled on her skirt and top over her tankini, and breathed a sigh of relief as Dylan put his shirt back on too. Half-naked Dylan on the beach was one thing—sitting at lunch was another entirely.

They headed up towards the boardwalk that ran along the edge of the beach. Brushing dry sand from their feet, they put their shoes back on and Sadie led him past the first few restaurants and cafés to the one she had in mind.

'Finn loves the seafood platters here,' she said, as they waited to be shown to a table. 'You'd think a four-year-old would balk at calamari and battered prawns and such, but he loves them.'

'It's sounding pretty good to me too,' Dylan said. 'Perfect for a light lunch after a morning on the beach.'

Sadie smiled up at him. 'Then that's what we'll have.'

Their table was at the front of the restaurant, and the glass doors that spanned the length of the space had been thrown open. Sadie sat back and listened to the waves, enjoying the cool shade on her hot body as they waited for their food. Her skin felt almost too sensitive now, like it was still being touched all over. She glanced across the table at Dylan and found his eyes already on her.

Maybe that was why.

It wasn't until they were tucking into their seafood platter that Sadie spotted the small flaw in her plan. 'I was going to take you out for seafood tonight,' she said, remembering suddenly her booking at the restaurant on the marina that had such good reviews. It was fancier than this place, and probably had less sand on the floor, but she'd be willing to bet their seafood platter wouldn't have been as good as the one they were enjoying anyway. 'Guess I'd better come up with something else after this. What do you fancy?'

Dylan paused with a prawn halfway to his mouth, looking at her just a moment too long to be entirely comfortable.

'Actually, I've got plans for tonight.'

Oh. How stupid to assume that he'd want to spend the whole day with her and have dinner too. Just because he had the previous day.

'Plans for us,' Dylan clarified, and relief warred with anxiety within her.

'Oh?' she said, as lightly as she could. 'I thought *I* was supposed to be showing *you* the town.'

'And you've been doing a great job,' he said. 'But now it's my turn.'

'Where are we going?' Sadie asked, because she couldn't really ask 'Is this a date?' without sounding incredibly idiotic if it wasn't—and terrified if it was.

'It's a surprise.' Dylan's smile was almost wolfish, and it sent a shiver across the surface of her skin. 'Just dress fancy, be in the lobby at eight, and leave everything else to me.'

Leave everything to him? If Dylan was in charge she shouldn't be worried about it being a date.

She should be scared—or prepared—for it to be a seduction.

CHAPTER NINE

BACK AT THE AZURE, Dylan hung behind as they arrived in the lobby, waiting for Sadie to disappear before he put his last-minute plan into action.

It only took a moment to realise that Sadie was doing exactly the same thing. The woman was incurably curious.

'Go on,' he said, making a shooing motion with his hands. 'You go get yourself all dolled up for tonight.'

'You're sure?' Sadie remained hovering next to the reception desk, her hands clasped in front of her. Behind the desk, the woman on Reception rolled her eyes in amusement. 'You don't need me to call and book anything? What about a taxi?'

'I have it all in hand,' Dylan assured her. Which was only partially a lie—he knew exactly what he needed to do to get it in hand. Sadie just had to leave the area first. 'And if I don't, the lovely…' He waved at the girl behind the desk.

'Esma,' she filled in promptly.

'Esma here can help me. So go. Get ready.' For a moment he thought she was about to object again, then she nodded sharply and started to head for the lifts.

He should let her go. Anything else would just make her more curious, more determined to find out his plans. But still…

'And, Sadie?' he called after her. She paused and turned back to face him. 'Don't wear black tonight.'

Sadie's frustrated expression was its own reward.

Once he was sure she'd really gone, and the lift lights had ticked up to the higher floors, Dylan turned to Esma.

'Okay, here's the thing. I have a plan, but I need a little help.'

'Whatever you need, sir,' Esma replied cheerfully, and he wondered if she'd been ordered to give him anything he wanted, just to make sure he invested. Probably, he decided. No one who worked with people all day was ever naturally that cheery by late afternoon.

'Great,' he said. 'Here's what I need...'

A few phone calls later and it was done. Cars booked—thanks to Sadie's reminder about taxis—and the best table reserved at the restaurant of the swankiest and newest hotel in Kuşadasi. As an afterthought, he'd also booked a room. Not—despite the voice at the back of his head telling him what a great idea it would be—to try and convince Sadie that friendship wasn't enough.

No, if Sadie was serious about coming up with a new plan, and doing whatever it took to save the Azure, then she needed to know what she was up against. And so did he. The Paradise Grand Hotel was the place to go for that. By the time she'd taken a good look at the place and its rooms and restaurant, Sadie would know exactly how much work they had ahead of them.

Letting himself into his suite, he headed straight for the shower, whistling as he went. Everything was coming together nicely.

It wasn't until he was lathering up, water sluicing down around him, that it occurred to Dylan that *Sadie* might think the evening could be something other than just business.

And would that really be so bad?

They'd made it past the memories of last night and through the strange, close moments on the beach. If he wasn't mistaken, there had been a definite…softening in Sadie's attitude to him since he'd confessed to the almost-kiss she apparently couldn't remember.

Maybe this *was* more than just business. Maybe it could even be a second chance at something he'd never really had a first chance at.

But no. Tonight wasn't the night.

Even if he did want to try and win one night with her, one glorious stolen moment, it couldn't be tonight. Before anything at all could happen between them, they had to hammer out the work side of things. Mixing business and pleasure never ended well, in his experience.

But once their plan for the Azure was secure, he'd have a whole new proposal to put to Sadie.

He couldn't just take his usual, casual approach to a hook-up—because Sadie wasn't like his usual conquests. They had history, for a start. And she'd been clear on the friendship front, for good reasons. Her place was here in Turkey, with Finn and her memories, much as he wished he might be able to persuade her to move on from that. He couldn't compete with the commitments she'd made—and even if he could, would he really want to? So he'd be upfront about what he could offer—and it wasn't forever. He was a short-term fix at best—in business or otherwise. That had to be clear before he could take things further, otherwise it wouldn't be fair—on either of them.

Tonight would be all business.

Decision made, Dylan shut off the shower and told himself that putting on his best suit for the evening was all about the destination, not the company.

* * *

Don't wear black. What kind of fashion advice was that? And who was Dylan Jacobs to tell her what she should or shouldn't wear anyway?

Except…if tonight was about them for once, instead of business, maybe this was just his way of hinting at that. Letting her know she was off duty tonight; that she could retire the black suit, relax and just enjoy being there with him.

She had to admit it did sound appealing.

Eventually, she picked out a navy halterneck cocktail dress that showed off her slightly pink shoulders, and slid it over her showered and lotioned skin. It was fancier than anything she'd have worn to the restaurant at the Azure or to a bar, but not too over the top. And he had said to dress up…

With a decisive nod, Sadie picked out her highest silver heels and added a little eyeliner to her usual make-up.

When she finally made her way down to the lobby, she was glad she'd made the effort. Hanging off the arm of Dylan Jacobs could be enough to make a girl feel positively plain by comparison at the best of times, but the suit he'd chosen for the evening only made things worse. Charcoal grey and perfectly cut, it accentuated all the wonderful things about his body that she'd tried not to stare at on the beach that morning. With a crisp, white shirt open at the neck he looked the epitome of relaxed elegance.

Sadie stood up a little straighter and hoped she didn't fall over in the unfamiliar heels.

'You look fantastic,' Dylan said, leaning in to kiss her cheek. 'And navy—'

'It's not black,' Sadie interrupted quickly. 'That was your only stipulation.'

'Is definitely your colour—that was all I was going to say.' Dylan flashed her a smile as he took her arm. 'Come on, the car is waiting.'

'Okay,' Sadie said, once they were both settled in the back seat of the car. 'I'm dolled up, we're in the car—*now* will you tell me where we're going?'

'What's the best, most luxurious and prestigious hotel in Kuşadasi?'

'The new Paradise Grand,' Sadie answered promptly, then frowned. 'Wait. Why are we going there?'

'To check out the competition,' Dylan said. 'If you're really ready to go with a new plan to save the Azure, you need to know exactly what you're up against.'

She should have worn a black suit.

Hopefully the car was dark enough that he couldn't see her embarrassed blush. What had she been thinking, imagining this could be anything more than just business? Wasn't that what they'd agreed? And what she'd insisted on from the start?

This was why he was here, in Turkey. Anything else was completely incidental. She had to remember that.

'Here we are,' Dylan said a while later, as the car pulled to a halt. Jumping out, he headed round to open her door before the driver could, and she took his hand as she stepped out of the car.

At least now she knew what she was really there for, she could give it her full attention.

The new Paradise Grand Hotel was on the outskirts of town, a little further than most tourists would like—but there the similarities with the Azure ended. Sadie was pretty sure that any guest would put up with the mildly inconvenient location in return for the splendour the Paradise Grand offered.

The hotel building rose out of a garden of palm leaves

and greenery, all glass and steel and white stone. Her hand on Dylan's arm, Sadie climbed the steps and the automatic doors opened with a swoosh.

Inside, the lobby was every bit as impressive as the exterior. The centre of the building was open all the way to the glass roof—some twenty storeys up—and every floor had a balcony overlooking the majesty of the central foyer. An ostentatious fountain burbled in the middle, surrounded by more local flora. Sadie swallowed as the chattering sounds of what had to be a full-occupancy hotel filled her ears.

Yeah, nothing like the Azure at all.

They were led through to the elevators by one of the several concierges, then up to the restaurant on the top floor. Their table, Sadie was hardly even surprised to note at this point, was right by the window, looking out over the town of Kuşadasi and the ocean beyond.

She wondered if she could see the Azure from there...

'So, what do you think?' Dylan asked, after the waiter had taken their wine order and left them to peruse the menu.

Sadie shook her head. 'The Azure is nothing like this.' And, quite honestly, she wouldn't want it to be. Yes, the Paradise Grand was impressive, and luxurious—but it wasn't her dream. Or Adem's.

'That's because this place is brand-new,' Dylan said. 'Shiny as the day it came out of the box. That's what some customers want.'

'But not all.'

'No, not all.' He leant back in his seat, looking out over the admittedly glorious view. 'But before you decide what your customers want, you need to know what *you* want. If it isn't this, fine. But what is it? What do you want the Azure to be? What makes it special to you? What's the big dream?'

Wasn't that the million Turkish lire question? The one she knew she *should* know the answer to already.

But she didn't. Because it had always been Adem's dream, not hers. She'd gone along with it, listened, been supportive, helped where she could…but she couldn't say what the goal was or the vision, because he'd held all that in his head. All she had were the plans he'd left behind and they'd already established that they weren't enough.

'Adem wanted…' she started, but Dylan shook his head.

'I'm not interested in what Adem wanted for the place. If you truly want to save it, to give it a new future against competition like this, it has to be *your* dream. Not his.'

Sadie stared at him, knowing he was right but still not knowing the answers.

How could she admit to him that her commitment to the Azure had more to do with memories of the past than the future?

Watching her, sitting across the table in that beautiful dress, her shoulders bare and her skin golden in the candlelight, Dylan wished heartily that this could be what it must look like to outsiders—a romantic meal for two. But he was in Turkey to do a job—to help her. And he couldn't let his personal wants get in the way of her very urgent business needs.

Not yet, anyway.

Still, seeing her struggle to answer what should have been the first question he'd asked on arrival, he wished more than anything that wasn't the case.

'I…I don't know,' Sadie finally admitted, the frustration in her expression showing him exactly how much those words had cost her.

'Okay. Try this,' he said. 'Imagine yourself at the Azure in five years' time. How does it look? What's its best features?'

'Five years…' Sadie's eyelids fluttered closed as she considered. 'Finn would be ten.'

Finn. He'd asked her to think about the business, and she'd instantly thought of her son. Dylan frowned. What was he missing here?

'Sadie,' he said, and her eyes flew open again. His gaze locked onto hers, and he knew this was his best chance to get at the truth. 'Tell me honestly. Why do you want to save the Azure?'

'For Finn,' she said, the words coming so quickly he knew she hadn't had to think about them at all. 'Because it's the only thing left of his father that I can give him. It's Adem's legacy.'

A noble reason, but Dylan knew it wouldn't be enough. She had to want it for herself, too. 'What about you?'

'I…I love the spa. That was always *my* place, *my* dream. But the hotel…it was all Adem.' He'd suspected as much, but from the relief that shone out of Sadie's face he had a feeling this was the first time she'd admitted to herself that, in truth, she didn't really want to be there. 'To be honest, without him there, some days it's hard to remember why I stay at all.'

'Sadie…' Dylan's heart clenched at the loss and confusion in her voice. No wonder the place was crumbling all around her. A project as big as the Azure needed love, not just obligation. It needed passion, not just vague enthusiasm. It needed what Adem had felt for it, and Sadie obviously didn't.

'I shouldn't have said that.' Sadie shook her head, as

if she could wipe away the words with the movement. The waiter arrived with their wine, and she took a large gulp the moment he'd tasted it and it had been poured.

'Are you ready to—?' the waiter started.

'Another few minutes, please.' Neither of them had so much as looked at the menu yet. Besides, he wasn't going to let Sadie use ordering food as an excuse to drop this line of conversation. Not when there was so much more to say.

As the waiter backed unobtrusively away, Dylan fixed Sadie with a determined look. 'You were saying?'

She took a deep breath before answering. He wondered if that was a sign that what was coming was a lie. He wasn't used to Sadie lying—or perhaps he'd just never noticed her lies before.

'The Azure is a wonderful hotel,' she said. 'It has huge potential, plenty of history and an awful lot going for it businesswise. But more than that, it's our future—mine and Finn's, I mean. It's my son's inheritance. And I'm committed to saving it.'

'Even though it's not your dream?' She didn't understand. Sometimes commitment wasn't enough. Sometimes commitment made people miserable, made them yell and scream and cry—until they just gave up on it and walked away, like his father had done.

He really didn't want to see that happen to Sadie.

'Only little girls believe that dreams will come true.' There was a scathing note in Sadie's voice, but Dylan ignored it. Because he knew different.

Sadie had believed in dreams once. He'd seen it in her eyes the day she'd shown him her engagement ring for the first time, and again on her wedding day. The first time she'd held out her baby son to meet him. She'd believed in happily ever after, in possibilities and greatness, even if she'd wanted them all with another man.

Finally, he'd found something about new Sadie he didn't like as much as old Sadie.

He sighed. How to make her understand? 'Look. I could give you all the money your current business plan calls for. I could help you come up with a new plan and fund that instead. I could bulldoze the Azure and rebuild it from the ground up, if you decided that was what you wanted. But none of it will make a bit of difference if you don't want it enough.'

'I just told you I—'

'Commitment and obligation aren't enough,' he interrupted her. 'You're not a multinational conglomerate, and you're not trying to build a heartless, soulless place like the Paradise Grand. The Azure is about charm, heart and home—those are its selling points. The personal touch. And if it's not home to you, if you don't love it…' He shook his head.

'So you're saying you won't help me.' Sadie straightened her cutlery beside her napkin and avoided his gaze.

'I'm not saying that,' he said. 'But I want you to really think about what it is you want, whether the Azure truly is your home, before we go any further with this.'

It was a risk—both personally and professionally. He was testing her commitments to the past and, knowing how she'd felt about Adem, it was entirely possible she was going to send him packing. So, yeah, big risk.

But he knew it was also the right thing to do. The only thing.

As the tension stretched between them he reached for his menu and opened it.

'Come on, let's order. That very discreet and professional waiter over there has been hovering for at least the last ten minutes.'

Sadie nodded, and turned to the first page of her own menu, but he wasn't sure she was actually reading it at all. Instead, she looked completely lost in thought.

Dylan just hoped that they were good thoughts.

Sadie ate her meal in silence and, for once, Dylan seemed content to let her. Maybe he knew she had too much to think about to make conversation at the same time. Or maybe he was just preoccupied with whatever message had flashed up on his phone. Either way, he didn't seem particularly interested in her.

So much for her thoughts that tonight might be more than just business. She really should have known better.

The worst part was admitting that, for a moment, she'd hoped it could be something more. That maybe, just maybe, this might be a chance for her to start moving on. To follow Rachel's advice and get back out there. A totally out of character, one-night stand to reboot her chances at romance. Just this once.

Dylan was the king of short-term flings. If she wanted something short and sweet to kick-start her new life, he'd be perfect. As long as they could be upfront about what it was and wasn't, and could keep it separate from business.

But it seemed that *nothing* trumped business for Dylan.

As she finished up her last mouthful of dessert—which was, she had to admit, delicious—Sadie pushed the plate aside and prepared to call time on an altogether depressing evening. Not only had she completely misread Dylan's intentions, the more time she spent at the Paradise Grand, the more convinced she became that the Azure could never be anything like this.

'Do you have a car booked back to the Azure,' she asked, 'or shall I get the concierge to call us a taxi while we pay for dinner? They can take a while on busy nights.'

Dylan looked up from his phone and grinned. 'Sorry, am I ignoring you?'

Sadie shook her head. 'I'm just thinking about getting back to work.'

'Actually, there's one more thing I want to see here first.' He slipped his phone back into his jacket pocket and smiled again, slower this time. Sexier. With his full attention on her, Sadie couldn't stop the warmth that seemed to cover her skin under his gaze. Really, who could blame a girl for getting ideas when he looked at her like that?

'What's that?' she asked, but Dylan was already standing.

'Let me settle up here,' he said, eyes dark with promise. 'Then you'll find out.' He flashed her one last smile as he signalled the waiter over, and Sadie swallowed despite her suddenly dry throat.

Get a grip, Sadie, she told herself firmly. She was imagining things. He'd made it perfectly clear that tonight was about business only. Nothing he did next would convince her otherwise.

Or so she thought, until he led her out of the restaurant to the elevator, stopping at the twelfth floor and pulling out a room key card.

'You got us a room?' she asked, as he slipped the key card into the lock and, with a flash of green, the door fell open. He stood aside to let her in, and Sadie entered, staring around her. 'A room with champagne. And rose petals. And chocolates.'

Okay, maybe she hadn't been entirely imagining the vibes. After all, who booked a hotel suite complete with built-in seduction supplies if they didn't have plans other than business for the night?

In a split second Sadie made her decision. Even the fear and anxiety burning through her veins couldn't compete with the rising tension between them. For twelve years she'd wondered what it would feel like to kiss Dylan Jacobs—and since the moment in the elevator after their night on the town that curiosity had grown beyond all reasonable proportions.

He wanted her. What more proof did she need than rose petals on the coverlet and champagne chilling beside the huge king-sized bed? Maybe he'd just wanted to get business out of the way before they moved on to the more…personal part of the evening. She could understand that, even if she wished he'd shared his plans with her earlier. Except she'd never have concentrated on work if she'd known she had this waiting for her.

And, God, why was she still thinking?

Sucking in a breath, she turned, only to find Dylan right behind her. Her hands came up automatically to rest against his chest and she looked up to see heat in his eyes. No doubt at all, he wanted this too.

'You booked us a room.' Her voice barely sounded like hers—it was too breathy, too sultry.

Dylan nodded, his gaze fixed on hers like she held all the power here for once. Sadie kind of liked it.

Seizing the moment, she stretched up onto her toes, bringing her mouth just millimetres away from his, savouring every moment. 'Good idea,' she murmured, and leaned in to kiss him.

From the moment their lips touched, bliss filled Sadie. Every inch of her body fizzed from finally, finally kissing Dylan Jacobs. And she knew, in her heart, that this was right—that she could move on, that there was a future for her beyond always being a widow. That she was still a woman, too.

Until Dylan stepped back, breaking the kiss, his hands on her upper arms holding her away.

'Sadie…no, I'm sorry…'

Normally, the sight of Dylan lost for words would have amused her. As it was, it just enraged her.

He'd ruined her fizz.

'If you tell me you booked this room to compare it to the Azure…'

'I didn't ask for the champagne and stuff!' He waved an arm around wildly, encompassing the room. 'They must have…misunderstood.'

'Just like me.' Sadie bit the words out, too furious to say more.

'No! I… It's just, this needs to be business first between us, Sadie.'

Because everything was, for him, wasn't it? Nothing mattered more than the next project, the next shining opportunity. Certainly not her.

'Of course.' With a deep breath, Sadie gathered the tattered remains of her dignity around her, and gave thanks that she hadn't wasted her best red dress on this disaster of an evening. 'Well, I think I've seen all I need to here. If you'll excuse me…'

She didn't care if he had a car booked or plans to look through some slideshow on the Azure's future. Sadie was going to the bar, drinking one more glass of wine to wipe away this evening, then getting a cab back home, where she would go straight to bed. No champagne, no rose petals, no Dylan. Alone.

'Sadie, wait.' He tried to grab her arm again, but she dodged him.

'I'll see you in the lobby in the morning as normal,'

she said. Maybe if she pretended nothing had happened tonight, he'd forget—like she had, apparently, after that wedding so many years ago. 'We've got plenty of work ahead of us.'

And that was all. Just work.

CHAPTER TEN

THIS NEEDS TO be business…

Sadie woke with the same words echoing in her head that she'd fallen asleep to, and a familiar burn of embarrassment coursing through her body.

What on earth had she been thinking, trying to kiss Dylan? Maybe she could just blame the wine.

Lying back against her pillows, she ran through the night before in her head. The part before everything had gone crazy and wrong. There had to be something she could salvage from her utter humiliation.

The business message had certainly got through loud and clear. So, how did she show him that she was back to work mode today, and that last night had been a minor blip? What had he told her she needed to do to live up to the luxuries of the Paradise Grand?

The other hotel had certainly been impressive, she had to admit, and the food *almost* as good as the Azure's. But it didn't feel homely or comfortable…

Suddenly, Dylan's words came back to her.

'The Azure is about charm, heart and home—those are its selling points. The personal touch. And if it's not home to you, if you don't love it…'

Maybe he had a point.

In fact, she decided as she headed for the shower, even

if last night hadn't been exactly what she'd been hoping for, maybe it had given her something more. Not another notch on Dylan's bedpost, which in the cold morning light she could only agree was a good thing. She'd lost her mind, briefly, but she was back in control now. This was all a business proposal—not a fantasy romance or a glimpse of possibilities that never really were.

Instead, he'd given her a way to prove to him, once and for all, that he should invest. All he wanted to know was that this place truly was her home, her passion.

And she knew exactly how to do that.

Suddenly, the day didn't seem quite so hopeless.

She met him in the lobby as usual, knowing he'd clocked her casual dress immediately. His eyebrows rose, just a touch, as he smiled a greeting at her. Was that nervousness she saw behind his eyes?

'So, boss lady, what's the plan for today?' Boss lady. He really wanted to make sure she didn't forget this was business, didn't he? Well, that was just fine by her.

'Have you eaten breakfast?' she asked, too focussed on her plan for small talk.

'Sort of.' His forehead crinkled up a little in confusion. 'Some fruit and cereal. I wasn't all that hungry after last night's feast. Why?'

'Perfect,' she said, ignoring the question. 'You don't want a heavy stomach for today's activities.'

'Now I'm really intrigued,' Dylan admitted.

Sadie flashed him a bright, fake smile. 'Good. Then follow me.'

He'd seen the whole hotel on their tour on the first day, so by the time she'd led him down the stone stairs and towards the corridor to the spa he'd already figured it out, which shouldn't really have surprised her. He was a bright guy.

'A spa day?' he asked, a hint of incredulity in his voice.

'The spa is one of the Azure's biggest attractions,' she reminded him, as they reached the heavy wooden door that led to her own personal sanctuary. 'It makes sense for you to spend some time here, see what all the fuss is about.' She pushed the door open, the heady scent of oils and steam filling her lungs as she stepped through. 'Besides, you'll need to lock your phone up in the lockers here. It'll do you good to switch off from your other business and concentrate on the Azure for a few hours.'

'I need to stay in touch with the office—' Dylan started, but she cut him off, more determined than ever.

'Not today. You want proof that the Azure is a safe investment? I'm about to give it to you. So I want you paying attention.'

'If you insist.' Dylan sighed, and followed her through the door to the spa reception desk. 'Okay, I'm game. So, what? You're going to give me a massage?'

Sadie wished she could blame the heat in her cheeks on the higher temperature of the spa rooms. Sadly, she knew herself better than that.

'Not me. We have an excellent trained staff here to see to your every need. But I'll show you around first, explain the different rooms to you.' Smiling at the spa receptionist, Andreas, she added, 'Andreas here will take you through to the male changing rooms and lockers, show you where everything is. I'll meet you on the other side.'

Slipping through to the women's changing rooms, Sadie didn't waste time, stripping off to her swimming costume quickly and locking everything up in her personal locker. Wrapping a robe around herself, she headed straight through to the spa, pleased to beat Dylan there by even a few moments. He looked faintly uncomfortable in the fluffy white robe, the towelling material making his shoulders look broader than ever. Still, she decided, it was good for him to go outside his comfort zone now and then.

He looked around him and Sadie watched his face for reactions as he took in the creamy marble, with hints of brown and rust red, which covered the walls. Above them, a domed and mural-painted roof belied their location underneath the hotel, making them appear to be in some ancient Turkish bath instead. The soothing splash of water from the pools toned nicely with the gentle music playing over the hidden speakers.

'So, where do we start?' Dylan asked.

'With the Turkish bath, of course,' Sadie said.

If that didn't relax him into handing over the cash, nothing would.

'This is the warm room,' Sadie explained, as she paused by a steamed-up glass door and slipped off her robe, hanging it up. 'Traditionally, this is where you would start a proper Turkish bath.'

She pushed the door open and Dylan shucked his own robe and followed her through, silently cursing the steam that rose up and obscured the beautiful curve of her behind in her swimsuit.

It had taken every grain of restraint in his body not to kiss her back the night before—and now she was tormenting him with *this.* A whole day in her barely clad company, trying to *relax.* And she'd made it perfectly clear it was all business. Just the way he'd wanted it.

The woman was a demon.

Inside, the warm room was empty of other people—which Dylan appreciated. Sadie took a seat on the tiled bench seat that ran around the outer edge of the room, and he followed suit, choosing to sit opposite her instead of beside her—something he regretted when he realised the steam hid her almost completely now.

He shuffled round a little closer, until he could make out the outline of her face at least.

'So, what do we do here?' he asked, settling back as the heat rolled over him, the steam already dripping off his skin as well as the wall behind him.

'We sit. We relax.' Sadie sounded different here already, like her words could take their time coming out. Like there was no rush for anything any more.

Dylan fidgeted, switching position to try to get a little more comfortable against the tile. 'That's it?'

'That's it,' Sadie said, apparently very satisfied with that state of affairs.

She'd tilted her head back against the wall, and as far as he could tell her eyes were closed. He watched the beads of water roll down the long line of her neck for a moment. No sign that she found this in any way frustrating. Clearly, she was enjoying the peace and quiet.

He gave it a minute before he decided that was too bad. He had questions.

'So, is this a traditional Turkish spa?'

'Yes and no,' Sadie answered, without moving or opening her eyes. 'I wanted to incorporate some of the aspects of a traditional Turkish bath, but I knew I couldn't compete with the authentic Turkish baths in the town. So, instead, I decided to go with a spa that would feel familiar to the visiting tourists—especially the Western ones—but would still feel a little exotic, too.'

'The best of both worlds.'

'That's the idea.'

Listening to her talk, even absently, about the plans she'd had for this place, it was easy to see exactly what was missing in her plans for the Azure. Here, she'd known instinctively what she wanted to do, what was important to the guests, what would work well. This was her comfort zone. The hotel wasn't.

Tilting his head back to copy Sadie, he stared up at the mosaic-domed roof, picking out patterns through the steam. Then, when that grew boring, he went back to watching Sadie instead.

She looked so much more relaxed here. Like she had swimming in the sea the day before. She truly was a water nymph.

'When was the last time you came down here?' he asked. 'Not just in a suit to check on the business either.'

'Too long,' Sadie admitted, turning her head to smile at him. 'I think everyone needs a day in the spa now and then.'

Her eyes fluttered shut again, and he followed suit, trying to find the same boneless relaxation she seemed to here. Letting the heat seep into his bones and the steam soak his skin, he let his shoulders drop and his mind zone out.

Maybe there was something to this relaxation malarkey after all.

Almost too soon, Sadie stirred beside him. 'Okay, time for the hot room.' She stood, gracefully.

Dylan peeled himself away from the tile with rather less finesse. 'This wasn't hot?'

'This was nothing,' Sadie told him, opening the door.

The hot room felt even hotter after the brief blast of normal spa temperature between the two rooms, but they didn't stay in the second room as long, which he appreciated. As they emerged back into the main spa, Sadie plunged herself into the circular pool in the centre of the room, letting the water sluice over her.

With a shrug, Dylan followed suit.

The ice-cold water hit his overheated skin like a thousand pins, and he rose gasping out of the water to find Sadie already out and perched on a wooden recliner beside it. She, somehow, managed to look refreshed and a little smug. Clearly this was revenge for the night before.

'You could have warned me.' He levered himself back out of the pool and reached for the towel she held out to him,

'Where would be the fun in that?' The impish gleam in her eyes made it hard to even pretend to be mad at her.

'Where indeed?' He sat down on the recliner next to her. 'Well, this has been lovely, but—'

'Oh, we're not done yet,' Sadie interrupted him.

'We're not?' Dylan shook his head, cold water droplets falling from his hair. 'What's next?'

'Traditionally, you'd be scrubbed clean by a bath assistant,' Sadie said. 'But today I think we'll let you off with just the massage. You can meet me in the pool afterwards.'

As a member of the spa staff, neatly dressed in white shorts and polo shirt, appeared to lead him to the massage room, Dylan saw another approach Sadie with a clipboard in hand. In a moment, all the relaxation he'd seen in her disappeared as she frowned at the paper in front of her, shoulders stiff.

'This way, sir,' the staff member said again, and Dylan hurried to catch up.

Left alone to settle face down onto the massage table, with just a small towel covering what was left of his modesty, Dylan tuned out the tasteful music and thought instead about Sadie.

She seemed so in control there in the spa—utterly unlike the uncertainty he saw in her when she talked about the hotel itself. Obviously, that was why she'd brought him there—to demonstrate that there was one place she felt totally at home here in Turkey. Here, she had passion and certainty.

The only problem with that was it just made it all the clearer that she didn't want to be running a hotel. She should be taking charge of a chain of spas, perhaps even in other hotels.

Maybe even in his new and burgeoning hotel chain.

Already the idea was taking hold, making him want to jump at the chance to make it happen. Sadie would have a career she truly dreamed of, and they could work together, seeing each other as often as possible…

But she'd have to leave the Azure. Break her commitment to Adem's dream. And there was the sticking point.

The door opened behind him, and Dylan stirred from his plotting as a familiar scent approached. He listened hard, recognising the pattern of her breath, the touch of her footfall.

Sadie.

Whatever she'd said about not giving him his massage, he had absolutely no doubt about who was standing behind him right now.

'Are you ready, sir?' she whispered, obviously trying to disguise her voice. 'I'm going to start with a simple massage. Let me know if the pressure is okay.'

She didn't want him to know it was her. But how could he not, when the first touch of her oiled fingers against his back made his whole body spark with excitement? Every movement she made was utterly professional—he'd never expect anything less from Sadie. But the feelings it left him with…

He was pretty sure that no massage in history had ever been less relaxing than this one.

* * *

This was torture. Actual cruel and unusual punishment for a crime she didn't fully remember committing.

Keeping her hands as smooth and steady as she could as they moved across the planes of Dylan's back, Sadie kept a running stream of mental curses going in her head. Mostly cursing the poor staff member who'd been sent home sick, leaving them short-handed. But partly cursing herself, too, for saying she'd take care of Dylan's massage.

She was the boss. She could have ordered anyone else to swap with her or take care of it. Instead, she'd decided to put herself through *this*.

She really was a glutton for punishment.

Staying professional, that was the key. It wasn't like she hadn't massaged beautiful people before, even a few famous ones. The trick was to treat them exactly the same way you'd treat anyone else. A body was just a body, when all was said and done, and they all needed the same care, love and attention to work away their worries and their aches.

It was just that *this* body was one she'd been thinking about for far longer than she cared to admit.

Focussing on the muscle groups helped, remembering every lesson she'd ever been taught about effective massage. She knew just where to press and where to hold back. She was *good* at this. She was a professional.

She was absolutely not thinking about what was underneath that very small towel.

Eventually, her time was up, and hopefully Dylan would never ask why he'd only had a back massage instead of a full-body one.

Stepping away, her heart still pumping too fast, Sadie murmured, 'I'll leave you to dress.'

'Thanks, Sadie.' His words were almost slurred, like he was too relaxed to articulate properly, but still they caused every muscle in her body to stiffen.

'How did you know?' she asked.

'I always know when you're near me.' Adjusting his towel to cover him, Dylan levered himself up and swung round to sit on the edge of the table. 'I always have.'

It was too much. The softness in his voice against the heat in his eyes. The implications of his words and the knowledge that just moments before she'd had her hands all over his body. Knowing that they were so close now he could touch her almost without moving. Her blood seemed too much and too hot for her body—hotter than it had ever been in any of the steam rooms.

All too, too much.

Business. That's all this was.

Sadie stepped back, away, and cleared her throat. 'Um, we have someone off sick, so I've been called in to cover. So I'll let you get on with enjoying the pool and so on. It'll be good for you to, uh, keep relaxing.'

Dylan nodded, slowly. 'Or maybe I'll just try the cold plunge pool again.'

'Whatever works.' She refused to think about why he might need the ice water, even for a moment.

'Will I see you for dinner?' he asked.

She wanted to say yes, but she couldn't. The wanting in his eyes…she knew exactly where that could lead, if they let it. And even if she'd thought last night that was what she wanted, seeing it now terrified her. This wasn't what she'd brought him to her spa for, not at all.

Dylan didn't do commitment, and she'd already committed too much. Wasn't that why she'd brought him there in the first place? To show him exactly how much she belonged at the Azure? So what good could come from giving in to those feelings now?

'Not tonight, I'm afraid,' she said, trying to sound apologetic. 'I need to type up my proposal for you, remember? But there's a Turkish night in the restaurant. I've booked you a table.'

'Fantastic.' Sadie ignored the total lack of enthusiasm in his voice. 'What about tomorrow?'

Tomorrow. His next-to-last day. She couldn't leave him alone again, but whatever they did needed to involve a lot more clothes than the last couple of days had. And preferably no easy access to a bed.

'Ephesus.' The word blurted out of her. 'I thought I'd take you to see the ruins at Ephesus.'

'Another big tourist attraction, I suppose.' How was his tone still so even, so steady when her own voice seemed to be getting squeakier by the second?

'The biggest. So, I'll see you in the lobby in the morning. Usual time.'

'If that's what you want.'

It wasn't. What she really wanted was to jump him, right here in the massage room. But what she needed to do was get back to work and put this whole afternoon behind her.

'It is.'

She'd do a shift in the spa, remind herself why she loved it so much. Then she'd spend the evening on Skype with Finn and her parents and dealing with the hotel admin.

She needed to remember all the things that *really* mattered in her world. And forget the feeling of Dylan's cool skin under her hands.

Or else she might go insane.

CHAPTER ELEVEN

DYLAN PACED THE lobby the next morning, waiting for Sadie. Who was late. Very late. For the first time since he'd arrived in Turkey.

Turning as he reached the automatic doors, too late to stop them opening for him, he headed back towards the large windows showcasing that brilliant view of the Aegean Sea. He tried to appreciate the view, but his mind was too preoccupied with wondering how the day was going to play out.

The rules had changed yesterday, that much had been obvious the moment he'd sat up on that massage table and looked into her eyes. The heat and want he'd seen reflected there had echoed his own so perfectly he couldn't help but think it was only a matter of time before they had to do something about it or explode. This wasn't a drunken attempt at a kiss in a lift, or a moment of madness brought on by a romantic hotel room. Sadie Sullivan wanted him, maybe as much as he wanted her. And despite every complication, every reason he knew he shouldn't, Dylan wasn't sure he'd make it out of Kuşadasi without doing something about that.

Except she was late, and he didn't know which Sadie was going to turn up today—buttoned-up business Sadie, old friend Sadie, or the Sadie who'd tried to kiss him the other night.

Yes, the rules had changed, to the point that Dylan wasn't even sure what game they were playing any more. If they were playing at all.

Ephesus. That was the plan for today. Ancient ruins, stones and sand and history. A big tourist draw, sure, but he couldn't shake the feeling that wasn't why Sadie was taking him there. More likely she was trying to get him somewhere safe—away from temptation and lost in someone else's history instead of their own.

Pity it would never work.

Besides, he wasn't interested in history today. He wanted to talk to her about the future.

Dylan had spent his solitary evening making plans, researching and brainstorming. He'd been looking for a way to set the hotel chain he'd recently taken over apart from the norm, and a spa range of the calibre of Sadie's could be just what he needed. Sure, it wasn't unique, but it *was* good and profitable, according to his preliminary research. He'd know more when his assistant got back to him with the stats and figures he'd requested.

Then he'd just need to talk to Sadie about it. He liked to hope she'd be excited about the new opportunity, but knowing Sadie he suspected that pulling her away from the old one would be the real challenge.

Turning to head back towards the doors, he caught sight of the Azure logo on the reception desk, and almost smiled. Just a few days ago seeing the name would have been enough to make him scowl. But now... Sadie had changed the way he thought about the Azure. About many things.

The lift dinged and the doors opened, revealing Sadie in a light and breezy sundress, a straw hat perched on her head. 'Sorry I'm late,' she said, without much apology in her voice. 'Let's get going.'

Dylan followed, trying not to read too much into the fact she'd barely looked at him.

In the car, Sadie switched the radio on before she even fastened her seat belt, turning the volume up high enough to make conversation next to impossible. Dylan smiled to himself as he settled into the passenger seat. So, that was the way she wanted to play it. Fine.

He was willing to bet there were no radios at Ephesus. She'd have to talk to him then—for a whole day, trapped inside some ancient ruins.

Of course, she'd probably try to just lecture him on the history of the place. Which was fine by Dylan; he knew she couldn't keep it up forever.

Eventually, they were going to have to talk about the heat between them.

Satisfied, he sat back to enjoy the drive, watching the foreign landscape skimming past the window. He had to admit Turkey was a gorgeous country.

Beside him, Sadie let out a little gasp—just a slight gulp of air, but enough to alarm him. All thoughts of the scenery forgotten, he jerked round to see what the matter was.

On the wheel, Sadie's knuckles were white, her fingers clinging so tight there was no blood left in them. Her face had turned entirely grey. But it was her eyes, wide and unfocussed, that worried him most.

'Sadie? What is it?' No response. The car kept rolling forward in its lane, falling behind the car in front as her foot slackened on the accelerator. 'You need to pull over. Sadie. Sadie!'

The sharpness in his voice finally got through to her

and, blinking, she flipped on the indicator. Dylan placed his hands over hers as she swerved onto the side of the road, ignoring the beeping horns of the cars behind them.

The car stalled to a stop, and Dylan let out a long breath as his heart rate started to stabilise. 'Okay. What just—?'

Before he could finish his sentence the driver's door flew open and Sadie flung herself out of the car, inches away from the passing traffic. Without thinking, Dylan followed suit, jumping out and rushing round to find her already leaning against the rear of the car.

He slowed, approaching her cautiously, like an unpredictable and possibly dangerous wild animal. God only knew what was going on with her, but he knew instinctively that this wasn't part of the game they'd been playing since he'd arrived. This was something else entirely.

She didn't stir as he got closer, so he risked taking her arm, leading her gently to the side of the car furthest from the road.

'Sit down,' he murmured, as softly as he could. 'Come on, Sadie. Sit down here and tell me what the matter is.'

Bonelessly, she slid down to the dry grass, leaning back against the metal of the car. Dylan crouched in front of her, his gaze never leaving her colourless face.

'What is it?' he asked again. 'What just happened?'

'I forgot…' Sadie's said, her voice faint and somehow very far away. 'How could I forget?'

'Forgot what, sweetheart?'

'That we'd have to drive this way. Past this place.'

'This place? Where are we?' Dylan glanced around him but, as far as he could tell, it was just some road. Any road.

Oh. He was an idiot.

'This is where it happened?' he asked.

Sadie nodded, the movement jerky. 'Adem was driving out to some meeting somewhere, I think. A truck lost control along this stretch…'

And his best friend had been squashed under it in his car. He hadn't stood a chance.

'I haven't been this way since it happened,' Sadie said, her gaze still focussed somewhere in the distance. 'When I suggested Ephesus…I wasn't thinking about this. I wasn't thinking about Adem.'

The guilt and pain in her voice made him wince—and feel all the worse because he had a pretty good idea exactly what she *had* been thinking about at that moment.

'We don't have to go on,' he said. 'We can just go back to the hotel. I can drive.'

But Sadie shook her head. 'No. I want… This is the worst of it. I just need to sit here for a moment. Is that…? Will you sit with me?'

'Of course.' He shuffled over to sit beside her and lifted his arm to wrap it around her as she rested her head against his shoulder. He couldn't offer her much right now, but any comfort he could give was hers. Always had been.

'It's crazy, really,' she said, the words slightly muffled by his shirt. 'That one place—one insignificant patch of road—can hold such power over me. There are no ruins here, no markers, no information boards. Just me, knowing that this…this is where he died.'

'We don't have to talk about it.'

'Maybe I do.' Sadie looked up, just enough to catch his gaze, and Dylan almost lost himself in the desolate depths of her eyes. 'I haven't, really. Haven't talked it out, or whatever it is you're supposed to do with the sort of grief that fills you up from the inside out until there's nothing left. I just…got on with things, I suppose.'

He could see it, all too easily. Could picture Sadie just throwing herself into the Azure, into making sure Finn was okay, and never taking any time to grieve herself. For the first time he found himself wondering if *this* was the real reason Neal had asked him to come.

'If you want to talk, I'm always happy to listen,' he said. Whatever she needed, wasn't that what he'd promised himself he was there for? Well, any idiot could see that she needed this.

'I don't know what to say.' Sadie gave a helpless little shrug. 'It's been two years… It seems too late. There was just so much to do. Taking care of Finn, the Azure, all the arrangements… He's buried back in England, near his family, you know? Of course you do. You were there, weren't you? At the funeral?'

'I was.'

'So it really is just me and Finn here.' She sounded like she might float away on a cloud of memories at any moment. Dylan tightened his hold on her shoulders, just enough to remind her to stay.

'And me,' he said.

'You're not permanent, though. You're like…in Monopoly. Just visiting.' She managed a small smile at the ridiculous joke, but he couldn't return it. There was no censure in the accusation, no bitterness at all. But that didn't change the way it stung.

Even if every word of it was true.

'I just don't know how to be everything Finn needs,' Sadie went on. 'Mother, father, his whole family… I don't know how to do that *and* save the Azure. But the hotel is Adem's legacy. It's the only part of him left here with us. So I have to. And I'm so scared that I'll fail.'

Her voice broke a little on the last word, and Dylan pulled her tighter to him. *Whatever she needs.*

'I'm here now,' he said. 'And I will come back, whenever you need me. Me, Neal, your parents, your sister… we're all here to help you. Whatever you need.'

It wasn't enough; he knew that even as he spoke the words. He wanted to promise he'd stay as long as she needed him. But he had a rule, a personal code, never to make promises he couldn't keep.

Everyone knew Dylan Jacobs couldn't do long term—him better than anyone.

'I'm here now,' he repeated, and wished that would be enough.

I'm here now.

Sadie burrowed deeper against the solid bulk of Dylan's shoulder, and ignored the fact that, even then, he couldn't bring himself to say he'd stay.

She was glad. He wasn't her boyfriend, her lover, wasn't anything more than a friend. She wasn't his responsibility. And even if she had been…it would have been a lie to say he'd stay, and they both knew it. Better to keep things honest.

She stared out at the scrubland before them and tried to ignore the sound of cars roaring past behind her. How could she have forgotten that driving to Ephesus would bring them this way? No, scrap that. She knew exactly how. Because all she'd been thinking about had been getting Dylan away from the hotel, fully clothed. Putting temptation out of reach before he fought past any more of her defences.

And yet here she was, clinging to him as if for her sanity, giving up all her secrets.

Maybe she should get some of his in return.

'Why do you hate the name of the Azure?' she asked, more for something else to focus on than any other reason. The fact that it probably led to a funny story with another woman—and a reminder why she couldn't become too reliant on him—was just a lucky bonus.

But Dylan said, 'My father walked out on us in another Azure Hotel. I was ten. We were there with him on some business trip. He just got into the car and drove away.'

'I'm sorry.' Sadie winced. Great way to lighten the mood.

Dylan shrugged, and she felt every muscle move against her cheek. 'It happens. He…he wasn't good at commitment. He stuck out family life as long as he could, then one day he just couldn't take it any more. I've never seen him since.'

'What did you do?' Sadie tried to imagine ten-year-old Dylan standing alone in the foyer of some strange hotel, but in her head the image morphed into two-year-old Finn, watching her cry as she tried to explain that Daddy wasn't coming home.

'I took my mum's purse and bought us three bus tickets back home—for me, Mum and my sister Cassie.'

'You became the man of the house.' She could see it so easily—Dylan just taking over and doing what was needed because there was no one else to do it. He'd been bogged down with commitment since the age of ten. No wonder he avoided it so thoroughly as an adult.

'I was all they had left. Mum didn't deal with it well.' From his tone Sadie could tell that was a huge understatement. 'By the time she could cope again I pretty much had it all in hand.'

Suddenly, a long-ago conversation came back to her. 'I remember Adem joking about all those dreadful part-time jobs you had at university. You were sending money home to your family?' Dylan nodded. 'That's why you shared that awful flat in London with Neal too, right?

Even after you were both earning enough to move somewhere nicer.'

All those puzzling facets of Dylan Jacobs that had never made sense fell into place to make a perfect diamond shape. A whole shine and side to him she'd never even considered.

'I'm like my dad in a lot of ways,' Dylan said, and Sadie frowned.

'Doesn't sound like it to me.'

'No, I am, and I know it.' He shrugged again. 'I've come to terms with it, too. I always want to be free to chase the next big thing, just like him. Difference is, I'd never let myself get tied down in the first place. I don't ever want to let anyone down the way he did.'

'You wouldn't,' Sadie said, knowing the truth of it in her bones.

'Anyway. He'd already abandoned my mum and sister. I couldn't do the same, so I took care of them however I could. Besides, they're not like you. They're hopeless on their own.'

'Oh?' Part of her felt warmed that he didn't consider her helpless and hopeless. But one small part of her brain wondered if he'd stay if he did. She stamped down on that part pretty quickly, before it could take hold.

'Yeah. My mum's on her third marriage, my sister's on her second. Every time something goes wrong I have to fly in and help pick up the pieces.' He shook his head. 'We *really* don't do commitment well in my family.'

Except for his commitment to them, which he seemed to hardly even recognise. 'I think commitment is something you have to practise every day,' she said. 'Every morning you have to make your commitment all over again or else it fades.'

'Maybe you're right.' He looked down at her, his expression thoughtful. 'I mean, you're the most committed person I know, so I guess you must be.'

'The most committed person you know? Is that meant to be a compliment?'

'Most definitely,' he assured her. 'Anyone else would have given up already, chucked in the towel and gone home. But not you. You committed to Adem and you won't let him down, even now he's gone. You're incredible.'

'Or possibly insane.' She shifted a little away, uncomfortable at his praise. Hadn't she let her husband down already, by being so distracted by fantasies of his best friend that she'd forgotten to even think about him today? Dylan being there confused her, made her forget to recommit every morning. He made her think of other paths, other possibilities—just as he had twelve years before.

To Sadie, that felt like a pretty big betrayal in itself.

'There's always that possibility too,' Dylan said. 'But either way…I admire you, endlessly. You should know that.'

Sadie looked away, pushing her hands against the dirt ready to help herself stand.

'Ready to move?' Dylan jumped to his feet. 'We can still go back to the Azure…'

'I want to show you Ephesus,' Sadie said stubbornly. That was the plan after all.

'Fallen-down buildings it is, then.' He reached out a hand to pull her up and she took it tentatively. But once she was on her feet he pulled her close into a hug before she could let go. 'Sadie…your commitment—I meant what I said. It's admirable. But don't let it lock you into unhappiness either, okay? Adem would hate that.'

'I know.' The truth of his words trickled through her, fighting back against the guilt.

Dylan kissed her forehead, warm and comforting. 'Come on, then. Let's go and see some history.'

At least, Sadie thought as they got back in the car, this history belonged to other people. Her own was already too confusing.

CHAPTER TWELVE

SADIE SWUNG THE car into the dusty, rocky car park at Ephesus and smiled brightly at him, as if the scene at the roadside hadn't happened at all. Dylan was almost starting to doubt it had himself; it had been such a strange moment out of time when he had seemed to look deeper into the heart of Sadie than he ever had before.

That sort of revelation should have added some clarity to the situation, he felt. Instead, he was more confused than ever.

He hadn't meant to confess all his family's dark and depressing past to her, but somehow, with her sharing secrets, it had only seemed fair that he give back too. He'd tried to keep it as factual and unemotional as possible, knowing that the last thing she'd needed had been him falling apart too. She'd just needed to know that he'd understood, and that he cared. Hopefully he'd given her that.

But just reliving those moments had stirred up something in him he hadn't expected—something he'd barely had to deal with in years. The small boy left alone in charge of a family seemed so many light years away from where he was now that he never really drew a comparison day to day. He could almost forget the way the horror had slowly crept through him as he'd realised what had happened, and the searing pain that had followed, always when he'd least expected it, over the months to come, when it had struck home again what it had meant for his future.

Dylan shook his head. The moment had passed. No point dwelling any longer on things he couldn't even change twenty-odd years ago, let alone now.

They walked up through a street of stalls and cafés, selling hats and tourist tat, more scarves and costumes. Dylan ignored the sellers, but focussed in on the nearest café. Maybe something to eat and drink would do them good.

'Are you sure you want to do this now?' he asked. 'We could stop and grab a bite to eat before we go in.'

But Sadie was already striding ahead towards the ticket booths. By the time he caught up she had two tickets in her hand, ready to pass through the barriers.

Apparently, nothing was going to stop her today. Least of all him.

'Come on,' she said. 'There's masses to see, and we've already lost time.'

Dylan gave thanks for the bottled water and cereal bars in his backpack, and followed.

The path led them through scrubland littered with broken stones—some plain, some carved, all seriously less impressive than he suspected they would have been once. Information boards told them about the area, what had been here before Ephesus, and what had happened to the geography of the place.

'Did you know, there have been settlements in this area since six thousand BC?' Sadie asked.

'I didn't until I read that same information board.' Was she seriously going to talk history for the rest of the day? He supposed he could understand the need to put some distance between now and that heartbreaking conversation at the side of the road, but still. At some point they were going to have to return to the real world. 'Come on, I want to see the city proper.'

As they continued along the path, recognisable buildings started to appear—ruined and worn, but with walls and doorways and even decoration in places. Sadie stopped to read every single information board—often aloud—to him, despite the fact she must have been here plenty of times before. Dylan was sure it was all fascinating, but he had other things on his mind.

She'd admitted that she hadn't dealt with Adem's death, not really. He should have seen that sooner, or at least been more mindful of it. Was that why she was clinging so hard to the Azure?

And, if so, what would happen when she finally *did* deal with everything? Would she be ready to move on? Maybe even with him, for a time?

They turned off the path into an amphitheatre, and Sadie went skipping down the aisle steps to the stage, standing in the middle and calling out a line from some play or another, listening to the words reverberating around the stones.

Dylan took a seat on the carved steps, right up at the top, and watched her explore. Leaning back, he let the sun hit his face, the warmth soothe his body. Sadie wasn't the only one to have confessed all that morning, of course. He'd expected to feel shame or be pitied or something after telling her all about his family. But instead, next to her emotional outpouring, his ancient pains seemed like nothing. Still, somehow it felt good to have shared them. And it had helped Sadie too, he thought. She seemed lighter after her confessions that morning.

Maybe she really *was* ready to let go at last—not just saying the words to win his support and his money.

And if so…hopefully what he had planned for the night would help her make that leap.

The Library of Celsus might just be her favourite part of Ephesus, Sadie decided as she ran her fingers along the delicately carved stonework. It never ceased to amaze her, just imagining all the learning and history the place must have held once. One of the later buildings, from the Roman period, its magnificence had only lasted one hundred and forty-two years before an earthquake and ensuing fire had destroyed it, leaving only the façade—and even that had perished a couple of hundred years later, in another earthquake.

Strange to think that the beauty she stared at now had been rebuilt by modern hands; that they'd found a way to bring some life back to a pile of rubble. But they had. Maybe she could, too.

Turning, she saw Dylan standing at the bottom of the library steps, staring up at the columns and statues. Smiling, she trotted over to join him. She'd known that Ephesus would be just the distraction they needed—especially after that morning. No business, nothing personal—just ancient history.

'It's pretty incredible, isn't it?' Sadie moved to stand beside him, looking back at the façade again.

'It's certainly impressive,' Dylan agreed.

'So much history… A whole different world really.' Just where she wanted to be today.

Dylan turned to her, eyes obscured by his sunglasses. 'You know, I don't remember you being so much of a history buff when we were younger.'

Sadie shrugged. 'Maybe I wasn't, back when the history around me was so familiar. But here…the history here blows me away. I want to know all of it.'

'Why?' Dylan asked, and she frowned at him. She should have known Mr Next Big Thing wouldn't get the appeal of bygone days. 'No, seriously, I'm curious. Why does it matter so much to you?'

'I guess because...well, it shows us where we came from. Where we've been and how far there still is to go. There's a lot of lessons in history.'

'Perhaps.' Dylan looked away, back at the library again. 'But I'm not so sure it can tell us what happens next.'

'You've never heard of history repeating itself?' she asked.

'Of course. But I like to think that we're more than just the sum of what has happened to us.'

Sadie followed his gaze back to the library façade. Suddenly she could see the cracks, the places it had been repaired, and where parts were still missing, in a way she never had before.

She was also pretty sure they weren't talking about the Ancient Greeks and Romans any more.

Was he right? Were they more than their history?

How could he say that when everything he'd told her that morning—about his dad, his family—had so clearly formed him into exactly the sort of man he was? Of course he didn't believe he could do commitment, coming from a family like that. It had even explained to her why he was so desperate not to miss chances—how many opportunities must he have given up to look after his mother and sister? It was a miracle he'd ever made it to university to meet Adem in the first place.

'Come on,' Dylan said, tugging on her arm. 'Let's keep going or we'll never see everything.'

Side by side, they climbed the paved hill through more terraces and temples and half-reassembled mosaics through the rest of the town.

'I mean, look at the people who lived here,' Dylan said suddenly, and Sadie frowned, trying to cast her mind back to the conversation they'd been having.

'What do you mean?'

'Well, they built this fantastic city, survived invasions and slaughters, were Greek, Roman, Byzantine…then the river silted up, the earthquakes hit, and the place started falling apart. And I bet you they never saw it coming—even though it had all happened before—however well they knew their own history.'

'I guess there are always twists and turns we can't predict,' Sadie admitted. 'And maybe sometimes we just choose to hope for the best instead.' Like she had, hoping for a long, happy life with her husband.

'You know that better than most, huh?' He gave her an apologetic half-smile, even though he hadn't done anything wrong, not really. She just wasn't meant to live happily ever after, it seemed. Not his fault. 'It's just kind of sad to think of all those people watching the harbour silt up, losing their access to the Aegean—the only thing that made this place matter—and realising there was nothing to stay for any more.'

Nothing to stay for... The words pricked at her mind, and she knew she'd been right, back at the library, to think they weren't really talking history any more.

'Is this some convoluted way of telling me that you think my harbour is silting up?' she asked sharply, stopping in the middle of the path and not even caring about the tourists behind who had to swerve suddenly. The anger bubbling up as she reran his words in her head mattered more.

Dylan glanced back at her and stopped walking himself. 'Your harbour?' he asked, voice laced with confusion.

'The Azure,' Sadie snapped. As if he didn't know what she was talking about. 'Look, just lose the metaphor. If you think there's no future for my hotel, that it can't be saved, tell me now.'

'You're wrong.' Dylan shook his head.

'Am I really?' Folding her arms across her chest, Sadie tapped one foot against the ancient stones and waited for him to deny it again.

If he dared.

Had the woman actually lost her mind this time?

Dylan grabbed Sadie's arm and pulled her away from the middle of the path into the shade of a gnarled old tree beside a tumbledown wall. Maybe the heat was getting to her. He fished in his bag for a bottle of water and handed it to her.

'Drink some of this,' he said, sighing when she managed to do so without breaking her glare at him. 'Look, I believe the Azure can be saved, okay? I'm just not sure that you're the person to do it.'

She lowered the bottle from her lips, her expression crestfallen. 'You don't think I can do it.'

He bit back a curse. That was not what he'd meant. God, how many ways could he mess this up? 'I'm very sure that you can. But I'm still not convinced that you really want to.'

'We're back to this?' She shoved the bottle back into his hands and cool droplets dribbled out onto his fingers. 'I've given you a million reasons—'

'And none of them are "because it's the work I know I was born to do".'

'Who has that? No one, Dylan. No one else expects that from their job.'

'You should.' He took a long drink of water. 'The difference between you and most people is that this isn't your only option. And obligation isn't passion, Sadie.'

'Fine.' She shook her head, stepping away from him. The extra distance felt like miles instead of inches. 'If this is too big a project for you, too big a commitment, just say so. I'll find some other way to save the Azure.'

She would too, he knew. Sighing, he rubbed a fist across his tired eyes. How had a simple sightseeing trip grown so complicated?

'I know things have been weird between us this week.' Her tone was softer now, and it only made him more nervous. 'But I swear I'm not asking for anything beyond your business and financial support, if that's what you're worried about. I…I think that maybe there could be something between us, yes. But I'm not trying to tie you down, or drag you away from your other opportunities.'

Something between us... Wasn't that the understatement of the year?

'I never thought you were.' At least he hadn't. Until she'd said that.

'Well…good.' She shifted awkwardly from one foot to the other, and he was pretty sure the faint pink flush on her cheeks wasn't just to do with the sun. 'So. Are you in, or not?'

She wanted an answer now. After days of dancing around everything between them—history, business, attraction—suddenly she needed to know. Of course she did.

'Can we discuss this at dinner?' he asked. If he'd read things right, tonight would be the perfect time to present his whole proposal in one go. A chance for them to maybe think about the future for once, instead of the past.

And he reckoned the odds on her saying yes were much better there than here at the side of the road through an abandoned city.

But Sadie stood her ground. 'No. I need to know now. Will you recommend investing in the Azure to your board?'

When had she got so stubborn? Or had she always been this way? Was it one of the things Adem had loved about her? He could hardly remember. The Sadie that had been had almost entirely given way to the new one, the one he'd spent the last week falling for.

He took a deep breath and dived in.

'I have a proposal for you,' he said, wishing his heart wasn't beating so loudly.

'Another one?'

'Yes. I'll help you save the Azure, if that's what you really want.'

'It is.' The words came fast enough, but did he hear a flicker of doubt behind them?

'You might want to wait and hear me out before you make that decision.'

She shook her head. 'I'm sure.'

'Really? Because I think you want something more. And I can give that to you.' He could see her considering it, the temptation on her face clear.

'What?' she finally asked, a little grudgingly.

And here they were. His one chance to win her away from this place. 'I recently took over a chain of hotels—mostly in the UK. I want to turn them into luxury spa hotels—and I think you'd be the person to help develop the spa aspect of them.'

Temptation gave way to shock as her eyebrows rose, frozen high on her forehead. 'I don't… I don't know what to say.'

Which meant she was considering it, right? Time to press the advantage.

'You'd be home in Britain, with your family,' he said, knowing he was sweetening the deal with every word. He'd spent enough time with her that week that he knew what she wanted—even if she wouldn't admit it. 'Finn would have your parents close too. You'd have support, help—and a generous, regular salary. If you really wanted, we could bring the Azure under the chain umbrella, put a new manager in charge…but it would still be yours and Finn's.' He had no idea how that would even work, or what his lawyers would say about it, but he'd say anything to get her to take the deal.

To have a reason to keep her close, to see her regularly, to have her in his life. However he could get her.

But it was more than that, he insisted silently. It was the right thing for her, too. And an opportunity most people would bite his hand off for.

Not Sadie, though. She still looked torn.

'Just think about it,' he said, and she nodded absently, her lower lip caught between her teeth.

He couldn't resist. The timing was wrong, nothing was as he had planned, they still had business to resolve, but he had to kiss her now. Before he went insane with wanting it.

CHAPTER THIRTEEN

SHE KNEW WHAT he was going to do a split second before he moved, could see it in his eyes, the way they softened and warmed. And, just like last time, Sadie knew she should pull away, back off, escape.

Except she didn't.

His hand came up to her waist and she let it, drawing a breath that burned her lungs at the touch. And when he dipped his head, she raised her chin to meet him, her lips aligning perfectly with his, as if they were meant to be kissed.

As if she'd been waiting her whole life for this.

Had that small, contented noise really come from her mouth? From the way Dylan wrapped his other arm around her, hauling her tight against his body as he deepened the kiss, she suspected it had. And she knew, without a shadow of a doubt, that their whole week together had been building up to this. She didn't know if it was history repeating itself, or the future imposing on her determination to cling onto the past, but this, this moment, this kiss, had always been inevitable.

It was what followed that was completely unclear.

After long, long, perfect moments Dylan pulled back, just enough to allow air between their lips again. His face was still so close that she could see every fleck of colour in his eyes, every hint of worry in his expression. He didn't know what happened next either, and somehow that made her feel a little better.

'So you'll think about it?' Dylan cleared his throat. 'My business proposal, I mean.'

Her eyes fluttering closed, Sadie let out a low laugh. All business, this man. 'Yes. I'll think about it.'

His hands dropped from her waist and she stepped back, sucking in the air that seemed to have disappeared for the length of their kiss.

'We should get back,' Dylan said. 'I have something great planned for tonight, and you're not going to want to miss it.'

Something more spectacular than that kiss? Sadie doubted it. 'There's not much more to see anyway. Just the gift shop. If you think you can live without a magnetic Library of Celsus…'

'I don't think I need anything more to remember this day by,' Dylan said, his gaze fixed on hers. 'I won't be forgetting our time in Ephesus in a hurry.'

'Neither will I,' Sadie admitted.

They made their way slowly back down the hill, inches separating them. Sadie wondered if she should be holding his hand—back when she'd last kissed someone for the first time, that had been the sort of thing you did afterwards. But, then, Dylan had never struck her as a handholding type.

She had too much to think about to make conversation on the drive back to the Azure, or do more than clench her jaw a little tighter when they passed the spot where they'd stopped earlier. Dylan's offer, for one, quite apart from that heartstopping kiss.

Why was he offering her this now? He'd come here to help bail out the Azure, but now it seemed he had other plans entirely. And as much as she appreciated him thinking of her…she couldn't help but wonder if this was just his way of keeping her close without actually having to commit to her in any way.

It was a stupid thought. They'd shared one kiss, that was all. But if they did decide to take things further… what happened next? What *could* happen, when Dylan had made it very clear that he wasn't the sort of man who stuck around?

Maybe she needed to separate the business from the personal—except that was impossible when her late husband's legacy *was* her business, and his best friend's job offer might just be a coded message for, 'Let's be friends with benefits.'

No, that wasn't fair. Whatever there was between her and Dylan, it was more than that, she could feel it. What was between them *mattered.*

But not enough for him to change his whole life philosophy—if she even wanted him to.

She sighed. If she took the job, it would mean abandoning her commitments here. And even if it was what she wanted to do, was it worth the risk to her heart? Dylan Jacobs had held a tiny corner of it for a very long time, she finally admitted to herself, and if she let him take more…well, she might not get it back.

And that was a big risk to take, for anyone.

'You okay?' Dylan asked.

She nodded, then realised she was already parked outside the Azure. When had that happened?

'What's the plan for tonight?' she asked unenthusiastically. She needed a long bath and an early night to think about her options, but it was Dylan's last night.

He flashed her an enigmatic smile as he climbed out of the car. 'Just meet me in the lobby at eight. It's a surprise.'

Just what she needed. More unexpected things happening in her life. 'Can you at least tell me what I should wear?'

'Anything you like.' He leaned back inside the car and pressed a swift kiss to her lips. 'You always look beautiful to me.'

And then he was gone, skipping up the steps to the Azure Hotel and leaving Sadie feeling more confused than ever.

Dylan refused to pace the lobby this time. The car was waiting outside, he was suited and booted in his best dinner suit and a crisp, new white shirt. Everything was going to be perfect.

As soon as Sadie showed up.

She didn't keep him waiting too long. He turned as the elevator let out its familiar ping and watched breathlessly as the doors opened and Sadie stepped out.

'Wow.' He'd been aiming for something more eloquent, but from the pink that hit her cheeks, honesty worked just as well. 'You look spectacular.'

'Thanks.' She looked down at her red cocktail dress and swirled her hips a little, making it rise and fall. The movement made every muscle in Dylan's body tighten.

If he didn't know better, he'd say that Sadie had plans for tonight, too.

'I've been saving it for a special occasion,' she said, taking his arm as they walked out of the hotel together. 'I thought that tonight might fit the bill.'

'I hope so.' Now that he was close enough he could feel the slight tremor in her hands, hear the tiny wobble in her voice. Dress aside, she wasn't as confident as she was making out. It made him feel a little better, actually—

because his confidence was giving way to nerves by the second.

'I, uh, I emailed you the proposal. For the Azure, I mean.' Had she? He hadn't checked. And that in itself told him that his priorities were shifting. 'We could look through it later tonight, if you wanted…'

Dylan shook his head. 'It can wait until tomorrow.' Tonight couldn't be about business, he could sense that. It needed to be about them. But the two were so closely linked…would they really be able to untangle them?

The car he'd hired sped them down to the marina, and he tipped the driver generously when they got out. If everything went to plan, they wouldn't need him until the next morning.

'The marina?' Sadie asked, looking around her at the lights. The whole town seemed lit up in the almost darkness of the autumn evening. 'What are we doing here?'

'I have a friend who has a yacht—and he owed me a favour,' Dylan explained, leading her towards the vessel in question. 'So tonight we shall be dining aboard the *Marie Bell*, catered by one of the finest chefs I've ever met. And, if it's okay with you, I thought we might take her out for a spin out on the Aegean.'

Her gaze shot to his. 'Overnight?'

'Yes. She has two bedrooms, and is fully equipped with anything we might need for an overnight stay, but if you'd rather come back sooner…' He trailed off. 'This can be anything you want, Sadie. I just wanted to give you a special night.'

She nodded slowly, her teeth tugging on her lower lip again in that way that just made him mad to kiss her. 'Okay.'

The yacht was every bit as spectacular as his friend had described, and watching Sadie stand at the prow as they motored out of the marina, staring out at the darkening water, Dylan knew he'd made a good choice in bringing her there. They needed tonight—even if it was all they ever got.

And just in case it was, he intended to make the most of every single moment.

Grabbing a bottle of champagne and two glasses from the bar, he headed out on deck to share it with Sadie.

Sadie stared out at the water, dark and constantly changing under the moonlight. Dinner had been beautiful—all four courses of it—and more than made up for their skipped lunch at Ephesus. The conversation, too, had been light and easy—after Dylan had declared a moratorium on business talk the moment they'd sat down. And neither of them had seemed inclined to discuss the past after the day they'd spent together.

Instead, they'd talked about Finn, about cities Dylan had visited recently, places she'd love to go one day, her sister and parents—anything except what was happening between them, or anything that mattered.

It almost felt like a first date.

But now dinner was over and she had to decide what came next. She could tell Dylan was leaving it up to her—which was probably why he'd removed all their other issues from the evening.

It was just them now.

No hotel, no history—no husband. Not any more.

She shivered, and Dylan wrapped his jacket around her shoulders without a word.

Out here at sea, it was just Sadie and Dylan. And it was up to her to decide what that meant.

But only for tonight.

That, she was sure, was the main reason he'd brought

her so far from the real world. Not just to give her a treat at the end of his visit but because, whatever she decided, once they returned to shore it was all over. He'd move on. They'd be business partners perhaps, or maybe not. She hoped they'd still be friends, whatever happened.

But nothing more.

'You're thinking too hard.' Dylan rested against the rail beside her, leaning back to get a good look at her. The lights from the boat lit his face, but hers must be hidden in shadow, she assumed. Yet still he stared at it. 'You're supposed to be relaxing.'

Sadie turned, her back to the water, and he shifted nearer, until he was half in front of her, so close against her right side that she could feel his muscles against her body, even through two layers of clothes.

No pretending this was anything other than it was now. And not even a hint of a suggestion that they might be using that second bedroom.

Sadie sucked in a breath, the scent of him mixed with the sea air filling her lungs, an intoxicating combination. God, she wanted him so much. It felt good to admit that, after so long.

Maybe she always had. But want and love were very different things—and she'd loved Adem.

Strangely, it was that thought that made it all feel possible. This wasn't love—and never would or could be with a man like Dylan. For him, love was commitment and thus impossible. However he felt about her, he'd never let it move past tonight—so neither would she.

Sleeping with him wasn't the same as betraying Adem's memory, not in the way she'd been afraid it would be. Not unless she never planned to sleep with another man again for the rest of her life. At thirty-two, that seemed a little impractical, even to her.

She could have this. She could have one night and no more. She could give in to that curious want that had plagued her since she'd met this man—and that had only worsened over the last week.

As long as she walked away with her heart intact in the morning. And her heart was buried in England with her husband.

Decision made, Sadie rose up on tiptoe before she could change her mind. Dylan's eyes widened, just a fraction, and his arms tightened around her. But he didn't move closer. He was still leaving this up to her.

Sadie closed her eyes, raised her lips to his, and took what she wanted.

The first kiss was gentle, tentative, like the one in Ephesus. But within moments it changed.

'God, Sadie,' Dylan muttered against her lips, and his arms hauled her up against his body so her bottom rested on the higher rail and she could barely touch the deck with her toes. It should have felt unsafe but with Dylan's arms so tight around her body she knew there was no chance of her falling.

She knew he'd never let her go.

'I can't tell you how long I've waited for this,' he murmured, as she placed kisses across his jaw and down his throat.

'About as long as I have,' she admitted, pressing an extra kiss to the hollow of his collar bone, as thanks for discarding his tie and undoing those top shirt buttons after dinner.

His thigh pressed between her legs, her bright red dress rising up high above her knees, and the pressure almost made her lose her mind.

'Really?' he asked, dipping his head for another kiss. 'You wanted this too?'

'Always,' she admitted. 'I just never thought I could have it.' Or should.

'Because— No. Not tonight.' He kissed her firmly. 'Tonight is just for us. No ghosts, no history, nothing between us.'

Sadie looked up into his eyes, almost black with wanting her, and kissed him in agreement. 'Just us. Just for tonight.' She swallowed, hunting down that last bit of courage she needed. 'So, how about you show me the bedroom you promised me this place had?'

Dylan grinned, a wolfish look on his face. God, what was she letting herself in for? And how would anything after it ever live up to tonight?

'Your wish is my command,' he said, and Sadie knew none of it mattered.

Just for tonight she was going to live in the moment, and enjoy every second of it.

CHAPTER FOURTEEN

DYLAN WOKE TO the feeling of something missing. Forcing his tired eyes to open, he waited for them to focus then frowned at the sight of Sadie already pulling that glorious red dress over her even more spectacular body. Without looking back at the bed, she began hunting around for her shoes, pulling them on as she found them.

Huh. Talk about a rude awakening.

Last night had been everything he'd ever dreamt it might be, and more. He could never have imagined the way they moved together would be so in tune, so perfect. He didn't know what had changed that week but, whatever it was, it had only brought the two of them more in sync.

But apparently that perfect connection was over with the sunrise.

'Morning,' he said, levering himself into a seated position and letting the sheets fall away from his torso.

Sadie jumped at the sound of his voice, which gave him some small satisfaction. 'You're awake.'

'As are you. And dressed, too.'

'Yeah, well…we're back in the marina,' she said. He wanted her to come and sit beside him on the bed, just enjoy these last few moments away from the real world, but the look on her face stopped him short of suggesting it. What was it he saw there? Uncertainty, a hint of fear, maybe a little sadness? Or was he just projecting his own feelings onto her expression?

'Time to get back to the real world, then, huh?'

'I guess so.'

'You should have woken me,' he said, trying to inject lightness into the words, to try and break the strange new tension in the room. 'Before you put all those pesky clothes back on, for preference.'

'I suppose you're usually the one slipping out of a borrowed room the morning after, huh?' Her smile suggested it was meant to be a joke, but the words fell flat between them as Dylan felt his mood worsening.

'You were slipping out on me?'

'No!' Sadie said, too fast. 'I mean, it's not like you wouldn't know where to find me, right?'

Was that the only reason? God, what had happened in her head between him falling asleep boneless and sated and the moment he'd woken up this morning? Dylan had no idea—and he wasn't sure he was going to be allowed to find out.

'So it's back to the Azure, then,' he said. Apparently their moratorium on business was over, too. 'That's what happens next?'

'I think it has to be,' Sadie said. 'I mean, you have a flight to catch this afternoon, and you still haven't checked over the Azure proposal. I think I included everything we've talked about, but if you have any questions it would be good to deal with them sooner rather than later. I'm leaving for England in a couple of days to fetch Finn home, remember.'

Home. So Turkey was still home to her. Good to know.

Dylan reached for his pants. Talking business naked just felt wrong. 'Never mind the Azure proposal right now. Have you thought any more about my proposition?'

he asked, wishing the moment the sentence was out that he'd chosen any word other than 'proposition'.

'I…I'm not sure it would be the best idea.'

'Because of last night?'

'Because of lots of things.' She bit her lower lip, and Dylan had to sit on his hands to stop himself reaching for her and kissing them back to last night again. 'Will you still present the Azure proposal to your board for investment? Even if I'm still in charge?'

'Of course,' he said, the words almost sticking in his throat. 'You've certainly demonstrated the potential of Kuşadasi and even the hotel itself as a viable investment. I'll talk to them as soon as I get back.'

'Great. Thanks.'

Awkward silence stretched between them until Dylan thought he might snap. Grabbing his shirt from the floor, he tossed it over his shoulders before striding across the luxurious cabin towards the bathroom. 'Why don't you go see if you can go scare us up some breakfast?' he suggested over his shoulder. 'I'll be there in a few minutes.'

If it was back to business as usual, he needed a shower, some food and plenty of coffee. Hopefully one of those would fill the yawning gap that seemed to have opened up in his chest.

Sadie kept it together until they reached the hotel, a feat she was rather proud of. It would have been so easy, that morning, to turn over and back into Dylan's arms. To let their one perfect night stretch just a little further. But it would have only prolonged the agony.

Because for all her arguments to herself the night before she had no doubt that letting him go again was going to be excruciatingly painful.

How was she supposed to go back to business, or even to being friends, now that she knew how it felt to have his skin against hers, his body pressing hers down into the bed with glorious pleasure? How was she supposed to even *think* about anything else?

But she had to. Because no matter how miffed he might have looked at being upstaged in the casual morning-after stakes, Dylan didn't want anything else. Oh, he might convince himself that they could be something more—but it wouldn't be a commitment, not from him. He wasn't Adem, and she had to remember that. Keep it at the front of her mind at all times.

Or else she had a horrible feeling she could slide so easily into love with the man.

And that *would* be a betrayal. Maybe not of her wedding vows—she knew that if Adem had lived she would never have taken this step, never have had this chance to explore what could be between her and Dylan—and not even of her husband's memory, not really. Rachel had been right in that at least—Adem would rather see her happy than alone.

But she'd be betraying herself. Betraying what she wanted—no, needed—from her own future. Maybe Dylan had been right when he'd said the Azure wasn't her dream, but he couldn't see that it was a part of something bigger. A chance for her to live her life with her son—and she didn't want that life to be confused and clouded by a man who came, made them love him, but never stayed. She wouldn't do that to Finn—or to herself.

Maybe Dylan would change one day, find something or someone worth committing to. But she couldn't take the chance that the thing or person he found might be her. Not when it would affect Finn too.

And it would, she knew. Her own fluctuating emotions

after one week, one night told her that. She needed to be solid and steady for her son, and Dylan Jacobs made her the opposite of both.

'I'd better pack,' Dylan said, as they stood in the lobby of the Azure, more than a metre of marble floor between them.

Sadie nodded her agreement. 'Your car will be here at two. I'll come down and see you off.'

'You don't have to.' He sounded so distant Sadie had to swallow a large lump in her throat before she could answer.

'Yes, I do.'

'Fine. I'll see you then.' He strode off towards the lifts, without looking back.

Sadie took a deep breath and went to check in with the front desk for any important news or messages, hoping they wouldn't comment on how overdressed she was for the task.

Then she was going up to her room to take a bath and break down in private.

The second hand ticked around the clock face seemingly slower than ever, but still inexorably working its way towards two o'clock. Sadie smoothed down her black suit one more time and tucked her still-damp hair behind her ears. At least the make-up seemed to be holding strong—her eyes weren't nearly as blotchy as they'd been a quarter of an hour ago.

In—she checked the clock again—twelve minutes' time she'd go down to the lobby. That, assuming Dylan arrived early too, would give her ten whole minutes to say goodbye to him.

It wasn't enough, but Sadie was starting to worry that no amount of time would be. She'd been so focussed on the fact that he'd be walking away the next day she hadn't spent enough time considering the fact that she wouldn't be able to—not from the memories and not from her feelings.

Dylan might not be the committing sort, but she was—and she should have remembered that before she'd fallen into bed with him. She'd never been the one-night stand sort, so why on earth had she thought she could start now?

She sighed, and sat back down on the bed. Because she'd wanted it so badly, that was why. She'd wanted that one night—and now she'd had it she couldn't give it back. And, truth be told, she wasn't sure she even wanted to.

A sudden hammering on the door jerked her out of her thoughts. Blinking—and hoping the waterproof mascara was still holding up—she quickly crossed the floor and opened the door.

'Dylan.' She was supposed to have another eleven minutes before she had to face him. What unfairness was this?

Without a word he pushed past her into the room. Sadie shut the door behind her; from the furious expression on his face she had a feeling this conversation wasn't one she wanted to share with the rest of the hotel.

'Okay, I'm leaving in, like, fifteen minutes, but I need to know something first.' He had his hands in his pockets, but from the look of the material they were bunched into fists. 'What happens next?'

'Next?' Sadie gulped. The question she'd been avoiding. 'Well, like we said, it's back to business. We can be business partners, hopefully, and friends for definite. I hope Finn and I will be seeing more of you in the future.' Even if it tore at her heart every time. Dylan was part of Adem's life too, and Finn deserved the chance to know him. She just needed to make sure she guarded her emotions more carefully—something that would certainly be easier with her son present.

'So last night was…?'

'Wonderful,' she admitted, with a small smile. 'But I told you, I never expected anything more. I'm not trying to tie you down or make you commit to anything. Well, anything more than saving my hotel.'

'You make it sound like everything that has happened between us this week was only about you getting my investment.'

'You know that's not true,' Sadie admonished. Whatever he might think of her today, he had to know she wasn't the money-grabbing woman his words suggested.

'Do I?' he asked, one eyebrow raised.

'I bloody well hope so!' Her own temper started to heat and rise to match his. Ten more minutes and they could have avoided this completely, parted civilly. But, no, he had to storm in here and demand the last say, didn't he?

'In that case, I can only assume that you slept with me as some sort of personal experiment,' Dylan said, the words sharp. 'A chance to find out what you could have had. And now you're burying yourself back in your old life, the tired old plan that wasn't working.'

'Sounds to me like you don't like being treated the way you've treated God knows how many women over the years,' Sadie bit back. 'What, it's okay for you to indulge in one night and call it quits, but God forbid a woman tries to do the same to you.'

'That's not what this was!' Dylan yelled. 'What we had—'

'Was a mutual attraction we worked out of our systems last night.' The lie hurt even to speak it, but what other option was there? Ask for more and watch Dylan flounder when he realised he couldn't offer it? She might have hurt his manly pride, but that had to be better than letting him destroy any self-respect she had left.

'It was more than that, and you know it.' His tone was low now, dangerous, daring Sadie to deny it.

She couldn't.

'Even if it was,' she said softly, 'it was never going to be anything more than this week, and it's not fair of you to pretend that it was. I have Finn and the Azure to think about, and you have your business… You're leaving any minute now, for heaven's sake.'

'But I'll come back. I said I'd come back.' He made it sound like a huge commitment. Probably because he had no idea what a real one looked or sounded like.

'And there'll always be a friendly welcome for you here.'

'Friends.' He barked a harsh laugh. 'You really think we can go back to that?'

'I think we have to,' Sadie said pragmatically. 'Because, Dylan, you can't offer me anything else.'

'I offered you a new career. A chance to start over.'

'What I want most is the chance to have a future with my son.' The truth, if not quite all of it.

'And what about me? Are you really going to let your dead husband and this bloody hotel stop you from moving on and being happy?'

She could have laughed at the cruel irony of it. Here he was, the ultimate playboy, asking for more—and she couldn't give it to him, however much she wanted to. Because he didn't even know what it meant.

'Are you honestly telling me you're ready to become a father—to a little boy you've barely met?' The sudden shock on his face was answer enough. 'Exactly. Dylan, you're not Adem, and I never expected you to be. I went into this with my eyes open. But you don't do commitment and I need that in my life—for Finn, as well as myself. We need stability and certainty more than ever now. And you can't give us that.'

You're not Adem.

Wasn't that what it always came down to? In the end, it wouldn't have mattered who'd met her first, who'd loved her most, who could give her what—he wasn't Adem. So he was always going to lose.

'I'm not even second choice to you, am I?' he murmured, watching her eyes widen. Could she sense the fury building inside him? He hoped so. But he also knew he needed to get out of there before it exploded. He'd never hurt her, but if they wanted to remain even business acquaintances there were some things they couldn't come back from. 'I'm no choice at all.'

'Finn is my choice,' Sadie said, but he knew what she meant. She would always choose Adem—even his memory—over moving on with him. Over giving him a chance to see if maybe, just maybe, this time he could stick at something. 'Yours is the next big thing. It always has been, and it always will be. You know that, Dylan.'

'Just like my old man, huh?' He knew it himself, always had. But it still hurt to hear it from her—the one woman he'd thought, for a moment, that he could be something more for. Someone better.

'That's not what—' Sadie started.

'Yes,' he replied. 'You did.'

So, really, what was there left to say?

'My assistant will be in touch about the investment proposal in due course,' he said. 'I'm sure it will go through without a problem.'

Sadie nodded but didn't speak. He supposed she'd got

the only thing she wanted anyway. At least one of them was ending this week happy.

'Goodbye, Sadie.' He turned on his heel and walked out, hoping his car was already waiting downstairs.

He didn't let himself believe that the sound he heard behind him as he shut the door was a sob.

CHAPTER FIFTEEN

SADIE DROPPED HER suitcase onto the spare bed in her parents' back bedroom and began rummaging through it for a cardigan. England might be colder than she'd remembered, but it was still good to be home, however temporarily.

Anything was better than moping around the Azure Hotel alone.

At least she had Finn back now. Once they headed home to Turkey, it would be the two of them against the world again, and everything would be fine. Just one look at his beaming face as he'd waved his 'Mummy' sign, surrounded by pictures of aircraft, when she'd arrived at the airport had told her that she'd done the right thing. When he'd wrapped his little arms around her neck and hugged her tight she'd known there was no other choice she could have made.

Finn was the only thing that mattered now. All she had left.

'Knock-knock.' Her sister Rachel appeared in the open doorway, both hands occupied with cups of tea. 'Mum thought you might need this after your journey.'

'Definitely.' Family, a cup of tea, familiar surroundings...this was all exactly what she needed.

A whoop of excitement from outside caught her atten

tion and she moved to the window, cup of tea in hand. In the back garden Finn and his cousins appeared to be playing some sort of game involving a football, three hula-hoops and a garden chair. Whatever the rules, he seemed to be having fun, even wrapped up in his coat and scarf instead of still being in tee shirt and shorts, as he would have been in Turkey.

'The kids have loved having Finn here to play with,' Rachel said, following her gaze. 'It's been lovely for them to all have some time together.'

'I know.' A flicker of guilt at keeping Finn so far away from his family ran through her. 'And I know Adem's parents enjoyed having him for a sleepover last weekend.' More people they didn't see enough of.

'I bet. It must be even harder for them.'

'They came out to visit in the spring,' Sadie said defensively.

'Not the same as having him round the corner, though, is it?'

No, it wasn't. Sadie sank to sit on the edge of the bed and blew across the top of her tea to cool it. 'Finn asked me if we really had to go back to Turkey,' she admitted. 'He's loved being here so much.'

Rachel winced as she sat beside her. 'Sorry. Didn't mean to make things worse.'

'It's the truth, though, isn't it?'

'But not all of it. If you're truly happy out in Turkey then Finn will be too. You know kids, they're always happiest exactly where they are, never ready to move on to the next thing. Especially if it's bedtime.'

The exact opposite of Dylan. Sadie huffed a tiny laugh into her mug at the thought.

'How are things at the Azure anyway?' Rachel asked.

'Any luck with the investment guy—personal or professional?' She nudged Sadie gently in the ribs.

'Dylan's going to present my proposal to the board, but he thinks they should go for investing.' There. She'd said his name without crying. A definite improvement. And the proposal was good—she'd worked on it with Neal before Dylan's arrival for weeks, and had tweaked it to fit everything she and Dylan had talked about on his visit. It was just what he'd wanted, she hoped.

'And personally?' Rachel pressed. 'Come on, Sade. I saw you all dressed up for him, remember? There was definitely something going on there.'

'Well, if there was, it was for one night only,' Sadie said.

Rachel frowned. 'That idiot walked out on you after one night?'

'Yeah. Well, no. I…I guess I walked out on him.'

'That doesn't sound much like you.'

'It was a pre-emptive strike,' Sadie explained. 'He doesn't do commitment, and it was more important to me that we stay friends and business partners. Apart from anything else, Finn doesn't need any more uncertainty in his life.'

'And how's that working out for you?' Rachel asked doubtfully.

'It's fine,' Sadie lied. 'It's for the best.' She just had to keep telling herself that. And not acknowledge the secret fear that kept her awake at night—that she had gone a fallen head first in love with Dylan Jacobs.

Even she couldn't be that stupid, right?

'He did offer me a different business proposal, thoug she said. Better to get the conversation back on prof sional terms. 'It would mean working back here in t UK, putting a manager in charge at the Azure.'

'That would be perfect!' Rachel bounced a little on the mattress. 'You and Finn could come home and still keep the Azure! Have you told Mum and Dad yet?'

'I turned him down,' Sadie admitted, with a wince.

Rachel stopped bouncing. 'Because you slept with him?'

'Because…it didn't feel right.' Of course, nothing had felt right since Dylan had left either. But how much harder would this be if she had to see him all the time for work, too? No, much better this way, with her safely tucked away in Turkey and him travelling the world, popping in for the occasional friendly visit. Knowing Dylan, they'd be lucky to see him more than once a year.

Another depressing thought.

'Well, I suppose you know best,' Rachel said, although her tone clearly said otherwise.

'I hope so,' Sadie whispered.

Otherwise it was entirely possible she'd made the biggest mistake of her life, sending Dylan away.

'Well, you're in a foul mood,' Dylan's sister Cassie said. He dropped into the wooden chair beside her, exhausted after an hour or more racing around the scrubland that surrounded her home with her two boys.

'Hey, you should be nicer to the guy who's been keeping up with your two tearaways for the past week.' Not that it was a chore particularly. Keeping two six-and nine-year-old boys entertained took energy and concentration, and worked marvellously as a distraction. Of course, it helped that it was also fun.

Much more fun than dwelling on how things had ended with Sadie anyway.

Cassie handed him a cold beer and he took it gratefully. 'Want to tell me about it?'

'I don't know what you're talking about,' Dylan lied.

'Seriously?' Raising her eyebrows at him, Cassie put her own bottle down and ticked her observations off on her fingers. 'First, you arrive here with no warning. You drag the boys off to play outside whenever they ask you questions about your travels. You haven't been to see Mum, even though you've been here for days. And, most importantly, you've almost drunk all my beer.'

'I'll buy you more beer.'

'That's not the point.' Cassie sighed. 'Go on, I'm listening. Detail your boring work problem and I'll make the necessary sympathetic noises as needed. Unless it isn't work…' She sat up straighter. 'In which case I might be much more interested.'

'It's nothing.' Dylan took a swig of his beer, glad it was a million miles away from the local wine he'd drunk with Sadie in Turkey. The fewer reminders the better right now. He'd spoken to the board, had got them to approve the investment and had handed the whole mess over to his assistant before he'd left for his sister's place in Sydney. He just wanted to move on.

'Which means it's a woman,' Cassie guessed. 'Okay, let me see… She's married to someone else? Or just not interested. Oh, Dylan, did you finally find a woman who *doesn't* want you?'

'Not exactly.' Although, really, wasn't that the truth? Sure, she'd wanted him for one night, but that had been it.

Dylan sent up a silent apology to every woman he'd ever spent just one night with, even if he'd been upfront about it from the start. Being on the opposite end showed him exactly how much it sucked.

'So what happened?' Cassie pulled her feet up under her on her chair, just like she'd done when she'd been little. 'You've got me all curious now. Don't leave me hanging.'

Dylan sighed. Cassie had always been stubborn. There was no way he was getting out of this conversation without giving up at least the basic facts.

'I went to Turkey to see an old friend, to see if I could help her business out. We…connected in a way we hadn't before, that's all.' He shrugged. No big deal, no drama, no hole in his chest filled with a swirling vacuum of rage and confusion and disappointment. Nothing to see at all.

'That's all?' Cassie asked sceptically. 'So, what, you slept with her, left as usual, and now you're, what? Missing her?' She shook her head. 'You're such an idiot.'

'Thanks for the pep talk.' His little sister always did know how to kick a guy when he was down. At least, that was what her first husband had said. Her second hadn't commented on it so far. Dylan liked him a lot more than the first.

'Seriously, Dyl, when are you going to stop running before you even have a chance to see if there could be something there?' Cassie waved her bottle at him accusingly. 'You're always the same. You find someone you like, indulge in a fling or whatever, then walk away before it can go anywhere. And this time it really looks like it could have! I haven't seen you this bummed since that deal in London went wrong.'

'What's the point in staying?' Dylan asked. 'I mean, we all know that I'll be leaving eventually, right? When the next big opportunity comes up, I'll be on my way. Why make that harder than it has to be?' He couldn't even deny the accusations Sadie had thrown at him. He didn't stay—and she wouldn't go. Permanent mismatch.

'That's just horse droppings!'

'You've been watching your language around kids too long.'

'I'd use stronger if I thought it would make you listen!' Cassie sighed, and settled onto the edge of her chair, staring earnestly up at him. 'Did you even think about staying and fighting for her? That's what you do, you know, when you love someone. You stay and figure things out. Every morning you wake up and decide to try harder. That's all there is to it.'

'She told me to leave. She has a son…commitments. There was no place for me there.' Even if it had felt, just for a moment, like he could have fitted into their lives perfectly.

'Honestly, Dyl, if you believe that you're stupider than even I ever thought. Just because Dad left doesn't mean you will. Of course you can settle down, *of course* you can commit, when you find the right thing.'

'And how, exactly, do you know that?' Because he sure didn't.

'Because you've already done it once.' Cassie sat back in her chair, a smug look on her face.

Dylan blinked. 'How do you mean?'

'You did it for me and Mum. You spent years taking care of us, committed to making sure we were okay even when we went out of our way to mess that up.' She smiled gently at him, and Dylan felt some of the truth of her words sink into his bones. 'You never thought about walking away, did you?'

'No. I suppose I didn't.'

'And you've never stopped either. You still check up on us both. You're always there for my boys—and I know you always will be. That's why I named you their guardian in my will.'

'You did?' Why hadn't he known that? Unless Cassi

had thought the idea of it would have freaked him out. Which, before this week, it probably would have.

Cassie nodded. 'Too right. I wouldn't trust anyone else with them.'

'Thanks. I think.'

'And I bet we're not the only ones,' Cassie went on. 'What about your friends? I mean, you said you went out there to help this old friend out. You've always done that, too. Whatever your friends needed, you were there. That's commitment too, you know.'

'I never thought of it that way,' Dylan admitted. All those years, he'd committed to the people who mattered to him—his friends and family.

The truth struck him hard in the chest. Friends and family? Sadie was already both, in his heart.

He was already committed, and he hadn't even noticed.

Now he just needed to convince her of that.

Maybe he wasn't Adem. But maybe he could be what she needed now instead.

And maybe, just maybe, he could be what Finn needed too. After all, he knew better than anyone how fundamental having a father figure in a boy's life could be. Maybe he could even give Finn what he and Cassie had lost when he had been ten.

Cassie took another swig of her beer. 'Little sisters are always right, you know. So, need me to book you a ticket to Turkey?'

But Dylan was already on the phone to the airline.

Sadie hung back from the gravestone, flowers held awkwardly in her hands. Her dad was waiting in the car with Finn, ready to take them back to the airport, so she didn't have long. But coming to the churchyard had seemed like the right thing to do before she left.

But now she was here, staring at a stone that spoke about a beloved father, son, husband and friend, she didn't know what to do next.

Adem wasn't here, not for her. She knew his parents felt better having him close, but for her no motionless, cold stone could ever represent her warm, loving, enthusiastic husband. She felt his presence far more in the heat of a Turkish summer or in the halls and rooms of the Azure.

And maybe that was why she needed to be here. To ask for his blessing, or advice, or something. To tell him that she needed to move on at last.

'I'll always love you,' she said, placing the flowers carefully by the stone. 'But I think you know that anyway.' She'd told him often enough in life.

Sighing, she crouched down in front of the flowers. 'We had a wonderful life together, didn't we? And we made the most precious little boy. But…I don't think you'd want me to stay in this limbo. And I'm starting to think I can't.'

She swallowed, fighting back the tears that pooled in the corners of her eyes. 'I need to move on. I'm not quite sure what to yet, but I don't think that matters as much as being ready to take the chances as they come.'

Just because Dylan wasn't an opportunity it didn't mean there wouldn't be others. In work, as well as in love.

'You always said that your instincts were the most important compass you had,' she went on. 'That if you trusted your instincts nothing much could go wrong. You said…' A choked sob escaped her throat. 'You said that asking me to marry you when we were so young, with no prospects, was the biggest ever test of that. And me saying yes…that was the last time I truly trusted my own instincts instead of yours.

'Well, that changes now. I don't know what's going

to happen next but… Dylan's assistant called. We have the investment we need to save the Azure. So I'm going to make that happen and then I'm going to find someone I trust to manage the place when I'm away. I'll take Finn back often, I promise, and it will be there for him when he's old enough. But in the meantime my instincts tell me we should be here, in England, with our families. And then…well, I guess we'll see. I have faith that the right thing will come along at the right time.' She managed a lopsided smile. 'It always did for you after all. Until the last.'

Adem's life had been too short and their happiness cut off before its time. But the happiness they'd had together would be hers to treasure for always. And she would.

Kissing her fingers, she pressed them against the stone. 'Love you,' she whispered.

Then, wiping her eyes, she turned and headed back towards the car, and her future.

CHAPTER SIXTEEN

SADIE SIGHED WITH relief as the car from the airport turned up the road that led to the Azure Hotel.

'Nearly there,' she told Finn, who snuggled down further on his booster seat, arms wrapped around his favourite teddy. 'Nearly home.'

Home for now, anyway.

The flight had been long and tedious, with a change in Istanbul that had dragged on as they'd waited for a delayed plane. Finn had been brilliant, really, but the journey had been trying for *her,* let alone a four-year-old. Still, with the help of plenty of snacks, a new toy or two saved for the occasion, and a well-timed nap on the last leg, they'd made it.

If nothing else, all the time in transit had given her time to think—to start to form plans, ideas that she hoped would come together as the weeks went on.

She was returning to Turkey prepared for her fresh start, ready to jump at the right opportunities as they presented themselves.

Of course, some sign as to what the right opportunities were would be appreciated, but Sadie figured that was part of trusting her instincts—figuring that out for herself.

'We're here,' she whispered to Finn as the car drew to

a halt. He blinked at her a couple of times then opened his eyes wider.

'The Azure?'

'That's right. You ready to get back to your room and your things? I know Esma's been missing you.'

Sadie opened the door and let him hop out onto the pavement, following as the driver retrieved their bags.

'Thanks,' she said, stopping for a moment to look up at her hotel. *Her* hotel. She liked the sound of that.

The familiar Azure sign shone above the glass doors and she smiled at it as she lowered her gaze…and felt her heart stop.

As Esma rushed out and tried to whisk Finn away, chattering loudly about milkshakes and special sweet bread in the kitchens, Sadie stared at the man standing under the Azure sign.

Dylan Jacobs.

Well, she'd asked for a sign.

'What are you doing here?' She stepped closer, leaving her bags on the pavement as the car pulled away.

'Mum?' Finn asked, looking between her and Dylan. Esma shot Sadie an apologetic look. 'Who's this?'

Dylan crouched down beside Finn and the smile on his face was a new one to Sadie. Friendly, warm and with no edge, no demands. No business.

'You probably don't remember me, but I was one of your dad's best friends.'

'You knew my dad?' Finn's face scrunched up, just a little. 'If you were friends with Dad and Uncle Neal, are you Dylan?'

Dylan held out his hand. 'Dylan Jacobs. At your service.'

Finn shook his hand solemnly, his fingers tiny around Dylan's bigger ones, and Sadie felt her heart contract at the sight. 'Uncle Neal tells me stories about you and Dad sometimes. How come you never come and see us, like he does?'

'I've been…' Dylan trailed off before he could finish the sentence, but Sadie was pretty sure the missing words were 'too busy with work'. Wasn't that always the case? But then he started again.

'I'm sorry, Finn. I should have done. I should have visited more. And I'd like to start now, if that's okay with you.'

'I guess so.' Finn tilted his head to the side. 'Do you like milkshakes?'

'Love them.' Dylan grinned. 'Maybe we can grab one together later? After I speak to your mum?'

Finn nodded. 'Okay.' Esma took his arm again and this time he didn't object as she led him off to the kitchens. Sadie sighed with relief—until she realised that left her alone with Dylan.

Just what she was trying to avoid. 'There's really no need for you to be here,' she said. 'I told your assistant I'd get the forms to him by—'

Dylan shook his head to stop her, standing up from his crouch. 'I'm not here in a professional capacity.'

How she'd missed that voice. Warm and smooth and caressing—even when he was chatting with Finn or when they were talking business. Just seeing him again made her want to reach out and grab him, to hold on and never let him go.

This was why she'd needed not to see him again. When she was near him it was impossible to deny that she'd fallen ridiculously in love with him.

'Then why are you here?' she managed to ask through her muddled thoughts.

Dylan stepped closer, taking a breath so deep she saw his chest move under his shirt. 'I'm here to commit.'

'To what?' Sadie asked, blinking. Because he couldn't possibly mean what she thought he did. Could he?

'To whatever you need to be happy,' Dylan replied. 'If that's me thousands of miles away, then I'll commit to that. If it's still the Azure, I'll work like the devil to make that happen with you. If it's England with Finn, I can make that work too. All I want is a chance. A chance to prove that I can be part of your plan, of your future.'

'That's it?' Was this really the same man who had walked out on her in such a fury?

'That's it,' Dylan confirmed. 'I know I'm not Adem, and I never will be. But I can be more than you think of me. All I want is a chance to be with you, however you need me. To be there for you and Finn. And I know that can't happen all of a sudden—he needs to get used to me, we need to figure out things between us… So, a new proposal, okay? No jumping in feet first, just a slow, measured plan you can back out of any time you want. The sort of plan you like, I promise.'

The ultimate commitment-phobe was offering to commit. The man who *always* leapt at the next big thing was promising to stick to just one plan. Her plan.

Hope blossomed deep in Sadie's chest, like the cherry tree in her parents' back garden in England, flowering with hope and possibility in the spring.

But… She shook her head. 'I'm sorry, Dylan. That won't work for me.'

That was it. With just those few words she'd dashed any hope Dylan had ever had of committing again, he was sure. The heaviness in his chest sank lower and lower until…

He blinked. Was she smiling?

Sadie stepped closer and he let just a little chink of hope back in.

'This time…' she said, reaching up to place her hand against his cheek. 'This time I'm trusting my instincts. I'm taking all the opportunities I can to be truly happy again. And I think I know what that means, at last.'

'You do?' Then he wished to God she'd tell him because he had no idea what was going on.

Sadie nodded. 'I want Finn to have the Azure when he's older, but I don't want to run it myself. Once we've got things set up here and on the road to recovery, I'm hoping you'll help me find a manager we can trust so that Finn and I can move back to England.'

'Of course. Does that mean you've reconsidered my job offer?' Was this business? Or pleasure? Her closeness suggested the latter, but her words didn't. And he'd already been caught out by that before.

'I've reconsidered a lot of things,' she admitted. 'I want to run my own spas, I know that. And if we can work together on that…well, that would be great.'

'That all sounds good,' Dylan said cautiously.

'But that's not all,' Sadie went on. 'I'm afraid I'm greedy. I want more than just my family near, my son happy and a dream business. I want you, too.'

His heart stopped, just for a moment. 'I thought you said—'

'I said that slow and measured wasn't going to work for me any more,' Sadie corrected him. 'I know we can't rush too much officially because of Finn—I need to be sure that he's ready for there to be someone else in my life, and that he's happy for it to be you. So, officially, fine, we go with your plan.'

'But unofficially?' He didn't care. He'd say yes to anything right now if it meant being part of her life. Hers and Finn's.

'Life's too short, I've seen that first hand. You have to take your chances for happiness when they come. So just between you and me… I hope you were serious about wanting to commit…'

'I was,' Dylan assured her.

'Good. Because…' She took a deep breath. 'Dylan Jacobs, will you marry me?'

Pure joy spread through his body at her words. This was one opportunity he had no intention of missing.

Reaching into his pocket, he pulled out the ring box he'd acquired in Sydney and flipped it open between them. 'Great minds?' he said, as Sadie laughed.

'I should have known the slow-and-steady thing was a bluff.' She took the ring from the box and stared at the diamond, mesmerised. 'You never did anything that way in your life.'

'Oh, I don't know,' Dylan said, as he slid the ring onto her finger. 'It took me thirteen years to find the right woman to commit to.'

'But now you're sure?' Sadie asked.

'I'm beyond certain,' Dylan promised, leaning in to kiss all her doubts away. 'You're my next, last and only big thing. Your love is the only thing that matters to me. You, Finn and I are going to be the happiest little family ever, I'm committed to that. And I plan to spend the rest of my life proving it to you.'

Sadie smiled, and kissed him back.

And in that moment Dylan knew, bone deep, that proposing to Sadie was worth more than the chance at any million-dollar business deal, and that marrying her would give him more opportunities for happiness than one man could ever use in a lifetime.

EPILOGUE

CHERRY BLOSSOMS BLEW across the garden from the tree at the far end, and Sadie watched, smiling, as Finn tried to catch them, Dylan swinging him up in his arms to reach higher.

In the kitchen behind her, her parents were putting the finishing touches to a Sunday roast—and didn't need any help at all, thank you. Ordered to relax, Sadie had retired to the garden to enjoy the spring sunshine and just be with her family. At any minute her sister would arrive with her brood, and they'd all be together.

In the six months since Dylan had first arrived at the Azure, life had changed beyond recognition—and into something Sadie had never even hoped for. It hadn't all been easy, and business had intruded more than she'd have liked. But Finn had taken to Dylan instantly—and his awed admiration seemed to be reciprocated. Some nights, when Dylan was staying with them—always in the spare room, as far as Finn was concerned—she'd catch Dylan sneaking into Finn's room just to watch him sleeping. The amazed love in his eyes always made her want to kiss him harder.

They'd finally broached the topic of becoming a real family with Finn the weekend before, despite Sadie's anxieties. His little five-year-old nose had scrunched up at the idea.

'So, Dylan would live with us?' he'd asked.

'When he didn't have to travel for work, yes,' Sadie had answered nervously.

'Good. I like our house. I can walk to Grandma and Granddad's from here, and to school, and Phoebe and CJ can visit me lots.' Dylan had shared a small smile with her at that. When she'd tried to insist on finding a place to rent on her own, maybe in Oxford, he'd pointed out that she'd only have to move again in a few months when they finally let everyone else in on their engagement. The whole point was to be near her family—so together they'd found the perfect house just across the village from her parents'.

It already felt like home should.

'So, you wouldn't mind me marrying your mum?' Dylan had asked, and Sadie had heard the nerves in his voice even if Finn hadn't. He'd come such a long way from the man she remembered as Adem's friend. And he was so much more now, to her and to Finn.

'Will I have to wear a stupid suit?' Finn had asked. 'My friend Riley did when his mum got married.'

'You can wear whatever you like,' Dylan had promised, his relief obvious.

Finn had tipped his head to the side, studied Dylan for a moment, then clambered up into his lap for a hug. 'Then I think it would be pretty great.'

As far as Sadie was concerned, it already was.

A commotion came from behind her and Sadie knew that Rachel had arrived with the kids. Finn came running towards her, cherry blossoms forgotten, Dylan following. As he passed, Sadie grabbed Finn around his waist and pulled him up into her lap.

'Mum!' He wiggled, trying to escape. 'CJ and Phoebe are here!'

'I know,' Sadie said. 'So, how would you like to be the one to tell everyone the big news?'

'The wedding news?' Finn whispered conspiratorially.

Sadie nodded, smiling at Dylan over Finn's head.

'Okay!' He jumped down and ran into the house. 'Guess what, everybody! Mum and Dylan are getting married!'

Dylan held out a hand to pull her to her feet. 'Better put this on, then.' He fished in his pocket for a familiar-looking ring box and handed it to her. 'It'll be good to see it on your hand permanently at last.'

'It'll be good to wear it.' She let him slide the ring into place then reached up to kiss him as her mum's squeals of joy rang out from inside.

'When do you propose to tell them our other news?' Dylan murmured against her mouth, his hand brushing across her middle.

'We've got a few weeks yet,' Sadie whispered back. 'Let's let this one sink in first.' In truth, she was enjoying the secret. 'Besides, I want Finn to know before anyone else. Being a big brother is a big job.'

'That it is.' He kissed her again, and Sadie felt a warmth flow through her that had more to do with love than spring sunshine and cherry blossom.

She was home at last, exactly where she was meant to be, and all her plans for the future looked golden.

* * * * *

HEART SURGEON, HERO...HUSBAND?

SUSAN CARLISLE

In Raina's memory

Special Thanks

To my Tuesday night critique group for steering me in the right direction each week, especially Lisa and Claudia.

To my editor, Flo Nicoll, for seeing something in my writing that showed promise and encouraging me until that something showed through. I appreciate you.

To Darcy for saying you should write this. You were right.

To Sia for sharing your writing knowledge. I'm better for it.

To Carol for reading, re-reading, and taking care of me. Couldn't have done it without you.

To my mom, my husband and my kids for being so supportive. I love you all.

CHAPTER ONE

"A HEART TRANSPLANT? My baby's only two years old." Hannah Quinn stared at Dr. Scott McIntyre, the cardio-thoracic surgeon who sat across the conference room table from her. His familiar Mediterranean-Sea eyes were sympathetic, but his face remained somber.

The shock of seeing Scott again was only surpassed by the pain of his words. Her son was dying.

When had she slipped down the rabbit hole to this horror at Children's General Hospital? As if that weren't torment enough, she now faced a mother's worst nightmare, and the news was being delivered by Atlanta, Georgia's supposedly best cardiothoracic surgeon, a man who had hurt her badly years before.

In the movies this would have been called a twist of fate, horrible irony. But this wasn't some screenplay, this was her life. Her child, who always had a smile, her little boy, who giggled when she kissed him behind his ear, was in serious danger.

"He was doing fine. I was taking him for a scheduled check-up. Next thing I know his pediatrician has ordered an ambulance to bring us here." Hannah covered her mouth, damming the primal screams that threatened to escape. Moisture pooled in her eyes, blurring her vision of Scott…now Jake's doctor. "You have to be wrong."

He glanced at Andrea, the heart-transplant coordinator, sitting beside him, before he reached across the table as if to take Hannah's hand.

"Don't." She straightened. He withdrew.

That night eight years ago had started with a simple brush of his hand. She couldn't go there, wouldn't go there again, or she'd fall apart. She had to hold it together until her world righted itself. And it would, it had to. "I knew that a valve replacement might be in his future sooner than I had hoped, but a heart transplant? Your diagnosis can't be correct."

Scott ran a hand through his wavy hair. The soft, silky locks had gone from light to golden blond with age. His fingers threaded through his hair again, a mannerism Hannah remembered from when they'd been friends, good friends. They'd shared warm banter when he'd come to work on the step-down floor. The banter between them had developed into a friendship she'd valued, and had thought he had too.

Leaning forward, he brought her attention back to why they were sitting in this tiny, barren room, acting as if they'd never known each other intimately.

"I'm sorry, Hannah," he murmured with compassion. His voice strengthened with the words, "But the diagnosis *is* correct. The condition is called cardiomyopathy."

"Isn't that when the heart has become enlarged?" Hannah asked.

"Yes, it is. In Jake's case, he must have contracted a virus that went undetected. It settled on the valve he has had from birth—the one that wasn't working correctly. His heart is inflamed and is no longer pumping efficiently."

"He's had nothing more than a little runny nose. I assure you that if it had been more, I would've taken him to see a doctor."

"I'm not questioning your care for your son. The virus may have looked like something as simple as a cold, but it attacked his heart, damaging it. Sometimes it takes weeks to manifest itself and sometimes, like in Jake's case, only days or hours. There is no way to know how or when it will happen. But you would know that, being a nurse."

"Most of my work experience has been on an adult orthopedic floor and, anyway, I'm not nursing at present."

His head canted questioningly, but he said, "Still, you should understand the only thing we can do for your son—"

"His name is Jake." The words came out frosted. She wouldn't allow Jake to become a hospital number, just another patient in a bed.

Scott's gaze met hers. "Jake needs a new heart." His voice softened. "He needs to be listed right away."

Could she melt into the floor? Disappear? Maybe run so fast reality couldn't catch her?

"There has to be another way. Isn't there medication you can give him? I want a second opinion."

The skin around Scott lips tightened. He shook his head slightly, forestalling any further argument. "Hannah, you're welcome to get a second opinion. But we can't waste any time. Jake will die without the transplant. He might only have a few more weeks. The first thing we'll do is see that he is put on the United Network for Organ Sharing list."

She wiped away the dampness on her cheek. The framed pictures of the smiling children lining the walls of the tiny room mocked her. Her child should be one of them. Instead, he lay in a bed in the cardiac ICU, fighting for his life.

"I've examined Jake. He's stable for now. We're giving him anti-clotting drugs to prevent blood clots, which are common with cardiomyopathy, and watching for any arrhythmia."

Her eyes widened. "Blood clots! Arrhythmia!" She leaned toward him, hands gripping the edge of the table. "I want Jake listed now."

"Before we can do that, you'll need to have a psychological exam."

Her dazed look met his. "You have to be kidding. Jake is dying and you want me to have a psychological test? There's nothing wrong with me. It's your job to get Jake a heart, not see if my head's on straight."

Scott shifted in his chair, one of his long green scrubs-covered legs bumping against the table support. Despite being terrified by what he was telling her, Hannah couldn't help but compare the man in front of her with the one she had once known. A tall man years ago, his shoulders had broadened since she'd last seen him. Cute, in an all-American way then, now he was handsome as a man with power. Maturity and responsibility had added fine lines to his face, which she bet only made him more appealing to the nurses.

Scott still possessed the air of confidence that had made him the shining star of his medical class and the desire of the female personnel in the hospital. She, fortunately, had managed to remain immune to his playboy-to-the-core charm for a while, but not long enough.

"You need to calm down. Take a couple of deep breaths."

"Don't patronize me, Scott."

"Look, the visit to the psychologist is protocol. You'll be asked questions to make sure you understand what's involved with a transplant. The care afterwards is as important as the transplant itself. We need to know you can handle it."

She pushed back in her chair and crossed her arms over

her chest. "I assure you I can take care of my son, both as a mother *and* as a nurse."

Propping his elbows on the table, Scott clasped his hands and used his index fingers to punctuate his words. "Hannah, I don't doubt it and I understand your frustration, but there are procedures."

At least he sounded as if he cared how she felt, unlike how he had acted years ago. Known for his excellent bedside manner then, in more ways than one, she'd never dreamed she'd ever be on the receiving end of his professional conduct.

"I have no interest in your procedures. I'm only interested in Jake getting well."

"If you really want that, you're going to have to work with me to see that it happens." His words had a razor-sharp edge, leaving her no room to argue.

"Okay then, I'm ready to do the interview." Hannah looked him directly in the eyes. "How much is all of this going to cost?"

He returned the same unwavering look. "Let's not worry about that. Keeping Jake healthy enough for the surgery is my primary concern."

Scott addressed Andrea. "Can you see that everything is set up for Han—uh…Mrs. Quinn's psychological?"

"I'll take care of it," Andrea responded.

Pushing the metal chair back, Scott stood. "I'll speak to you again soon. I'm sorry this is happening to your son." He hesitated as if he wanted to say something further but thought better of it.

Wishing this situation would just go away, she gave Scott a tight smile.

"Andrea also has some forms that need to be filled out, so I'll leave you with her."

With that, Scott made a swift exit. She shouldn't be surprised he'd showed no more emotion. He'd done much the same thing the next morning after she'd made the mistake of succumbing to his charms. Their friendship had died, and so had her faith in him. Hannah let her brain shut down, and answered Andrea's questions by rote. When Andrea had finished, Hannah asked, "How good a surgeon is Scott, I mean Dr. McIntyre?"

"He's the best," Andrea stated, her voice full of assurance.

Was she just another woman who had fallen under Scott's spell and could sing nothing but his praises? "I can't let Jake die."

"Mrs. Quinn." Andrea placed her hand on Hannah's arm. "Dr. McIntyre is a brilliant surgeon. He'll take excellent care of your son. You can trust him."

Andrea guided Hannah to the waiting room and to an area away from the other parents. Hannah sank onto a blue vinyl sofa and put her head in her hands, letting pent-up tears flow. She understood what she'd been told, but she wasn't entirely convinced. Hannah couldn't afford to be blindly accepting where her son's care was concerned. He was all she had.

Hannah studied the blue square pattern of the carpet. She had no idea that Andrea had sat down beside her until she laid a comforting hand on Hannah's shoulder.

Andrea said, "You'll get through this. Why don't you go back and see Jake? Visiting hours will be over soon."

Entering the cardiac unit, Hannah checked in with the clerk at the large circular desk situated in the middle of an enormous open room. Of the twenty or so beds around the wall, only one interested her, the third one on the left, where her little boy lay so still.

Her precious child looked small and pale stretched out

on the white sheet of the big bed. Wires ran from him to the surrounding machines. She'd seen this before, during nursing training, but this time it was *her* child lying there.

It's just you and me, honey. Don't leave me. Jake's usually sparkling blue eyes were clouded with fear as they pleaded for reassurance. Hannah took his tiny hand in hers, careful not to touch any of the IV lines. Her chest tightened. She placed a kiss on his forehead before stroking his dark baby curls while making a soft cooing sound that settled him.

"Mrs. Quinn?" A young woman stepped to the foot of the bed. I'll be Jake's nurse for today. You may come back to visit any time during the day but you need to call first and get permission."

What if something happens while I'm not here? Could I live with myself if it did? Would I want to? Her hands shook, and her stomach jumped. Wrapping her arms around her waist, she squeezed. "Can I stay with him tonight?"

She sensed instead of saw Scott step beside her.

"I'm afraid not." His words would've been harsh except they were said in such a low, gentle tone that they came out sounding compassionate, regretful.

"I don't see why not. I'm a nurse."

"But as Jake's mother you need to take care of yourself. Rest. Leave a number with the nurse and she'll call if you're needed." He gave Jake's nurse an appreciative smile.

The fresh-out-of-nursing-school girl blinked twice before she said in a syrupy tone, "I'll put it on his chart, Dr. McIntyre."

"I don't see—" Hannah began.

"Those are the rules. You have to be out of here by seven and can't come back in until eight in the morning," Scott said in a flat, authoritative tone.

"I guess I don't have a choice, then."

"No, you don't." Scott's words came out even and to the point.

Enunciating the numbers to her cellphone with care, Hannah watched to make sure each one was written correctly. The way the nurse was acting around Scott, she might make a mistake.

As Hannah gave the last digit Scott approached his patient's bed. "Hello, Jake. I'm Dr. McIntyre. You can call me Dr. Mac."

Jake didn't look at Scott's face, but focused instead on his chest, reaching his hand out.

Hannah moved around the bed to stand opposite Scott to see what Jake was so engrossed in.

"Oh, I see you found my friend." Scott smiled down at Jake. "His name is Bear. He rides around with me. Would you like to hold him?"

Jake's eyes lost their look of fear as they remained riveted on the tiny animal. His fingers wiggled in an effort to reach the toy.

Unclipping the toy from his stethoscope, Scott offered it to Jake.

Scott's charm obviously extended to his young patients. Jake didn't always take to new people but Scott had managed to make her son grin despite the ugliness of the place. Hannah sighed. Scott looked up and gave her a reassuring smile. She didn't like the stream of warmth that flowed through her cold body. Still, a kind, familiar face in her life was reassuring right now, even if it was Scott's.

"My bear hasn't been well. Could he stay with you?" Jake gave Scott a weak nod before Scott handed Jake the bear. "I need to listen to your heart now. I'm going to put this little thing on you and the other end in my ears, okay?"

Small creases of concentration formed between Scott's

eyes as he moved the instrument across Jake's outwardly perfect chest. She'd always admired Scott's strong, capable hands. The same ones that were caring for her child had skimmed across her body with equal skill and confidence. She shivered. Those memories should've been long buried, covered over with bitter disappointment.

She'd been around enough doctors to recognize one secure in his abilities. Scott seemed to have stepped into the role of pediatric surgeon with no effort. He certainly knew what to do to keep Jake from being scared, at least she'd give him that much. Maybe she could put her hope in him professionally, if not emotionally. She wanted to trust him. Desperately wanted to.

Jake's eyelids drooped but he continued to clutch the toy.

Scott removed the earpieces, looping the stethoscope around his neck.

"Scott, thanks for giving Jake the bear. He looked so afraid before. I still can't believe he needs a heart transplant," she said in little more than a whisper that held all the agony she felt. "He doesn't look that sick."

She prayed his next words would contradict the truth she saw on his face.

"I realize that by looking at him it's hard to believe, but it is the truth."

Hannah's knees shook. With swift agility, Scott circled the bed, his fingers wrapping her waist, steadying her.

She jerked away. The warmth of his touch radiated through her.

As if conscious of the nurse nearby, he dropped his hand to his side.

"I'm fine." For a second she'd wanted to lean against him, to take the support he offered.

Hannah peered at him. Had hurt filled his eyes before

they'd turned businesslike again? The unexpected look had come and gone with the flicker of his lids. Had she really seen it? Could she trust herself to interpret his looks correctly?

"You need to understand a heart transplant isn't a fix. It's exchanging one set of problems for another. Jake will always be on meds and have to come to the hospital for regular check-ups."

"I understand that. I'll take care of him."

Scott placed a reassuring hand on her shoulder.

"Don't touch me."

He dropped his hand. "Hannah, I know this is rough. But we were friends at one time. Please let me help."

"Look, Scott, the only help I need from you is to get Jake a heart."

"Hannah, we're going to get Jake through this."

"I hope so. My son's life depends on you." She couldn't afford for him to be wrong, the stakes were much too high.

"Hannah, with a heart transplant Jake can live."

Like before? Would he still squeal when she blew on his belly? Would he giggle when she blew bubbles and they burst above his head? Her sweet, loving child was dying in front of her eyes.

Scott was saying all the right things, but could she believe him? "It's not your kid, so you really don't have any idea how hard this is, do you?"

The muscle in his jaw jumped, before he said, "No, I guess I don't. But I do know I'm a skilled surgeon and this is an excellent hospital with outstanding staff. We can help Jake and we will."

"I'm counting on that."

In his office, using the time between surgeries, Scott waded through the stack of papers cluttering his desk. He leaned back in his chair. Hannah's face with those expressive green eyes slipped into his mind for the hundredth—or was it the thousandth?—time in the last few hours. She'd looked just as shocked to see him as he'd been to see her. It had required all his concentration to stay focused on what they had been discussing.

He couldn't have been more astonished to find a red-eyed Hannah looking at him expectantly as he'd entered the conference room. Andrea normally arrived ahead of him but she'd had to answer a page. He'd stepped into the room, and back through time.

Hannah's hushed whisper of his name had made him want to hug her. But she'd made it clear she'd never allow him. Guilt washed over him. Of course she didn't want his comfort. He'd hurt her, and for that he was sorry, but he'd believed it was for the best.

He'd wanted her desperately that night eight years ago, and she'd come to him so sweet and willingly, trust filling her eyes. If he could have stopped, he would have, but, heaven help him, he hadn't been able to. He'd handled things poorly the next morning. She had been too young, in her second year of nursing school. He had been an intern with a career plan that wouldn't allow him to be distracted. He'd refused to lead her on, have her make plans around him. He hadn't been ready to commit then, and he wouldn't commit now.

Andrea had entered before he'd let his emotions get out of control. Regret had washed over him, for not only what he had to tell Hannah but for what life would be like with a sick child and for their lost friendship.

Based on her reaction today, he'd killed whatever had been between them. She'd not been cool to him, she'd been dead-of-winter-in-Alaska cold toward him. Compared to the way she used to treat everyone when they'd worked together, almost hostile.

Not the type of woman that made men do a double-take, Hannah still had an innate appeal about her. He'd known it back then and, even while telling her the devastating news of her son, that connection between them was still there.

Speaking to any parent about their deathly ill child was difficult. Sending a child home with smiling parents after a life-giving transplant made it all worthwhile. Scott's intention was to put such a smile of happiness on Hannah's face.

Scott shook his head as if to dislodge Hannah from his mind. He let his chair drop forward, and picked up an envelope off the stack of mail on his desk. The familiar sunshine emblem of the Medical Hospital for Children in Dallas, Texas, stood out in the return spot. A surge of anticipation filled him as he opened it. Was this the news he'd been hoping for?

A quick tap came at the door and Andrea entered.

The statuesque, older nurse had worked with way too many young surgeons to be overly impressed by him when he'd arrived at Children's General. Still, she'd had pity on him and had taken him under her wing, helping him when he'd needed to navigate the ins and outs of hospital politics. They had become fast friends.

"Is that the news you've been looking for?" Andrea indicated the letter.

He'd been talking to the administrator at MHC for months about starting a heart-transplant program there. He opened the flap and pulled out the letter. "Not quite. They're still looking at other candidates. They'll let me know of their decision soon."

"You're still top man on their list, aren't you?" Andrea asked.

"Yeah, but they want to review a few more of my cases." He'd geared his entire career toward this opportunity. To set up his own program, train a team, and make the program in Dallas the best in the country.

"Don't worry, boss. I'm sure they're impressed with your skills."

With years of experience as an OR nurse, Andrea didn't look like she had a soft touch, but she had a talent for making parents feel comfortable. That was a gift he valued. Appreciative of the skills she brought to her job, Scott intended to persuade her to become a part of his new team in Dallas if he was offered the position.

"Thanks for the vote of confidence."

"I've got the latest blood work on the Quinn kid. You wanted it ASAP."

Scott took the lab sheet and studied it. "We shouldn't have a problem listing him right away."

"None that I can think of." With a purse of her lips and a glint of questioning in her eye, Andrea said, "I know I came into the meeting late, but I've never known you to call a parent by their first name. So I'm assuming you two know each other."

"Yes, we met while I was in med school, just before I left for my surgical training." Meeting her look, he refused to give any more information.

Andrea raised her brows. "Oh. Interesting spot you're in, Doc. She didn't sound particularly happy to see you again. History coming back to bite you?"

Few others would've gotten away with such an insubordinate question.

At his huff, she grinned and slipped back out the door.

Scott might have found some absurd humor in the situation if it wasn't such a serious one, and if he hadn't been so afraid that Andrea was right.

Hannah was the one nurse that had mattered, too much. The one that had gotten under his skin, making him wish for more. He'd pushed her away because she'd deserved better than he'd been able to give. He still couldn't believe Hannah had re-entered his life and, of all things, as the mother of one of his patients. Life took funny bends and turns and this had to be one of the most bizarre he'd ever experienced.

But it didn't matter what their relationship had been or was now. What mattered was that her son got his second chance at life.

Hannah made her way to the snack machine area on the bottom floor during the afternoon shift change. She was sitting in a booth, dunking her bag in the steaming water, when Scott walked up.

Her breath caught. He was still the most handsome man she'd ever known. His strong jaw line and generous mouth gave him a youthful appearance that contrasted sharply with the experienced surgeon he surely was. There was nothing old or distinguished about him, not even a gray hair to indicate his age.

He still wore the Kelly-green scrubs covered by a pristine white lab coat, which meant he'd been in surgery. She couldn't see the writing on the left side of his coat, but she knew what was printed above the pocket.

Embroidered in navy was "Scott T. McIntyre, MD" and under that was "Department of Thoracic Surgery." Reading those words over and over during their meeting had been her attempt to disconnect from the surreal turn her life had taken. She'd almost reached across the small table and traced the letters with a finger. He'd gotten what he'd wanted. She couldn't help but be proud for him.

Scott stepped to the coffee-dispensing machine and dug

into his pocket. Pulling his hand out, he looked at his open palm, muttered something under his breath and spilled the coins back into his pants.

"Here." She offered him some quarters in her outstretched hand.

Blinking in surprise, he turned. "Hey. I didn't see you sitting there."

"I know. You were miles away."

With a wry smile, he accepted the change. His fingertips tickled the soft skin of her palm as he took the money.

A zip of electricity ran up her arm. It was a familiar, pleasant feeling, one that her body remembered. But her mind said not to. She put her hand under the table, rubbing it against her jeans-clad leg in an effort to ease the sensation.

Scott purchased his coffee then glanced at her, as if unsure what to do next. She couldn't remember seeing him anything but confident. He appeared as off-kilter as she.

He hesitated. "Do you mind if I join you?"

"You know, Scott, I'm not really up to rehashing the past right now."

"I really think we should talk."

Hannah took a second to respond. Could she take any more emotional upheaval especially when she'd just started believing she could breathe again after their last meeting?

Her "Okay" came out sounding unwelcoming.

One of his long legs brushed her knee as he slid into the booth. That electric charge sparked again. She drew her legs deeper into the space beneath the table.

"I've just seen the psychologist. Is Jake listed?" Hannah asked into the tense silence hovering between them.

"I put him on a few minutes ago." Scott's tone implied it was no big deal, an everyday occurrence, which it might be for him. For her, it was a major event.

She breathed a sigh of relief.

Scott sipped his coffee, before setting the paper cup on the table. He looked at her. “I have to ask: where is Mr. Quinn?”

“That’s not really your business, is it?”

“Yes, and no. If he’s going to be coming into the hospital and making parental demands and disrupting Jake’s care, yes, it is. For the other, I’m just curious.”

“There’s no worries where he’s concerned.” Her look bored into his. “He left us.”

Scott’s flinch was barely discernible. “When?”

“Just after Jake was born.”

“You’ve no family?”

“None nearby. My sister is living in California now. I told her to hold off coming. I don’t know how long we’ll have to wait on a heart.”

His sympathetic regard made her look away. “There’s no one that can be here with you?”

“No. When you’re a single parent with a small child, relatively new to town and you have to work, it leaves little time to make friends.”

“I understand. Doctors’ hours are much the same way.”

“As I remember it, you didn’t have any trouble making time for a social life.” She softened the dig with a wry curl of her lips.

He chuckled. That low, rough sound vibrated around them and through her.

She took a sip of her tea.

Scott drained his cup before looking at her again. “Uh, Hannah, about us…”

“There *is* no us.”

“You know what I mean. You have to admit this situation is unusual at best.”

She placed her cup on the table. “Scott, the only thing

I'm interested in is Jake getting a new heart. Whatever we had or didn't have was over and done with years ago. You're Jake's heart surgeon. That's our only relationship." She probably sounded bitter, but she didn't have the energy to deal with her emotions where he was concerned. Particularly not today. She needed time to think, to sort through her feelings. Scott twisted his coffee cup around, making a tapping noise on the table.

"Hannah, I shouldn't have left like I did. I thought I was doing the best thing for you. I was wrong not to tell you I was leaving town."

She put up her hands. "Let's just concentrate on Jake. I don't have the energy to rehash the past."

He gave a resigned nod, but she didn't think the subject permanently closed.

"Then would you at least tell me why you're not nursing?"

"I took a leave of absence when Jake started getting sicker. I didn't think he needed to be in a day-care situation, and I couldn't find private care close enough to home to make it work."

"That's understandable. I thought you had quit altogether. I remember how much you enjoyed it. What a good nurse you were…are."

"Yeah, I still love it. I'll get back to it when Jake's better."

He'd made no attempt to be a part of her life in the last eight years, and now he was interested in her personal life? Picking up a napkin on the table, she wadded it into a ball.

Hoping to avoid further questions, she asked, "How about you? Where did you go…uh…for your surgery residency?" She'd almost said "after you left me alone in bed. Without saying a word."

He pulled his legs out from under the table, extended them across the floor, and crossed one ankle over the other.

"Texas, then to Boston for a while. I took a position here a couple of years ago."

"You always said you wanted to be a heart surgeon. You didn't change your mind."

"No. After hearing my first baby's irregular heartbeat during my cardio rotation I've been set on it. It took me years to qualify, but it was the right move." His gaze met hers. "But it meant making some tough decisions."

"So, is there a Mrs. McIntyre and any little McIntyres?"

Hannah held her breath, waiting for his answer. A part of her wished he'd found no one special, while another part wanted him to be happy.

"There's no Mrs. McIntyre or children."

Hannah released the breath she'd held. Why'd she feel such a sense of relief? "Why's that?"

"A surgeon's life doesn't lend itself to a peaceful private life. Somehow my patients always take precedence over anything or anyone else."

A dark shadow crossed his face that she didn't quite comprehend. Had he almost married? What had happened?

"As the mother of one of your patients I'm grateful you make them a priority. I believe that would be a part of being a great doctor. " She took a sip of tea. "So, are you still seeing a nurse on every floor and in every department?" The question had a sting to it that she couldn't help but add.

He chuckled. "You don't have a very high opinion of me, do you?"

Hannah chose to let that question remain unanswered. "Did you know that the joke in the nurses' station was that, when you had rotated to our floor, you'd asked for an alphabetical listing of all the single nurses and were working your way through the list?"

"I did not."

"What? Know or ask for the list? Because you sure as heck worked your way through the staff. I watched you. With the last name of Watson, I had time to see you coming." Heavens, she'd gotten what she'd deserved. She'd seen for herself what a player he had been.

"Yeah, and you refused to play along. That was one of the many things I liked about you. You made me work to get your attention."

"I wasn't interested in being another nurse you scratched off your list."

Scott's hand covered his heart. "Ouch, that hurt."

She grinned. "That might have been too harsh."

He smiled, oozing Dr. McDreamy charm. "Same Hannah. You never cut me any slack. But as it turns out, believe it or not, being a surgeon doesn't leave me as much free time as being a med student did. As for an answer, I hope I've grown up some."

"I know I have. I understand things I didn't use to." Like how it felt to be drawn to the bright fire that was his charisma and get burnt. He was speaking as if they'd shared nothing more than a casual meal all those years ago, instead of a friendship that had ended with a night filled with passion. She had repeated the same mistake with Jake's dad.

"I'm sorry, Hannah, for everything." His beeper went off, demanding his attention. "I have to see about this. Thanks for the coffee." He picked up his cup, crushed it and pitched it into the nearest trash can.

Scott moved down the hall as if he was a man in command, a man on a mission. He'd been intense and focused as a medical student. That didn't seem to have changed, but he also had the ability to laugh and smile effortlessly, which drew people to him.

Taking a deep breath, she slowly released it. She needed to think. Put things in some order in her mind.

Jake. Heart transplant. Waiting. Cost. Die. Scott. The words ping-ponged off the walls of her mind.

CHAPTER TWO

SCOTT peered over the unit desk toward Hannah, who sat at her son's bed. Her head had fallen to one side against the back cushion of the chair. Even with the burden of worry showing on her features, she caught and held his attention. Her chestnut-colored hair brushed the tops of her shoulders and hung forward, curtaining one cheek. If he'd been standing closer, he would've pushed it back.

Puffy eyes and stricken looks were so much a part of his profession that he had become impervious to them, but telling Hannah about Jake's heart condition had been the toughest thing he'd ever done. She was no longer the impressionable nursing student he'd once known. Hannah was now a mother warrior fighting for her child. He believed her strength and spirit would see her through.

She'd made it clear that their only association would be a professional one. He could be there for her as a friend, for old times' sake. The only sensible choice was to keep their relationship a professional one. Being involved with a parent on a personal level was a huge ethical no-no anyway. Lawyers didn't represent family members, and surgeons didn't treat loved ones, or, in his case, family.

Hannah shifted in the chair and shoved her tresses out of her face. She looked tired, worn and dejected. She stirred, causing her hair to fall further across her face. With effort,

Scott resisted the urge to go to her, take her in his arms and whisper that everything would be all right. She'd always brought out the protective side of him. She'd never believe it but he'd left her that morning all those years ago in order to protect her. Even then medicine had been his all-consuming focus. He'd gotten that trait from his father.

As a small-town doctor, his father had been on call day and night. Scott had watched him leave the supper table numerous times to see a sick child after eating only one forkful of food. More than once Scott had heard him return to the house in the early hours of the morning after seeing a patient. Their family had even returned early from a vacation because an elderly woman his father had been treating had taken a turn for the worse and was asking for him. Scott had never once heard his father complain. All Scott had ever wanted was to be like his father. He had thought he was the finest doctor he'd ever known.

Hannah woke with a start, blinking fast. Daylight had turned to darkness outside the window but the fluorescent lighting made it bright in the room. She straightened.

"Mommy."

She hopped up and went to Jake's bedside.

"Hi, sweetheart. We both had a little nap." She brushed his hair back from his forehead. "How you doing?" She kissed him.

The nurse pushed medicine into the port of the IV located at the side of Jake's tiny wrist. Giving the IV set-up a critical look, Hannah realized old habits did die hard. She still wished she could take a more active role in Jake's care. As long as he was in CICU she had to remain on the sideline.

"Would you like to hold him for a while?" the nurse

asked as she punched buttons on the IV pump and it responded with small beeps.

Moisture filled her eyes. "Could I, please?"

"Sure. You have a seat in the chair and I'll help you get him situated."

After a little maneuvering of IV lines and moving of machines, Hannah had Jake in her arms. It was pure heaven.

"Go home," Jake mumbled as he settled against her.

"I wish we could, but hopefully you won't be here long."

She looked over Jake's head at the nurse as he played with his toy bear.

The nurse spoke softly, "You know, Mrs. Quinn, I've seen some very sick kids come through here who are doing great after having a transplant."

The words reassured Hannah somewhat. At least she was getting to hold him. That more than satisfied her for the time being.

"If you don't mind, while he's sitting with you I'm going to step over to the next bed and help another nurse with her patient. Will you be okay?"

"Sure." Hannah's gaze shifted to Jake again. He looked like a small cherub. His lips were getting bluer, though. She had to admit Scott was right. Jake needed a heart. *Soon.*

She put her cheek against Jake's. "I love you."

"I luv 'oo."

Moisture filled her eyes. *Loving...was...hard.*

Her head jerked up at the sharp insistent beeps of the monitor that turned into an alarm. Staff rushed into Jake's cubicle. Scott came with them. "Hannah, let me have Jake." Scott took Jake from her and laid him on the bed, all the while issuing orders.

Hannah stepped to the bed. Her hands gripped the

rail. "What's wrong?" she whispered, fear coiling in her middle.

Scott looked at her as he listened to Jake's chest. "Hannah, you need to leave." His authoritarian tone told her he'd accept no argument. His attention immediately returned to Jake.

She was a nurse, Jake was her son. *She could help.*

But as much as she wanted to stay, Hannah knew he was right. She'd been involved in enough emergencies to know that the fewer people around the bed the better. If she wasn't allowed to assist then she would be in the way. Slowly, she stepped back.

Scott's gaze caught hers. "I'll be out to talk to you when Jake is stable."

Hannah walked toward the doors but took one final look over her shoulder as she left the unit. Jake's bed was no longer visible because of the number of people surrounding it.

Finding one of the small conference rooms off the hallway empty and dark, she stepped inside, not bothering with the light. Her eyes ached from the dry air and the bright lights. She dropped onto one of the chairs situated as far from the door as possible.

Unable to control her anguish any longer, Hannah's dam broke and her soft crying turned into sobs.

Now that Jake was resting comfortably, Scott needed to find Hannah. He paused in the hall.

What was that sound? There it was again. It was coming from the consultation room. He stepped closer to the entrance. Dark inside, no one should be in there. Was that someone crying?

He couldn't ignore it. In a hospital it wasn't unusual

to hear crying, but this sounded like someone in physical pain.

With tentative steps, he entered the room. "Hello?"

A muffled sob filled the space.

"Are you okay?"

"I'm fine. Please go away." The words were little more than a whisper coming from the corner, followed by a sniff.

Even when it was full of sorrow, he recognized her voice. *Hannah*. The stricken look on her face when he'd ordered her to leave still troubled him. He'd been surprised she hadn't put up more of a fight.

"Hannah?"

A whimper answered, then a muffled "Please leave" came from the corner. Moving into the room, he gave his eyes time to adjust to the dim light spilling in from the hallway. Scott had seen patients in pain, but her agony reached deep within him. Hearing Hannah sobbing knocked the breath out of him. It was killing him to stand behind professionally closed doors where she was concerned.

But if he did open that metaphorical door, would he be able to step through? Could he help her? Did he have the right to get involved so deeply in her life? What he did know with unshaking certainty was that he couldn't walk away. He couldn't make the same mistake twice. The consequences could be too great.

Coming toward her, Scott lowered his voice. "It's Scott. Hannah, honey, Jake is fine. He had a reaction to the new med. He's all right now."

Her head rose enough that he could see her eyes over the ridge of her arm. The rest of her face remained covered.

"Go. Away." The words were sharp and wrapped in pure misery. She turned her back to him and lowered her head again. "I don't need you."

Those words stung. Scott touched her and she flinched. He removed his hand. It wounded him that she wouldn't accept his help. Was she really that untrusting of him? "He's resting now, really."

Scott sank into the chair beside hers. He'd dealt with parents besieged by strong feelings. It was part of his job, but Hannah's pain reached deep to a spot he kept closed off. A place he shouldn't go with the parent of a patient, especially not with her. Somewhere he wasn't comfortable or confident in going.

Then again, his failure to recognize how distressed his mother had been when his parents had divorced had had disastrous results. He'd promised himself then to never let that happen again to someone he cared about. He wasn't leaving Hannah, no matter what she said or how she acted. Her obvious pain went too deep to dismiss.

Hannah made a slight shift in her seat toward him, then said in a hard voice, "I don't—want you here. Go away and leave me alone."

She was in so much pain she was contradicting herself. He could resist a lot, but Hannah's pain brought down the final wall. He had to do something, at least try.

A feeling of inadequacy washed over him. What could he say to make it better? Could he help her? Scott placed a hand on her shoulder, feeling the inflexible muscles. As if she were a troubled child, he began moving his hand in comforting circles along her back.

"Scott, stop." She twisted her shoulders back and forth, but he refused to let her have her way. He may not have the correct words or be able to change the situation but he could hold her, be there to comfort her.

"Hannah, I'm not leaving."

She stilled.

"Look, you're a fighter. And if Jake is anything like you, he is too."

He wrapped an arm around her shoulders and pulled her to him. She stiffened and pushed against his chest. "Let me help you get through this." His grip tightened and he tucked her head under his chin. Holding her as close as the chairs would allow, he said in a tender voice, "Let me be your friend. You need someone."

She remained rigid, but he refused to ease his hold. Taking several halting breaths, she gave up the battle and relaxed against him.

Hannah's distress was difficult to witness. He didn't flinch when he opened a child's chest or when making life-and-death decisions but he couldn't stand seeing Hannah in so much pain. He wanted to make it go away, make it his own.

"Why won't you leave me alone?" she murmured against his chest.

"You need to be held, and I'm going to do that. Cry all you want. I'll be right here when you're ready to talk."

Having her in his arms went beyond wonderful, even with her crying and heartbroken. It felt right. He'd not only stepped over the invisible don't-get-personally-involved line, he'd jumped. But he'd see to it remained one friend comforting another. He wouldn't, couldn't, let it become personal.

Holding her firmly against him, he made calm reassuring noises that made little sense. With his voice low, he spoke to her as if she were a hurt animal. After a few minutes she quieted. Pure satisfaction coursed through him like brandy on a cold night.

He placed a fleeting kiss to her forehead, which smelt like fresh apples. She still used the same shampoo. Wit his cheek resting against her hair, he took a deep breath, letting her scent fill him.

Neither spoke. Her breathing gradually became even and regular. The sensation of her body pressed against his made his thoughts travel back to what could have been. Was he taking advantage of her vulnerability? Yeah, but he still couldn't resist resting his lips against her skin again.

Scott comprehended for the first time in his life what it meant to want to carry someone else's burden. He longed to take Hannah's hurt away. Fix her problems. Yet he could never be her knight. His duty to others would always be pulling him off the horse.

With a sigh of resignation, she completely relaxed against his chest. She had to be drained in both body and mind.

Having Hannah in his arms brought back memories of that night. Even then he couldn't help but touch her, hold her. Now she needed to be held, desperately, and he was afraid that he needed the contact just as much. Everything about Hannah pushed his common sense away.

Heavens. She was being held by Scott.

"Better?" he asked.

In a quick movement Hannah straightened and shifted back into her chair. She should've never let him touch her. Mercy, it had felt wonderful. She was so tired of being alone, carrying the load for Jake's care. At least with Scott she had a partner until the transplant was done.

Under Scott's scrutiny, she refused to meet his gaze. "I've never fallen apart like that before," she muttered.

"Are you positive you're okay?" He sounded as unsure as she felt.

"I'm better now," she said, though her words lacked confidence. "You can go."

"Have you eaten today?"

Why wouldn't he leave her alone? She closed her eyes, then lifted them, looking through her lashes. "If I answer you, will you leave?" She didn't want to have a reason to start caring for him again.

Scott said nothing but gave her a hard look.

"Okay, I had a bowl of cereal this morning. I was going to eat during shift change…" she sighed "…but I just wasn't hungry. Satisfied?" Where was the ever ever-present sound of his pager going off when she needed it?

He shook his head. "You're one of the most intelligent women I know so I expected better from you. What did I tell you about taking care of yourself?"

"I heard you."

"But you don't plan to follow orders." Cynicism wrapped his words.

She straightened her shoulders. "I don't have to follow your orders. You're Jake's doctor, not mine." At his chuckle, she realized he'd baited her on purpose to make her show some kind of animation.

"That might be, but if you'd followed my orders…" He cocked his head to the side in question.

"It must feel good to be a know-it-all."

"It does have its advantages. Let's go get a bite to eat."

"Us?"

"Yeah, us. I eat too. I certainly can't trust you to see to feeding yourself. Anyway, I like to share a meal with someone when I can. I eat too many dinners alone."

"That's hard to believe. You can't find a nurse to eat with?" She'd never known him to have trouble getting dinner dates. Had he really changed that much?

"I did. You."

She huffed. "You know what I mean."

"I do, but I'm pretending I don't. Come on. Keep me company."

"I don't really want to go, but you're not going to give up until I agree, are you?"

He grinned and shook his head.

She'd consider it payment for him giving her a shoulder to cry on. And she was just too tired, too scared and too emotionally drained to fight him off. Besides, having one meal with Scott wouldn't change anything between them.

After a long moment she nodded her agreement. "But I'm going to check on Jake first."

"I never thought any different." He took her elbow and helped her stand. The pad of his thumb skimmed across the bare skin of her forearm. She shivered and stepped away.

Tugging at the hem of her pink T-shirt, she said, "I'm fine now."

He remained close as they moved toward the door. Her head seemed to be on straight again, but having Scott so near was making her nerves fire in double time.

What was happening? She'd given up acting like a schoolgirl long ago. Given up on him. She hadn't needed anyone in a long time, but she'd fallen apart in Scott's arms. Hannah shook her head to remove lingering feelings of being cherished while in Scott's embrace. Years ago he'd acted as if he cared, and she'd been crushed. She wouldn't let it happen again.

Jake was sitting up in the bed, playing with the toy that Scott had given him, when they walked into his cubicle.

"Mommy." He reached his hand over the rail of his bed.

She took his little hand in hers and placed a quick kiss on the top of it. "Hi, sweetie."

"Hello, Jake," Scott said, as he move around to the other side of the bed from Hannah. "While you're talking to your mom, I'm going to give you a little check. It won't hurt, I promise."

Scott slipped two fingers around Jake's wrist, feeling for his pulse before he stepped to the end of the bed. Pulling the blanket back, Scott placed the tips of two fingers on the top of Jake's foot to check his *dorsalis pedis* pulse.

At Scott's finger skimmed Jake's skin, her little boy jerked his foot away.

Scott looked up at Jake and smiled. "Do you like to be tickled?"

Jake nodded.

Cupping Jake's heel, Scott ran a finger down the bottom of Jake's foot. Her son laughed. Scott's low rumble of mirth joined Jake's.

Hannah couldn't help but smile. Her heart lightened. For the first time all day she believed Jake might get well.

Her laugh drew both males' attention as if they'd forgotten she was even there.

The overhead lights dimmed.

"It's time for your mom and me to let you sleep," Scott said to Jake as he pulled the blanket back over the tiny foot.

Hannah squeezed Jake's hand and kissed him on the forehead. "I love you, honey."

Scott nodded to a nurse standing behind her, who she'd not noticed until then. The nurse inserted a needle into Jake's IV port and emptied the syringe's contents.

"That should help him sleep," Scott said as he came to stand beside Hannah. "He'll have a comfortable night, so don't worry."

"Yeah, that's easier said than done." Hannah watched Jake's eyelids droop. When she felt his hand go limp, she placed it on the bed. Pulling the blue hospital blanket up she tucked Jake in.

The urge to scoop Jake up and take him home to his own bed had never been stronger.

"Come, Hannah," Scott said in a sympathetic voice. "It's time to see about yourself. You need to eat."

As they waited for the elevator to go down to the cafeteria, Scott kept glancing at her. He'd been wonderful with Jake, but he was making her nervous now. Did Scott think she was going to fall into his bed again just because he'd made her son giggle?

She curled her hands together and intertwined her fingers again.

As close as they'd been at one time, they were little more than strangers now. She'd changed, was a mother now, and had been a wife. Maybe Scott had changed too. Relief flowed through her as the elevator doors slid open. Hannah stepped in and stood in a corner. She was glad that Scott chose to stand on the opposite side.

The jerk of the elevator as they dropped to the bottom floor made her grab the rail on the wall.

Scott moved nearer. "Are you okay?"

"Yes."

His gaze met hers then moved to her lips and lingered.

Her mouth went hot-summer dry. Her head spun. Had someone turned off the air-conditioning?

The elevator stopped and the doors slid open. Scott's eyes lifted. A smoldering look filled them. Hannah blinked. Gathering her wits, she slipped by him. As she exited, his warm breath ruffled her hair against her cheek.

He followed. "Let's go to the cafeteria instead of the snack machines. Wednesday is fried chicken day, the best thing they make."

Scott spoke as if the intense moment in the elevator had never occurred. Had having her back in his life affected him at all? Perhaps it hadn't.

"I think I'll just have a BLT and a cup of hot tea," Hannah said.

"I'm going for the chicken. Find us a table. Tell Lucy at the register that I'll pay for yours when I come through."

"I won't let you do that," she said as she stepped toward the grill line. "This isn't a date."

He held up his hand and grinned. "Okay, okay."

His boyish smile made her feel like she was sitting in the sun on a spring day, pure bliss. Her heart fluttered. He still had that devastating effect on her.

Don't stare. *Think.*

Hannah forced herself to turn around and go to the sandwich line. The mundane business of selecting a sandwich and the physical distance from Scott helped to settle her nerves. She'd moved into the register line when Scott came up behind her. Bending down, he said, "I'm getting yours."

He was too close. She was too conscious of him. He paid before she could form a protest.

Outside the high arched windows a slow, steady rain began to fall. The water on the concrete walk shimmered in the glow from the security light. The weather reflected her life. Dark, with hints of brightness.

Moving toward the dining area, she selected a table in the center of the room, if only to put a physical object between them as a way to regain her equilibrium. Scott glanced at an available booth and shrugged. His mouth lifted into the beginning of a grin before he took the chair opposite hers.

Hannah concentrated on keeping the bacon between the pieces of toast while Scott ate his fried chicken. It amazed her that after the heated moments earlier they could still manage a comfortable silence between them

They'd slipped back into that easy place they'd enjoyed when he'd been in medical school.

Cleaning his plate, Scott sat back with a sigh, giving her a quizzical look. "Feel better now you've had some food?"

Her heart skipped a beat. He'd caught her staring. "Yes, much. But I do insist on paying for my meal."

"I owed you for coffee. Anyway, can't two old friends eat together without fighting over the bill?"

"We're just acquaintances." She fiddled with her glass a second before pinning him with a look. "True friends don't leave without saying a word."

His lips formed a tight line before he said, "Hannah, I realize you're still angry with me and I don't blame you."

She opened her mouth to speak.

"No, please hear me out. I know you don't want to go into the past. I appreciate that. You're having a rough time and I'd like to help if you'll let me." He laid a hand over hers, blanketing it.

Her heart thumped faster. She didn't know how to force her body to be sensible where Scott was concerned.

It would be nice to have someone to lean on. It was tempting to accept his offer, for at least a little while, until she could right her world long enough to think straight. But could Scott be that person, with their past looming between them?

And he was Jake's doctor.

"I guess we can try." They'd been friends before, maybe they could be again. She was just too exhausted in spirit and mind to argue. "But you'll have to earn my friendship and that will be *all* there is between us. Friendship." She tugged her hand from beneath his.

The stiffness in his body eased and, with a gentle smile, said, "I understand."

With one finger, Hannah circled the salt shaker sitting in the middle of the table. She rolled it from side to side. The base of the glass knocked against the wood.

Scott took the shaker, setting it aside. "I wish I could make the situation with Jake easier for you."

"I appreciate that." She gave him a weary smile. "I hate not being able to help care for him. I am his mother and a nurse."

Scott opened his mouth to speak, but she forestalled him.

"I know. Protocol. I understand it, but don't like it."

He laughed softly. "And I understand where you're coming from. I know that right now it seems like all you're doing is sitting around, watching and waiting, but once Jake goes to the floor I promise you there'll be plenty to do. Plenty to learn."

"I hope I don't sound too whiny. I've been Jake's sole parent for so long it's hard to relinquish control. I understand why I'm not allowed to do more but that doesn't mean my heart accepts it."

He nodded. "So, do you plan to return to the same position when Jake recovers, or do you want to work elsewhere? Maybe a satellite clinic?"

Hannah leaned back against the chair, pulling her lower lip between her teeth. "I hadn't thought about doing that. Working at a clinic isn't a bad idea. The hours are better, and it may be easier to arrange care for Jake if I did." She sat up again, crossing her arms and leaned on the table. "Have I satisfied all your questions?"

"No, but I'll save some for another time." Downing the rest of his drink, he asked, "Are you ready to go? I've an early morning and you've had a hard day. We both need to get to bed."

At her surprised look he realized what he'd said. "I'm sorry, that didn't come out right."

She laughed. "I knew what you meant. Scott, I'm not holding a grudge against you. I got over what happened between us a long time ago. That's water down the river."

His blue gaze bored into hers and he said softly, "I wish that wasn't true."

Hannah swallowed. Her words weren't completely honest but she didn't want him to know that. Truthfully, their night still hung between them, but now wasn't the time to get into it.

As they left their trays on the cleaning rack Hannah said, "Thank you for the meal. It hit the spot." She looked up at him. "Even with the questions."

"You're welcome. I'd like to make one more start toward earning your friendship by seeing that you get home safely. I'll get someone to take you home. You don't need to be driving, but I'm on call and can't leave."

"There's no need."

"You're worn out. You need to go home."

"I'm staying here."

Scott leaned forward. She could see the lines around his eyes, indicating he'd smiled a lot through the years. Probably at all the women he'd seduced. She'd do well to remember that.

"Hannah," he said earnestly, "you need to rest, which you won't do here. Wouldn't you like to sleep in your own bed? Pick up some clean clothes? Take a hot shower?"

He'd known what would get to her. A shower sounded heavenly.

After sighing deeply, she said, "I'll go. For tonight."

"I know you'd like to see Jake one more time before you leave. I'll call up and let Jake's nurse know you're coming. While you're gone I'll arrange your transportation and meet you in the lobby."

Hannah made her way through the maze of corridors back to CICU. At a set of automatic doors she spoke into the monitor on the wall and requested entrance into the unit. She'd never been more acutely aware of hospital rules. It was her son in there, and she had to ask permission to see him. As a nurse, she'd never realized how much control she'd had over a patient's life.

At Jake's bed, she whispered goodnight to her sleeping child and gave him a kiss.

Her baby…needed…a heart. If not…

She refused to let that thought catch hold.

Scott stood at one side of the lobby, talking on his phone, when Hannah approached a few minutes later. As if he sensed her arrival, he turned and looked at her. He ended the conversation and started forward.

Watching him saunter down the long corridor of the hospital used to be a favorite pastime of hers. She still found it absorbing.

As he approached, he smiled. "Your carriage is waiting."

Taking her elbow, he ushered her out the sliding glass doors at the front of the hospital. Waiting beside one of the hospital's vans was a security guard.

"Hannah, this is Oscar. He's going to be escorting you home."

The large, toothy man smiled. "Nice to meet you, Ms. Hannah. Climb in." Oscar opened the door nearest her then went around to the driver's side.

"I thought I was taking a taxi."

"Hush and appreciate the ride. Oscar believes he owes

me a favor, so this is my way of letting him think he's paying me back."

"I'm grateful for the ride, but I don't understand why you're going to so much trouble."

"Let's just say I need to do it for me more than you. This way everyone wins." Scott helped her into the van. "You get a safe ride home with someone I trust, and Oscar gets to feel good about what he's doing. I'll see you tomorrow. I'll keep an eye on Jake and let you know if you're needed. Trust me."

Trust him? She'd trusted him one time with her affection and her body. He'd disappointed her. Could she trust him with Jake's life?

Oscar returned to her house early the next morning to bring her back to the hospital. He informed her that Dr. Mac expected it. Hannah agreed to the service, not wanting to hurt the sweet man's feelings.

At the hospital, she killed time in the waiting area until she could visit Jake. Her heart skipped when she saw Scott. She stepped toward him, pushing panic away, and asked, "Has something happened to Jake?"

His hand cupped her shoulder. "He's fine. I've spent most of the night in the unit, so I've been close by. He was sleeping when I left. You can go back to see him just as soon as shift change is over."

Hannah released an audible breath.

Scott held out a box of donuts. "I was hoping to find you. I thought you might like these. The 'Hot' sign was on."

"Did you go out especially to get these?"

"Yeah, but the bakery is just a few miles away. I promised the nurses I'd bring them some today. And I remember how crazy you were about them."

Hannah took the box. "You are really going above and beyond the call of duty on this being-a-friend thing." She looked up at him. "I really can use one right now. Ah, and they're still warm. Thanks for remembering." She brought the box up to her nose and inhaled deeply.

"I remember everything about you." He smiled, as a pensive look came over his face.

Heat rushed to her cheeks and she avoided his gaze. She didn't want to be sucked in by his charisma again, but he was making it awfully difficult not to be. "I thought you could use a blast of sugar to keep you going today. I've got a couple of minutes before I have to be in surgery. How about sharing those…" he nodded his head toward the box of donuts "…and a cup of coffee with me?"

"Sure, the parents' lounge has a coffee machine and a table and chairs. How about we go there?"

"Sounds great." He grinned.

It was still early enough in the day that they had the lounge to themselves. Scott's bulk filled the small area, making her conscious of how large a man he was, his scent reminding her of being outdoors after a rainstorm.

He sat at the small table after her. Hannah placed the box of donuts in front of him, and grinned as he struggled to work his long legs under the table. He gave up and stretched them out in front of him.

Sharing an intimate breakfast with Scott was something she'd expected to do that morning after they'd made such passionate love. By a twist of fate, instead she was sharing a meal with him years later in a pitifully utilitarian room of a hospital with nothing more than tentative friendship between them. She forced the emerging hurt to one side.

She crossed to the automatic coffee machine and poured two cups of coffee.

"You don't have to pay?"

"No, this is here for the parents." She smiled. "Maybe they'd let you get a cup here the next time you're out of change and I'm not around."

A disquieted look came over his face for a second, and then he said, "That's a thought. I'm going to remember this place."

Placing their cups on the table along with some napkins, Hannah took a chair at the table. She really looked at Scott for the first time that morning. Absorbed his appearance. He looked incredible, even after a night with little sleep. He'd always been intriguing, larger than life, and that hadn't changed. If anything, he'd become more appealing.

Dressed in jeans that had seen better days and a yellow snug-fitting T-shirt with "Come Paddle with Me" printed in bright red letters across his chest, Scott looked nothing like the white-coated doctor she knew him to be. His hair was a crowd of unruly waves, with a lock falling over his forehead.

Did he still spend his days off kayaking and rafting? He'd loved the water and adventure when he'd been in school. After rounds, he had sometimes come by the nurses' station and told her a funny story about something that had happened on one of his trips down the river. She'd always looked forward to those stories, because he'd shared them with such flair, making her wish she could go with him some time.

"You're not dressed like you're going to work. More like you're going to the river."

Somehow the thought that he might not be around for the rest of the day bothered her. What if Jake needed him?

His soft laugh filled the room. "These are my spare clothes. I keep them in a locker for nights like last night. Nothing was wrong with Jake."

Relief filled her. He wasn't going anywhere.

"You must be getting plenty of time in down the river because you haven't changed much in the last eight years."

"Why, thank you for noticing." He dipped his head in acknowledgement. "I don't kayak as much as I'd like but that's where I usually spend my days off."

"I see your ego is still in good shape."

"It isn't as large as you might think," he said softly.

Had something happened that had damaged his confidence? "Was your night so difficult that you didn't go home?"

"Not bad, just constant."

From his causal demeanor, she would have never guessed he'd spent the night at the hospital.

"We got a new patient."

It made her chest tighten to think how the parents of the child must be feeling. Had it just been yesterday morning that she'd been in the same spot?

Scott opened the green and white box containing the donuts and pushed it toward her. "Ladies first."

Hannah picked out one sugary ring. She took a healthy bite and shoved the box toward him.

"You know what I've been doing for the last few years—how about you?" He picked out a chocolate-covered one.

Hannah didn't want to talk about the last few years. The future was what she was interested in, one where Jake was better and at home. She'd tell Scott the bare facts to satisfy him, and hope he'd leave the subject alone.

"Well, since we worked together I received my MBA in nursing, got married, got pregnant, got divorced and moved to Atlanta after getting a job at Fulton Medical. And here I am." She raised her hands in the air in a dramatic pose.

That sounded like a well-rehearsed litany of events, even to her ears.

"Have you tried to contact his father since Jake was listed? I'd want to know if my son needed a transplant."

"No." The word came out jagged and tart.

"Why?"

Yes, why? Why wouldn't he leave it alone? "He wouldn't be interested." She couldn't conceal her bitterness.

"Why not?"

Hannah took her time finishing the bite of donut she'd just taken before she said, "He left us." She paused. "I shouldn't have married him to begin with. I think I just fell in love with the idea of being married. For him, I think his mother thought I could settle him down. By the time I realized we had no business being married, I was pregnant. Turns out I didn't have to leave him. He packed his bags and was gone. I found out later he already had someone else by then."

Scott's harsh, crude words filled the space between them.

"I couldn't agree with you more. He wasn't too sure about having children to begin with and when Jake was born with a heart problem he couldn't get past the idea that his child wasn't perfect. His answer was to run." She made it sound like she was giving a statement to a newspaper reporter. Just the facts. "Anyway, I have Jake, and he's the best thing that has ever happened to me. He's my life. All I've got. I won't lose him too."

"We'll do our best to get Jake out of here soon."

"I sure hope so." She picked out another donut. Her eyes closed in delight as she took the first bite out of it.

"Like these, do ya?" The words were filled with Scott's mirth.

She opened her eyes and nodded as she licked the sticky sweetness from her upper lip, and began to flick away the grains of sugar that had fallen on her chest.

Scott's laughter stopped as his eyes followed her movements.

An uncharacteristic warmth settled over her. The fine hairs at the nape of her neck stood as straight as corn on her granddaddy's farm. She tried to concentrate on what she was doing. Seconds ticked by.

His gaze rose and locked with hers, held.

Scott's pupils had widened and darkened, giving him the intent look of a predator. Suddenly, the light button-down top she wore seemed heavy and hot against her skin.

Mercy, she was in over her head. He could still do it to her. She placed her donut on a napkin and stood. "Um, I think I need some cream for my coffee. Can I get you some?"

She needed to move away from him, get out of the room, but she had to pass Scott to do so. His intense look still clung to her.

"It hurts you don't remember I take my coffee black," he said in the indulgent voice of a man who knew she was trying to escape and why.

Hannah moved to step over his legs at the same time he drew them in. Her feet tangled with his. Falling, her head landed on his chest. The quaking of Scott's low rumble of amusement only added to her frustration, compounded by the molten heat she felt from being against him.

A zing of awareness zipped through her. It was happening again, just like it had all those years ago. Despite her embarrassment, Hannah longed to stay. She struggled not to show a response to the continued emotional assault, but she had to stop this now. If she didn't, it would end no differently than it had last time. With heartache—hers. Pushing against Scott's muscular thighs, she made an ineffectual effort to stand.

"Hannah, stop struggling and I'll help you up."

The words reverberated pleasantly beneath her ear. She stilled. He gripped her shoulders, pushing her away until she found her footing.

"Thanks," she murmured.

Scott stood, maintaining eye contact. "My pleasure. I rather like having you sprawled across me." As he closed the bottom button of his lab coat he said, "I'd better go check on a patient."

The nuance of his words and the heat of his touch lingered well after he'd disappeared down the hall.

CHAPTER THREE

WATCHING the clock, Hannah called to see if she could see Jake the second the minute hand clicked to eight. The clerk said she could come in, but she would have to stay at least thirty minutes because Scott was doing a procedure on a patient and couldn't be interrupted.

The automated doors swooshed opened when Hannah pushed the silver entry button on the wall. She went straight to Jake's cubicle. He was still asleep. Hannah placed a kiss on his forehead and the nurse told her that he'd had a good night.

She wanted to believe that a heart would be available soon. Scott had spoken with such confidence that one would be found. For her own sanity, she was desperate to trust him. Searching for something positive to cling to, Scott's optimism was all she had. Yet Hannah wasn't ready to believe him without question. If she lost Jake…

Dropping into the chair next to Jake's bed, she looked out into the unit. From her vantage point, she had a direct view of Scott.

He'd changed into scrubs. Holding a mask in his latex-covered hand, he said to the nurse beside him, "Has she been given meds?"

"The morphine and Pavulon are on board," the young nurse responded.

Donning the mask with the nurse's help, Scott gave calm orders in a crisp tone that generated an instant response.

Hannah was impressed by the way he managed the situation, but not surprised. Scott demanded attention out of respect, without being dogmatic. Being witness to how he remained cool in a literal life-and-death situation reassured her. The staff followed his lead.

These attributes were priceless in the operating room. No wonder she'd heard such glowing reports about his abilities. A surgeon had to have the respect of the people who worked with him.

Scott raised the edge of the dressing covering the child's open chest. "Patch."

The nurse at his right handed him the six-by-six white bandage. He placed it over the incision.

Despite her lingering cynicism, Hannah appreciated Scott's efficient but tender manipulations as he worked with the infant child. She'd always admired the way he'd had a gentle touch for his patients and had gone to great lengths to make them feel comfortable.

Scott had done the same with Jake and herself. He'd been nothing but caring and helpful towards them both.

Over his shoulder, Scott spoke to the clerk behind the desk. "Call OR. Tell them we're coming down in fifteen." He turned back to the nurse. "Thanks for the help."

The nurse nodded and smiled.

Scott stepped away from the bed, pulled off the mask and gloves, then removed his gown with minimal effort, before tossing them into a basket. The actions were automatic. Hannah found the ordinary spellbinding when Scott was involved. It was like watching a thoroughbred horse go through his paces. She couldn't help but be riveted.

Going to the row of sinks on the wall, he scrubbed before moving to another patient's bed, where he spoke to a nurse. When he was finished, he approached Hannah.

She stood and asked in a hushed voice, "Is the baby going to be all right?" As irrational as the thought pattern was, when another child wasn't doing well, Hannah felt like it might rub off on Jake. As if heart problems were contagious.

"Yes, she should be fine with time. How's Jake doing?"

"Sleeping peacefully, but I think he may be breathing heavier."

"Let me have a listen."

Hannah watched as he examined Jake.

When Scott had finished he turned to her. "He may be having a little more difficulty. I'll have the nurse keep a closer eye on him."

Scott flipped the stethoscope around his neck and took her by the elbow, leading her away from Jake's bed to a corner of the room where they couldn't be easily seen.

His look sobered, telling her he was debating whether or not to say something.

"What's wrong? You're scaring me."

"I wasn't sure if I should tell you, but I had a call about a possible heart for Jake a few minutes ago."

Hannah grabbed his arm and squeezed. "You did?" It was the first time she'd voluntarily touched him. Scott just wished it had been for another reason.

He wanted to reassure her, make her understand. "Yes, but it wasn't good enough. I had to turn it down."

Disappointment, disbelief, and fear all showed in her eyes before anger pushed them away. Her fingers tightened on his arm, biting into his skin. "What? You can't do that." She glanced around as if she were caged and looking for a way out.

Scott hated having to telling her. He'd anticipated this

reaction. Unable to wrap his arms around her, he took her hand. "It'll be fine." Softening his voice as if to calm a scared animal, he added, "I want the best heart we can get for Jake. The right one will come."

He believed that, but wanted her to accept it as truth. To have faith in him again.

She pulled her hand away, clasped her hands together and looked straight ahead. "I hope you're right."

The sharpness of her voice cut him.

"Hannah, I can't imagine how hard this must be." His fingers wrapped her forearm, unable to keep from touching her. "I'll take good care of Jake. I'll get him the right heart. Trust me."

"Dr. McIntyre," the clerk called.

Scott let his hand drop and stepped away from Hannah.

"Dr. Stevens would like to speak to you and the OR called to say they're ready," the clerk finished, giving them a speculative look.

Scott regretted the interruption. "Please tell Dr. Stevens I'll call him as soon as possible and let the OR know I'll be down in a few minutes." He shocked himself. He'd never said anything but, "I'll be right there."

Hannah needed him and neither of the other issues was an emergency.

"Hannah, please sit down." She eased into a chair, and he pulled a rolling stool up close.

He unclasped her hands, taking one and smoothing her fingers out across his palm. Lowering his voice, he said, "The perfect heart for Jake will come. You just have to believe that. He's stable for now. We have to wait on the right one."

"I know. I understand. I just don't like it."

He ran a finger along her jaw, making her look at him. "That's my Hannah, tough when you have to be. I hate to leave you but I have to go. I have a patient waiting in surgery."

"I know. I understand. That little baby needs you. I'll be fine."

Guilt gnawed at him for having to leave her when she needed him but he had no choice. When duty called he would always go.

Scott entered the large open area of the waiting room and stopped. The nurse had said the parents were here. He wished he could delegate this job to someone else, but that wasn't the way he worked, or would let himself work. Despite feeling inadequate, it was still his responsibility to talk to the mother and father of his little patient.

He'd let his mother down when she'd needed him, and he wouldn't do the same with the parents of any of his patients. Sometimes he wondered if his struggle to speak to the family was his penance for failing his mother so miserably. Was it his way of atoning for past mistakes, to involve himself so totally with his patients?

The surgery on the girl had been more difficult than anticipated but the medical whys and wherefores wouldn't mean anything to the girl's parents. They were only interested in him fixing the problem and making sure their daughter went home with them. It wasn't, unfortunately, that simple.

He understood their fears, sympathized with them, sometimes to his own emotional detriment. Caring so profoundly made him a sought-after surgeon but it left nothing to give to others. He'd heard that complaint on more than one occasion from a woman.

Scott searched the area again. He scanned past a person, and came back. *Hannah.* He'd not seen her since earlier that morning.

His gaze met hers. She sat up ridged in her chair. *She thinks I've come to give her bad news.*

Summing his most reassuring smile, he watched as the tension drained from her like a rubber band being released. Her chest rose as she took a deep breath and let it out slowly. She met him halfway across the room.

"Jake's fine. I just checked on him. He was even sitting up and playing with his bear."

"Thank goodness." Hannah gave him a weak smile. "From the look on your face, something is wrong. Are you okay?"

"I should be asking you that."

"I'm all right. Just don't be turning down too many hearts."

"I won't, I promise."

"So what's putting that frown on your face?" Her hand made contact with his forearm for a second.

The simple gesture calmed him, giving him confidence. Telling him it was all right to care. "How did you know?"

"I've always been able to tell when you were upset."

"Yeah, you were good at that. You were the one nurse who was willing to go with me when I talked to parents."

"Thankfully, that didn't happen too often."

Scott glanced around the room and found the couple he'd been looking for in the far corner. "I've got to speak to those parents."

As he turned to leave, Hannah touched his arm again. "You're better at talking to parents than you think. The truth is always hard to take, but they'll want to know it and will appreciate you giving them honesty."

"Thanks." Hannah's words were gratifying, making what was coming seem less daunting. She made him believe he was up to the task.

He'd always cared too much for his own good about his patients, unable to keep a professional distance like other physicians. It became more of an issue after his mother's overdose. The next morning in the hospital she'd made some ugly accusations about him. When she'd shouted that he'd abandoned her for his own patients, just like his father had, and she didn't need Scott any more either, he'd felt like he'd been slapped.

He'd seen that she received the care and services she needed and became absorbed in his work. Their relationship still wasn't what it should be. He wished for more but it was difficult to put the unpleasant words she'd thrown behind him completely. If he had a question about his ability to manage a high-pressure career and a solid relationship, after that morning he'd known beyond a shadow of a doubt he couldn't. Even his own mom wanted little to do with him after he had disappointed her.

But he refused to disappoint his little patients' families. Squaring his shoulders, Scott made an effort to look less like a man bearing bad news and walked toward the girl's parents. Hannah watched Scott approach the couple. They stood, but he waved them down before he sat. He raked his hand through his hair, leaving a wavy lock hanging across his forehead, adding to his vulnerable look.

Elbows on knees, Scott leaned forward, occasionally raising a hand to punctuate a point. He maintained eye contact with the mother and spoke in a low tone. One filled with compassion, she was sure. She'd heard the caring there when he'd told her Jake needed a heart.

He appeared confident, but she knew better. In the past, they'd talked a number of times about how difficult it was for him to speak with parents. She'd tried to reassure him, telling him that feeling so deeply for the patients and their families was part of who he was and what made him a good doctor.

The mother's shoulders jerked up and down and Scott

reached out and touched her. She turned to her husband, and he took her in his arms.

Hannah's sympathy went out to the three. Scott looked like he was the one that needed a friend. She was tempted to go over and take Scott's hand, be his moral support.

She'd had a taste of his bedside manner when he'd held her. Based on what she'd learned about him during their reacquaintance, he wouldn't be a doctor who didn't tell it like it was, even if he had bad news. He'd always felt more deeply than he let on. They'd talked about different patients' problems in the past. Hannah had been able to tell by the tone of Scott's voice when he'd taken a patient's issues more to heart than he should have. Not being able to heal every person had worried him more than it had the other interns.

Scott was a soft touch with a hard outer covering, and was careful not to let that gooier side show. If he appeared weak, then the patient would feed off that. Their will to get better would be diminished and Scott wouldn't allow that. She'd often wondered if he was so cavalier in his personal life because he was trying to compensate for how deeply he cared for his patients.

He might have been, maybe still was—despite his implied remarks in the negative—a playboy but he'd always had a kind heart. She wasn't sure why he had treated her the way he had. Had she done something wrong to make him leave that morning? Only looking back on it, that really hadn't been like him.

Scott rose and spoke to the mother again. The woman nodded. Scott didn't even look in Hannah's direction as he left. He hurt for the parents, and that about Scott hadn't changed.

He'd comforted her yesterday. Today she wanted to run after him, reassure him. Maybe she'd been too hard on him? He'd been a great friend before and he seemed to be trying hard to be one again.

Who did Scott go to when he needed to talk through his problems?

Maybe she could at least make an effort to meet him halfway. She could use a friend right now, a shoulder to lean on. Could he also use one?

Hannah remained in the waiting room a while longer before going to visit Jake. It was quiet in CICU but she noticed two nurses and one of the interns standing beside the bed of a patient. It must be the child Scott was concerned about.

The parents had to be terrified.

She found her usual chair and settled in. Already she'd slipped into a hospital routine. The hours of waiting dragged by and the sky darkened as the sun set. The only thrill in the day was when she got to hold Jake for a short while. She craved the closeness of having him in her arms. Even now she missed his little body nestling next to hers.

Jake's nurse pulled Hannah out of her staring stupor with the statement, "I need to change Jake's IV. It's not flushing as it should."

Light-headed when she stood up, Hannah shook it off and moved to the bedside opposite the nurse. Hannah watched as the nurse removed the old IV port and began inserting a needle into a vein near Jake's wrist. Bright red blood dripped from the port onto the bed before the nurse could cap it off.

Hannah's stomach rolled like a wave hitting the shore. She'd witnessed IV ports being placed hundreds of times, done them herself more often than she could count, yet this was her son's blood.

Come on, Hannah. Keep it together.

She gripped the bedrail.

This is nuts. I'm an experienced nurse.

Closing her eyes, her head spun. Her body swayed. Opening her eyes wide, she focused on a spot on the white wall and took a gulp of air. Her grip on the rail became painful. The whirling worsened.

Her world went black.

Was that a hand pushing her hair off her forehead? There it was again. Opening her eyes a slit, Hannah could only make out a tiled ceiling. There was also a hard bed beneath her. Where was she? How had she gotten here?

Fainted. She'd fainted. She couldn't believe it.

A scraping noise of metal chair legs being moved across the floor caught her attention. Turning her head towards the sound, she saw a pair of khaki-covered legs.

Her gaze lifted past sprawled legs, to the hem of a white pressed cotton lab coat with an unfastened bottom button. Her eyes followed the row of secured buttons to the open neck of a light blue shirt that looked familiar, over a square chin covered in enough evening shadow to be TV sexy, to full lips where a faint smile rested below a Roman nose and arresting eyes. They peered at her with a mixture of frank concern, humor, and maybe…longing.

Scott.

Could she be more embarrassed? Putting her hands over her face, she said between her fingers in a strangled voice, "Oh, no."

"Are you all right?"

"I'm fine. Just mortified." She groaned. "I've never fainted before in my life."

His soft chuckle would've made her knees go weak again if she'd been standing. He propped an elbow on a knee and put his chin in his hand, bringing his face closer. His eyes twinkled. "It's okay. Don't worry about it. We see it in the unit pretty often."

She shook her head in denial. “But I’m a nurse. It shouldn’t be a problem for me!”

After a tap at the door, an aide entered with a soft drink can in one hand and a glass of ice in the other. Scott took both, setting them on a table.

“Is there anything else I can get or do?” She glanced at Hannah with concern.

“Thanks, Susie. No, I think Mrs. Quinn’s going to be fine.”

The aide left, closing the door behind her.

Hannah moved to sit up. Scott put a hand on her shoulder in gentle deterrence. The heat of his hand seeped through her cotton top like the sun on a hot day. That comforting warmth was becoming addictive.

“You need to stay put a few more minutes. We don’t want you to fall and hurt yourself.”

Resigned, Hannah settled back. “Where am I?”

“In the on-call attending’s sleep room.” Scott stretched back in the chair, extended his legs and folded his arms across his chest. He acted as if he was in no hurry to leave.

“How’d I get here?” Hannah murmured.

He gave her a cheeky grin. “I carried you.”

“You did?” She hid her face. She hated the thought of facing the people in CICU after that show.

“Yeah. I was coming through the doors when I saw your knees buckle. I managed to catch you before you hit the floor.”

“Th-thanks,” she stammered.

“I wish I could say I’ve always been as aware of people’s needs, but I can’t. I was just lucky to be in the right place at the right time.”

“Whatever it was, I appreciate it. How’s Jake?”

“He’s just fine. Fared much better than you. He’s a tough kid.”

“I guess you think I’m a complete basket case after yesterday’s show and now this today.”

"Truthfully, I'm impressed with how well you're holding it together. I know of others with much less stress that haven't coped nearly as well as you."

The compliment brought a glow of pleasure. Had he been thinking about an old girlfriend, friend or family member?

"Let's see if you can sit up now." He reached out and helped by supporting her back as she righted herself, though Hannah wasn't sure the physical contact wasn't putting her further off center.

"I'm fine. You don't have to baby me, even if I seem like one." She moved away from his hand.

She didn't want to contemplate her strong reaction to Scott's touch. Heaven help her, having Scott's attention was getting to her. Maybe this thing she had about him was her mind's way of helping her remain sane. Giving her something to dwell on besides Jake.

Scott stood, pushing his chair out of the way. Pouring the soft drink into the cup, he offered it to her.

Hannah looked flushed, but beneath it a healthy color had returned. Was the pink from embarrassment or because he remained so close? Maybe both?

Setting the cup on the table, she tried to stand. She plopped back on the low bed.

The next time he slid his hand around her waist as she stood. "Let's try that again, a little slower." He left her no opportunity to move away from him. "Better? Head bothering you?"

Scott sucked in a breath as the gentle heat of her body pressed against him. The yearning to lean into her grew. Under his scrutiny, Hannah looked away but, using a finger under her chin, Scott brought her focus back to him. Her moss-colored eyes had darkened, and she blinked.

Heaven help him, he wanted to kiss her. Unable to stand the tug of need any longer, he leaned towards her.

Hannah's eyes widened as his mouth lowered to hers.

Fearing she might push him away, he placed his lips lightly at the corner of her mouth, tasting, testing, and asking for her acceptance.

A hot flare of desire flashed through him. History was repeating itself, and he was incapable of stopping it.

Scott wanted Hannah as much as he had that night so many years ago. His hands shook with the depth of it. She was a soft yet demanding siren, drawing him. Her vulnerable appearance masked an iron strength he admired. He'd fought his desire once but he couldn't do it twice. His emotions drove him, his mind was no longer in control. He had to savor her once more.

Her lips parted, and he gave thanks for the opportunity. He took the invitation offered and pulled her tight against him, bringing his lips down to completely capture hers.

Seconds ticked by before her hands ran along his arms, stopping at his biceps, squeezing them slightly as if to steady herself.

She tasted of tea, lemon, and well-remembered Hannah. He felt a quake of emotion ripple through her as her fingers flexed on his arms. No longer able to hold himself in check, his desire flowed over its banks. Without constraints the kiss escalated into a crushing assault.

Hannah shivered, and Scott groaned low in his throat. This was going to get out of hand if he didn't put a stop to it. He didn't need to ruin the cautious friendship they were building again.

Hannah clung to him. Having her in his arms was a heady feeling.

He had to put a stop to the fever threatening to become wildfire out of control. Easing his mouth from hers, he tenderly brushed his lips across hers as he murmured, "What are you doing to me?"

He knew he'd missed their friendship but he'd not realized how much he'd missed touching her, having her in his arms. "I've thought a lot about kissing you since this morning," he muttered. "You make eating a donut look incredibly sexy." He glanced at the hard, narrow bed behind her. *The* question flickered in his gaze.

Hannah squirmed and he eased his hold. He watched the rapid throb of her pulse on her delicate neck.

If he asked the question out loud, would she?

Long, sizzling seconds hung between them. Scott closed his eyes then opened them again. Remorse washed over him. He'd promised friendship, she'd made her expectations clear. She was the mother of one of his patients. What he was suggesting was wrong on many levels.

Scott stepped back, releasing her. "I'm sorry. I shouldn't have done that. You had my word we'd remain just friends. I think we're both experiencing emotional overload." The words came out flat and measured. "Please, forgive me."

She smiled shakily. "You're forgiven. I think it's the least I can do for someone who brings me hot donuts."

Hannah was on her way through CICU to visit Jake for the last time that evening. She'd relived the kiss between her and Scott numerous times. She understood he was just being human, that maybe he'd needed someone after the day he'd had. As a way to let off steam. But somehow his apology for kissing her felt worse than being left in bed alone.

She couldn't be mad at him. He'd been so wonderful with Jake and had cared for her when she'd needed a shoulder to cry on. That tenderhearted person she'd known before had still been in him when he'd spoken to those parents.

As she reached Jake's cubicle a deep baritone growl filled the air. The sound was followed immediately by a roll of giggles she recognized. *What was going on?*

She stopped short at the sight of Scott sitting in a rocker with Jake in his lap. Scott held a book so Jake could see the pictures. Neither of them noticed her as she stood in the doorway.

"And the pig goes..."

"Oink, oink, oink," Jake said with a big smile. "You do."

"And the bear goes grrrr..." Scott drew the sound out.

Hannah had never expected to find Scott taking the time to read to any of his patients. She enjoyed listening to his rough voice as he read to Jake. The sight and sounds of the two of them having a good time together soothed nerves that had been piano-wire-taut.

"And the horse goes?"

"Me do, me do. Heehaw, heehaw."

Scott's deep chuckle made her feel mushy inside. He was enjoying himself as much as Jake was. Her heart softened. She ran a finger under her eye. Once again Scott had managed to push the unpleasantness of what was happening to Jake away for just a few minutes. Her son was a kid, instead of just a patient.

"More. Me do," Jake said as he helped Scott turn the page.

"Okay, how does the chicken go?" Scott said as he smiled down at Jake.

"Cluck, cluck, cluck."

"Yes, that's right. Cluck, cluck, cluck. Smart boy."

Jake clapped his hands.

Scott looked up. Hannah couldn't help but grin at his disconcerted look. He shrugged his shoulders and grinned.

She smiled back, hoping to convey her appreciation. "Hi, guys. You two sound like you've been having fun."

"Mommy." Jake lifted his arms toward her.

"Hi, sweetheart." She stepped over to take him from Scott, being careful not to get tangled up in the IV lines. She pulled the little boy close for a hug. Jake was warm from being held by Scott.

"So, have you been having a good time with Dr. Mac?" she asked against his cheek before kissing him.

Jake nodded up and down. "He funny."

She looked at Scott and grinned. "He is, is he?"

Jake bobbed his head with enthusiasm.

"I was here when the Child Life lady came by with the books and the next thing I know I'm making animals noises."

She nibbled at her boy's neck. "Jake loves to have someone read to him."

Jake yawned.

"I think you might have had too much fun," Hannah said as she moved to Jake's bed and laid him down. His eyes were already closing as she kissed him on the cheek. He had such a small energy reserve. Despite the earlier lift to her spirits they were suddenly dampened by the reminder of why he was here.

Scott came to stand beside her. "He's a wonderful kid. You've done a great job with him, Hannah."

"Thanks. I think he's pretty outstanding too." She pulled the blanket up around Jake.

She looked away from him a few seconds later when she thought she'd heard Scott say Jake's mother was pretty amazing also, but he was gone.

* * *

Scott didn't want to tell her, but he had to. Hated what he had to say. Hated to see the little boy who had such a cute personality so sick.

Some patients he connected with better than others but Jake had captured his heart. Scott wanted to say it was because he was Hannah's son but that wasn't all there was to it. Jake's willingness to be held by him, to giggle when he was around, made Scott feel taller and stronger for some reason. It made his heart swell to see the boy grin up at him.

Hannah should be waiting on him in one of the consultation rooms down the hall. He'd had the clerk call her soon after she'd left the unit, asking her to wait for him. She had to be scared to death, wondering what was wrong. He lengthened his strides.

She was pacing the room when he opened the door.

"What's wrong? Can I see Jake?"

"He's okay but—"

"But what?" Fear sharpened her voice.

"I've given orders for Jake to be put on the respirator." He stepped closer to her. "Things are under control. He just needs a little help breathing."

She took a couple of halting breaths, and let out a soft moan.

"Hannah, honey, this is just a precaution. Jake's all right." His chest clenched at seeing her upset. He'd give anything to take the burden away.

She looked up. Even in the dim light he could see the moisture glistening in her big, sad eyes.

"W-w-will he be okay?"

Hannah was struggling bravely to keep her composure. Scott took her in his arms, pulling her securely against him. A tremor went through her, and a sob escaped. He couldn't really know her fear. He wasn't Jake's father. F he could comfort her, let her know she wasn't alone. When he placed a kiss on her temple, she made a soft, incoherent sound.

"We've got everything under control," Scott whispered as he took a handful of silky hair and moved it out of her face. "The fellow is a good man. He'll take care of Jake tonight." He tipped her chin up, drawing her focus. "This is nothing more than a precaution. Jake's breathing became labored and we don't want him to wear himself out before surgery. Hannah—" his tone gained her complete attention again "—a heart will come."

"I don't know how much more of this he can take. Or I can take," she murmured.

Scott skimmed a tear from her cheek with the pad of his thumb. "You're strong. You'll get through this. Trust me, we're doing all that can be done."

She leaned into him as if she was drawing strength from him.

Scott liked having her next to him for any reason. He tightened his embrace, needing the contact almost as much as she did. He lowered his voice to soothe and comfort. "We have everything under control." He sure hoped he was telling her the truth. All that could be done was being done, but sometimes things went wrong. He ran a hand across her shoulders and down her back. "You can—*we* can—get through this together."

He desperately needed her to feed off his confidence. To believe in what he said, in him. He wanted to be her haven, someone she turned to. Hannah nuzzled her cheek against his chest. Dampness touched his skin. "I hope you're right." She shuddered against him, as if she was accepting that with him was where she should be.

Holding her close, he continued to whisper nonsense. spite all his skill as a surgeon, there were times he still felt helpless. He wished he could prevent what Jake was going through, but that was out of his power. Hannah needed support, and he would see that she got it.

He wasn't going to make the same mistake twice with someone he cared about. He'd misread how emotionally depressed his mother had been, and he refused to take the chance of doing the same with Hannah. The first time there had been major repercussions to his inaction. He would not repeat it. He couldn't promise that he'd be there for her for ever, but the least he could do was to be here for her now.

This time he would make time. At this moment he had no doubt he was needed, and he refused not to act on it. Regret was something he wasn't prepared to live with. But there was a major difference between the two women. His mother had demanded his attention and Hannah was pushing him away.

He breathed a sigh of relief when she moved. She turned her back to him, took a deep breath and squared her shoulders. "I'm okay now." He couldn't help but admire her. She was already gathering courage, preparing to fight her fears bravely again.

"Hannah," he said softly, "I know you're going to hate this suggestion, but I think you need to stay at my place tonight."

She spun to face him. "What? I can't do that!" The words had a ring of panic to them.

"Calm down. Hear me out. It's late and you're upset. Tired."

"I don't plan to go home. I bought a bag with me this morning. I'm staying at the hospital."

"No, you're not. You need a good night's rest. You'll stay at the hospital a lot after Jake's transplant. Anyway, my place isn't far away. You can be here in no time if you're needed. You can use my extra room."

A yawn escaped her, confirming visibly how drained she was. She covered her mouth. "I'm staying here."

"I don't think so." The words were said in a firm, blunt tone. His voice softened with the next ones. "Be reasonable Hannah. If you stay at my place you can visit a few minutes before shift change tomorrow morning."

"That's blackmail."

"Yes, it is. Now, come on."

CHAPTER FOUR

SCOTT'S condo was in a nice upscale area, but nothing over the top. Done out in beiges, tan and a touch of black, it had a masculine appearance, with the only hint of a woman's touch being two bright orange pillows on the sofa. What girlfriend had been responsible for those?

Outdoors magazines were strewn across the dark wood coffee table and the black leather sofa, and a shirt hung over a chair next to the door. The room had all the markings of bachelor living, of a person who didn't have time to waste on the small stuff in life.

She liked the place. It suited Scott.

"How about something to drink before we call it a night?" he asked as he threw his jacket on a chair and dropped her small overnight bag on the floor.

"A glass of iced tea would be nice, if you have it."

"Sure."

Scott led her to a kitchen lined with windows. It would be a perfect place to enjoy a leisurely breakfast but he probably never had time to do so. He pulled a pitcher of tea from the refrigerator and opened a cabinet. He was taking out two glasses when his cellphone rang.

"Hey, hold on a sec," he said into the phone, and then told Hannah, "I need to get this. Help yourself. I'll be right back."

"The hospital?"

"No, honey. It's one of my kayaking buddies. I'll be right back."

She had to stop overreacting every time Scott's phone rang. Relieved but with her nerves still unsteady, she began filling a glass with ice from the fridge door. As she placed the glass on the counter, it toppled and began rolling over the edge, leaving ice in its wake. She bent and fumbled with the glass, taken aback when an arm brushed her breast. A quiver like that of a bow with the arrow just released went through her. Scott clasped the glass before it shattered on the floor. Reaching around her, he put the glass back on the counter.

His body heat blanketed her from head to foot. Her body came to full attention.

She strengthened and looked at him. Their gazes met and held.

Scott's hands came to rest on her waist. Why she didn't argue, she couldn't fathom. Maybe because her mind was fuzzy, so completely filled with him. Or because she didn't want to.

He nudged her backwards, until her bottom pressed against the cabinet. Caging her in with an arm on each side, he trapped her between the hard surface of the cabinet and the equally firm plane of his body.

She should be pushing him away, but it felt good to be sharing someone's warmth. Being in Scott's arms calmed her nerves, pushed the worry away for a while.

His hands cupped her face. The slight tremor to his fingers made her understand the effort he applied to control his need. The pad of his thumbs caressed her cheeks. In a low and raspy voice he said, "I know I promised...but I can't quit thinking about this—you." He gathered her into a firm embrace before his mouth claimed hers.

Hannah made a soft sound of acceptance, and wrapped her arms around his waist. Her eyelids fluttered closed as her fingers kneaded his back. She leaned into the warm, sweet taste of his lips. The memory of how he'd made her feel years ago and the sensation of his lips on hers earlier mingled together and made this kiss even sweeter.

The pressure of his mouth intensified, taking on a sense of urgency. Excitement filled her at the thought she made Scott spin out of control. He held her so tightly it was almost painful. The demand of his lips against hers was hard and unrelenting as he thrust his tongue into her mouth. A flurry and churn like that of a rocket going off swelled within her. Caught in the spinning sensations, she met his powerful demands with those of her own, and hung on for the marvelous ride. A pleasure-filled way to escape.

After the initial combustion of their lips meeting, Scott eased the kiss into a tender caress. Soothing, sinful and sensual all at once but Hannah missed the throbbing pressure and heat. She wanted more. To replace the debilitating fear and heartache, even if only for a few minutes.

Bringing her hands to his head and spreading her fingers to run through his hair, she guided his mouth closer, opening her own. Scott took and countered with a challenge of his own. He shifted closer, making the evidence of his longing clear.

A steady hum of pleasure built upon itself until it became an unrelenting, pulsating yearning. Unaware of anything else in her world, Hannah's only reality became what Scott's lips were doing to her.

She made small purring sounds.

Scott lifted her to sit on the counter. There was a clank as the glasses tumbled along the counter behind her.

He lifted his mouth. Resting his forehead against hers

for a moment, he took a deep breath and let it out. He looked as regretful as she that they'd been interrupted.

Scott's gaze met hers. His eyes had turned a dark, velvety blue. "I think I'll pass on the iced tea and go for you." Still in a Scott-induced haze, Hannah fought hard to comprehend what he'd said. He'd twisted her thoughts around like a tornado going.

Hannah shook her head and looked away. Heaven help her, she was no more immune to his charm and desire than she had been as a young nurse. She had to clear her mind. "I think I'd better get down."

His mouth dipped towards hers. She stopped the motion with a hand on his shoulder. He didn't immediately back away but soon helped her down. She wobbled as she moved, then swayed. Scott released a low chuckle. Putting out a hand, he steadied her and with the other hand he swiped the ice cubes into the sink.

"As much as my ego would appreciate believing you're weak in the knees from my kisses only, I'm afraid some of it's because you're worn out. Come on. I'll show you where you can sleep." He kept a hand on her elbow as they moved down the hallway.

He stopped, opened a door wide and turned on the light.

"I'll go get your bag. That door over there is the bathroom. Make yourself at home. You should find everything you need in there." His arm brushed her as he pointed. "My mother usually keeps extra here for when she visits."

Hannah's breath caught. She balled her fingers to keep from reaching out and touching him. If she couldn't control her growing attraction, she'd embarrass them both. They needed to be comfortable around each other, for Jake's sake.

Just friends. That's what they were. If she repeated

it enough maybe she would believe it. Despite the red-hot kiss.

Before she could do something she'd regret, he'd turned and headed toward the living room. She wanted to call him back. Beg him to kiss her again. Instead, she watched as his loose-hipped strides took him away.

Hannah sucked in a breath. *This has to stop.*

Scott looked confident and relaxed, while her insides quivered. She must've developed brain rot to have agreed to come to his place. He was too much. Heck, he made her feel too much.

Hannah stepped into the bedroom. It had the basics—bed, end table, and dresser. The navy spread and curtains were the out-of-a-package kind that could be found in any large household chain store. The room had the look of a functional but otherwise forgotten space.

Scott returned and handed her the bag.

"If you'll toss the clothes you have on into the hall, I'll throw them in the wash."

"Scott, I've needed a friend and you've gone out of your way to be a good one. I appreciate it."

He nodded. "You're welcome."

The husky thickness of his voice beckoned her. She wanted to step into his arms. Feel safe. The heat of their earlier kiss hovered, waiting to flare up again, like a spark starving for fuel.

He made no move to leave. "Hannah?"

As if he willed it, her gaze lifted to meet his.

"I'm sorry I treated you so badly back then, that you had such a lousy marriage, and that this is happening to Jake."

Hannah nodded, unable to say anything as he closed the door quietly behind him.

Going to the bed, she lay on it and covered her eye

with an arm. Her thoughts bounced around like ping-pong balls inside a lottery machine. She was caught up in the vortex called life. Jake needed a heart and Scott's mind-numbing kisses were becoming additive. The emotional pressure of having a child waiting on a heart transplant and this, this…

She couldn't even put a name to it. A crush? An attraction? Sexual desire? Why did these emotions have to be swelling all at the same time? It would be hard enough one after another. Her feelings were all tangled. Scott and Jake. Jake and Scott.

Scott cracked the door open, allowing a dim shaft of light into Hannah's room. Had he heard her call out?

"No, no, no," she cried as she tossed, kicking at the covers.

She was having a nightmare. He hurried to her. Sitting on the edge of the bed, he gathered her into his arms. She trembled. The musky, warm smell of sleep surrounded her.

The T-shirt she wore left an exposed expanse of slim thighs. Scott stared, feeling the first stirring of arousal. He couldn't have stopped looking for the world. His eyes remained riveted to where the edge of the T-shirt barely covered her panties. He summoned the presence of mind to say in an even tone, "Hannah, wake up. You're having a nightmare."

She opened her eyes but he could see she wasn't completely focused on him. "Scared."

"I know, honey. But I'm here now."

"Stay," came out in a pleading whisper.

His heart jerked to a stop before it found its pace again.

"Hold me."

Her quiet, pleading words tore at Scott's heart. He could help this time and he wouldn't let her down. He was being a friend. But they couldn't remain friends if she continued to snuggle up against him like he was her savior. It was difficult to keep her at arm's length physically as well as emotionally. His wasn't that strong. Taking a deep breath, he vowed to comfort her—nothing more.

Scott scooped her into his arms and placed her in the middle of the bed before crawling under the covers and snuggling her to him, her back against his chest. He'd never spooned with a woman before. Never stayed long enough to form a bond. Women had asked him to stay but he had always refused. His affairs had been more about physical release. Because he'd guarded his emotions so closely and refused to open up, all his relationships had slowly dissolved over time.

Hannah had already broken through one of the barriers he'd erected to distance women. He'd never experienced this kind of confusion before where a woman was concerned.

It felt good to have Hannah cloistered under the sheets alongside him as if he were fighting off her fiery dragons. She wriggled closer, then sighed deeply. Seconds later her breathing became soft and regular. He couldn't give in to his growing desire, refused to make promises he couldn't ever keep.

What would be next? Would she expect more from him? Would he be disappointed if she didn't? He wouldn't like it if she was the one pushing him away.

He'd seen the damage a job like his did to a relationship. Others managed, but it wasn't in his genes to handle it. The chance he might fail Hannah and Jake was one he wouldn't allow himself. He couldn't have two people depending on him emotionally, just medically. He refused to let the demands of his career ruin their lives, because he couldn't reset his priorities.

Still...wouldn't it be heaven to have Hannah to come home to after a long night of emergency surgery?

Pain and pleasure warred within him. There would be no more sleep for him tonight.

Hannah woke with a start. She needed to check on Jake!

Snugly tucked against warmth, she wished she didn't have to move, but she had to find her phone. Riding quickly behind that thought was the realization that Scott's arms surrounded her. The solidness of his chest resting against her cheek was a sweet contrast to the gentle hand stroking her arm. Hannah felt a tender, dewy touch at her hairline. He'd kissed her.

She'd fallen asleep in Scott's arms! Even asked him to stay with her. In her bed. There were no social guidelines for what to do when you've begged a man to join you in bed. She had to maintain her self-respect, but checking on Jake took priority.

"Hannah?" Scott asked. The warmth of his voice swept across her cheek.

"I need to call the hospital."

The mattress shifted as he rolled away and back again. He handed her the cell phone she'd left on the bedside table. "I've already checked on Jake, but I know you want to hear for yourself."

Hannah punched the speed-dial number for the hospital. The phone rang.

Her heart beat in double time. Scott's arms no longer encompassed her, but he remained close enough that she could still feel his heat. She almost broke into hysterical laughter. How many mothers of transplant patients slept with the surgeon?

The nurse assured Hannah Jake was doing fine.

Had the nurse noticed how fast and shallow she was breathing?

Hannah disconnected the call, keeping her back to him.

"Are you all right?" Scott asked. "Jake is fine?" She could tell he'd moved out of touching distance.

"Yeah."

"Look at me," he said, sternly enough that she complied.

She tugged on the sheet as she sat up. Scott stood before her in a pair of red plaid boxer shorts. Her gaze moved past his bare chest, which she ached to run her hands across, and lifted until it met his eyes.

"You needed someone to lean on last night. You've nothing to be embarrassed about. So don't act as if you do."

She said nothing, her gaze locked with his. She licked her suddenly parched lips.

"Hannah..." Scott stepped toward her, passion flaring in his eyes. He halted beside the bed and looked down at her. The question hung in the air.

Time stood still between them.

She'd been forced by circumstances to trust Scott with her son's care, but had he changed enough that she could trust him where her heart was concerned? Could she take that chance again?

When she said nothing he took a deep resigned breath and said, "Why don't you get dressed? We still have time to get to the hospital before shift change. We can check on Jake together."

CHAPTER FIVE

SCOTT stepped into the bedroom, carrying Hannah's freshly laundered clothes as he'd promised. The hairdryer was buzzing in the bathroom so she was still in there. He laid the clothes on the bed. What would her reaction be if she stepped out and found him there?

Those precious, heartbeat-suspending seconds when he'd stepped toward the bed slipped into his thoughts. A tingle of anticipation still lingered. He'd wanted to return to her warmth, had all but begged to. Had she had to force herself to say no? From the look in her eyes, he thought she might have. What had kept her from saying yes? Did she still not trust him? If he had been in her shoes, he probably wouldn't either.

Was she still embarrassed about last night? To have her begging him to join her, to hold her had been so out of character for her. He was glad he'd been the one here when she'd needed someone. She was no weak ninny who pleaded for comfort often. If she was out of control enough to ask him to stay then she was really hurting. This morning she had to be working to regain her pride.

He'd tried to put her at ease in the kitchen, which was next to impossible since he was humming with need like a taut wire in the wind. He'd held her because she'd needed it, despite it being unbearably difficult for him to stop there. She'd needed companionship and caring, not a lusty male. He'd been the gentleman last night that he should have been years ago. At least he'd made sure he'd still been there when she'd woken up this time.

His eyes lingered on the bed a second before he walked out the bedroom door.

Five minutes later Hannah entered his living room. Dressed in jeans and a red T-shirt with a sweater draped around her shoulders, she looked like a fresh-faced sorority girl out for an afternoon of shopping. She carried her bag in her hand. He'd not seen her look lovelier.

With a gruff "Let's go," he took the bag from her and opened the front door. She gave him a quizzical look but said nothing. If he just didn't touch her again he could make it without turning around and pulling her back into the bedroom.

As they approached his car, Hannah said, "I see you got that BMW you were always talking about. You've definitely moved up in the world."

"Just a little."

She gave a little huff of disbelief. "From that worn-out car you used to drive to this beauty is more than a little."

Warm pleasure at her appreciation filled him, and he smiled. "I bought it after I finished my surgical training. The old car had given its all, so I had to let go."

"That happens with people too."

Scott studied her a moment. Was she thinking about how badly he'd treated her after she'd given him her virginity?

He didn't want to believe that. Guilt had become something that he lived with every day, but he wanted to believe that Hannah really had forgiven him.

Opening the passenger door, he let her scoot in before closing it, then put the bag in the backseat. He climbed in behind the wheel. Hannah had already buckled up and was running her hands across the leather seat.

He smiled. At least she liked his car.

The sky was just turning pink on the eastern horizon as Scott drove to the hospital. He and Hannah spoke little on the way. Scott let her out at the front door, saying he would meet her outside the unit.

"Okay. Uh...thanks for your—uh—help...last night."

"No problem." Scott waited for her to close the door before he drove away. He hated having to leave her there. Didn't like the feeling they were sneaking around. After all, nothing was going on.

Yeah, right. He had to be fooling himself. If she'd said the word they would be in bed together right now.

Scott watched as Hannah came down the corridor from where he stood waiting for her. "I've cleared it for you to stay for just a few minutes."

They walked together to Jake's bed. A machine making a puffing sound with a long tube leading to Jake's mouth was the new fixture beside his bed.

"I hate this machine."

"I know, but you also understand it is necessity."

Jake's small chest rose with a huff of the pump. His eyes were opened but were glassed over from the drugs Scott had ordered to keep him calm. His small fingers flexed as he strained against the Velcro strips that secured his hands to the bed, preventing him from trying to pull out the tube. He struggled to speak and looked frustrated when he couldn't.

Hannah put her index finger in his palm. She trailed the back of her finger down his pale cheek. "Shh...honey, Mommy's right here. I love you." She repeated the words almost as a chant.

Jake fell asleep as they stood watching him. Seconds ticked by. Hannah glanced over her shoulder at Scott.

"You really are a wonderful mother. Jake's a lucky little guy to have you," Scott said softly.

"I'm just doing what any mother would do."

Scott knew better than that. "No, you're not. You're here, letting him know you love him, no matter what, and that's the important thing. You're always thinking of him and not just yourself."

"Doesn't every mother?"

"No." The word came out harsher than he'd intended. "Some mothers reject their children because they aren't what they want them to be." His mother certainly had.

She gave him a thoughtful look, then said, "I can't imagine ever doing that to someone I love."

"I don't imagine you could." Hannah loved too freely and unconditionally for it to be any other way.

"I don't feel like a very good mother right now. I can't do anything to help Jake."

"You will soon. A new heart will come." Scott picked up the chart on the end of the bed and looked at it. "He's just getting a little help. We don't want him to wear himself out. He's on half a liter of oxygen and five breaths."

"You do know Jake's more than what you read on that darned chart."

"Yes, I'm aware of that." A tone of sadness entered his voice. "I hate to see him this way too."

"I'm sorry. I shouldn't have said that. I know none of this is your fault. It's just nerves talking." She looked at Jake.

"I won't hold it against you."

She gave Scott a wry smile, and he tried to return a reassuring one.

Her smile grew and reached her eyes. "Thanks, I appreciate that. No more falling apart for me. I'm going to be a big girl."

"I think you're doing just great." He raised his eyebrows in a wolfish manner. "I don't mind helping out at all."

Hannah looked away, but he didn't miss her pink cheeks. "Hey, there's a hospital event being held downtown tonight to raise money for a new cardiac MRI. I have to attend. I was wondering if you might like to go with me?" Scott tried to insert a casual friendly tone to cover his eagerness to spend an evening with her.

"I don't think that would be a good idea."

He wasn't going to give up easily. "I'd have more fun if I were with someone, especially if that person was you." What he didn't say was that he only wanted to go with her. "You can't stay with Jake at night anyway. Come, please. Food and dancing. No pressure, you've my word." He put his hand up as if he were taking a pledge in court.

"I don't have anything to wear."

Scott's mouth lifted at the corners. "Searching for an excuse, are you? All you need's a nice dress. These events are usually fun and it'll take your mind off Jake for a couple of hours."

She shook her head. "I don't—"

"Look, we'll go late. At nine. After you have to leave CICU. It's not good for your health to be sitting and stewing twenty-four seven. Look what happened yesterday. I'm alone. You're alone. So why can't we do something together? For old times' sake?"

"I don't know..."

"A heart won't come any faster because you're sitting here day and night. I'll be paged if anything happens."

"Scott, you and I shouldn't be going out. I don't need any more emotional upheaval in my life." She laid her hands on the rail of Jake's bed.

His heart flip-flopped. "So I cause you emotional upheaval?" He lowered his voice. "Come on, Hannah. Just because you're taking a break from here doesn't mean you care any less about Jake."

She wrinkled her nose and pursed her lips. He grinned. That dig had hit home.

"I think our relationship should only have to do with Jake and the present."

Scott said nothing for a few of seconds, letting the space and time between them grow. "But it's not, is it? I don't normally have mothers of patients to my home. This thing between us is too powerful to ignore."

Hannah blinked, and blinked again. She was aware of the *thing* he was talking about.

He stepped closer. "You don't want me to have to go alone, now, do you?" He purposely sounded like a little boy pleading for his first puppy. "You've got some pretty intense days ahead. Why not have one night of fun while Jake's in good hands? It might help keep you sane." Scott shifted from one foot to the other. Was she going to turn him down? He'd never been more anxious to hear a yes to a date invitation.

"Okay, but only this one time."

He grinned in triumph, tempted to give the air a high five. "Gee, that's not the most enthusiastic response I've ever received but I'll take it. I'll have Oscar take you home. He'll be waiting out front. I'll see you at eight?"

"I thought you said nine."

"I did, but you don't need to be here after shift change anyway."

"It's nine or not at all. I want to stay until Jake goes to sleep."

"Okay, I'll accept that if you will make an effort to at least try to enjoy yourself this evening."

"All I can promise is that I'll do my best."

She gave him a slight smile. Genuinely relieved to hear a positive answer, he decided to leave well enough alone. He wasn't used to feeling insecure when asking someone out on a date.

The clerk and tech gave him a curious look as he left. Had they noticed his special interest in Hannah?

The single desk lamp provided the only illumination in Scott's windowless office. Resting his elbows on the desk, he covered his face with his hands. What was happening to him?

He'd promised Hannah they would keep it simple and easy. He shouldn't push for more. They had no future. He'd known all those years ago that she was the type of woman who would want to settle down and have a family. She would expect and deserved someone that could be there full time. Not someone with divided loyalties.

What would happen when he could no longer step away? She and Jake were slipping under his defenses. That didn't matter. He still had to let them go.

Heck, he'd not only fallen for the mother but her kid. Jake had managed to wrap him around his finger as well. Scott felt like a car being pushed by another one. No matter how hard he applied the brakes, he was still moving forward. He was in deep with no hope of getting out gracefully. Was it possible for him to have a solid relationship and still be the kind of doctor he wanted to be?

Hopefully if he got the position in Dallas, that would solve the problem.

He didn't want Hannah to be hurt again. When she'd made that comment about being let go he wasn't sure she'd been referring to years ago. Her ex had hurt her too. No wonder she was so cautious.

Scott understood why Hannah had been angry and distrustful of him initially, but she acted as if she was coming around. He'd been honored she'd trusted him enough to ask for help during the night.

It would've been fabulous to be inside Hannah's warm, welcoming body. Instead, he'd been left with a hunger that might drive him mad. A cold shower had been his reward for being a gentleman.

He'd not stayed around long enough the last time they'd been in bed together to enjoy the ruffled morning look that was so cute on Hannah. Now he wished more than ever he'd crawled back into her bed the morning after they'd made love.

Kissed and bedded the mother of a patient. It wouldn't have been a quick consoling trip down memory lane. He hardened at the memory of the vulnerability and longing that had been in her eyes. Once he'd started kissing that generous pink mouth, he wouldn't have stopped until they had both been satisfied. He'd have missed rounds for sure. And he never missed rounds.

Despite the gnawing longing, he refused to take advantage of her need for simple human contact. She was alone, in a stressful and fearful situation. She'd only been in his home because of her son. He wanted Hannah to desire *him*, not just let him into her bed because she needed someone.

Tapping on the open door drew his attention. Andrea entered. "Daydreaming, boss?" she asked with a grin.

If the truth be known she was more his boss than the other way around. As his right-hand woman, she kept him on track.

"Just thinking. Did you let UNOS know that Jake Quinn had been placed on the respirator?"

"I called just a few minutes ago."

"Good. I was…wondering if you would do me a favor."

"What's that?"

"Would you sit with Mrs. Quinn while the transplant is taking place? She has no one and I think she should have someone with her while Jake's in surgery. I need to know she is taken care of."

The protective part of him had been more pronounced since Hannah had re-entered his life. When he'd seen those sad, sorrow-filled eyes he'd wanted to take all her cares away.

"Sure, boss. I'll be glad to. This one's getting to you, isn't it?"

"Yeah, this transplant needs to go smoothly."

The one way he could achieve that goal was to make sure that Jake got better, and soon. He had no control over the allocation system, or the number of children on the waiting list, but he had control over the type of care Jake received. Confident in his abilities as a surgeon, he'd been right when he'd told Hannah not to worry. The odds were in Jake's favor.

"I wasn't referring to the patient."

Scott didn't respond. Andrea gave him a knowing smile and left him alone with his thoughts. He needed to face facts—his greatest fear wasn't for Jake, but for his own heart when he had to give Hannah up. And he would give her up because he did care so much for her.

Scott groaned. He couldn't go around half-aroused all day. He leaned back in the chair and raked his fingers through his hair. The sexual tension between Hannah and himself was like no other he'd ever known. What he didn't understand was how she'd managed to flip his ordered and planned world upside down in a matter of days.

The doorbell dinged again.

"I'm coming," Hannah yelled, managing to make it

into the living room just after the third ring. Swinging her front door wide, Hannah stood stunned by the sight of Scott, dressed in a navy suit.

Gorgeous. Breathtakingly handsome. All healthy male.

Scott looked like the cover guy on a magazine. The color of the suit deepened the blue of his eyes. The ones twinkling at her now.

His broad shoulders filled the entrance. She swallowed a "Wow," trying not to embarrass herself. A crisp white button-down shirt and a silk tie in striped shades of blues finished his impeccable appearance. He'd shaved that evening. She caught a hint of his earthy aftershave. She liked it.

What would he do if she ran her palm across the plane of his cheek? She shoved her hands into the pockets of her robe.

Scott's hair had been trimmed, but the thick waves were mussed. She grinned. He'd been running his fingers through it. He did that when he was anxious. Had he thought she wouldn't let him in?

He represented sophistication right down to the bouquet of yellow roses in his hand. Her favorite color. Right now Scott appealed to her more than a chocolate sundae on a hot Saturday afternoon. She could almost taste him.

"That good, huh?" A grin lined his full lips and broadened to a smile.

Hannah bit the inside of her cheek to keep "Yum" from seeping through her lips. "Good-looking suit."

"Just the suit?"

She waved her hand at him as if dismissing the question. "Stop fishing for compliments."

Scott's smile and laughter were a lethal combination, hard to resist. He was pulling her under his spell again, making her revisit all those feelings she'd long hidden, making her think, *What if?* Making her remember why they had been such good friends at one time. Why she'd enjoyed his company so much. Hannah hoped he had no idea of the magnitude of her mental and physical reaction to him.

She didn't want to feel anything for him. She'd already been there and done that, and had the broken heart to show for it.

"Come in. I'm not quite ready. I still need to put my dress on." She sounded more out of breath than she should've been.

"I don't know, that furry thing you have on looks interesting," Scott drawled as he entered. "I particularly like those silver shoes with it." He nudged the door closed with a foot and offered her the flowers.

Hannah took them, inhaling their sweet smell. She smiled. "They're wonderful." She sighed with delight. "Thank you. I love them. Let me get a vase. I'll only be another sec. Have a seat."

When had she become such a chatterer?

"We've plenty of time," he said, chuckling.

He knows he rattles me. I've got to be on guard or I'll be overwhelmed.

In the kitchen, Hannah pulled a chair toward the counter below the cabinet where she stored vases. She removed her shoes. With her robe gathered in her hand, she stepped on the chair, opened the cabinet and reached in for a container.

"Hey, let me help with that." Scott stood beside her. Effortlessly, he grabbed the largest crystal container from the shelf, then closed the cabinet door. The vase clinked as he placed it on the counter.

Scott's gaze dropped to the long expanse of her exposed

leg, then lifted to meet hers. Appreciation, heat, and humor warred to dominate, making his eyes darken.

Hannah released her bathrobe, letting it drop to cover her thighs.

Humor won, leaving a twinkle in his eye. "Let me help you down." His hands circled her waist, lifting her. Her hands automatically braced on his shoulders and she could feel muscles bunching beneath the fabric of his suit jacket. She longed to explore their breadth, but resisted the urge.

Their gazes locked, held as she slid at a snail's pace toward the floor. Her toes were inches from touching when he pulled her against his solid frame.

Acutely conscious of her body's reaction to his nearness, Hannah made no effort to be released. Her core heated, glowed, grew brighter and flowed outwards, like a river of lava. Would she burst into flame? Her fingertips kneaded his muscles, asking for something she wouldn't put into words. Scott's quick, heavy breaths mingled with her expectant ones.

The air crackled around them.

For one beautiful, suspended moment Hannah thought he'd kiss her. Hoped he would. Instead, his hands tightened at her waist as he eased her away, letting her feet rest on the floor. Scott stepped back, his hands falling to his sides. Disappointment washed over her. Hannah missed the pleasure of his touch and the promise of his kiss. She shook her head, clearing the cotton-candy fog.

"I'll take care of the flowers. You go get dressed." His words had a rough edge to them, as if he were in pain.

Hurrying across the living room, she closed the bedroom door and let out a soft sigh. Her heart thumped in double time. Darn the man. He didn't seem rattled at all. Would it be considered irony if a heart doctor caused a heart attack?

Keeping her hands off Scott would prove difficult. She'd never responded to another man the same way as she did to him. *That* thrill had been there before, and had returned with a vengeance. She stood stock still. The truth of that reality would mean heartbreak but she was older and wiser now. She'd handle it. Her vow just to remain friends was like a stick that had been thrown into a fast-running river. Long gone.

Hannah slipped her dress over her head. It was the nicest thing she'd ever owned. She'd bought it as a splurge. Had fate known she'd meet Scott again and need it? With a fluttering heart, she took a deep breath. The effort did nothing to calm her anxiousness.

At the mirror, she checked her hair. She'd pulled it into a loose French twist. Tendrils fell to frame her face. Ignoring them, she added a princess strand of pearls to her neck and single pearl studs to her ears.

Taking another fortifying breath, holding it for seconds before letting it go, she stepped out to meet the man that flustered her and sent her heart racing.

While he waited, Scott wandered the living room, trying to get his libido under control. It was becoming almost impossible to maintain the "just friends" concept between them. Sweat nearly popped out on his brow from the effort he made not to touch Hannah whenever she came near. Taking a deep breath, he tried to focus on something beside the woman dressing a few feet away.

Her condo was small, but adequate for a mother and young child. Floral artwork hung on the walls, adding a bright hominess to the rooms. The furnishings spoke of comfort first, looks second. There was a bit of a backyard where toys of all shapes and colors were strewn. A sandbox was tucked away in the corner. Knowing how Hannah needed space, it was no surprise she'd found a home that would give Jake a place to play.

Framed pictures of Jake and Jake with Hannah rested on tables throughout the room. Scott picked up one where Jake was giving Hannah a kiss on the cheek. Jake looked full of life and Hannah's face held an almost angelic appearance as she smiled with pleasure. It was heartwarming to see such love between a mother and child.

He remembered seeing pictures of his parents with him and his brothers as small children, but as they'd grown it always seemed his father had been too busy to make time for the family portrait appointment. It wasn't only those his father had missed. The picture taken after Scott's winning run in baseball didn't have his dad in it either.

Scott had tried to understand. He'd known what his father did was important, even admired him. Still, it had hurt when his father hadn't been there for the state baseball play-offs. At first, Scott had thought that if he went into medicine then he would have a connection to his father, but had soon realized that he loved everything about the profession. That, after all, he was his father's son.

He studied the picture of Hannah and Jake again. *What would it be like to be encircled in that glow of emotion?*

He didn't have any business having those kinds of thoughts. He shouldn't be thinking of Hannah in regard to a future. It couldn't include him. He had hurt Hannah before but this time whatever happened between them would also affect Jake. He wouldn't do that to them.

Scott carefully returned the picture to its spot.

Hannah came into the living area. "I'm ready." Her words tumbled out as she reached for the tiny beaded clutch lying in one of the chairs. With a self-conscious flourish, she faced him.

Scott didn't miss the smallest detail as his eyes took in

the amazing vision before him. Hannah must be what angels in heaven look like. Air left his lungs as if he'd been sucker-punched, while his heart rate kicked up ten notches. All his good intentions had fled.

Supported by thin straps at the shoulders, her dress left an expanse of her smooth skin bare. From there the palest of pink fabric fit like a glove across her high breasts, and along her slender waist, to create a cloud of folds that swirled down around her hips and ended an inch above her knees.

He'd never had a lovelier date.

The same rose tint of her dress rested on her cheeks. She was nervous, self-conscious. A feeling of satisfaction filled him to know that it mattered to her what he thought. He grinned. She refused to meet his gaze. The small jingle of the linked chain of her purse made the lone noise in the room as she wrapped it around her fingers, undid it, and rewrapped it in rapid succession.

His whistle was low and appreciative. "You look amazing."

"Thank you, kind sir. You don't look half bad yourself." Her eyes had a shy look, but her words indicated her confidence was returning. "Shall we go?" She stepped toward the door.

From her head to the tips of her delicate feet, she was perfection. Except for...

He stooped and picked up her thin strapped shoes. They dangled on the ends of two of his fingers. "I believe you might need these." She'd forgotten them when she'd left the kitchen. With a question in her eyes, she looked at him, then down at her feet. He watched with satisfaction as she blushed crimson, making her even more becoming. *She's absolutely captivating.*

Scott liked the strong, demanding Hannah and the give-as-good-as-you-get one, but this sensually unsure Hannah was the best yet. It would be extremely difficult to keep his promise of no pressure when his body was already making demands to have her.

"I guess I do need those." She took the shoes, making an obvious effort not to touch his hand.

Sitting in an armchair, she adjusted the straps around her feet, treating him to a fine expanse of her shapely legs. She caught his appraising stare and pushed her skirt down, effectively closing the curtain on his view. Finding her tiny bag, she stood. "I think I'm ready now."

"I'll have the best-looking woman there on my arm. My colleagues are going to be jealous."

She smiled. The first unwavering one he could remember her having that evening.

"I do believe you're flirting with me, Doctor."

Scott grinned wickedly. "You might be right." He held the door for her. She slipped past him, and Scott had his first view of the back of her dress. From each of her shoulders, the folds of chiffon dropped to scoop below her waist, leaving her back bare.

The rise in his body temperature was instant, probably high enough to break a glass thermometer. He feared he would combust on the spot.

Breathe man, breathe. His mouth went dry. With effort he remembered to put one foot in front of the other as they went down the walk. All he could think about was placing a kiss on the ridge of one of those golden shoulders while his hand glided along every silky inch of her back.

"That dress is incredible."

"It's not too much for this event, is it?" The insecurity in her voice reminded him of a girl on her first date.

"No, it's perfect, absolutely perfect," he said with almost too much enthusiasm. Taking her hand, he pulled it through the crook of his arm and gave her a broad smile. "And so are you."

She returned the smile with a bright one of her own.

Unaware of her sex appeal, Hannah exuded it with no effort or consciousness. Did she realize his libido was running wild because of her? His body sang in response. His reactions were displaying themselves like a flashing billboard, but she didn't seem to notice. If he didn't focus on keeping the evening light, he could scare her off.

Guiding her to his car, he opened the door and helped her in. The least a mere mortal could do for this celestial being.

Hannah settled into the supple leather seat as Scott maneuvered the low sports car through the late-evening traffic. A tangy smell encircled her. She inhaled, appreciating Scott's own special essence. He smelled like a combination of sun and rain, with a hint of pine. She resisted the yen to lean closer.

"Hey, I'm sorry I gave you a hard time about coming tonight," she said. "It does sounds like a good time, but I'm not sure I'll be much fun. I seem to be unhappy at the hospital and miserable when I'm away. Until Jake gets a heart I'm not sure I'll be satisfied anywhere."

Scott reached for her hand and briefly squeezed it. "Why don't you try not to think about that for a few hours and attempt to enjoy yourself?" He flashed a smile.

One of her favorites. But each of his smiles was jockeying for a spot as favorite. This smile wrapped around her like a blanket on a cold winter day, making her believe that all could be well. A fluttery feeling developed in her stomach. Afraid she might be learning to love more than his smiles, she didn't dare let herself go down that path. "I'll try."

"These events are always laid back and fun. There'll be games, a silent auction, dancing with a good band. We should have no problem finding something distracting to do."

In no time Scott had pulled up in front of a building with massive glass windows. Inside a huge ballroom a band played a fast rock and roll number. Enormous records and pictures of movie stars blown up bigger than life decorated the area. An old '53 Chevy with girls in poodle skirts and guys with slicked-back hair greeted them.

"The fifties. My favorite decade." Hannah smiled, giving Scott's arm a slight press in her enthusiasm. The band struck up the first notes of another song. She swayed to "Earth Angel." With a sheepish grin on her lips, she looked at him from under lowered lashes. "What?"

"I was thinking how appropriate that song is. I've my own earth angel."

Tongue-tied, Hannah could only stare at him.

Scott suppressed a smile…barely. He said close to her ear, "Knowing you, you need to eat before we play."

His lips brushed the shell of her ear, making her body quiver. Her breath caught. Did he have any idea what he did to her? Her stomach did loop-di-loops. She was hungry for more than food.

Scott took her hand. "Let's go and see what's on the buffet."

They wove their way through the crowd towards a group of tables set up on the far side of the room. Her hand fit comfortably into his as if it belonged there. Scott held her hand tight enough to be possessive but not so tight she couldn't have removed it if she'd wished. Her heart missed a beat when he gave it a gentle squeeze, as if he knew what she was thinking.

* * *

With their meal completed, Scott took Hannah's hand again as they headed toward an area set up for games. His body needed some type of physical contact with hers, otherwise it felt like a piece of him was missing. He spoke to a couple of his colleagues as he and Hannah walked across the large room. He introduced her only as an old friend, leaving out that she was the mother of one of his patients.

In the game area, they waited their turn after he'd talked Hannah into playing a round of table tennis. He watched her remove the silver shoes, finding the artless action very sexy. Keeping things light was turning into work.

"Did I mention I've been the Watson family reunion champion three years running?" She grinned at him across the expanse of the green table.

"You failed to share that information."

"Don't let that intimidate you."

"I'll try not to." He served his best fast ball.

"Not bad." She nodded with approval. "All those hours in the interns' hideout in the basement of the hospital must've paid off."

"Just serve, Quinn, and know I'll be giving no mercy."

Hannah grinned, obviously pleased with her efforts to rattle him. At least he'd succeeded in helping her forget her problems for a few minutes.

After a couple of spirited games Scott had a newfound respect for Hannah. She didn't beat him but managed to hold her own.

"You don't feel the need to let my male ego go undamaged by letting me win?" It wasn't a trait he'd normally found in the women he'd been out with.

"No. Why should I? My motto is 'Let the best man or woman win.' Your ego is the last thing I need to feed."

He pulled his lips back in mock pain. "You always did

tell me like it is. That's one of the things I always liked about you."

Scott took the final game, barely. Coming around the table, she gave him a quick hug of congratulations. Their laughter merged.

The tinkling sound that he loved placed him hopelessly and completely under her spell. He wanted to hold onto this moment for ever. His days were spent with such serious matters. It was nice to laugh and have fun for a change. Her sharp wit and love of life was infectious.

"That'll show you not to mess with me. That was fun," she said after most of her mirth had dissipated. "I needed to do that. You always could make me laugh. Even when I was having a tough day on the floor," she said. "That's a gift, you know."

"My pleasure." And it was. He always liked her laugh. It reminded him of a breeze moving through wind chimes on a hot summer day. He had an idea she'd not laughed much in the last few years, certainly not in the last few days.

It was nice to see her smiling, letting go a little. She needed to. Her emotions had to be swinging one way and then the other. She needed a release.

"What?" she asked, sounding a little ill at ease.

"I was just contemplating what an interesting woman you are."

"How's that?"

"Well, you play table tennis like a demon, love donuts, you're evidently a self-sufficient single mother, you appreciate nice cars and you like the oldies."

Scott noticed the worry lines on her face had decreased. For that he was grateful. She had looks that went beyond attractive. Hers was still a wholesome beauty, the kind of loveliness that came from the inside. The type that had drawn him to her in the first place, making him want to get to know her, and later to consider the impossible.

Turning her shoulder in a saucy manner toward him, she said, "What more could a man want?"

"I can imagine."

She immediately flushed red, making her even more desirable.

"Don't be using that charm on me, Doctor. It won't work. I've seen it in action too many times. That's just a figure of speech."

He chuckled. "Yes, Hannah, I know what you meant." It was nice to see that some of the spunk that had attracted him when they'd first met hadn't disappeared. His plan was working. He'd been right to insist she accompany him. She needed fun in her life. If he could, he would have it be that way for her always.

"I'm thirsty." Her eyes shined as she smiled.

"Then let's get you something to drink." He hoped none of his colleagues saw the sappy grin on his face. He could imagine the unmerciful fun they would make of him. The grapevine would no doubt run with that information. "Don't forget your shoes."

Hannah found them under the playing table and slipped them on.

"I think it adds something to your dress when you're barefooted." Hannah's nervous laughter sent heat to a part of his body that didn't need any encouragement. "Come on, hotshot, I think there's a soda stand over this way." He pointed to a red and white awning.

As they made their way across the room, Hannah exclaimed, "I thought you meant a place to get a cola! This is a real soda parlor."

They found a small empty table. A young man, dressed

in a yellow striped shirt, took their order. She wanted a chocolate shake. He ordered vanilla.

"I'm really enjoying myself." Hannah's eyes sparkled. "There must be thousands of nurses wishing you'd invited them."

"I think it is more like a hundred." He gave what he hoped was his best wolfish grin.

She laughed. "At least."

The young man returned with their shakes. Hannah stuck her straw into hers. Her cheeks drew together as she sucked. A look of pure joy touched her features as she drew up the rich liquid. He grinned. Releasing the straw, she ran her tongue with slow deliberation across the curve of her top lip. Closing her eyes, she made a sound of unadulterated pleasure.

Had all the air been sucked out of the place? Scott couldn't breathe. Captured by the sight, he wished he'd been the one to put that look of delight on her face.

Hannah's smiled broadened. "I'll race you to the bottom. On your mark, get set, go."

He shoved his straw into his glass. The thick liquid moved up their straws at a slow pace. Watching her over the top of the glass, Scott raised a brow, taunting her. Smirking around the straw, he continued to suck hard.

"You won't beat me." Determination filled her eyes as her lips drew on the straw again.

Scott put his hand under the table and caressed her knee. Hannah's eyes widened in surprise, then narrowed. He beamed. She shoved his hand away and moved her knee to where he couldn't touch her with ease. With a negative movement of her head and a gleam in her eye, she continued sucking with gusto.

He broke contact with his straw and let out a laugh that came from his belly. It was loud enough that others sitting around them stared. The last noisy slurp of nothing being left in her glass could be heard by the time his mirth had died into a chuckle.

"I won." Hannah clasped her hands over her head in a victory sign. "And you tried to cheat!"

Scott laughed again, feeling no guilt. "Yeah. In the end you got the better of me. I could tell that, no matter what I did, you planned to win this contest."

"You're right." Hannah grinned. "We should've set a prize."

"How about this?" Not allowing her time to answer or caring if he was seen, Scott slipped a hand behind her neck and pulled her to him.

Her lips were cool under his. In a slow, methodical motion his tongue slid over her lips, not wanting to miss any of the sugary flavor. Hannah brought her hand to his shoulder and made a low sound of acceptance. Her mouth heated under his. Long, perfect seconds went by before he lifted his mouth.

CHAPTER SIX

Scott's hooded eyes and the sensual curve of his lips made Hannah's blood speed through her veins. A blur of shapes and colors whirled around them. Scott was the only person who remained in focus.

Her gaze locked with his blue one. The air snapped round them. He leaned toward her. Her lips parted.

A man moving between the tables jostled Scott's chair. Pulling back, Scott sat straighter. The moment evaporated. He'd been thinking about kissing her again. She would've let him.

"I think, no, I know, kissing you could get out of hand and I promised no pressure."

As far as Hannah was concerned, he could forget that pledge. She wanted him and she wanted to feel wanted. Even if it was just for a little while.

"There's a silent auction going on. I read a trip down the Colorado River through the Grand Canyon was being offered. I'd like to bid on it. After we check that out, maybe we could dance, if you'd like," he said, standing.

Scott sounded a little formal all of a sudden. The abrupt shift in his attitude made her feel a little lost. He'd been so warm minutes before. Had that kiss affected him as much as it had her?

Lifting a finger, Hannah touched her bottom lip. She

should be grateful for the interruption. It gave her time to get her emotions corralled.

As they strolled side by side toward the auction area, she noticed the number of admiring looks that came Scott's way from other women. Hannah glowed with feminine one-upmanship, knowing he was with her.

The area where the auction was set up was quieter. A few other couples strolled around the tables. Scott located the Canyon trip and wrote his bid on the sheet. Hannah coughed to cover her gasp of shock when she saw his bid amount.

He must've known what she thought because he said, "It's for a good cause."

"Yours or the hospital's?" she asked with a grin.

"Both."

Hannah realized he could afford it. A reminder of how different their worlds were.

They continued down the line of tables filled with auction items. An exquisite blue floral teaset caught Hannah's eye. Picking up the cup, she checked the bottom to find it had been made by a quality British company. She ran the tip of her index finger along the scalloped rim of the fragile cup. Returning it to the matching saucer, she lifted the pair to admire what a beautiful pair they made.

"It's beautiful." She spoke more to herself than Scott. The magnificent set was one she'd enjoy owning and using.

"Would you like to bid on it?" Scott asked from behind her.

She'd been so engrossed in admiring the set she'd not seen Scott put down an autographed baseball and join her.

"No. No. I was just looking." Even the starting bid was way beyond what she could afford.

"I'd be glad to bid for you." Scott studied the auction sheet.

"No. I don't even have a good place to put it," she assured him. "And I've a small child. Nothing like this would survive long in my home."

"You're probably right. How about a dance now or would you rather play some more games? I could let you win this time."

"Funny. It's not a real win unless you earn it." She looked at him. "But let's go and see if you're as good on the dance floor as you are at table tennis."

He draped her arm through his. She'd noticed he'd made a point all night not to touch her back. During the last few days she had especially liked him placing his hand at the small of her back, like an old-world gentleman. Why wouldn't he touch her back now?

The music became louder as they approached the tile-covered dance floor.

"I wonder if my *must-attend* cotillion lessons when I was thirteen will stand up to this." His lips curve into a boyish smile.

"You'll be better than me. My skills come from dancing in the living room with my father. Most of the time on his feet."

"As a kid I use to watch my dad swirl and twirl my mom around the house. Mother always wanted my father to take her dancing. She loved to dance. Still does."

"That's a nice memory."

He didn't say anything for a second, as if he'd never thought of it like that before. "You know, it is. Come on, let's give it a shot. What do you say?"

"Lead on, Mr. Astaire." She beamed up at him

Scott placed his hand low, but not too low, on her back. Hannah's breath jerked to a stop for a second. Heat radiated out from where his hand moved over her skin. Maybe it'd been a good idea for him not to touch her. It'd been a long time since she'd allowed an adult male's interest.

He maneuvered them across the floor to where other couples were preparing to dance. A fast tune began. It took a few steps for Hannah to adjust to Scott's closeness and the rhythm of the music. She settled into his lead. He was an excellent dancer. With his lithe and athletic body, he moved across the floor with natural grace. Scott twisted her in his arms, spun her one way then another and even dipped her following one number.

"How about a cold drink?" he asked after a set of songs. She nodded her agreement and he took her hand, leading her off the dance floor.

"Please. This is the most exercise I've had in days," she said, breathless from exertion and being in his arms. "I should've known when you suggested dancing you would be good at it."

Scott found a cart selling sodas, and then they located a spot out of the way where they could sit.

"Thanks," she said when he handed her the drink. "I thought you said you didn't dance well."

"No, what I said was it'd been some time." He smiled down at her. "I'm rusty at it. I don't have much spare time to go dancing."

"You're still a great partner. Mr. Astaire wouldn't be disappointed in you."

"Thank you, ma'am." He gave her a regal nod. "As are you." He took a swallow of his drink. "I was wondering why I never took you dancing."

"I wouldn't go out with you, remember? I saw you for the womanizer you were." She grinned at him. "Anyway, if we'd gone out it would've ruined a friendship. I wanted more than a date. What happen between us proved I was right."

"I see your point. I'm sorry. I handled things badly." His words seemed to include more than not taking her on a date.

"You can stop apologizing. I've grown up. Moved on. I have Jake to be concerned about. Men that come into my life affect him too. It's not just me getting hurt any more, it's Jake too."

"You're a strong woman."

"I don't know about that. I'm simply a mother doing the best she can for her child. He has no one else but me." She took a swig of her drink, and put her cup down.

He nodded in understanding. Slipping his hand in his pocket, he pulled out his cell phone and handed it to her. "Here, why don't you call and check on him? The hospital is number one on speed dial."

"I'm not surprised." His eyes clouded over for a second. Had she said something wrong?

"I would be paged if there was a problem, but I know you wouldn't be happy unless you heard he was fine from the nurse."

"You know me so well."

"Not as well as I would like to." His voice took on a suggestive note. Time held still between them then he said, "You go find someplace quiet enough to check on Jake, and I'll go and have a look at how the silent auction is going. I'll meet you back here by Elvis."

"I won't be long," she said over her shoulder as she walked away.

Ten minutes later they were both standing beside the life-size Elvis cutout.

"How's Jake?" Scott asked as she joined him.

"Resting. And I know you want to say I told you so but please don't."

"You're a great mom. I see a lot of mothers who

shouldn't have the job. It's nice to see a parent who has a connection to their child. Sadly, it doesn't always happen."

"Thank you. Sometimes I think I'm fumbling around in the dark."

"You're more in the daylight than you know." A slow song began and the lights dimmed above the dance floor. "Would you like to see some of my best moves?" he asked, his voice going low. He led her into the center of the already overflowing floor.

"I can't imagine them being any better than what I've already experienced."

Gathering her into his arms, Scott placed a hand on her back. She couldn't help but tense at the stimulating contact, but soon relaxed enough to lean into him. One of her hands found his and the other slid along his arm to rest at his shoulder. When another couple bumped them, Scott flexed his arm at her waist bringing her closer.

The solidness of his body met hers from head to toe. Hannah had a sense of being protected from the ugliness of the world. His hand dipped low on her waist before it moved inch by tantalizing inch up the length of her spine to her neck. A hot trail of consciousness flowed through her as his fingers paused at each dip in her vertebrae then worked his way down again. She simmered in the heat his touch created in her. His hand came to rest in the bow of her back.

His lips touched the sensitive spot behind her ear, sending a jolt of awareness rocketing through her.

"Scott..."

"Shh, let me enjoy having you in my arms."

Hannah's hand gripped his upper arm. Every fiber of her being strained toward him, hyper-responsive to each nuance of Scott's touch. His chest rose and fell against hers. When his heartbeat increased, she felt it. Skimming her hand over his shoulder, she curled her fingers into the waves of hair at the nape of his neck. Stepping closer, she breathed deeply, taking him in. A soft sound of pure pleasure escaped.

Scott groaned, pulling her tighter. His thigh slipped between her legs as they swayed slowly to the music. Scott no longer led to the beat of the music, but to his personal one.

His fingertips followed the edge of her dress along her back until his hand came to rest in the folds. He slowly slipped his fingers under the material to settle near the curve of her breast.

A tingle ran through her. Her nipples strained upward, pebble hard. Her step faltered. Scott compensated with a flawless move, holding her snug against his length, his desire hard against her belly.

His pager vibrated between them, bursting the blissful, sensual balloon they'd been floating in.

He expelled a scalding word and eased his hold.

Her body throbbed with need left unmet.

Scott unclipped the phone from his waistband, glanced at the screen, then muttered a blunt curse under his breath.

Hannah put more space between them. "Is it about Jake? Is something wrong?" she asked, fear filling her voice.

"I don't know yet, honey. Let me answer this." His voice was husky with disappointment. He led her off the dance floor and into a quieter area.

"This is McIntyre," he said sharply into his phone. "Yes. Can you see to it? Yes. That sounds good." His manner had turned all business.

She put a hand on his arm, and caught his gaze. "Jake?" She whispered the plea.

Scott put his hand over the receiver and mouthed, "He's fine, honey," before continuing his conversation.

Hannah took a deep breath and released it, listening to the low rumble of Scott's voice. If the call had come an hour later they would've been making love. She would've been a willing partner. Very willing. The tornado of sensations still swirled through her. Scott had set her on fire. She'd never before experienced the all-consuming need he elicited from her.

Now he stood discussing a patient. His mood had shifted lightning quick. She'd been forgotten. He'd morphed into doctor mode. But with something as simple as catching her hand, she'd be lost again.

Her feelings overpowered all logical thought, shocking her. Maintain control, that's what she needed to do. Think first. Not to expect more than Scott could give. None of that mattered. Scott had already left his mark.

Hannah watched as his jaw tightened and he looked off into the distance. His questions came out short and succinct.

As if he suddenly remembered she was there, Scott reached for her hand and pulled her close, wrapping an arm around her waist. Already her plan had a huge hole in it. She couldn't control Scott. The heat from his body surrounded her.

"I'll be there within the hour." He flipped his cell phone closed, and turned her so she could look at him.

"Something has come up that will require our attention. He curved his lip into a confident smile. "We think we've found a heart for Jake."

"Oh, thank God."

He squeezed her shoulders. "Now, remember we're in the beginning stage, and it'll take hours before we know for sure, but the heart looks promising."

"Please let this be the one," she whispered.

"I'm going straight to the hospital to review the information about the possible donor and check on Jake. Timing is everything now."

"I'll go with you."

"No," he said firmly, "you don't need to be sitting and fretting at the hospital. I'll drop you at my place. That way you'll be close. It could be hours before I know more. I'll call you."

She refused to let him dictate whether or not she should be there for her child. "I'm going with you. Jake's my son and I want to be with him as much as I can. Anyway, I have a change of clothes at the hospital and a sleep room in my name. It makes more sense."

He nodded his agreement but didn't appear happy about the arrangements.

In a hurry, Scott left her where the hallway divided, one hallway going to CICU and the other to the waiting room. She missed the security he represented the second he was out of sight.

With Scott gone, Hannah stood in the middle of the corridor, suddenly unsure what to do next. She couldn't move. This was it, what she'd prayed for. Only she'd never have dreamed she'd be involved emotionally with the doctor who would be saving Jake's life. She'd stopped thinking straight the minute Scott had arrived earlier that evening. With the possibility of a heart for Jake, the situation had become more desperate.

Change. That's what she needed to do. She rode the elevator to the upper floor and found the small sleep room she'd been assigned that afternoon. She'd made arrangements for it so she wouldn't be tempted to stay at Scott's. The room held a single bed and end table. It wasn't much, but it was close to Jake. Withdrawing her bag from the locker where she'd stored it earlier, she dropped it on the bed and began to change.

A flood of heat washed over her as she removed her dress. She overflowed with longing. If it hadn't been for the tremors of Scott's pager she'd no doubt be in his bed right now. Her heart rate quickened. A flood of hunger washed over her as if Scott was near.

She couldn't deny she'd been as willing a participant as he. No way could she place all the blame on him.

Pulling a pair of comfortable jeans out of the bag, she slipped them on, added a favorite T-shirt and tennis shoes, grabbed a sweatshirt, and hurried out to check on Jake.

"Mrs. Quinn wants to come back. Is that okay?" the clerk asked the midnight shift nurse.

Scott, standing by the desk, looked up from the chart he'd been reviewing. He'd asked her to wait. It figured she wouldn't listen. Hannah had certainly never been intimidated by him. The nurse looked at him and he nodded his consent.

The clerk had hardly replaced the phone receiver before Hannah entered the unit. She glanced at him but continued straight to Jake's bed.

Scott appreciated the view of Hannah's shapely backside as she stretched and leaned over the rail of the bed to place a kiss on her sleeping son's head. He needed to get his thoughts off the mom and on the son.

To give her some time alone with Jake, Scott waited before he approached. "Hannah." The word came out sharper than he'd intended. Lowering his voice to a more mellow level, Scott said, "I told you to wait until I came to get you."

Hannah glared at him. "I couldn't wait." She turned

back to Jake. "I had to see him." Her voice caught. She was in protective mode.

"You're right." Scott understood her feelings because he felt that same need to protect her. He admired her strength. There was no begging and pleading or demands on her part. She just did what had to be done because she loved her child.

The desire to wrap her in his arms pulled at him, but he would have an audience. The best he could offer, though inadequate, was the reassurance of knowing what she could expect in the next few hours. He moved to the other side of the bed in order to put some space between them. Hannah had a way of making him do things he'd not planned to whenever she was within touching distance.

She looked at him in expectation with a gleam of moisture in her eyes. Her hand clasped one of Jake's.

"Let me explain what's happening and going to happen. Right now, we're waiting on the family of the possible donor to agree to donation. Most of the time the recipient family never knows this far in advance about a possible donor."

"You get to know sooner if you're out dancing with the surgeon," Hannah said, averting her eyes.

His lips became a thin line. The acute sting of the remark registered.

Hannah brought her eyes back to his. "I'm sorry. That was uncalled for."

Glancing to see if anyone watched, Scott reached across the bed and captured one of her hands. His thumb brushed over her knuckles before he released it. "I understand, but don't regret what almost happened between us. I certainly don't."

She gave him a wry smile.

"As I was saying, the family will have to agree, which

will probably take place in the morning. Afterwards there'll be more tests, and it may not be until tomorrow..." he looked at his watch "...or I mean this afternoon, before things will really start moving along. The thoracic fellow will go after the heart. I plan to stay here with Jake. He won't go into surgery until after the fellow has left. We'll be in constant contact until the fellow walks into the OR with Jake's new heart."

"Will I know what's happening?"

"Yes. Andrea will be coming into the OR and I'll be sending messages out to you."

"So nothing may happen until tomorrow evening?"

He nodded. "That's why I insisted you didn't need to be here."

"I couldn't stay away."

"I realize that now. It's just part of who you are. If I hadn't had my mind on other matters I might've been thinking more clearly."

Even in the dim light he could see her blush. She knew exactly what he'd been referring to.

"So why don't you go up and try to get some rest? I'll call you when there's something new to tell. I'm even going to bunk in the attending's room for a few hours so I'll be ready for surgery."

"You don't have to stay right here?"

"No, they'll call me with any questions. We're good at transplants here, Hannah. My staff knows their jobs and they do them well."

"Dr. Mac, Lifeline is on the phone," the clerk called, holding the phone out.

Hannah spun around to look at the nurse.

Scott circled the bed, stopped beside her and said, "Wait for me outside the unit. This call shouldn't take long. I'll walk you to the elevator." He made a few steps and stopped, turning back to her. "Please wait," he pleaded softly. "Jake is hopefully going to have his new heart soon."

Hannah kissed her sleeping child, wishing she could hug him close, and left the unit. She lingered outside the CICU doors. "Still thinking of me?" Scott quipped as he came out, a slight grin on his lips.

He was obviously trying to add some levity to this anxious and unsure time. "Mighty confident of yourself, aren't you?" Her smile grew, despite her effort to control it.

His grin disappeared and his look turned solemn. "Not where you're concerned."

Scott's intense gaze bored into hers for a long moment before he took her arm and directed her down the corridor. They walked in silence, with uneasiness hanging between them. At the elevator Hannah pushed the "up" button.

"I want to kiss you." Scott's words were a husky demand.

Hannah's body tingled. Her pulse pounded. Her fingers itched to touch him. "I…I…don't think that's a good idea. I think we both should focus on Jake."

Scott stepped away, his jaw tight. "Jake will be getting my very best care. In no way will I let what I feel for you affect my performance as a doctor."

"I didn't mean to imply—"

"Hannah, I know you're beating yourself up over what was happening between us on the dance floor. I wish you wouldn't. I know all the negatives to this relationship. You still don't completely trust me and I understand. I can't make you any promises, but I also know there's something special between us."

She remained silent. There was something amazing between them. She felt it too. But she needed to be sure about her next move. She'd misread him before, had completely missed the mark with her husband, and she couldn't afford to do it again. Scott had convinced her to trust him with Jake's heart but she still didn't know about hers.

"Try to get some sleep. I'll call you as soon as I know something more concrete."

Scott turned, going back toward the unit. She'd wanted him as much as he'd wanted her. Scott wanted her sexually, but she was looking for someone to share her future. He hadn't been willing to do that during medical school. Could he feel differently now? If she invested her heart, she had to know he wanted the same things in life she did. She owed it to Jake, and to herself.

The trouble was, she was weak around Scott, and so very alone.

In the hospital the next morning, Hannah's cell phone hadn't completed a full note before she snatched it up. Her heart jumped when she heard Scott's voice.

"Hannah, we think this is the heart for Jake." His tone sounded professional, somber. "But it'll be hours before we'll go to collect it. Jake's resting and everything looks good on the donor end."

"Thank goodness." She closed her eyes and said a silent prayer.

"I'm sorry I can't tell you more. I'll see you later. I've gotta go."

His abrupt end to the conversation startled her. She wasn't sure she appreciated the return of his all-business manner. She'd come to enjoy, anticipate, the warmer version. It had become part of her comfort zone.

Despite her jumbled emotions, the chain of events leading to Jake getting a new heart registered. On a human *and* parental level she knew another family had lost their child in order for hers to live. Her chest constricted. As wonderful as Jake getting another chance to live was for her, at the other end of the spectrum was the donor family's devastation. Moisture blurred her vision. The thought of what those parents must be feeling was almost impossible to endure. Their two families would be forever linked.

Clutching a pillow, she caught herself wishing for the security of Scott's arms. He'd really been wonderful and supportive, not only with her but with Jake. She had to admit she'd felt a twinge of jealousy when Scott had managed to get Jake to laugh. She hadn't been able to do that. Wiping tears away, she took a fortifying breath. There were things to do, calls to make.

Phoning her sister in California, Hannah told her about the available heart. Despite the distance, Hannah felt better just talking to her. Jake was getting a new heart. She could scarcely comprehend it.

Scott managed to get a few hours of sleep at the hospital between calls from Lifeline and thoughts of Hannah creeping into his dreams. The long hours leading up to a transplant were often tedious. Reviewing the donor's history, checking the heart size to see if it would fit into the chest cavity and assessing blood work were a few of the many details he'd organized that morning.

A heart transplant took careful and well-timed actions. An amazing life-and-death dance. It never ceased to fill him with awe that he had a part in something so phenomenal.

Dancing. For ever after, dancing would be synonymous with Hannah. He loved holding her, wanted her in his arms again. Soon. It had hurt when she had refused to kiss him at the elevator, but she'd made the right call. They needed to take things slower.

They were on two different paths. Her life was hearth and home, and he couldn't commit to that. He wasn't capable of giving Jake and Hannah what they needed or deserved. It would be another failed relationship to add to his list.

The life he'd chosen made it impossible for him to be doctor and family man. He couldn't foresee doing both well. He already carried the heavy weight of guilt from letting his work get in the way when his mother had needed him. Hurting Hannah or Jake was something he wasn't prepared to accept. Some people could manage different parts of their life effectively, but he couldn't. The McIntyre family history bore that out.

He was just too much like his father. His patients had always come first, and Scott felt the same way about the children he cared for. That the idea he and Hannah could have more even crossed his mind came as a surprise.

It would be late evening or early morning before the major part of his day would be complete. Now wasn't the time to consider what-ifs.

Scott looked up to see Hannah coming through the CICU doors. He met her beside Jake's bed.

Jake's eyelids opened a moment and then slid closed again.

"I've ordered something to make him sleep. Jake needs to be well rested before going into surgery," Scott said. "Did you get any sleep?"

He stood close enough to catch a whiff of the fresh apple smell of her hair when she turned to him. Scott ached to pull her into a dark corner and kiss her until her cool demeanor fell away. Until the hot passion he knew she held in check boiled over.

"Some," Hannah said, before taking Jake's hand. "Is there any news?" she asked, her attention totally focused on her son.

"Yes. The family has agreed to donate. Now Lifeline

has to see that all the organs being donated are placed before the retrievals."

"All the organs?"

"Yeah. The family can agree to give other organs."

"Other children will share the same donor as Jake?"

"They could. Depending on what organs the family agrees to donate. I think we'll be going after the heart around six this evening." Scott forced his voice to remain flat, showing none of the concern he felt about the upcoming surgery. He'd grown attached to the little boy. This would be one surgery where he couldn't leave his feelings at the door.

"Where's the heart coming from?"

"I can't say, but not too far away. A heart has to be transplanted within four hours so that doesn't let it travel a long distance."

Hannah nodded, and he watched her thick hair bounce around her shoulders. His fingers flexed and curled in an effort to keep him from succumbing to his longing to touch it.

They stood by Jake's bed, doing nothing more than watching her sleeping boy. Scott practiced equal care and concern for all his patients, but this particular little patient had become a personal case despite his efforts not to let it happen. He wanted to save Jake's life. He must.

"It won't be long now," he said with all the confidence he possessed.

"Mrs. Quinn?" Andrea placed a light touch on Hannah's arm long hours later.

Hannah blinked. "What?"

"It's time to get Jake ready to go down. You need to say goodbye to him." Compassion filled her voice. It held something encouraging in it, maybe a note of excitement

"He's going now?" Jake needed the transplant, but it was difficult to let him go. At least now he was alive. He might not live though surgery. The known was better than the unknown. The terror of losing Jake filled Hannah's body like a sharp wind on a bitter winter morning.

"No. He'll actually go down in about an hour. It takes a while to prep him," Andrea said.

Hannah tensed. A film of wetness blurred her view. She needed to absorb him, afraid this would be her last memory. Studying every detail of Jake's precious face, she wanted to remember him happy and smiling, laughing with Scott...

Stop. She inhaled, letting the breath out in measured puffs. Jake had to live.

Sedated and on a respirator, her precious son had no idea what was happening. Jake lay pale against the white sheets of the bed, the only color in his face being the dark circles under his eyes. She wanted to drop to her knees and cry, howl at how unfair it all was.

"I love you, honey. Be strong. See you soon." Kissing his cheek, she released his tiny hand and cringed when it fell limply on the bed. She refused to use the word *goodbye.*

Jake would be fine. She'd accept nothing less. She believed Scott would allow nothing less.

"Mrs. Quinn," Andrea said in a low, gentle voice. "They're expecting him in the OR. Why don't you go on down to the surgery waiting room? Do you know where it is?"

"Yes." The word came out as a croak.

"Good. I'll be down to join you in a little while."

Hannah balanced on her toes, leaned over the rail and placed a kiss on Jake's forehead. A tear dropped onto his face. Hannah wiped it away. "I love you, sweetie."

Andrea put a hand on her shoulder. The comfort was appreciated. "I'll tell Scott where you are. He'll want to talk to you before going into the OR." Hannah wiped her cheek with the back of her hand as she made the long, lonely walk to the waiting room.

Her chest tightened. Would she be able to draw another complete breath until Jake came out of surgery?

Be positive. Straighten up. Jake will be fine.

Taking a seat in the far corner of the waiting room, Hannah settled in for the night. A few minutes later Andrea entered and took a seat close by.

"You'll see a big difference in Jake right away," Andrea said.

Hannah appreciated Andrea trying to make conversation while at the same time she just wanted to be left alone. "That's what the nurses tell me."

Scott came through the door dressed in blue scrubs with his ever-present white lab coat. Hannah stood, meeting him in the center of the room. If he'd opened his arms, she wouldn't have thrown herself into them, but he didn't.

Instead he said, "Let's sit. We need to talk." He placed his hands lightly at her waist, turning her. Hannah wanted to lean into his strength, but found her chair again as directed. Scott sat in the one beside her, which put Hannah between him and Andrea.

He took her hand. Desperate for his offered comfort, she didn't pull away. Looking into her eyes, he promised, "I'll take good care of Jake."

"I know you will," Hannah whispered, making her trust evident.

"Jake's getting settled in surgery. He's had his first dos of Prograf, which is the anti-rejection medicine. The te going after the heart has been gone almost an hour. I' in touch with them at regular intervals until they return. As close as I can to the heart's arrival, I'll open Jake's chest."

Hannah winced. He shifted closer, giving her hand a squeeze.

"You need to understand this is an iffy process right up until the new heart gets to the OR. Something could happen to the heart, the time could go too long, or we might find out at the last minute that the heart isn't good enough. There's a chance we may not be able to do it tonight."

She looked at him, saying nothing, praying, *Oh, God, please let it be tonight.*

Scott tightened his hold on her hand. "Surgery will probably take around four to six hours. Don't expect to see me any time soon. I'll be out when Jake's ready to go up to the unit."

He glanced at Andrea. Standing, he pulled Hannah into his arms. Hers went around his waist, absorbing his warmth, strength and assurance. His confidence and support was like balm to her nerves.

Scott ran his hand over her back, making no move to leave. He brushed his lips across her temple, then released her.

Hannah gripped his upper arms. Tears, swimming in her eyes, blurred his handsome face. She silently begged him to tell her that everything would be okay.

Scott's hand cupped her cheek and he looked directly into her eyes for an extended moment before he said, "Next time you see me, Jake will have his new heart."

CHAPTER SEVEN

SCOTT stood at the surgery wash basin, running a small white brush beneath his fingernails. The antibacterial soap formed froth.

He'd performed numerous heart transplants. Being well trained, he knew what to expect. Yet he hadn't been this nervous since his first surgery.

It added pressure to an already hyper-sensitive situation. Why hadn't he at least waited until Jake was out of the hospital to get to know Hannah better?

He'd tried to resist her, but it seemed like he was always there when she needed help. Touching her had become addictive. He didn't understand this unfamiliar emotion. She'd slid his world sideways.

His heart had soared when Hannah had said she trusted him. Looking in the mirror above the basin, he saw the amazed look on his face. He loved Hannah.

Scott stood shock still. Muttering an inappropriate word for a children's hospital, Scott's foot slipped off the water control, stopping the flow over his hands. How had he let this happen?

What was he going to do? He couldn't act on that emotion. He refused to. Loving someone meant making them happy, and he could never make Hannah happy.

Pain squeezed his heart. He'd never be really happy

without her. She'd become his world. But he would never tell her so.

The surgery nurse next to him cleared her throat, drawing his attention. She handed him a sterile towel.

There was no time or energy to waste dwelling on the revelation. His needed to focus on Jake getting his new heart.

Another nurse helped him into gloves before he shouldered through the door of OR Four. The coolness of the room surrounded him. He'd soon be grateful for the lower temperature. It not only kept the heat from the operating lights reasonable, but helped slow the patient's blood flow. Right now he was glad to have the cold bring his mind back to the job at hand. He knew this routine. Understood this world. He had control here.

Jake lay on the operating table with his hands held securely and under sterile drapes. Scott didn't make a habit of viewing a patient, but he couldn't help but look at Jake. The boy's soft laugh as he himself had made animal noises came to his mind. He touched one of Jake's hands briefly. Like a punch in the stomach, the realization came that he'd fallen for this little guy as well.

This surgery *must* go well.

The anesthesiologist sedating Jake sat at his head. "Mac, are you okay?"

Scott nodded. He had to get in the zone and let his training take over from his emotions. Jake's life was in his hands. "Is everyone ready?" he asked. The smell of sterilizing solution wafted through the brightly lit OR.

The phone on the wall rang.

"Heart's on its way. It looks good. It should be here in two hours. They'll call back when they're in the air," the nurse announced.

Flipping down the small but intense light stationed between surgical magnifying glasses, Scott stated, "Let's get the chest open and this young man on bypass. Scalpel."

He made an incision down the center of the chest, opening it. The heart looked exactly as he'd told Hannah it would. Large and flabby.

"Needs a new one," one of the assisting fellows remarked from across the table.

"Let's see that he gets it." Scott glanced at the clock.

The shrill ring of the phone drew his attention. The team was in the air. Forty minutes away. No time to waste.

"Let's get him on bypass," Scott stated.

Minutes later the swishing and bumping of the heart-lung machine became a constant sound in the room.

The phone rang again.

"The helicopter's on the roof. The heart's on its way down," the nurse said.

"We're ready." Scott concentrated on his patient.

Minutes later the door swung open and a two-man team entered with the new heart. One man carried a small white cooler. On top, printed in red, were the words "Live Organ."

Looking at the heart with care, Scott said, "Looks good. Time?"

"Two hours, eighteen minutes."

Great. He had leeway. He'd have time to get the heart into its new home and some to spare.

"Scalpel." With skilled precision, Scott removed Jake's damaged heart and replaced it with the donated one. "Nice fit. Sutures."

The new heart looked wonderful. Strong. Healthy. The tests indicated the match was a good one but, still, you never really knew for sure until the heart was in place if the body would accept it. The match needed to be good enough Jake wouldn't have any major problems with rejection but there were never any guarantees. Despite medical advances, heart transplants were still medical miracles.

"Coming off bypass."

The rhythmic sound of the heart-lung machine ceased as the transplant team stood around Jake, holding a unified breath.

"Releasing the clamps," the fellow said.

Blood flowed through the new heart.

It quivered.

It shifted.

With a jerk, it began to beat.

Scott always felt a sense of awe when he watched a transplanted heart begin beating on its own. It took a few seconds before the heart moved into a steady pace of thump...bump...thump...

Surgery couldn't have gone more textbook perfect. Scott felt like a weight had been lifted off his shoulders.

"Andrea, you can let Hannah...uh...Mrs. Quinn know that the heart is in and looks great. Jake is stable."

Hannah saw the smile on Andrea's face as she came through the waiting-room door. She could tell the woman had good news and Andrea's words confirmed her confidence in Scott.

"Thank God," she cried in relief, as joy bubbled up and escaped.

She hugged Andrea. "What happens now?"

"Scott will watch closely for bleeding and then close." Her tone was reserved, but she wore a smile.

"How long will that take?"

"If all goes well, about an hour." Her look turned more serious. "We still have some hurdles to get over. Jake's not out of the woods yet."

Hannah sank into a chair, her knees going weak. *Jake has a new heart.*

With an impatient clasping and unclasping of hands, Hannah stared at the waiting-room door, then glanced at the clock on the wall. An hour had passed. Where was Scott? Was something wrong? Why didn't he come?

As soon as Scott entered the waiting room, Hannah jumped up. He grinned at her. *Jake was doing well.* In her happiness, Hannah wrapped her arms around Scott's neck. He felt solid and secure, safe. Scott pulled Hannah close, lifting her off her feet.

"Oh, Scott…" she whispered into his neck. "Thank you, thank you, thank you." He lowered her, letting her feet touch the floor. Taking her hand, he led her to a chair, indicating she should sit. He sat in the chair next to hers.

"How's Jake?"

"He's doing as well as can be expected." Scott gave her hand a reassuring squeeze. "I wanted to explain what'll happen next."

Andrea rose. "I'll let you two talk."

"Thanks," Scott said. "For everything."

"No problem, Mac. I'll be back in a few minutes to walk up to the unit with Hannah."

Scott gave Andrea an appreciative smile. "I owe you one."

She smiled. "Glad to be of help." Andrea went out the door.

Hannah's attention returned to Scott. "What was that about?"

"I asked her to sit with you during surgery. I didn't want you to be alone."

She gave him a grateful smile. "I'm glad you did. It was a long night and would've been even longer sitting here by myself." She scooted closer. "Now, tell me about Jake."

After taking both her hands in his, Scott said, "Jake did well through the surgery. The new heart looks great." He absently played with her fingers as he spoke. "The heart even started on its own, which is always a good sign. He's in CICU now. You can see him after he's settled. The plan is for him to be in the unit for three days, then be moved to the cardiac step-down unit."

Hannah sighed. "I can't wait." Some of her fear and worry fell away. "I'll get to hold him again. Take care of him."

Scott stood, and pulled her up beside him.

Slipping her arms around his waist, Hannah lifted her gaze to his. "I can't thank you enough," she said pouring all the gratitude she felt into the words.

He looked deep into her eyes and returned her hug. "You're welcome. You have to remember, Jake isn't out of the woods yet. He has to come off the respirator and be moved to the step-down unit before he's well enough to go home. There's rejection to be concerned about and med adjustments to be made."

Hannah refused to let her happiness be dampened. "I understand, but getting the heart was a giant step. He'll make it through the rest. I just know he'll be all right."

"That's what we're working towards." Scott followed the line of her cheek with the tip of his index finger. "I love your spirit."

At the insistent buzzing of Scott's pager Hannah moved away but remained in his arms. She was close enough to read 911 Quinn on the pager screen.

At Scott's look of alarm, her stomach dropped, and rolled. She clutched his arm. "Something's happen to Jake."

Scott pushed her away and set her in a chair. "I have to go."

Andrea returned as he rushed out the door. "Take care of Hannah," he called over his shoulder.

Scott ran along the hallway, took the stairs two steps at a time, ran down another corridor and shoved through the unit doors.

Oh, God. This can't be happening. Not to Jake.

His bed was already surrounded by staff working at a fast but efficient speed.

Frantic, Scott made his way into the thick of things. His heart had almost stopped when he'd read the page. What was going on?

He felt small beads of moisture popped out across his forehead as he pulled on plastic gloves.

"Report," he snapped.

"BP 80 over 20. Unresponsive," a female voice stated.

Keep your cool. Think, man, think.

"Push meds."

He jerked off his stethoscope from around his neck, placed it on Jake's chest, and listened.

The beats sounded strong but slow.

"Epi—"

"BP rising," someone called from behind him.

"Eighty over fifty. Ninety-three over sixty-five and rising."

Rolling his shoulders, Scott released the tension knotted there, hard as a baseball. He turned to Jake's nurse. "Give another dose of Prograf. Check level in one hour. Blood gases every fifteen minutes till the hour and then every thirty minutes if stable. BP?"

"Low but steady."

"Okay, we're going to let him rest. Let his body adjust to the new heart. Stop any possibility of rejection. Watch him carefully. Page me if I'm needed."

Scott's hands shook. He'd almost lost control. Now he had to tell Hannah that Jake still wasn't out of danger.

Andrea placed a hand on his arm and said in a low voice, "Hannah's in the hallway. She's almost hysterical."

Scott took a deep breath and let it out slowly. He must get his rattled nerves under control before he saw Hannah. He pushed through the unit doors.

Hannah leaned against the wall, her face drained of color. She looked like she'd slide down the wall any second. When he opened his arms she stepped into them. A tremble went through her as she clung to him. He tightened his embrace.

"Scott, what's happening?"

He ran a hand down her hair, smoothing it, allowing himself time to form the words he resisted saying.

"Jake is in rejection."

"Oh, my God, no."

Her tears dampened his shirt where her face was pressed to his chest.

"We've seen this before. But it'll be touch and go for a while. We may even have to relist him if the rejection can't be controlled. He'll have to be watched closely through the rest of the night. All we can do now is to wait and see if Jake's body will accept the heart."

Hannah pulled away and looked up at him. Terror, desolation and weariness filled her eyes. "Can I see him?"

"Yes, but only briefly."

Hannah noticed Scott's usual reassurance and confidence was missing. He wasn't telling her everything would be all right. A sick feeling hit her again. Scott was worried.

It was difficult to believe Jake had gotten his new heart and now it might kill him. She wanted to curl into a ball and hide, but she wouldn't. She had to remain strong, see Jake over this hurdle.

With effort Hannah prepared for what Jake would look like. She'd been warned he'd be swollen from being on the heart-lung machine. Tubes, a lot more than before, would be inserted into his body. It hurt to think of her small boy having to endure pain.

After washing her hands, she shakingly pulled on a gown and gloves. One of the nurses helped her with a mask. She found Jake behind glass doors, which were closed to form an isolation room.

The steady whoosh and puff of the respirator was ever-present. He was surrounded by beeping pumps and three of the staff. Hannah tuned all of it out. Taking slow, steady steps, she approached the bed. The light touch of Scott's hand at her back steadied her. He was her rock in the face of this ugly reality. She was thankful to have him there.

Jake wasn't as puffy as she'd feared. That was one positive. "He looks so pink," Hannah whispered. She hadn't seen such a healthy color on Jake's cheeks in a long time. The difference was remarkable. The dusky blue around his lips had disappeared. He looked beautiful. If only his body would embrace this heart.

The incision site made her flinch. Taking his small limp hand in her gloved one, she'd make do with meager contact until she could hold him.

Hannah looked at Scott and whispered, "This heart has to work." She refused to believe otherwise.

Scott's hand flexed against her back.

To Jake she whispered, "I love you, honey." She watched for any indication he'd heard her. "Hang in there."

"Tomorrow we'll know more," Scott said from behind her. "We'll let him rest, give him a chance to adjust to the heart. If he improves we can start weaning him off the respirator. But the next twelve to twenty-four hours are crucial. You'll want to stay close."

Hannah slumped against him as tears ran down her cheeks.

Apparently Scott no longer cared what the staff thought or what the grapevine would say in the morning. His arm supported her as they walked out of the CICU.

Hannah had asked Scott a couple of times during the wee hours of the morning if she could come into the unit. He allowed it once but the next time he had to say no. Jake's blood pressure had plummeted again. Scott feared they were losing him, but Jake came through the episode and started doing much better. It looked like the adjustment period was over.

He'd wanted to sit with Hannah and give her some much-needed support but Jake required his attention. He couldn't remember a time when he'd felt so torn. Scott managed to go to the waiting area and check on Hannah around six in the morning. The lights were still off, and he found her staring into space in the dark room. The TV was in snow mode.

He flipped the switch, doing away with the electric storm, and gathered her to him. She laid her head on his chest and a soft sigh slipped through her lips. They said nothing for a long time. He struggled with having to leave her all alone when it was time to return to the unit.

At midmorning Scott returned to the waiting room to find Hannah asleep sitting up. His heart went out to her. It was pouring with rain outside, and despite the weak light Scott could see the exhaustion on her face. The weariness had to be both emotional and physical. A person could only take so much, and she'd had more than her share.

Scott hated to wake her but she needed to be in a bed. Outside the hospital rest area. He gave her a gentle shake.

Hannah's head jerked up. "What?" A wild look filled her eyes. She rose quickly. "Is Jake okay?"

"He's fine, honey. Doing much better, actually. I thought you'd like to go back for a visit."

She blinked once, twice. Her hair was mussed and she looked adorable. He wanted to gather her into his arms, take her home and tuck her into his bed.

Unable to act on the impulse, he settled for taking her hand and walking beside her down the hall. "Jake needs to rest and stay quiet the rest of the day. If he's still improving by this evening, we'll start weaning him from the respirator."

After gowning up to visit, Scott followed Hannah to Jake's bed. "I've ordered he remain sedated to prevent pain and to let him rest. That'll put him in the best shape for when the respirator is removed. I've left orders for the meds to be decreased later this evening allowing him to wake up a little."

"Is he out of the woods?"

"I believe so, but I'll know more when I see him this evening."

"Thank God." Hannah leaned over, picked up Jake's unresponsive hand and brought it to her cheek.

Scott's chest constricted to see the love Hannah expressed. What did it feel like to be on the receiving end of that kind of devotion? His heart ached with longing for something that could never be. He needed to leave before he said something that might end up hurting her. "I need to check on another patient. I'll be a minute."

He went to the nursing station and glanced at his notes, not really seeing them. Inhaling deeply, he let the breath out slowly. His hands trembled slightly. Hannah and Jake made him wish he was a different kind of person.

The nurse seated beside him gave him a curious look. He managed a smile, hoping it looked more normal than his rattled nerves indicated. Taking another deep breath, he returned to Hannah. "It's time to go. You can come back later."

Her green eyes fixed on his. "May I kiss him?"

Scott couldn't say no. "Sure. Just be careful."

On her toes as far as she could stretch, Hannah leaned over the rail. The bed had been adjusted to a higher than normal position. She couldn't quite reach Jake's head.

Without hesitation, Scott circled her waist with his hands and lifted her. Hannah's lips touched Jake's forehead. Holding her a second longer, he lowered her. She glanced back at him, her eyes full of gratitude. His chest swelled.

A hand still at her waist, he said, "Let's go. You need to rest too. You're almost dead on your feet." He lowered his voice. "You're coming home with me."

She gave him a defiant look and said in a low whisper, "No, I'm staying here."

He grinned. She hadn't disappointed him. Even worn out, she could put up a fight. "No, you're not, and that's the way it's going to be." His tone left no doubt he meant it. "Think about it. If anything were to happen to Jake I'm the first person who'd be called, which means you'd know right away." With complete confidence he knew his statement would put a stop to any argument she might make.

They made their way to the parking deck in silence. As the elevator doors closed, he slipped an arm around her waist and gathered her close, tucking her against him. She accepted his support. He liked having Hannah next to him. She fit.

As they exited the elevator and walked to the car, Hannah made no effort to leave his embrace. He helped her into his car, and she rested her head against the seat. Exhaling a sigh of exhaustion, she closed her eyes and immediately fell asleep. Scott adjusted her head so it rested on his shoulder.

Scott and Hannah stood in his living room, watching each other. Indecision hung in the air as if they were two magnets pulled together while at the same time being pushed apart. His gaze lingered on Hannah's brown hair then traveled over the curve of her cheek, paused at her breasts before following the length of her jeans-covered legs.

He wanted her in his bed, but she'd get no rest there. It wouldn't be fair to her. A physical relationship would imply there could be something more between them. That wasn't going to happen. He would leave her. He had to.

His eyes returned to hers. Those expressive green orbs had gone wide. The tell-tale rapid pulse in her neck caught his attention. Hannah recognized his desire. He had to send her to her bed before he tumbled her into his. "Get some sleep, Hannah."

She said nothing, turned and walked down the hall.

Scott decided he needed a shower. An ice-cold one.

Needing rest after a long night, he'd installed the one thing that could keep him awake right next door to his bedroom. What had he been thinking?

On the way to his room, Scott hesitated at her closed door. He brought his fist up to knock, but dropped his hand to his side. It would be disastrous if she opened the door. He would lose control. His body ached to have her. All the tension, emotion and adrenalin of the last twenty-four hours would find release. With a force of will he hadn't known he possessed, Scott moved on down the hall. The firm click of the door closing behind him echoed in his too-empty bedroom.

Scott was stepping out of the bathroom a few minutes later when the door to his room opened. Hannah stood partially in the entrance, as if she wasn't sure she'd be welcome. She wore the same T-shirt she'd had on the other night. One sleek leg came into view. He wanted more.

His heartbeat rose, along with another part of his anatomy. He was grateful for the boxers he'd pulled on.

She didn't move. He waited. The next step had to be hers.

"I…uh…I don't want to be by myself." She made a movement towards him.

"Hannah, I can't just hold you."

"I know." The words were said so softly he almost didn't hear them. "I want to forget all the ugliness. To start living life again. To feel. I want you to make the loneliness go away for a little while." Scott enveloped her in a hug. Hannah wrapped her arms around his trim waist and pulled his warmth and strength closer. She wanted to burrow into him, to push the loneliness away. A ripple of awareness went through her, and she released a soft moan of pleasure. It felt wonderful, even right, to be in Scott's bedroom.

His look intensified. Drawing her snugly against the breadth of his chest, his lips came down on hers in a crushing kiss. Those same lips had brought her pleasure on many levels, smiling at her, reassuring her, making her laugh. A ripple of excitement raced through her body. She'd found her protective harbor.

Scott eased his hold, but his body remained tense, as if he was restraining his desire with effort. His kisses became a succession of gentle nibbles against her mouth. She leaned into him, asking for more, demanding it. Her hands slid up his arms to circle his neck, offering herself to him completely.

The sound of a man released from his pain surfaced from deep within Scott. He became the aggressor again. Giving her a couple of long caressing kisses, he then probed her mouth with a gentle flick of his tongue. She opened to him, surrendering. His tongue explored her mouth, conquering.

He lifted her, his hands cupping her behind. She tightened her arms about his neck.

A sound trickled out of her, a cross between a mewl and a hum.

She trusted him. Scott would take care of her.

Scott groaned in delight at the discovery Hannah wasn't wearing panties. He feared his need might pour over the dam wall of his control. Hannah had surprises. Sweet surprises.

His finger traced the place where a band of lace should've been circling her thigh, before his hand traveled over the curve of her hip. Hannah pulled away and searched his face for a suspended moment before bringing her mouth to his again. Her kiss became damp, dense and daring as she caressed his lips with her own, as her tongue searched and found his.

She fed his raging need. He surrendered with a growl of unadulterated male desire.

Hannah giggled. She had to know exactly what kind of effect she was having on him.

His mouth feasted upon hers. Their tongues dueled. The hot, forceful motion of her tongue tasting and exploring his mouth tantalized him, testing his control. His manhood stood ridged between them. He would have Hannah, and there was no going back.

"Hannah..." Scott drawled in a strangled voice when

she dragged her mouth from his. "You're so hot." He reached for her again, pulling her along the evidence of what she did to him. In a raspy whisper he said, "You do the sweetest things to me."

"You're kind of wonderful yourself." Her look was shy, sending a completely different message from the suggestive shift she made against him.

Her bashfulness ebbed and flowed. It was one of many facets of her personality Scott found intriguing. A lioness when fighting for her son, yet in a heated moment of passion she could still act and look like a lady. Someone he wanted to care for, protect. Scott found the combination of strength and timidity intriguing.

He studied her earnestly.

"What's wrong? Am I hurting you?" she asked, stirring as if she'd leave his arms.

He held her in place with a firm clasp of his hands under her amazing behind. Oh, yeah, she was hurting him, but in a good way. "Stay. I like you here. I want to look at you."

Hannah lowered her eyes then brought her gaze back to meet his.

"I want you in my bed." His words were little more than a husky sigh.

Her cool lips touched the fevered skin of his chest in acceptance, before moving her attention to his lips.

With her secure in his arms, Scott walked her backwards to the bed. Her lips remained tightly pressed against his as she followed his lead. Half seated, half lying, he brought her down with him. She shifted, gaining a more intimate position against him, pushing his ache higher. Searching her eyes, Scott found trust and openness and wanting there.

He needed to have her crave him as much as he did her. Something he'd never experienced before.

Scott found he was experiencing numerous firsts where she was concerned.

Hannah broke the heated kiss and smiled down at Scott. His lips curved into one of the sexy grins she loved so much. “Hannah…” The word drifted across her cheek like a sea breeze. Blood zipped through her veins. With a tender slip of his hand along her neck he guided her mouth down to meet his. She saw the reverence in his eyes before her lids lowered. The pure, perfect pleasure of his mouth against hers again made her heart soar.

His index finger crawled cross her thigh to the edge of her shirt, and slipped under. His hand gained her complete attention as it slid further up over her hip and across her back to settle at the curve of her breast. His fingertips danced away, leaving behind a straining ache to be touched.

She shuddered. The hunger throbbed low in her belly as primal as a native drum. Her hips lifted towards him, then pulled away and lifted again, before he brought her on top of him. The hard length of his desire pulsated against her belly. Their tongues touched, darted away, and came together to meet again.

Hannah’s fingers wandered across his chest. Warm and solid, her hand hovered over the fine mat of hair there. Scott shifted beneath her as she continued her exploration. His heartbeat thumped steady and strong under her palm. Ignoring his murmur of protest, she lifted her mouth from his and placed a kiss above his heart.

His chest stilled, his breathing faltered.

With a rumble of pure manly pleasure coming from deep within him, Scott flipped her. He pushed the shirt she wore up and off, exposing her breasts.

He placed a tender, reverent kiss on the soft curve of one of the exposed mounds before his mouth moved to hover over the tip of the other breast. Hannah inhaled and her nipple brushed his partially open mouth.

With the tip of his tongue, Scott flicked the nipple straining to reach him. A shiver moved through her. Her eyes widened. Was the hunger she felt reflected in them?

"Please," Hannah begged, as she pushed at his boxers.

Scott stood, letting his underwear fall to the floor. He reached into his bedside-table drawer, found what he needed and sheathed himself. He rejoined her, taking her mouth in a long and lingering kiss. Moving between her legs, he entered her slowly. Reverently.

Hannah welcomed him into her heat, basking in it. Wrapping her legs around him, she pulled him to her. She joined him in the special dance of life as they found a rhythm that was theirs alone.

She tensed, gripped his shoulders and voiced her pleasure before a rumble of satisfaction began deep in his throat and built like thunder rolling into the night to boom as he joined her in paradise.

A feeling of power swept over Hannah as she lay cradled in Scott's arms. She'd made the always-in-control doctor lose it. The knowledge fueled her desire.

She'd never been the aggressor in lovemaking but with Scott it had been different. It amazed her. The freedom he allowed her to be herself endeared him to her even more. The curtain surrounding her heart and concealing her feelings fluttered open after years of stillness.

She was in love. Mountain high, valley low and river wide, in love.

Scott pushed her hair away from her forehead and kissed her.

"That was wonderful," Hannah said against his chest.

"The kiss or...?"

"Fishing for a compliment?"

"No, actions speak louder than words."

Hannah nipped his skin with her teeth.

"Watch it. That might lead to retaliation."

She giggled. "I wouldn't mind."

His hand skimmed over her hip. "I wouldn't either."

Neither said anything for a few minutes.

Was this the time and the place to ask? She had to know. She'd wondered for years. If she asked it might ruin everything but if she didn't she might never know. She needed to understand why.

Hannah brushed her hand back and forth over the mat of hair on his chest. "Scott, can I ask you something?"

"Sure." The word came out slowly, as if he was drifting off to sleep.

"Why?" With her cheek resting against his warm skin, she felt the catch in his breathing.

"Why what?" His voice no longer sounded drowsy.

"Why wouldn't you talk to me after that night?"

He stilled. His hand no longer caressed her side. "Because it couldn't go anywhere," he said quietly. "I would've only hurt you more. It should never have happened."

Hannah twisted around so she could look at him. "You think I didn't know that? I'd watched you with all the other nurses. But I did think our friendship deserved more credit than you gave it."

He didn't say anything for a long moment. "You're right. You were a stronger person than I gave you credit for being."

"Self-esteem get in the way, did it?" The question had a bitterness to it she'd not intended.

"I'll admit I was a little more than confident about my success with women, as you know."

She smiled. "A little?"

"Well, if it's any consolation I'm not as confident as I used to be." He shifted, moving away from her slightly. "As for the way I acted, for the first time in my life I found something I wanted as badly as I wanted to be a surgeon—you. I had no idea you were a virgin. I couldn't believe you chose to give that gift to me. I knew you were the type of woman who needed a forever kind of guy. I wasn't prepared to be the guy. The truth is you scared me."

She swallowed hard. There was nothing to lose by asking, "And now? Do I scare you?"

"No, now I'm scared *for* you."

"Why?" she asked softly, fear prickling her heart. Something told her she wouldn't like his answer.

"Do you remember me telling you my father is a doctor?"

She nodded.

"He's a wonderful guy, and a great doctor who loves people. He still makes house calls. But my father has a problem. He can't say no. It made my mother miserable and in turn it made him miserable. When I decided to go to medical school my mother cried. Not with joy but in disappointment. She said I'd be just like my dad. Married to my job."

Hannah wanted to yell that Scott was different. He already proved it in so many ways. Their relationship had nothing to do with his parents' marriage. Scott needed to give them a chance. There must be another reason he wouldn't let her get close.

"That's not all there is to it, is it? Because all kinds of people have high-pressure careers and solid relationships."

"No, that isn't all. My parents divorced during my surgical fellowship. If anything, Mother got worse. She became more demanding, more in need of attention, but now it was from me and my brothers. Mother called us all the time, wanting this or that. During one period the calls numbered as many as ten or fifteen a day. My brothers have families so I tried to run interference and asked Mom to come and visit me for a few weeks. While she was staying with me she had an emotional breakdown and took an overdose of pills."

"Oh, Scott. I'm so sorry." She squeezed his hand. "Is she all right?" she asked quietly.

"She's fine now. Doing well. For the first time in a long time I really think she is starting to be happy."

He continued, as if he needed to talk.

"I had no idea she'd become so depressed. I should've known but I was so involved in my work I couldn't see it." He looked down at their clasped hands. "She called me, and I didn't go, didn't even answer her call. She'd gotten to where she was calling me almost hourly, day in, day out. Sometimes I answered, other times I didn't. I didn't want to encourage her.

"That day was no different. It had been a crazy day, with one patient going into cardiac arrest, two more being admitted. My voice mail was full of messages begging me to come home, but I still had afternoon rounds to make.

"I arrived home to find her passed out on her bed in her best dress with a pill bottle in her hand."

"And you've been blaming yourself ever since."

"Yeah." The word was said so softly she almost didn't hear it.

She cupped his face. "It wasn't your fault."

"It's easy to say, but I don't think I'll ever really believe it. The overdose was bad enough but Mom said she wanted nothing more to do with me."

"That can't be true!"

"Well, it was at the time. Now we do have some semblance of a relationship but we're just going through the motions. Both of us are dancing around the elephant in the room when we see each other."

"Have you sat down and really had a heart to heart with your mom?"

"No, I just want to forget and move on."

"I don't think you ever will until you two kick the elephant out the door."

He squeezed her to him. "You might be right." He hesitated. "It also hit home that horrible day that I was no different from my father. I knew then I had no business having a wife and family. I'm incapable of setting boundaries for myself. I'm too wrapped up in my work. My job will always come first."

Hannah wrapped her arms around him and gave him a hug. She said nothing for a long moment. She couldn't let him know how she felt. He was already starting to run. She was done being the goodbye girl. Maybe with more time she could convince him he was wrong about himself, that his mother had been speaking out of her own pain. For now she had to tell him what he needed to hear. "I don't expect any more than your friendship."

The tension in Scott's body eased.

CHAPTER EIGHT

NO LIGHT beamed through the bedroom window when Hannah woke up.

Jake. How's Jake?

She reached for her cell phone on the bedside table. The space beside her was still warm. Scott hadn't been gone long.

Battery dead.

Flinging the spread off, she looked for a phone. Finding none, she pulled on the first thing she saw. It was one of Scott's T-shirts. Her bare feet made a padding noise as she went to the door and pulled it open. A gurgle came from down the hall. Coffee-pot. Kitchen. There'd be a phone there. Her throat tightened as she hurried toward the sound. Panic welled. She had to check on Jake.

She stopped short at the sight of Scott at the kitchen table. He held a newspaper, a cup of coffee within his reach.

He glanced at her. "Evening," he drawled.

"I've got to call the hospital." She frantically searched the kitchen for a phone.

"Settle down. Jake's fine. I checked in. They're already starting to wean him from the respirator."

The calmness in his voice annoyed her, but her heart slowed its pace. "Really?"

"Yes. Really." He gave her a lazy smile.

Relief washed over her.

"I'm his doctor, remember?" Scott grabbed her arm and pulled her into his lap. His lips found hers. They'd slept and loved the afternoon away without Scott's beeper sounding an alarm. Even after the time they'd shared in bed, Hannah still hungered for him. He'd left her in bed again but based on his actions earlier in the day and again later in the afternoon she knew he wouldn't go far. Scott had been a wonderfully attentive lover.

She couldn't resist returning his kiss but she had to put a stop to this before she went past the point of no return. The truth was, though, that had already happened.

She pushed away and stood, moving out of his reach. "Uh, about last night, I mean today, I—"

"You needed someone and I was there. Being a friend. How about a cup of coffee or tea before we go to the hospital? Would you like something to eat now or wait until we get back?"

Scott certainly wasn't placing any importance on what had occurred between them. His calm demeanor almost made her smack him. Those had been the most amazing moments of her life and Scott was treating them as if they had been no big deal. If he could act cool about their lovemaking then so could she.

Resting back in his chair, with a slight grin on his lips, he acted as if it was a normal everyday occurrence to have her in his home. Despite the lack of sleep during the night and today, he appeared well rested. He'd already dressed. His royal blue polo shirt and khaki pants made him look like he was ready for a round of golf.

Heavens, she was wearing one of his thin white shirts. Her eyes dropped to what she wore. His shirt barely reached the top of her thighs. Heat rushed up her neck and settled in her cheeks. She crossed her arms over her breasts. Scott had seen much more, touched every inch of her, but she wasn't used to parading around half-dressed in front of a man.

"Why didn't you say something?" she squeaked. "I'm going to get dressed."

He raised an eyebrow and made a low chuckle. "Are you kidding? I was enjoying the sight of you in my T-shirt, in my kitchen."

She whirled to leave.

Scott pushed back his chair, stood and caught her arm. "I'll get you something to cover up with. Fix yourself a cup of tea. Settle for a minute." He left.

Going to the pot, Hannah found a teabag and poured water into a cup. After the stress of the last couple of days, and especially yesterday, on many levels, she needed to soothe her nerves. She was still standing by the counter when Scott returned.

He handed her a robe. Scrambling into it, she found it fell below her knees, giving her some sense of security. She pulled the belt tight. The tangy smell of Scott permeated the robe.

"Better?" he asked.

"Much, thanks."

Scott returned to his seat and picked up his coffee mug, still grinning. It was clear he was enjoying her discomfort.

Pushing against the leg of a chair, he scooted it out. "Come and sit next to me."

Hannah approached the chair with trepidation. The whole scene smacked too much of marital bliss. It made her wish for things Scott had said could never be.

She sank into the chair. "Why're we taking our time getting to the hospital? Don't you need to check on Jake? I need to see him."

"You didn't get much uninterrupted rest. I was giving you as much time as possible to sleep. Instead of doing that, you came storming through the door." His lips turned up at the corners.

Hannah flushed all over. Yes, he had kept her busy as if he'd held himself in check for all the years they'd been apart. "Please don't make fun of me. My first thought was of Jake. He's all I've got."

Scott's face sobered and the skin along his jaw tightened. He acted as if he was going to say something, before his face eased and he returned to his easygoing manner. "When you finish your tea, we'll go."

"I need to get a quick shower."

His eyes turned dark and his voice dipped low. "Would you like some company?"

Heat coiled within her. For a second Hannah was tempted to say yes. "No, I think I can manage by myself." She hurried out of the room, fearing she might change her mind.

Scott groaned.

How much could a healthy male take? Waking with Hannah's warm body nestled close and having her come into his kitchen with the scent of him lingering on her was one of the most erotic things he'd ever experienced. He longed for it all. Hannah, the job, a family. Could he have that ideal life?

She'd said Jake was all she had. He'd wanted to argue the point. Tell her she had him too. But could he honestly make that promise? Pulling out his cell phone, Scott checked on Jake and another patient in the hope Hannah would be dressed by the time he'd finished. He needed to get his mind on something else. If he didn't find a way to keep busy, he might do something stupid, like stepping into the shower with her. Or telling Hannah he loved her.

Would she welcome him with open arms?

Scott groaned. There were other problems. Jake's recovery concerned him more than he'd let on to Hannah. There was always a chance Jake could have difficulty getting off the respirator because he had been on it before going into surgery. Scott hoped and prayed removal went smoothly for everyone's sake.

"Ready?" Hannah had entered the living room without him noticing. A quizzical look crossed her face. "You're deep in thought."

There was a fresh, wholesome smell to her. Perfect. She wore a simple light green shirt and a short blue denim skirt that showed off her incredible legs. Scott resisted the urge to pull her to him and kiss her past all reason. If he did that, they'd never make it to the hospital any time soon.

She stepped closer. "Everything okay with Jake?"

Her question brought him back to reality. He had to leave. He'd never run away from a woman before, but he felt the need to put some space between himself and Hannah. "How about we see for ourselves?"

Scott pulled into the hospital parking lot a few minutes after seven. Hannah had to wait until after shift change before she could see Jake. Scott regretted he couldn't let her come back with him, but shift change was the one time of day the nurses' word was law.

When most of the patients' reports had been given, Scott asked Jake's nurse to call the waiting room and tell Hannah she could come through.

His lips curved upward as he watched Hannah hurry to Jake's bed. Her smile made him feel like the greatest man on earth. A superhero. His skill as a surgeon had helped to put a joyful look on her face. With that knowledge came immense satisfaction.

Scott moved to stand beside her. "Jake's making great progress so far. We'll be going down five breaths at a time over the next few hours and then try to remove the tube first thing in the morning.

"Nurse, I want a blood gas drawn every fifteen minutes. Cut back on the dopamine and Captopril." He made a notation on Jake's chart.

"He looks better than he did yesterday. Even his incision area doesn't look as awful." Hannah ran a caressing finger along Jake's arm.

Hannah showed her caring through touch. Scott especially enjoyed it when he was on the receiving end of emotion. The stroke of her hand had a way of making him feel as if he was the best man in the world for her. It was already killing him to think about having to let her go.

"During the night we will work toward removing the respirator. The longer we wait the harder it is to remove. Because Jake was on the respirator before surgery it's even more important he comes off it soon," Scott said. "You'll be surprised at how fast things will improve afterwards. We'll continue to keeping a close watch on him."

"Jake certainly doesn't need any additional problems."

"I don't want him to have any more problems either. He's a special little guy. I'm doing everything I know to see it doesn't happen. I think he's past the worst." Scott gave her shoulder a quick squeeze. Something as simple as giving Hannah a reassuring touch sent heat hissing through him.

She continued to look at her amazing little miracle.

"Do you think you could eat now?" Scott asked.

"Yeah. I'm starving, but I hate to leave him."

"His nurse knows we're but a phone call away. Hunger's a good sign your nerves are settling down."

His certainly weren't. A different kind of hunger gnawed at him.

After picking up a drive-through meal, they returned to Scott's place. With their dinner completed, Scott gave Hannah one of his piercing looks that said in no uncertain terms he wanted her. He scooped her up and carried her to his bed. This time their lovemaking was slow and sweet. Afterwards Hannah curled into him and settled into a peaceful, deep sleep, enhanced by dreams of what could be.

The next morning Scott left her with a swift, but fervent kiss before they parted in the stairway. With Jake improving and a kiss from Scott on her lips, Hannah's heart felt lighter than it had in years.

She'd barely been in CICU a few minutes when Jake's nurse asked her to leave. It was time for the respiratory therapist to remove the respirator.

Hannah sat, paced and sat again. Would Jake be able to come off? Would he stay off? What if he had to be put back on?

Stop.

She had to quit thinking. Thinking led to an all-consuming fear. Despite her efforts not to look at the clock, she watched each slow minute pass. With any luck this would be the last time she'd have to endure this type of wait.

The desk phone rang. Hannah stared at the pink-coated volunteer who answered it. She looked at Hannah. "The nurse says you can come back now."

The tube was gone from Jake's mouth. He lay at a slight angle, propped on pillows with an oxygen canula under his nose. A weak smile came to his lips as Hannah approached. Her heart swelled. It felt like years since she'd seen his lips curl upwards.

"Hello, honey." She beamed to the point that her cheeks ached. The bed had been lowered and she leaned across Jake, placing her cheek against his.

The nurse still had his hands secured. Hannah put her index finger in his palm and he wrapped his fingers around hers. His breathing remained labored, but not enough for her to be too concerned. He was breathing on his own. That was what mattered. Catching the corner of her shirt, she wiped the moisture away from her eyes. "I love you."

"M-o-m-m-y." He mouthed the word but she heard no sound.

"Do you have anything to put on his lips? They're so dry and cracked," Hannah asked.

The nurse handed her lip balm. Hannah applied it, welcoming the opportunity to have even such a small part in his care.

Jake's eyes focused on Hannah for a second before his eyelids drooped. The sparkle of his childhood had yet to return but it would soon. She said a prayer of thanks for Scott's surgical skills and for the family who had given her child life again. The knowledge of what the family of the donor was suffering troubled Hannah, but she was grateful for the gift of Jake's life. She would make sure their gift was honored by taking excellent care of Jake.

The nurse allowed Hannah to remain at his bedside most of the day. The time passed in a blur of activity, which was a relief from the mind-numbing worry and boredom of the past few days. Hannah hadn't seen Scott since earlier that morning, but knew he had to be in surgery. She missed him. He'd come to see them when he could, she had no doubt.

By the middle of the afternoon only one nurse was required for Jake's care. The central line had been removed, along with the catheter. The machines monitoring vitals, two chest tubes and a pacemaker were all that remained.

Scott finally made it by to see them in the early evening. The nurse smiled knowingly at Hannah and Scott then left them alone.

"Doesn't he look wonderful?" Hannah asked, unable to contain her happiness.

"He does." Scott's smile reached his eyes. "He's doing great. If tomorrow goes as well as today, he'll be going to the floor."

"Wonderful. I can stay with him all the time then."

"I'll miss having you next to me when that happens, but it's nice to see you happy." Scott's look turned solemn. "I wanted us to have dinner tonight, but I've got emergency surgery. Please don't stay too late. I don't like you being in the parking deck by yourself." His finger traced the line of her jaw. "Go to my house. Get some rest," he whispered, and slipped her keys.

Her heart contracted. She felt cherished, as if she had someone to stand beside her. It was wonderful to no longer be alone. Not having experienced those feelings for a long time, she wrapped the sensation around her and basked in its warmth. "I won't. I'll go after I see Jake, I promise."

Scott nodded, his gaze never leaving hers.

Hannah glanced around, then lowered her voice. "I appreciate you taking care of both my son and me. You've been a great friend. I'm glad you were here when we needed you." She gave him a bright smile.

"My pleasure."

In response to his husky tone, a sizzle of delight zipped through her.

In the same sensual timbre, he said, "I wish I could kiss you..." he glanced around "...but..."

She reached for his hand, catching his little finger for a moment then releasing it. "I do too."

He looked into her eyes for an extended moment filled with wishing, regret, and a promise before he left. The warmth that had surrounded her went with him. Hannah understood why he hadn't kissed her but that didn't keep her from being disappointed.

Much later Scott slipped into bed beside her. She scooted next to him. The contentment she'd been missing had returned, engulfing her.

"Shh...go back to sleep," Scott said softly in her ear as his arms drew her back against him.

"Jake?"

"He's fine, honey. Sleeping when I left."

She glanced at the clock. One a.m.

"Are you okay?" The blood hummed through her veins, being so close to him. The roughness of his beard brushed across her cheek.

"Yeah, tired. Sorry to wake you."

"A doctor's life isn't always their own. Coming home at all hours is part of my life. I understand."

"A lot of women wouldn't see it that way."

"Well, I'm not just any woman. I know firsthand what you do is important." His arms tightened around her for a second then eased. Goose-bumps popped up along her arms.

He placed a quick kiss behind her ear. "Thank you."

The words were thick with emotion, as if she'd given him a precious gift.

"Okay, we're off." Hannah made a buzzing noise like an airplane as she circled the white plastic spoon in a flying motion toward Jake's mouth.

He giggled. Like a baby bird waiting for a worm, he

opened his mouth. Hannah dipped the spoon into his mouth. Scott stood at the door, watching mother and child totally absorbed in each other. His chest swelled with pride. This was his reward for the years of medical school and lost sleep of his intern years. If only he could keep Hannah as happy for the rest of her life. He shook his head. He had no business contemplating such things. They were never to be.

Scott winced at the memories of his family meals. There had been a few nice ones early in his life, but as his parents' marriage had disintegrated during his teenage years, few if any had been peaceful. It was hard to remember the warmth that he felt in this small hospital room at any meal.

Hannah might understand now what his job entailed, but after a while his dedication to his profession would grow stale, start to divide them. He didn't want what had happened between his parents to happen to him and Hannah. That would be a pain he couldn't bear.

He ached to be on the inside of the love he was witnessing, instead of standing on the outskirts. Could he manage having a family and a growing transplant program at the same time?

What if he set boundaries? Learned to say no? Accepted help? Could he make his professional life different than his father's?

No. He wouldn't take the chance. He loved Hannah and Jake enough to protect them from him.

Scott left without disturbing them.

By the end of the day most of the tubes and lines attached to Jake had been removed. The two large chest tubes used to drain fluid and the pacemaker wires were all that remained. They would be taken out after he went to the floor.

Hannah disliked Jake's hands having to remain tied.

She *ached* to hold him. She'd have to settle for small hugs for a while longer. They weren't as satisfying as having him sit in her lap, secure against her chest, but that would come.

She'd thought Scott would've been by to see them before now. At least visit between surgeries.

Life would be busy during the next year. There would be little time to devote to a relationship, even if Scott wanted one—and he gave no indication of wanting that. She wasn't fooling herself into believing he gave any thought to a future with her. She wished she could get Scott to see they could be a family if he would open his mind to the possibility of a relationship. But it was more than she could hope for.

This thing between them had simply been a convenient interlude.

She had to stop driving herself crazy with what-ifs. One question still wouldn't go away. How had she let Scott become such an important and necessary part of her life so quickly?

"They're ready for Jake on the step-down unit," his nurse said, interrupting Hannah's musings.

Jake was sitting up in the middle of his bed with a smile on his face. His nurse had already loaded his belongs onto the far end of the bed.

"Ready to go, sweetheart?" Hannah asked him.

"Go, brrmm, brrmm," he said, driving his pretend car.

It was hard to believe how quickly he was recovering. Almost hourly he gathered more strength. His personality was returning too.

Hannah laughed. "Yes, brrmm, brrmm."

With Hannah's help, the nurse maneuvered the bed down the hall and into the elevator. It felt so good to be doing something active after so many hours of waiting and worrying. They pushed Jake's bed into a wing of the hospital Hannah had never seen.

The charge nurse met them in the hall. "We're glad Jake's doing so well. We've been looking forward to meeting you."

Hannah didn't understand the comment. Why would the nurses be interested in her? Had the grapevine been talking about her and Scott?

The nurse settled Jake into his room and checked his IVs. Hannah watched as the telemetry to monitor Jake's heart rate in the nurses' station was attached. His nurse also hooked him up to a blood-pressure and a pulse-ox machine.

Hannah scrutinized everything. Being a nurse was an innate part of her. She may not be nursing at present but she'd not forgotten the safety precautions.

"You'll need to continue to wear a gown and gloves," his nurse said.

"Even when I sleep?"

"You can go without covering if you sleep on the other side of the room. And there can be no visitors outside immediate family."

"That won't be a problem. There's just me." Those words sounded sad to even Hannah's own ears.

When Jake slipped into a peaceful sleep, Hannah went down the hall to buy a canned drink. On her way back she passed a partially open door to a patient's room. The respiration and heart monitor were buzzing. No parent was staying with the child. She'd mentioned the patient to Jake's nurse earlier, saying how difficult it must be for the parents not to stay with their child. Hannah was grateful she wasn't in the same situation.

Searching the hallway, she saw no staff members headed her direction. She looked into the room. A child of about two years old was lying on his back unmoving and turning a dusky blue.

Hannah pushed the door open as a man from housekeeping came around the corner.

"Get some help. Stat!" She didn't wait to see if he did as ordered. She plopped her drink on the table on her way to the bedside. Reaching the child, she pushed the nurses' call button. No answer.

She placed her hand on the child's chest. There was no rise or fall. Quickly lowering the bed rail, Hannah rolled the boy on his side. She placed her cheek near his mouth. No breath.

The beeping of the monitor still pierced the air, but she tuned it out. This child would die if she didn't do something. Had he aspirated into his lungs? She checked the child's airway.

She had to start CPR.

Where were the nurses? Why wasn't someone coming?

The boy was turning bluer. She couldn't wait.

Covering the child's mouth with hers and holding his nose closed, she blew enough air into his lung to raise the child's chest, then began compressions to the sternum.

Minutes crawled by. Still no one came. She continued working.

Where was everyone? Couldn't they hear the monitor? People as far away as Africa should be able to hear it.

She was going to have to use the defibrillator. Hadn't the crash cart been outside the door? It was her sole chance to save this child.

The housekeeping man stuck his head in the door and said help was on the way. There'd been a code blue at the other end of the hall.

"There's a code blue here," Hannah snapped between compressions.

The man stared at her.

"Two, there is, three, a cart, four, outside, five, the door, six, get it, seven, now."

The housekeeper didn't return pushing the crash cart. Instead Scott appeared.

"Hannah, I'll handle this. You push the meds. They're in the cart." He handed her a keyring with a key held between two fingers. "We'll worry about the legalities later."

She found the meds. Double, triple checking the dosage on the code card against what was in her hand, she stepped to the other side of the bed. Pushing the needle into the portal of the IV, she said words of thanks that it had already been placed. She pressed the plunger down slowly.

"Step back," Scott commanded.

He placed the paddles of the defibrillator on the child's chest.

With the electric shock, the boy's chest rose then fell, then rose and fell again on its own.

"Get the oxygen mask on him. Two liters."

"Yes, sir." Hannah unwrapped the plastic tubing and turned on the oxygen at the head of the bed. Fitting the small plastic mask over the child's nose and mouth, she watched as Scott checked the boy's pulse. Scott pulled his stethoscope from around his neck and began listening to the boy's chest.

"We've got him back. Good work, Hannah."

A charge nurse rushed into the room, stopping short. "I just heard."

"He's stable. A CBS, panel, and gases need to be drawn. Let Dr. Carter know what happened. This is his patient. Also let the supervising nurse know I'd like to see her," Scott told the nurse in a stern voice.

He turned his attention to Hannah. "You did a fine bit of

nursing here. This boy wouldn't have lived without you." He smiled across the bed at her as he reset the monitor and continued to check the numbers. "You can have a spot on my team any time."

She glowed under Scott's praise. He was right, they *had* worked well together. "Thanks. It was pretty scary there for a few minutes."

CHAPTER NINE

HANNAH glanced at her sleeping child when Scott opened the door enough to stick his head in. He'd been stopped by a staff member when they'd passed the nurses' station on their way back to Jake's room. Smiling, he backed out, returned with a mask in his hand then came inside and closed the door behind him.

The dark shadow along his jaw gave him a roguish look, a bad-boy appeal. She liked it. Her fingers itched to skim across his cheek while her heart raced at the sight of him. Hannah met Scott halfway across the room. A slow and sensual smile covered his lips. She had no doubt his thoughts were running similar to hers. They'd not really spent any time together in the last couple of days. She'd come to depend on him, accept him as part of her life. She'd missed him.

His smoldering eyes made her afraid she might flash-burn on the spot. Reaching for her, Scott took her hand and towed her toward the door. There they wouldn't immediately be seen by anyone entering the room or through the window to the hall. With his back against the wall and his feet spread apart, he pulled her close.

"I've missed you." His words rumbled as his lips skimmed over her cheek en route to her mouth as a finger pulled her mask down over her chin.

A tingle traveled along her spine. Hannah shivered as she molded her body to Scott's and brought her mouth to his. Scott took the invitation, grazing her lips, before he dipped to explore her more completely. The kiss pushed any thoughts away except for those hot and heavy with need that begged to be fulfilled. Scott's kiss communicated the same desperation.

A bolt of longing shot through Hannah. She gripped his waist. Molten heat pooled in the lower part of her body. With a sigh Hannah met his demands with those of her own. Her hands slid over the expanse of his chest to wrap around his neck. A fire blazed in her center. By the time Scott's lips had left hers, their breaths came in small gasps.

Hannah traced the nape of his neck with her fingertips. His hand scanned her ribs, down her hip until it cupped her behind. Shifting, he fit her more snugly to him. The light, caressing kisses Scott was placing down one side of her neck made her knees buckle. Pressed against him, she didn't have to guess at his desire. It was evident. Hannah shifted her hips forward. He held her securely, a moan originating deep in his throat.

The prickle of his whiskers sent a shudder along her spine. They brushed her sensitive skin as his mouth found the hollow of her neck and he murmured, "You sure taste good."

Heat simmered then boiled in her as it flowed to her center. She wanted to hold onto this feeling for ever.

Hannah surrendered her neck and pushed closer. Scott's hand aided her movement forward. A yearning built in her like a summer electrical storm. He retraced his path with tiny nips of his teeth. His low rumble of satisfaction brought her a wave of delight. Going up on her toes, she silently asked for more.

Scott's tongue followed the shell of her ear. A tingle shot

through her like water sizzling in oil. Her fingers dug into his back in an unspoken demand for more of everything.

"Mommy..." The soft call pierced the mist of sexual need. Hannah jerked away. Once again, Scott's hands had made her forget where she was. Scott groaned at the interruption.

"Bad timing?" Hannah giggled.

"You've no idea," Scott muttered. His body had some type of radar that zeroed in on Hannah's like a heat-seeking missile. The woman didn't have to be looking at him for his body to react.

"I think I might."

It was nice to know he wasn't the only one who forgot where they were when they were together. Hannah met his gaze and her hand cupped his cheek. Scott eased his hold but didn't let go of her. "I seem to lose control around you."

"Mommy..."

"Coming, honey."

What had he been thinking? Kissing his patient's mother in the little boy's room certainly showed poor professional conduct. That was just it, he didn't think around Hannah. He gazed down at her. Hannah's eyes were wide with expectation. Her sweet lips were plump and cherry colored. She had the look of a woman who'd been thoroughly kissed, and wanted more.

Oh, yeah. He'd like to do it again.

The need for her still throbbed within him.

He gave her a quick peck on the lips, then let her go. "I need to be a heart surgeon and check on my favorite patient." Pulling the mask out of his pocket, he fit it over his mouth before he approached Jake's bed.

"Hi, there, buddy," Scott said. "Remember me? I'm Dr.

Mac." Scott pulled down his mask and gave Jake one of his Hollywood smiles before replacing the covering.

Scott picked up the disposable stereoscope hanging on the rail of the bed and listened to Jake's chest. "I need to give your new heart a listen for a sec."

"Mommy," Jake whispered. Hannah turned to pick up her mask before she stepped beside Scott.

"I'm right here. Be real still for Dr. Mac."

Jake watched his movements with interest. He was a bright little boy anyone would be glad to call his son. It wasn't a thought he should be having.

"His heart has a strong, steady beat. But I do want to pace it for a couple of days." Scott glanced at Hannah and saw the look of panic wash over her face. "Nothing's wrong. If I pace the heart it'll fall into a solid rhythm. The pacemaker gives the heart a little help so it doesn't have to work too hard."

She nodded.

"I see you still have Bear," Scott said to Jake as he touched the toy clipped to the bed. "We'll get those chest tubes out today so you can get out of bed and play some." To Hannah he said, "I'll write the orders before I go back to surgery."

"You're going back to the OR? You look like you need some rest."

"That bad, huh?" Scott chuckled. He appreciated the concern in her voice. It felt good to have Hannah fuss over him.

"I didn't say you look bad."

His grin grew. "So I look good?"

"Oh." She swatted his arm. "You know what I mean."

"I do. But I like seeing you flustered." Hannah returned his smile. Scott looked back to find Jake watching them. "I've got to go. They'll be waiting for me in surgery. Hannah?"

Her eyes lifted.

"Have dinner with me?"

"I…don't know. I need to be here with Jake."

"What if we make it a late meal? Jake will be asleep. I'll order Chinese take-out and we can eat in the garden. We wouldn't be too far away."

She didn't answer right away.

Was Hannah trying to put some distance between them? He should be doing the same thing, instead of acting like the family man he could never be. But he couldn't back away yet. "Please. You don't have to stay any longer than you feel comfortable."

"Okay, but I want sweet and sour chicken, and fried rice."

He grinned. "You've got it. I'll see you around eight."

"Don't forget the fortune cookies."

He raised his thumb in the air and said goodbye to Jake before pulling the door closed behind him.

For Hannah the rest of the day was spent caring for Jake. The interruptions continued with doctors and nurses checking in. She and Jake did take a nap, but her peaceful sleep was sabotaged by thoughts of Scott. Where did she fit into his plans? Did she fit at all? Was this relationship going anywhere? She wanted him, but did he want her? Even with all the unknowns she still looked forward to seeing him again.

The thoracic surgery fellow came in to remove Jake's chest tubes. The nurse had warned Hannah it would be painful for Jake. The fellow asked Hannah if she wished to leave the room, but she declined the offer. She was a nurse. She'd be able to handle it. Besides, the fellow wasn't someone Jake knew. He'd be scared without her.

The fellow clipped the sutures holding the chest tubes in place then pulled them out with a steady motion. Jake's body tensed, tears streamed over his cheeks. His hands pulled against the restraints securing them.

Moisture welled in Hannah's eyes and fell. Never in her life had she wanted to scream "Stop!" louder or longer. Her hands gripped the metal rail until her knuckles turned white and her fingers blue. She knew this pain was necessary, but her mother's heart howled to have it done with.

"It'll be over soon, honey," Hannah said as calmly as she could in spite of the knot lodged in her throat.

As the fellow finished he told Hannah she could remove the restrains. Whimpering, Jake reached out to her. She lifted him into her arms, holding him tight as she cooed.

Exhausted, Jake soon quieted and fell asleep. Hannah settled into the wooden rocker, enjoying the feel of his small warm body against hers. Finally, she was able to hold her baby close.

When she finally put Jake down for the night he made a noise as if awakening. She patted his bottom until he settled again. Glancing at the clock, she saw she was running late and had to rush to change into tan slacks and a red cable sweater for her date with Scott.

The phone rang.

Her heart jumped. Was Scott calling to cancel?

The floor clerk was on the line, telling her Dr. McIntyre would be there soon. He was seeing a patient in CICU. Hannah's heart settled into a steady rhythm again, but her breathing remained faster than normal.

Twenty minutes later, Scott came to the door. "Sorry I'm late. I hate you always having to wait for me."

"I don't mind."

"You really don't, do you?"

"No. I know the importance of what you do. I'm just glad to see you."

Scott dressed in jeans and a striped button-down shirt reminded Hannah of how appealingly male he was. His shirt was tucked in, which emphasized his trim waist. His sleeves were rolled up over tan forearms. No man had ever looked better.

His smile reached his eyes. "It's nice to see you too. Our food's at the front desk. We'll pick it up on the way to the garden."

Hannah started in the direction of the elevator, but Scott took her hand and directed her into a stairway.

"Where're we going?"

"Down this way." He pinned her against the wall of the stairwell and his lips found hers. Long, lustful and luscious moments later he released her. "There's way too much interest in what I do around here. And I get a kick out of sneaking around, don't you?" He winked at her.

Hannah laughed and followed him down the stairs. Scott even made dinner at the hospital an adventure. She enjoyed seeing the kid come out in him. His job was a serious one. He needed a release from the life-and-death decisions that made up his world.

At the bottom of the stairs, Scott peeked out the door and gave her a quick peck on the lips before they stepped through it. "Wait here," he said in a conspiratorial tone, before walking across the lobby. Scott spoke to a woman behind the welcome desk. She smiled and handed him two big bags. "Thanks, Helen. I owe you one."

Scott charmed young and the old. He'd gone one better with her, he'd made her fall in love with him. Hard. Could she convince him to make her and Jake a part of his life?

Looking both ways, as if he were a spy, Scott returned to her and took her hand again. Hannah snickered at his antics. His lips lifted into a sexy grin. Her breath caught. He led her to the drink machines, where they made their selections.

The garden looked lovely in the dusk of the summer day. A few late-blooming flowers gave off sweet scents. The setting sun shone brightly on one side, while the other side of the garden remained encased in shadow. They followed a curved walk around to the most secluded area. At a stone bench, Scott stopped.

"Wait before you sit." He poked through one of the bags, pulling out a camping lantern and a green and yellow plaid blanket. Flipping the blanket a couple of times, he settled it across the bench.

Hannah watched in fascination as he lit the lantern and placed it on the ground in front of the bench. Bowing like a maître d', Scott offered her a place on the bench.

Picking up the other bag, he handed her a white box from it. "Sweet and sour chicken, ma'am."

"Thank you, sir."

He dug further and came out with another container.

"What did you get?" She leaned over to peer into the container as he opened it.

"Nosy, aren't you?" he teased.

"I am. What're you having?"

"Mongolian beef."

"Ooh, that stuff's hot."

"Yes, like me," he quipped, making his brows rise and fall.

Hannah laughed. Something she did a lot when Scott was around. There had been little laughter in the last few years in her and Jake's life. It was nice to have it back, even for a short while.

"Here's your fried rice."

Hannah took it. "This is nice, thank you. I'm glad to get out of the room for a while." She picked at her chicken with her chopsticks. "I haven't been out here before. I'll have to bring Jake. No, I can't. He can't be around people for a few months."

"I wish I could tell you it was okay, but we can't take any chances he might catch something."

"I know. I'll bring him when we come for a visit. By the way, why didn't you tell me taking chest tubes out was so horrible?" She screwed up her face at the memory.

"It's rough. That's why I didn't do it myself. I don't want Jake to have that memory of me."

"Why not?"

"I want us to be friends and removing chest tubes isn't a friendly thing to do."

Her chest contracted to think it mattered to Scott whether or not Jake liked him.

As they ate, Hannah enjoyed the deep roll of Scott's voice. They discussed the movies they'd seen. She learned they both enjoyed Westerns and wished more were being made. Another thing they had in common. When they'd finished, Scott started gathering their empty containers. He pulled a couple of small packages out of another bag, like a magician performing a trick.

"Want your fortune cookie now?"

"I'd love it."

Opening his, he laughed.

"What?" she asked, leaning over until her shoulder rested against his. "Let me see." She took the small sli of paper from him. "What's so funny?" She handed it ba

"Haven't you ever heard about adding 'in bed' t end of the fortune? 'Your talents will prove to be esp useful this week…in bed.'"

A flush covered her face. She couldn't meet his eyes. "It does give it a new meaning."

"Yeah, it does." The humor in his voice had disappeared, leaving it deep and raspy. She glanced at Scott from hooded eyes. His sea-blue gaze captured hers.

Hannah saw his desire. Hot, rich, deep. It pulled at her. But that was all it was, she had to remind herself, sexual desire. She couldn't let it drag her under. He'd made no promises. She wanted, no, needed more than a meeting of their bodies. Especially from Scott.

Scott leaned toward her as if planning to kiss her, but when a mother with a child in a stroller came around the curve in the walk, he straightened. Saying nothing, Scott began gathering the rest of the remains of their meal. Hannah helped. When her hand brushed his, Scott captured it, turned it over and kissed the inside of her wrist. A tremor rolled through her. With everything packed away, he took her hand and they slowly walked back into the hospital.

Hannah didn't want the evening to end. Scott seemed to agree.

In the stairwell, before he opened the door to the floor, they shared a passionate meeting of lips that was much too short. With a final kiss to her cheek, Scott said, "I'll miss having you in my bed tonight."

Her stomach fluttered. "I'll miss being there, but you know I have to be here with Jake."

"I do and I'd expect nothing less from you. You're a wonderful mother."

"Thanks for understanding. I know what it is to be left ' I'd never do it to Jake."

'rkness filled Scott's eyes.

'dn't mean you."

A dry smile came to his lips. “I realize you could mean me.”

Hannah cupped his cheek and smiled at him. “I could, but in this case I don’t.”

At Jake’s room, Scott stopped long enough to review the med chart posted on the outside of the door. Dressed to enter, they stepped toward the sleeping child’s bed.

Careful not to disturb Jake, Scott pulled off the sheet and checked the tube sites. “They look good.”

“I’m proud of him. He’s a trouper.” Hannah tipped her head toward Scott. “Thanks for your part in saving his life.”

“You’re welcome. I’ll let you both get some rest. See you tomorrow.” He pulled her to him and gave her a tight hug because having a mask on didn’t lend itself to kissing.

Hannah was returning to Jake’s room after breakfast the next morning, and noticed the door stood ajar. Someone was talking to Jake. She recognized the rich voice. Jake giggled. Her pulse went into overdrive.

She gowned up and pushed the door open. Scott sat in the rocker with Jake in his lap. Scott had his mask pulled down to his chin, and Jake was busy feeding Scott cereal.

Hannah’s heart stopped, and lurched again. It could be a Norman Rockwell picture. Jake let out a squeal of joy every time Scott lost a piece inside his mask. *Scott would make a wonderful father. If he would only believe that.*

He pulled at her heartstrings. Was he beginning to care for Jake less as a patient and more as a son? Would he ever consider being a parent of a heart patient when he worke[illegible] with them all day? Dared she hope so?

Scott smiled up at her. “Hey. Jake woke up when I [illegible] in, and I didn’t want to leave him here by himself[illegible]

"I went down to the cafeteria for breakfast. I thought he'd sleep until I got back."

"Would you like some of ours?" Scott asked.

She noticed Scott made no effort to hand Jake to her and Jake was content to stay where he was as well. Their coloring was close enough they could be family.

Jake offered the plastic bowl of cereal to her. Some fell to the floor. Both males laughed.

"Which ones are you guys giving me? The cereal off the floor or that in the bowl?"

Jake brought the bowl to his chest in a protective manner.

"The floor must be it," Scott said, with a grin. "Jake, I think we could be nicer to your mom."

Jake shook his head.

"I can see you're feeling much better this morning," Hannah told Jake. "Maybe too good. Dr. Mac might have done too fine a job on you." Hannah smiled at Scott.

Her heart swelled with the contentment of seeing her son so happy and comfortable with Scott. Hannah couldn't believe how quickly it had happened.

Jake and Scott had bonded. It would make it even harder when Scott stepped out of their lives. With all her heart she wanted this moment to last. But could it? Would Scott allow it? She didn't want Jake hurt by becoming too attached to Scott. That feeling she was very familiar with. Jake didn't need the loss of another man in his life.

"He's acting like a mischievous boy should," Scott said as he took another offered piece of cereal. Jake continued to stuff Scott's mouth with more than it could hold. He hewed and swallowed the mass before he rose with Jake his arms. "Well, I've got to finish rounds."

ke complained when he was handed over to her.

ching out, Scott tickled Jake's belly. He squealed.

"I'll be back to see you soon, bubby." Scott gave her a quick kiss on the lips.

Had she wanted to see a wistful look in Scott's eyes? Had it really been there?

Jake's day nurse entered soon after Scott left. She checked Jake's vitals and adjusted the settings on the monitors.

"Looks like Jake's doing great. He should be going home soon," the nurse said with stethoscope in hand as she prepared to listen to Jake's chest. "Dr. McIntyre's a great doctor. We're going to miss him when he leaves."

Bile rose in Hannah's throat. Her heart skipped a beat. She stopped rocking and sat up straight. "Leave? Where's he going?"

It was happening again. Scott was going to leave without saying anything to her again.

"The rumor is he's been offered a position as head of a transplant program in Dallas. He'd be starting the program from scratch, which is a big deal if you're a transplant surgeon," the nurse replied in an offhand manner.

Hannah's shoulders sank. Leaving? She couldn't believe Scott hadn't said anything to her. Why hadn't he?

She shouldn't have expected more, hoped for more. He'd made no promises. Hadn't he made it clear where he stood the afternoon they'd spent in bed? She hadn't wanted to accept it.

"When's he supposed to leave?" Hannah made an effort to make the question sound nonchalant, despite the tightness in her chest.

The nurse adjusted the blanket over Jake. "Soon, I think. It's pretty much a done deal, I understand."

Hannah not only wanted Scott around because she loved him but because he was Jake's doctor. It gave her a sense of security to know Scott was close by if Jake needed h

"Dr. Mac is such a great doctor I can't imagine him not getting the job." The nurse looked at her. "Uh, are you all right, Ms. Quinn?"

Hannah nodded, her stomach rolling like a ship in a storm.

"I thought you knew," the nurse said in an unsure voice.

"No, I didn't know and I'm concerned for Jake. Who'll care of him if Dr. McIntyre is no longer here?"

"Oh, don't worry there. We've other great doctors." She patted Hannah's hand, gave her a bright smile and went out the door.

A tear rolled down Hannah's cheek as she slowly started rocking again. It was the same old scene of the same old play. Scott hadn't changed. He planned to leave without saying a word. Again.

She knew what she had to do. End it.

Scott had managed to get out of the OR earlier than he thought possible and had every intention of spending the extra time with Hannah and Jake.

He took a few minutes to stop by his office to check his mail. While there he received a call from Dallas. Despite the short notice, they wanted him to fly out to speak with the committee the next day. Thankfully, his patients, including Jake, were doing well enough that he could agree. He made some quick travel arrangements.

He'd put off telling Hannah about Dallas because it wouldn't have mattered by the time he thought he would be moving. She would've gone on with her life, making it a non-issue.

Scott couldn't believe how fast Hannah had become important to him. Jake too. A chance to be with someone like Hannah didn't come along more than once in a lifetime. Well, maybe twice. He knew what he was letting go of, but still he had to do it.

In another few days or so Jake might be going home. Scott's relationship with Hannah would change then anyway. With Jake recovering, she wouldn't need him any more.

Could he and Hannah maintain a long-distance relationship? Would seeing her occasionally fill his need for her? He didn't think so. It didn't matter he had to be a different person than he was for it to ever work.

Hannah didn't stand to greet him when he entered and closed the door to Jake's room behind him. She continued to hold Jake and rock.

Scott leaned down to kiss her, but she only offered her cheek. "How's Jake been doing today?"

"He's had a great day." She sounded pleased, but the words were stiff. She didn't look at him.

Was something bothering her? Jake's nurse had said nothing about there being a problem when he'd stopped at the nurses' station. "Hannah, is something wrong?"

Hannah looked up at him. "Why didn't you tell me you were planning to move to Dallas? Was it a secret? You didn't have to hide it from me. You've made it perfectly clear we have no ties on each other. I understood. But *friends* don't keep secrets."

The knot forming in his chest ached. There were ties between them, but he couldn't tell her that. Scott raised his brows. "How'd you come by that bit of info?"

"The hospital grapevine works for everyone." Her eye remained fixed on him. "So, are you leaving?"

"I've been interviewed by a hospital in Dallas. The want to start a transplant program. It's been my drear head my own."

"When're you leaving?"

"I'm still in the discussion stage. But...I have to fly out first thing in the morning to meet with the committee."

"What about Jake?" Anxiousness crept into her voice.

His desire to help patients was already coming between them as he'd known it would. He didn't want her to live her life worried he wouldn't be there when she needed him. He was making the right decision, for both of them as well as Jake. "He's doing well. He'll soon be followed by Cardiology. My job is almost done." Scott tried to make the words sound matter-of-fact.

"I think, under the circumstances, it would be better for Jake if things remain professional between us. Jake doesn't need to get attached to you." She looked out the window as she spoke.

"Better for Jake?" His words came out softly.

She looked at him. "Okay, better for me. You're leaving, so what're we doing anyway? Having great sex? I want more, you don't or won't let yourself have more, so I think now is a good time to call it quits, before either one of us gets hurt."

Scott's chest felt like a band was being tightened around it. There was no longer an ache but a cavernous hurt. He had no one to blame but himself. "I told you—"

She shook her head, silencing him. "I know what you told me. The problem is you have issues that you need to resolve with yourself and your parents. I care for you more than you care for me. But I've been left behind or set aside for the last time. I have to think of Jake. He doesn't need to get attached to someone who won't be there for the long haul or want to see him make the first step. Jake deserves omeone who will stick with him and fight for him, and I too." The last few words had a bite to them.

cott said nothing. He couldn't refute anything she'd He wished with all his heart he could.

"Stupid me," she murmured. "I'd hoped this time you'd feel differently." She gasped, swiping her hand across her cheek. "It's been fun while it lasted. Nice seeing you again."

Scott stood looking down at her for a long moment. He wanted to argue with her, but how could he? She was right. "One of the other surgeons will see about Jake while I'm gone. I'm sure he'll be discharged before I return. Goodbye, Hannah."

"Thanks for taking such good care of Jake and for helping me get through some stressful moments. I wish you the best in Dallas. Bye, Scott." The last few words had an iceberg chill of finality to them.

The pain of leaving Hannah was so searing and deep Scott found it difficult to breathe. For the first time in his life he was asking if he was doing the right thing.

CHAPTER TEN

HANNAH'S next few days were spent preparing to take Jake home. Hannah was grateful to be busy because it left less time to think about Scott. She pushed thoughts of him aside the best she could. At unexpected moments, like each time the door opened, Hannah's heart raced, thinking it might be Scott. It never was.

She missed him. Hurt with the want of him. As disappointed as she was that he didn't need her, it didn't make her love for him disappear, which only intensified the pain.

Jake had his first biopsy to determine if he was rejecting the new heart the morning after Scott left. Jake would continue to have biopsies regularly throughout his life. Hannah waited in Jake's room while the nurse took him to the cath lab for the procedure.

Wringing her hands until they were almost raw, Hannah watched the clock as an hour crawled by. Dr. John Reynolds, the cardiologist now following Jake's progress, came in to see her. The test had shown no rejection and Dr. Reynolds planned to release Jake from the hospital the xt day.

he news was like the sun coming out after a long, inter. Elated with Jake's recovery, Hannah's first was to share the good news with Scott. It was too late for that. The day turned gloomy again. Her sense of loss seemed as vast as the ocean.

Hannah was packed and ready to leave before Dr. Reynolds made rounds the next morning.

Once back at home, fretting over missing Scott took a backseat to caring for Jake. She gave medicine four times a day, checked Jake's blood pressure, temperature and weight at regular intervals. Feeding Jake took extra time, coaxing him to eat enough to gain weight. His incisions required attention as well.

Jake napped a number of times during the day, giving Hannah an opportunity to take care of her everyday matters. Bills arrived daily, and there were phone calls to make and return. Holding Jake became the highlight of her day. Reminded of how much she'd almost lost, she was grateful for each precious moment.

The nights were different. They dragged. Thoughts of Scott wandered in and camped. She relived all the wonderful times they'd had together, and yearned for his breath-stealing kisses, his body next to hers, his lovemaking. Despite being exhausted, it took hours for sleep to find her.

As the days lapsed into weeks the loss of Scott became a dull pain Hannah learned to live with. Like splinters, barely touched memories would flood back with a sting when she saw a tall man wearing a white lab coat or heard shoes tapping across a tile floor. Thoughts of Scott never completely left her.

No one liked being left behind, but it was a part of life When had she become so scared of living? Chances had be taken if happiness was ever to be found. She wou have missed her time with Scott for anything. Th was worth those amazing hours she'd spent in h

Other people, sometimes more wonderful pe

enter to replace him. The secret was not to let fear close any door. She didn't want Jake to grow up with a mother fearful of life. She wanted to be a positive role model, strong, resilient, no matter what happened to her.

Hannah glanced at Jake as he swung in his swing and played with his bear. She wasn't the only one who'd been left behind, but her ex had given her a wonderful gift in Jake. Each positive report Jake received was a thrill. He'd grown since the transplant and was becoming more active. Still, the only time they left the condo was when Jake had an appointment at the hospital. She even had groceries delivered.

A thump of a toy falling on the floor and Jake's squeals made Hannah look up from balancing her checkbook. The toy Scott had given Jake had slipped from his hand. The little bear was Jake's constant companion.

Hannah smiled and leaned down to pick up the toy. Giving it to Jake, she kissed him on top of his head. "Time for meds, sweetie."

Hannah slipped into doing Jake's care as easily as putting on old shoes. Maybe Scott had been right. She should think about being a clinical nurse instead of working in a hospital. With a few extra courses, she could work with children. Perhaps working with transplant families would be a good place to consider. With leave pay still coming in for a while longer and her savings in fair shape, she had time to look into jobs when Jake had recovered enough to be left with a sitter.

Jake had been given a second chance at life and she [illegible]nned to live her life to the fullest, for her sake as well [illegible]ke's.

[illegible]rnoon the doorbell rang. Hannah answered it [illegible] a delivery man there.

"Hannah Quinn?"

A huge box sat at her feet with the word "Fragile" written across the top.

"Yes, but I'm not expecting anything."

The man in the brown uniform smiled at her, and handed her an electronic device for her to sign. The return address indicated it was from one of the best gift shops in the area. There had to be some kind of mistake.

Hannah pulled the box indoors and cut through the packaging tape. Picking up one of the items in the container, she removed the plastic bubble wrap. Beneath it, she found a teacup from the set she'd admired at the fundraiser. Gently, she set it back with the rest of the set.

Reaching for the invoice under another item, she located a phone number. Calling the store, the manager explained she couldn't return the set because it had been donated to the hospital. Her name had been identified as the highest bidder.

Hanging up the phone, Hannah sat staring at the box. Scott must have bid on it when she'd gone to call about Jake.

She removed each piece with loving care until the completed set was arranged on the coffee table. Spying a white gift envelope pushed against the inside wall of the box, she pulled it out. Opening the card, she read: "*Don't even think about returning it. Enjoy. Scott.*"

Hannah's hands shook and her eyes watered as she held the envelope to her chest.

Scott drummed his fingers on the desk as he waited to be connected with Dr. John Reynolds.

"Scott, how you doing?"

"I'm working more hours than should be humanly possible. What I was calling about—"

"You want to know how Jake Quinn is doing."

He was too transparent. John had to know Scott was checking on Hannah too. "Yeah."

"He's doing as expected, like I've told you every time you've called. His mom is taking excellent care of him."

"I appreciate the report." Scott smiled. Jake was doing great. Was Hannah? He couldn't ask. But if Jake was getting better, Hannah had to be happy. He'd have to find contentment in that knowledge.

"I'll be in Atlanta in a few days to clear up some business. I'll stop by."

"Sounds great. I'd like to hear firsthand how your program is shaping up," John replied, and Scott rang off.

Maybe he should make arrangements to see Jake while in Atlanta. After all, Jake had been his patient. Who was he kidding? He wanted to see Hannah. Needed to see her.

Scott shouldn't have had time to think of Hannah with the amount of work he'd done in the last two months but she crept into his thoughts continuously. During meals, he thought of their shared ones. At night, it took him hours before sleep found him. Even after he fell asleep, Hannah filled his dreams. He ached to touch her and ached to have her touch him.

His hunger for her hadn't died. If anything, it had intensified.

For the first time in his life he wanted more than to be a great heart surgeon. He wanted Hannah. And Jake. Wanted to be a husband, father, a family man. He would do whatever was necessary to convince Hannah to take a chance on him. Without Hannah and Jake, nothing mattered.

Hannah had gotten his attention about more than setting his priorities in regard to work. He needed to set things right between him and his mother. Hannah would expect that, want that for him.

With Hannah as his life partner he could find that balance between his professional and private life. She had already helped to do that. Hannah would keep him centered, support him, while at the same time reminding him of what was really important. They could make it work—together.

He wanted it all. Would fight for it, beg for it if he had to.

But would Hannah have him?

"We need to hurry honey or we'll be late," Hannah said when she hiked Jake further up on her hip as they went down the hall of the hospital. Jake, with a mask covering his mouth, looked like a miniature doctor as he bounced along in her arms.

"If Dr. Reynolds says you can go out in public, we'll stop and get some ice cream on the way home," she promised.

Absorbed in her conversation, Hannah didn't notice the man standing next to the door of the pre/post cath lab. She reached for the doorknob.

"Hannah."

Her breath caught. Had her name ever sounded sweeter? Her thoughts swirled, and her blood hummed. She looked up into the most beautiful blue eyes she'd ever seen.

"Hello," Scott said.

"Hi."

"Dr. Mac," Jake squealed and reached out to him.

"Hi, big guy." Scott opened his arms to take Jake. He jerked toward Scott in his eagerness to be held by him. Hannah let Jake go to him. "You look like you're doing well."

Hannah gave up trying to slow her heartbeat. "What're you doing here?"

"I'm visiting. I had a few loose ends to take care of in Atlanta."

"Oh." Hannah tingled from the tip of her fingers to the ends of her toes. Now was the time to sound intelligent. *Talk to him.* "By the way, congratulations. I heard you got the job you were after. That's great." She meant it. She was proud of him. He was an outstanding surgeon.

"Thank you." Scott studied her a moment. "It's good to see you." He captured her gaze. "You look wonderful."

Her heart fluttered, his words a soft caress.

Scott stepped forward, tentatively reaching out a hand to touch her but not doing so. Jake demanded his attention by pulling on Scott's tie.

Sharp disappointment filled her at the abandoned connection.

Jake put out his hand, showing Scott his toy.

"What've you got there?" Scott asked. "Is that Bear?"

Jake looked at the toy and smiled, pulling it closer to his side.

Hannah had tried for weeks to replace the little toy with another one, but Jake had refused. He had to have Bear with him when he came to the hospital or when he fell asleep. For Hannah, the toy had been another constant reminder of Scott.

"Does Bear go everywhere with you?" Scott asked.

Jake thrust the toy at Scott. He studied it. Looking up at Hannah, with a twinkle in his eye he said, "Bear has gotten a lot of wear."

"Jake won't let him out of his sight." She didn't meet Scott's gaze. Instead, she focused on his broad smile as he returned the animal to Jake.

"Um…I'm glad we ran into you," she said. "It's nice to—"

"You didn't run into me. I've been waiting on you."

A stream of warmth Hannah hadn't felt in months raced through her. She didn't trust herself to say anything, so she just waited.

"Could we meet somewhere and talk?"

"I guess so." She brushed Jake's curls back as he squirmed in her arms. "How long are you going to be in town?"

"Until tomorrow."

"Would you…uh…" she'd promised herself she'd take chances "…like to come to dinner tonight? I owe you one or two." If he said no, could her heart stand it?

A look of surprise crossed his face before the grin she loved so much found his lips. "I have some meetings this afternoon but I'll make it work. Thanks."

Delight filled her at the sparkle of pleasure in his incredible eyes. "Six okay?"

"I'll be there."

She returned his smile with a bright one of her own. Hannah reached out to take Jake again. "We have to go. They're expecting Jake for a biopsy."

When Jake whined about having to leave Scott he said, "I'll see you this evening buddy. We'll play then."

Her hand shook as she opened the door of the cath lab.

Hannah shifted the candle a little to the left, then moved a book back to its original spot on the end table. She'd blurted out her invitation to Scott without thinking it through. The delivery boy had had to make two trips from the grocery store before she'd had everything she needed for the meal. The boy's face had brightened at the large tip he'd received on the last trip.

After trying on a couple of outfits, Hannah settled on a pair of jeans and a peach-colored sweater. The one she'd been told looked particularly nice on her. Tonight she wanted to appear at her best.

Hannah wouldn't let her hopes get out of hand enough to expect things to be different between her and Scott. She wanted to pull off the evening without seeming pathetic or needy. If he wanted some kind of relationship more than friendship but less than marriage, would she take it?

With a final check in the mirror, she went to the kitchen to finish preparing their meal. She was preparing to put the shrimp with white sauce on the linguine when the doorbell rang. With a deliberate movement she laid the spoon down. She adjusted her sweater at her waist and walked to the door. The bell rang again. Jake squealed as she passed, and she stopped to pick him up. With more flourish than intended, she opened the door.

Scott stood on the front stoop, shifting his weight from one foot to the other as if he thought she might not let him in. He didn't look like a self-assured surgeon. Instead, he appeared uncomfortable. Surely he wasn't uneasy about seeing her again.

Had anyone ever looked more appealing? Dressed in a green knit shirt and tan slacks he filled out perfectly, Scott had never looked better, which was helped by the fact she'd missed him so desperately.

Her stomach quivered. Scott was there.

His smile reached his eyes before his gaze fell away. He ran his hand through his hair in that uneasy gesture she recognized. What could he possibly be nervous about?

Shifting Jake to the other hip and stepping back, she said, "Please come in."

As Scott entered, he cleared his throat and said in a raspy voice, "For you." He handed her a small gift bag.

He reached for Jake. "Why don't you let me take Jake while you finish supper?"

Hannah wasn't surprised when Jake gave no argument to switching rides. Jake had bonded with Scott. She left the room to the sound of her son's laughter as Scott sat Jake on his foot to play This Little Horsy. A feeling of rightness washed over her.

In the kitchen, she poured the noodle mixture into a bowl. She turned to the bag Scott had brought her and pulled the light blue tissue paper out. Inside she found a tin of tea leaves and a tea diffuser in the shape of a house. Warmth filled her. The gifts were perfect.

At the sound of footsteps behind her, she turned.

Scott, with Jake in his arms, stood in the doorway. Scott appeared less out of sorts as he stood there than he had at the front door. It was as if Jake had soothed his anxiousness. Scott looked like he belonged in her home. "I thought you could use them with your teaset."

"I love them." She beamed, hoping her smile showed all the delight she felt. "I should've said thank you for the teaset earlier. It's beautiful. You shouldn't have done this either." She dangled the diffuser from two fingers. "Did you pick it out yourself?"

He smiled. "No. The lady at the store helped me. I thought you'd appreciate them more than a bottle of wine."

"I do. They're wonderful."

Scott tickled Jake's belly, causing him to giggle. Looking down at him, he said, "Amazing, aren't they? How tough and resilient children are."

"Yes. Jake, come on. It's time to eat." She reached to take him but he clung to Scott.

Scott grinned. "Where does Jake sit?"

Hannah pointed to the highchair next to the table.

Their meal was pleasant, because she and Scott both

focused their attention on Jake. Hannah enjoyed having a man at her table but she had the feeling Scott was anxious about something. Was she reading too much into him being there? He'd said he wanted to talk. The anticipation kept her on edge and apparently he was too. The one time she relaxed and he did also was when she asked Scott about his new job and got caught up in his excitement.

"I've been working a lot of hours and hiring staff. I've also had to spend time writing procedures and going to meetings, which aren't my favorite things. But I think we'll have a great program that will help many children."

"You must be very busy." Probably far too busy to have thought of her.

"Yeah. It's been nice to get away for a few days."

The meal completed, Scott helped her clear away the dishes and clean the kitchen while Jake played with a pot and spoon. Scott watched TV while Hannah got Jake ready for bed.

As she rocked Jake to sleep, Hannah sensed Scott's presence. She glanced at the door and found Scott leaning against the frame with his arms across his chest. He had a solemn, contemplative look on his face. What was he thinking?

Happiness had filled her at having Scott there, but by the way he was acting it had been only to see how Jake was doing. Was he here to say goodbye for ever?

Hannah continued to move back and forth despite being hyper-conscious about Scott's presence. Jake shifted in her arms as if he was responding to her reaction to Scott. When Jake eyelids lowered, she kissed his sweet-smelling forehead and started to rise. Scott stepped over and took Jake, gently laid him in his bed.

Hannah joined Scott at Jake's bedside. "Thank you for this. For these precious moments I might not have had."

Scott offered his hand, and she placed hers in his. He smiled as he laced his fingers through hers and gave them a gentle squeeze. “Hannah, can we talk now?” His words were soft and earnest. Without releasing her hand, he led her to the living room. At the sofa, Scott said, “Let’s sit.”

To Hannah’s disappointment, he took a chair opposite her. Balling her trembling hands in her lap, she mustered up her courage. Hadn’t everything already been said between them? He’d given no indication he’d change his mind. Supper had been two friends sharing a meal.

“I was surprised to see you at the hospital today. I’m so glad your new job is going well. I know they’re glad to have you. Jake’s growing and happy. I’m so proud of him.”

Scott chuckled and moved over beside her. “Are you almost done? Can I speak?”

He smiled at the glow his comment brought to her cheeks. His heart lurched. *She hasn’t shut me out entirely.* Was she as unsure as him? Maybe he had a chance.

“I was just trying to see how—”

Apparently she wasn’t going to be quiet until he did something to get her attention. His mouth came down to claim hers, tugging at her full bottom lip until she opened for him. Scott registered her hesitation then acceptance and the moment she returned his kiss with complete abandon. He’d come home. With Hannah was where he belonged. What they shared weeks earlier still smoldered between them, and found oxygen again.

Before the kiss went beyond his control, he had to talk to her. Know what she was feeling. If she would take a chance on him—again. Scott ran his hands up Hannah’s arms, cupped her shoulders, and put her away from him. Their lips remained inches apart. She made a small sound of protest, which added fuel to his already raging desire

"I want..." Her eyes shined with a longing begging to be filled.

He smiled. "What do you want, honey?"

"You." The word came out like a caress.

Scott watched with pleasure as her face went crimson. "I want you too, but we need to talk first." He gave her another quick kiss, resisting the urge to take it deeper, despite Hannah's efforts to draw him closer.

Looking as if she'd been in a dream and reality had returned, she scrambled away and put some space between them. Her eyes were wide, her cheeks flushed and lips full. She'd never looked more beautiful, more desirable. His body throbbed for her. Battling the hunger roaring in him, Scott had to let her go. He couldn't carry on a rational conversation with her sitting so close to him.

He took one of her hands in his. Absently, he moved the pad of his thumb over the back of her hand. "We need to talk."

Her green eyes searched his, weary. She looked unsure. He'd not meant to make her feel anxious.

"I've been a plan follower all my life. The plan was working well until you showed up again. My life was no longer as clear cut as it had once been. But you didn't demand anything. You were strong and supportive of me even when your own child was sick. You understand the work I do and why it drives me. It has been made clear on more than one occasion you're nothing like my mother.

"Even when I woke you in the middle of the night, coming home late, you welcomed me, comforted me. I hadn't known how much I'd missed that in my life until then. I've realized that I share many wonderful traits with my father but I don't have to be like him in all ways. He should have set priorities, learned to say no, taken on a partner when he saw that his marriage and family were suffering.

"When I went to Dallas I knew I'd miss you but I had no idea how much. I ached with it. I dream about how nice it would be to come home to you and Jake every night. The comfort you would offer after a long, tough day." He grinned. "Or days. You wouldn't make unreasonable demands I couldn't meet. You would just take me in your arms and hold me."

Her eyes glistened with tears, and she squeezed his hand.

"I thought getting the position in Dallas would make my life perfect. It's everything I've worked for, sacrificed for. Today and this evening when Jake came so trustingly to me I knew I wanted to be his father, to feel that love every day. I couldn't return to Dallas without telling you how I feel. No job is worth sacrificing you for. Without you and Jake it means nothing. The most important thing in life has been missing in mine, and I found it with you and Jake. I want to settle down. Have a wife and a family.

"I want you and Jake. For Jake to have brothers and sisters. I wanted *that* with you. I love you."

Her lips parted and her eyes remained fixed on his. A knot of fear formed in his chest. Why didn't she say something? Had he misread her kisses?

With a sudden tiny squeak Hannah threw herself at him, wrapping her arms around his neck. Scott pulled her tight, his lips meeting hers in a searing kiss.

Her mouth left his, to slide across his cheek to his ear. "I love you so much. It almost killed me when you left. Please don't ever do it again."

His lips found hers again, the contact a gentle stroke of promise. He broke the kiss and looked straight into her eyes. "I know you have good reasons for being afraid I'll leave, but if you'll take a chance on me, I promise never to leave you again." His tone held all the sincerity he felt.

The kiss that sealed the pledge was sweet and spicy. After long, perfect moments Scott released her and his hand came up to brush her cheek.

Hannah's lips touched his palm.

Closing his eyes and breathing deeply, Scott labored to control his passion. Hannah was too close for him to think straight. He shifted, putting her at arm's length, but kept his hands on her shoulders.

With his gaze fixed on hers, Scott said, "I know I won't be around a lot at first and I'm already looking to bring another surgeon on to help. With you, I know I can find that balance between work and family. Together we can do anything. Please give us a chance. Marry me and move to Dallas?"

She wrapped her arms around his neck. "Yes, yes, yes." Scott's heart beat faster. A thrill better even than the one he had each time he saved a child's life.

He drew Hannah against him. His lips found the softness of hers. Her fingers fanned through his hair as she tugged him closer. Hannah opened her mouth, offering him the honeyed taste within. With a murmur of satisfaction his tongue reached out and found hers.

When Hannah broke away Scott tried to pull her back, but she stayed him with hands to his chest. His fingers settled with a light touch at her hips.

She beamed up at him. "What took you so long, you big lug?"

Scott grinned. The feisty Hannah he loved so much had shown up. Tightening his grip, he brought her hips against his. "I fought it at first. But I knew I was a goner when I found myself calling the hospital a couple of times a week to check on Jake. I convince myself that I was only calling to check on Jake. When I realized that I wanted to ask more questions about you than him, I knew I was in trouble.

"Thanks to you, I've spoken to my mother and really cleared the air between us. She's even planning to visit soon. Things are better now between us than they have been in years. Surprisingly, she and Dad are even talking."

"I'm so glad." She leaned over and gave him a quick kiss.

His hands moved upwards until he could skim the undersides of her breasts. His reward was a smoky come-hither look.

"I've been doing some thinking too," she said. "I believe you're right. I should consider working in a clinic situation. My appreciation for your skills has me thinking about how I can use my own."

"You know, I happen to need a good clinical nurse to work in the Dallas transplant program. Do you know anyone who might be interested?"

"I just might." With a grin on her face, she said, "I'd certainly have insight where others wouldn't." Her hands moved up over his biceps and across his shoulders. "Would *you* be my boss?" Her voice took on a Marilyn Monroe quality.

The combination of husky voice and twinkling eyes was intoxicating. Flirty Hannah sent a fire through Scott. He growled low in his chest. "You can count on it." He punctuated each word with small kisses.

Hannah guided his mouth down to hers.

Scott loved the way she couldn't seem to get enough of kissing him. As her lips traveled along his jaw, he said, "I've been living at the hospital the last few months. I've put off looking for a place to live in Dallas. Do you think you could help me find the right house? Maybe one with a big yard? A place for our kids to play?"

"I believe I can."

"In that case, I've something else I need your help with." At her expectant look, Scott chuckled. "But we'll need to find a bed."

"I know just where to find one." Hannah stood. Taking his hand, she tugged him down the hallway.

A feeling of pure satisfaction filled Scott. *I'm home.*

* * * * *

For exclusive extracts, competitions and special offers, find us online:

facebook.com/millsandboon

@millsandboonuk

@millsandboon

Or get in touch on 0844 844 1351*

For all the latest titles coming soon, visit millsandboon.co.uk/nextmonth

* Calls cost 7p per minute plus your phone company's price per minute access charge